THE LAST WOMAN IN THE FOREST

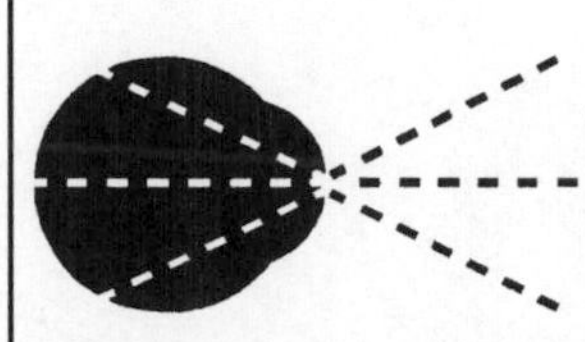

This Large Print Book carries the
Seal of Approval of N.A.V.H.

THE LAST WOMAN IN THE FOREST

DIANE LES BECQUETS

THORNDIKE PRESS
A part of Gale, a Cengage Company

Farmington Hills, Mich • San Francisco • New York • Waterville, Maine
Meriden, Conn • Mason, Ohio • Chicago

This is a work of fiction. Names, characters, places, and incidents either are the product of the author's imagination or are used fictitiously.

Thorndike Press® Large Print Basic.
The text of this Large Print edition is unabridged.
Other aspects of the book may vary from the original edition.
Set in 16 pt. Plantin.

LIBRARY OF CONGRESS CIP DATA ON FILE.
CATALOGUING IN PUBLICATION FOR THIS BOOK
IS AVAILABLE FROM THE LIBRARY OF CONGRESS

ISBN-13: 978-1-4328-6707-2 (hardcover alk. paper)

Published in 2019 by arrangement with Berkley, an imprint of Penguin Publishing Group, a division of Penguin Random House LLC

Printed in Mexico
1 2 3 4 5 6 7 23 22 21 20 19

For John Philpin

■ ■ ■ ■

Part One

■ ■ ■ ■

As soon as there is life there is danger.

— THE BARONESS DE STAËL-HOLSTEIN
(ANNE-LOUISE-GERMAINE NECKER)

PROLOGUE

VICTIM #1
Natasha Freeman

Natasha was the prettiest of all the girls, with long, reddish-brown hair, the color of brindle. She was a little over five foot six, and two inches taller in the boots that she wore. She wasn't from Montana, though that was where she had lived for the past four and a half years. Natasha was from Massachusetts, where her father still lived in Franklin, one town over from where the Patriots played. Natasha didn't care for Massachusetts, and she wasn't a Patriots fan. Natasha was interested in cowboys and had her heart set on marrying one. She didn't know anything about cattle or ranching, or cowboys for that matter, so she left Massachusetts five years after her mother passed away and drove to towns where cowboys lived. Lately she'd been thinking about moving back to Massachusetts, or somewhere close to Franklin, like New Hampshire, because she missed her father, who had never remarried, and the only cowboy Natasha had loved had left her for someone else.

She would save a little more money, finish her coursework. She would visit her father, find another job. Maybe schools would be hiring.

Natasha and the cowboy had been living on a gentrified ranch outside Montana City. The cowboy didn't own the ranch, but he helped take care of the cattle, and he and Natasha had a sweet spot in an apartment above the barn. Natasha was working as a teacher's aide in a second-grade classroom four miles from where they lived. She liked the children and hoped that soon she and the cowboy would marry and have their own family. Two evenings a week, Natasha made the two-hour drive to Missoula, where she was enrolled at the University of Montana. The cowboy paid for her classes. He'd said she'd make a good teacher. But he'd gotten lonely on the nights she'd been away, and on the other nights when he'd wanted her to come to bed and she'd stayed up at the kitchen table studying and drinking so much coffee that she didn't go to bed at all.

She might have forgiven him. He'd said a man had needs. She tried to tell him she was sorry, that she would cut back on her classes, that she would stop staying up so late. But the man wasn't interested in reconciling. He was interested instead in a woman he'd met, a cute little thing at the feedlot, who had been buying dog food for her allergy-sensitive Irish setter.

That was when Natasha left the cattle and the sweet spot above the barn. She moved into an apartment in Helena that she could afford on her teacher's aide salary. She continued to make the two-hour drive, two nights a week, to the University of Montana. She didn't think about cowboys or big skies or the smell of cattle. She'd think of her father and the picture of her mother on the bureau beside his bed. Brian Freeman, who told his daughter she had her mother's eyes, said he wasn't lonely even though he missed his daughter. He had his job and his friends. He watched the Patriots and went to church and threw office parties. Natasha wasn't like her father. She didn't have any friends. When the cowboy walked out of her life, she'd lost the only friend she'd had.

Natasha liked the class she was taking the spring after the cowboy and the little woman and the Irish setter moved in together. Creative Drama and Dance was offered through the theater department and was required for education majors. The course focused on the use of drama and dance as types of educational tools. Natasha was especially fond of the dance portion of the class. She enjoyed the way the music entered her body and rooted her someplace else, her childhood perhaps, when her mother would sway behind the steering wheel, to the melody of a song on the radio, and her fingers would tap out the tempo as she drove. Her voice would sing off-key and Natasha would change the station. Then her mother would swat her daughter's hand and laugh and change the station back.

Natasha wondered if her mother had been swaying to the music and singing off-key when she slid on the black ice and crashed into a guardrail. While paramedics rushed to the scene, Natasha waited to be picked up from her seventh-grade CCD confirmation class at St. Mary's Catholic Church. Natasha didn't own a cell phone then and everyone else at the parish had already left. She thought her mother would be arriving soon and continued to sit on the curb beside the parking lot. She finally gave up waiting when her fingers began to turn numb, and decided to walk the seven miles home. After thirty minutes, she saw Papa Gino's on her right. She went inside and asked to use a phone. A patron overheard her and said she could use his. She dialed her mother's number, but the call went to voice mail. Then she called her father. He picked up on the first ring. "Oh, God, oh, God." He was crying. He said he was sorry. He told her he'd be right there.

The Creative Drama and Dance class was supposed to end at nine. It often let out early, and Natasha would stop by one of the clubs where a local band would be playing. She'd order a margarita and find a seat somewhere toward the back of the room. She'd drink her margarita slowly to make it last and let the music loosen up something inside her, all that brokenness that she'd never paid much mind to. She'd find hope on those nights, a brief levity, like a rising tide that would carry her east along Interstate 90 to the exit for Highway 12. She'd head over the highlands, a fifty-mile stretch, to the small apartment she'd yet to call home. As she drove she'd hum tunes from whichever club she'd been at and imagine a life different from the one she had. Maybe she'd marry a teacher, or an electrician, or a dentist like her dad.

These were Natasha's thoughts on that cold Wednesday evening in early December. She'd been listening to music at the Top Hat on West Front Street. She'd even ordered a second drink. She'd liked the band that was playing. After she'd listened to the band and had begun to make the drive to Helena, she'd felt her sadness lift more than it had on previous days.

By the time she took the exit for Highway 12 it was later than usual for her, just past eleven, and there was little traffic, only a solitary vehicle here and there. That was why she was startled when a truck came up behind her and flashed its lights. She was a couple of miles outside the little town of Elliston, with about a half hour more to go to her apartment. She thought the driver behind her might want to pass, so she slowed down and veered onto the shoulder. But she'd forgotten about the warmer temperatures that day. She hadn't anticipated how soft the shoulder would be. Her right front tire sank a good several inches and then began to spin. Within seconds her back right tire was spinning as well. The truck that had been flashing its lights had already sped on. Natasha kept a shovel in the extra cab of her truck. She climbed out, opened the extra cab extension door, and retrieved the shovel. She wasn't worried. She'd gotten stuck before, and despite the fact that the sky was dark and she didn't have a lot of room on the shoulder to work, she was still in a good mood. She dug slush and mud out from around the right front tire, but no matter how much she dug, the ground remained soft.

For a moment she thought of the cowboy and wished she could call him for help. But then she thought of the cowboy's girlfriend. She would call for a tow truck before she would call her ex-boyfriend, even though she knew the tow truck would cost her more than what she had in her bank account.

After fifteen minutes, she heard a vehicle approaching from behind her and soon saw the headlights of a truck coming around the corner. She'd left her own vehicle running and the lights on so that other vehicles would see her. The truck pulled up beside her. The passenger window was rolled down. A man's voice spoke to her through the rolled-down window, though Natasha couldn't see the man's face.

"I've got a chain in the back of my truck," the man said. "How about I give you a hand?"

The man pulled up just ahead of her truck and got out. He lowered his tailgate and retrieved the heavy chain. He walked to the front of Natasha's truck, and as he did, she heard another vehicle approaching, this time from the opposite direction. The vehicle was a midsize SUV carrying an older couple. The passenger, a woman who looked to be in her sixties, rolled down her window and asked

Natasha and the man if they needed help.

"We're good," the man said.

"But thank you," Natasha said. She almost asked if the couple would wait until her truck had been pulled back onto the road. She wasn't sure how comfortable she was being alone with this man whom she didn't know. But she looked at her watch, and it was already going on midnight. The couple was no doubt tired and ready to get home, so Natasha just stood there and waved at the couple as they drove away.

The man said he'd have her on the road in no time. He hooked the chain to her truck's front axle. "Where are you coming from to be out so late?" he asked her.

She'd been hoping he wouldn't try to make conversation, but she didn't want to seem ungrateful or appear rude, so she told him about her class.

"I take night classes there, too," he said. "I thought you looked familiar."

Natasha felt herself breathe more easily then. This man was also a student, which she took as a good sign.

"What's your name?" he asked her.

While they stood there and talked, Natasha's truck was still running. Maybe it was because she was tired and it was late, or because of that second drink she'd had, but she'd forgotten how low on fuel her vehicle was. She climbed in her truck and shifted it into drive so that the man could pull her out of the soft shoulder. That was when she saw that the fuel gauge needle was just a hair above empty. She knew she might not have enough gas to drive the twenty miles or more over the mountains and back to her apartment.

She had enjoyed talking to the man. She'd already thanked him for pulling over to help her. She'd learned that he was taking classes in engineering, that he had an apartment in Missoula but was driving to Helena to visit his parents. She'd told him it was nice that he was close to his parents and that she missed her father, who was back home in Massachusetts. The man asked her about her mother, and she felt an awakened melancholy that the man seemed to register. "I'm sorry," he said. "Something terrible must have happened."

The man drove forward, pulling Natasha's truck back onto the road. At that time another truck approached from the opposite direction. Natasha waved the vehicle on when it slowed down.

Then the man who had helped her climbed out of his vehicle and walked back toward Natasha. "How are you holding up on fuel?" he asked her.

He looked at her fuel gauge before she had a chance to answer and told her to follow him up the road a ways to a pull-off. Then he would give her a ride back to the Elliston Store, which had a fuel station. He said he had a five-gallon gas container in his truck. At first Natasha insisted that she had enough gas to make it back to the store on her own. The man seemed concerned. What if she didn't make it, or the pump was out of order? He assured her he didn't mind giving her a ride. Natasha thought the man was handsome and she didn't want to offend him. She even thought they might be flirting with each other, which she told herself wasn't a good idea.

He removed the chain and returned it to his truck. As he pulled forward Natasha followed him. The alcohol had worn off and the sky was black. She'd stayed up way too late studying the night before. She was tired and eager to get back to her apartment and turn in.

In a few hundred yards, the man pulled off at a gravel section where in daylight people could view the Continental Divide. Natasha pulled up beside him. She could turn around and head back to Elliston on her own, and yet she was being foolish. She hadn't found a reason not to trust this man. She even entertained the thought of them meeting up after class one night and having a drink together.

She shut off her ignition, climbed out, and locked her doors. With her keys in her hand, she walked around her truck and over to the man's vehicle. She opened the passenger door and when she did the interior lights came on that allowed her to see into the extra cab, as well as the bed of the truck. She didn't see a fuel container. The air tightened in her chest for as long as a second. But then she saw a heavy coat in the backseat and thought there might be a fuel container beneath the coat. With that in mind, she climbed into the truck and shut the door. The man was smiling at her. His eyes looked kind and helpful. She realized once more how handsome he was.

"All set?" the man said.

Natasha nodded. She wore purple knit gloves on her hands. After she fastened her seat belt, she tucked her hands beneath her legs and stared straight ahead.

The man pulled back onto the highway and drove west toward Elliston. He continued to talk to her in a friendly way. How did she like her classes? What made her want to be a teacher, and how honorable he thought that was that she wanted to work with kids.

But then as they approached a gentle curve, the man slowed down more than Natasha thought was necessary. He turned left onto Little Blackfoot River Road.

Natasha's palms turned clammy inside her gloves and she asked the man what he was doing. He just wanted to check on something, he told her.

"This isn't the way to Elliston," Natasha said. She reached for the door with her right hand, but when she did so, she heard the locks click.

"I wouldn't do that," the man said.

She reached again for the door and tried to unlock it, but the man's arm shot out across her chest and pinned her to the back of the seat, and in his right hand was a knife with a blade about four inches long that was angled precariously close to her neck.

"Don't move," he said in a voice that was tight and loud.

She tried to speak calmly. "What are you doing?"

"We're going to help each other out," he said. "You help me, and I will make sure you get on your way."

When the truck stopped, she struggled to turn her shoulder away from the man. She reached for the door with both hands, but the man was quicker than she. He'd shut off the engine and whipped his right arm over her head and around her neck, the knife still in his hand, and pulled her away from the door. Now his left arm was free, and he wrapped that arm around her as well. He pulled her across the seat toward him. She screamed and kicked her feet against the glass.

"Shut up!" he yelled.

She tried to bite his arm, but he was still wearing the denim coat and leather gloves.

He dragged her out of the truck, kicked the door shut behind him, and pulled her around the vehicle, his left hand now held over her mouth. She smelled the rust from the chain he had held earlier and the cold air and her own fear. She tasted blood from her mouth from where she had bitten down on the inside of her cheek.

As he hauled her downhill into thick woods of Douglas fir, her cowboy boots carved deep gullies through the mud and snow. One of her boots caught on a rock and came off, sliding her wool sock down to the arch of her foot. Then the man stopped. All around them were dark evergreens and a few cottonwoods whose trunks and branches looked like bones. Natasha thought she could hear a river close by.

"If you try to run I will kill you," the man said. His breathing was heavy.

Ever so slowly he released the tight clasp of his arms around her. He held the knife in front of her face.

"Take off your clothes," he said.

Natasha listened for the sound of vehicles,

but she knew it was after one o'clock by now, and this road was mostly used for forest access. Even if someone were to drive by, the person would not be able to see this far into the woods and over the sloping decline. Nor would the person be able to hear her screams through the driver's rolled-up windows and heater and radio and the sounds of the nearby stream.

Natasha was cold and trembling. She unzipped her gold coat, a layer of thin down.

"Take it off," the man said.

She removed her jacket and handed it to the man. She didn't know when she had begun crying, but she became aware of the tears dripping off her cheeks and landing in the snow.

"Leave it," he told her.

Natasha dropped her jacket. "Please," she said. "Please don't do this."

"Take off your shirt."

Natasha continued to remove her clothes one item at a time. She continued to plead, her voice and skin and throat raw.

The man still held the knife. He stepped behind her. Again he wrapped his arms around her body, this time his mouth close to her ear so that she could feel his breath. The denim of his coat sleeves pressed against her stomach and her neck, and the cold metal buttons of his jacket dug into her back. Her bare feet tingled and were becoming numb.

"Please. I'll do anythin—"

His arm was quick, the pressure sharp. Her eyes widened. She could not breathe.

1
PRESENT: JULY 2017

Marian
Bull River, Montana

It's a terrible thing to have loved someone and not know the extent to which you'd been deceived, and a more terrible thing still to love someone and not know if you'd ever been loved in return. There is something shameful in that prospect, the kind of shame that can reduce a person to someone she no longer recognizes.

These were Marian's thoughts as she waded into the outer edge of the Bull River in Montana on that hot afternoon in July, as she carried a coffee tin poised in the crook of her left arm, which Marian thought ironic, as Tate didn't drink coffee.

It was a beautiful spot, the river wide enough to let in a nice expanse of sunlight. Tate had chosen this location, had sat on the rocky outcrop a few feet from where Marian stood now, had pressed the river rock against her palm and asked her to remember.

That was before the story Marian had believed in, the one she'd been certain had been written for her, had begun to change, like a kaleidoscope. Turn the cylinder one way, and the pieces shift, and a new image appears, as if each of her memories were a shard that could be rearranged to fit whichever story she chose to believe, and she wondered if truth existed at all. The only thing she could be certain of was that each day forward would carry the past.

"It will get easier," people had told her, well-intentioned people like her mother and her father, who had each lost a parent and had lost friends. "You will always miss him, but in time the pain will become more remote." But they didn't know. How could they? Her grief was a complicated one. It was a mystery as addictive as her love affair had been. There were nights as she prepared to turn in, as she peeled a shirt from her body and lifted it over her head, that she imagined removing the memory of Tate from her skin. She'd step toward her bed and crawl beneath the covers. But no matter where she slept or whichever air she breathed, she felt his presence, this man who'd told her they were cut from the same block of wood, like a giant sequoia, and had she ever seen a sequoia tree, and Marian had told him she hadn't. Only two weeks had passed since Tate had died, and now as she prepared to scatter what was left of his remains, she thought this was her crucible — all of it: her relationship with Tate, his death, the events that lay ahead.

Marian hadn't worn waders. She didn't own a pair. But she'd pulled on her Muck boots before she'd left the vehicle. Besides, the water wasn't deep in these parts, eighteen inches or a little more, and yet she knew from what Tate had told her that if she waded out any farther, the river could be well over her head, forty feet in some parts.

The water pressed against her calves and splashed inside her boots. Marian stood still and watched her shadow dance on the surface. "I love you, Tate. I hope you know that." Then she removed the lid from the tin and reached her hand inside the plastic bag. Slowly she sifted the fine ash and fragments into the water, watched the particles swirl downstream. Heat rose through her body despite the cool water, and her breathing became shallow because she felt everything. Then she shook out the bag and rinsed her hands in the river and returned the bag to the tin.

Her heavy boots sloshed through the water, and she almost fell but instead extended an arm out to the side to rebalance her footing. She stepped into the reed grass and hawthorn. With an awareness of her body, of its muscle and cartilage and bone, she wrapped a hand around the trunk of a young cottonwood and pulled herself up the embankment. And there might have been a breeze through the trees, cooling her damp skin, as she navigated her way back to the U.S. Forest Service road.

She'd parked the silver Xterra off to the side, along the ravine. The vehicle hadn't always belonged to Marian. Tate's name still appeared on the title. But ever since Tate's sister had visited to collect his things, Marian had been driving the SUV, eight years old and scratched and dinged and without a working radio, to pick up sundries, to transport one or more of the dogs, to remember the places where she and Tate had been.

The windshield faced the upper two thirds of the Cabinet Mountains Wilderness, its boundaries less than two miles away. Marian set the canister on the passenger seat and opened the glove compartment. Her fingers sorted through expired insurance cards and service records until she found the man's number that she'd written on a receipt.

She held the phone in her left hand and dialed the number. And as she waited, she half whispered, "I'm sorry, Tate," her throat an ache that burned down to her sternum.

Marian had not thought the man in Idaho would answer. She had thought she would leave a message. But he answered on the fourth ring, and when he did, Marian spoke too fast. She told the man who she was; she told him she was familiar with his work on the Stillwater cases. Eventually she told him about Tate and asked if her boyfriend had found one of the bodies of the Stillwater victims.

"Why now?" the man asked her.

Marian pushed her hair away from her face and off her sticky forehead. The phone felt too warm against her left ear, so she switched it to the other side. "Because I loved him," she said. "Because I wanted to believe him."

Nick Shepard wasn't from the West. He'd been born and raised in Detroit, to an alcoholic father and a family that was often on welfare. But he'd escaped the chaos of his childhood by earning good grades and getting a scholarship to college. He'd escaped Vietnam as well, a war he had vehemently protested, by receiving an occupational deferment for his work as an aide at a mental hospital. He was retired and reclusive now; his face appeared weary in his photos, like soft thunder, and Marian didn't have to know the man to see that he still felt the pain from dreams and childhood and the knowledge of too many disturbed minds. But there were good things in his life: a woman to whom he'd been married for forty-seven years, a grown son who was doing well. Nick enjoyed literature and music, studied the works of the great modernist poets Eliot and Cummings and Stevens. He even gardened some. Marian knew all of these things.

Marian looked out to the west as if she could see into Idaho, where this man lived, as if the distance between them weren't the two-hundred-and-something miles that it was. She thought of the images of the crime scenes, or rather the places where the remains had been found, and the pictures of the women's faces, young women, like Marian. She knew that if Nick Shepard agreed to work with her, she would be reliving her life with Tate all over again. "I need to know what is real," Marian said. "I don't know what is real anymore."

All the while Marian thought no one

could know she had made this call. She would even go so far as to erase it from her phone. There were the others to think about — Lyle and Trainer and Jenness and Liz and Dudley. And now there was Tate's sister to consider, as well. Yet more than Marian's concern for the others was her fear that Tate could read her mind, as if somehow he were all-knowing now that he was gone, his presence like breath and oxygen. And there was that lingering hope that she was wrong, that her speculations and misgivings, tentative at best, were nothing more than an active imagination.

"You won't tell anyone I talked to you," she said. She could end this call. She could say she had made a mistake.

"All right," Shepard said.

And so it had come to this. She did not know if she could trust this man, but there was no one else. "Will you help me?" she asked, because she could no longer do this on her own. Because there was no other way to find out the truth.

Yes, he would help her. He had too much time on his hands. He was interested. He said all of these things.

Then Shepard asked her, "When was the first time you felt something wasn't right with Tate?"

2
Almost Seven Months Earlier: January 2017

Marian
Edmonton, Alberta, Canada

When Marian met Tate, she didn't know that the story of her life was about to change. She didn't know of northern Rocky Mountain skies and moons that could cut her heart open to the bone or that his cool hands would burn rivers beneath her skin, and that when he'd tell her in so many ways that she'd been everything he'd been looking for, his voice would sound unmistakable and true and she would believe him. She had just flown into Edmonton two days after New Year's and would be joining a group of field technicians for the next three months on a conservation study. The study would be conducted in the Athabasca oil sands in northeastern Alberta, between Lac La Biche and Fort McMurray.

Marian passed through customs and stood with one of her duffel bags strapped vertically to her back and the other slung over her neck and hanging crossways in front of her. A messy braid fell over her right shoulder, and wisps of brown hair trailed from beneath her knit cap. She'd told Lyle, the program coordinator, what she looked like and had sent him a picture. He'd told her not to worry; someone would be holding a sign. But she didn't see anyone holding a sign, so she proceeded to follow the foot traffic that led outside the airport and onto the curb. She held her cell phone in her left hand and was about to check it for a text message or a missed call when she heard a male voice say her name.

That was the first time she saw him. He was standing against a white pickup truck with a black soft topper. And though he would later want her to recall the moment, to set it apart from all the other moments that had existed for her up until then, no matter how many times she revisited the memory, she would not be able to recall the same kind of specific details as he. It was morning in Edmonton. She had taken a red-eye flight and had slept on the plane. She had not had time to brush her teeth, and the coffee that she had been served before the plane landed was weak and had left her with a terrible headache, and she worried that she had packed too many clothes because the duffel bags felt heavier than she would have liked.

But she did remember how as soon as she raised her chin and smiled, relieved that she had arrived and that there was a person on the other end to get her where she was supposed to be, she'd heard the barking of a large dog from the back of the truck, and that the man had hurried toward her and had taken the duffel bags off her shoulders. Tate introduced himself and put her bags in the back of the truck with boxes of food and a crate that held an eager Labrador mix who barked and wagged her tail against the plastic housing of her kennel.

Marian lowered her face to the kennel. "Hi, there," she said, her voice a fairly high note, as if she were talking to a very young child, as if she were talking to her dog, Deacon, who would be staying with Marian's parents while she was away.

"Her name's Arkansas," Tate said. "She's a rescue dog from the Ozarks."

"How old is she?"

"We're not sure. Maybe five or six."

Marian had first learned about K9s for Conservation and that it was seeking applicants for an upcoming study in Alberta that past summer when, as a seasonal employee, she was living with Deacon and a group of other technicians in a small trailer on the north beach of South Padre Island, Texas. Her job had involved rescuing stranded sea turtles, rehabilitating them, and releasing them into safer areas. Marian had been reading through job listings for her next position, preferably one that would allow dogs, when she'd seen the posting for six detection dog handlers and six orienteers with no prior experience required. The job would involve hiking in Alberta in three feet of snow and taking helicopters into remote locations for the purpose of finding wolf, caribou, and moose scat during the winter's oil explorations.

The program, a part of the University of Washington, was operated out of a camp facility just west of Whitefish, Montana, and relied on high-energy rescue dogs who would work for the sole pleasure and reward of playing with a ball. The candidates who were accepted for the positions would be expected to arrive in Whitefish in October for two months of training.

Marian filled out the online application. She mentioned her studies in biology at the University of Michigan, where she had graduated four years before. She listed all of the seasonal jobs she'd held since then, including tagging and tracking brown-headed cowbirds in Illinois, spraying for noxious weeds in Oklahoma, and banding ducks and mourning doves in eastern Wyoming. She wrote about her bulldog, Genius, whom she'd grown up with. And she wrote about Deacon, a forty-pound cattle dog with too much energy whom she'd adopted from a shelter shortly after arriving in Texas.

But seasonal jobs for field technicians were competitive. Marian was not selected for an interview for the study in Alberta. When her summer employment with Turtle, Inc., ended, she'd been allowed to stay in the trailer through December in exchange for working in the non-profit's gift shop. The other technicians moved on to other jobs or went back to school. Marian strung Christmas lights outside the trailer and drank spiked cider on the beach with the local employees. She'd found a job with a fish hatchery program in Clinton, Missouri, that would begin in the spring, and had decided to move home to Michigan in the meantime, to spend time with her parents and her brother's family.

Then she received the call from Lyle. She'd just come in from a run with Deacon and was standing in the doorway of her trailer, the sweat of Texas moving down her body, the lights on her trailer blinking red and green. Did Marian have a DUI, Lyle wanted to know. How soon could she get to Edmonton?

Tate told Marian that he was one of the team leaders and that he had worked as a handler for the past ten years. Jenness, the other team leader, who managed the program's communications, had been with the program six years. "Jenness and I will be running the operations," Tate said. Marian already knew that Lyle would be staying in Montana at the program's base camp, or The Den, as it was called, to coordinate and prepare for other studies.

The crew had arrived in Edmonton three days prior, with ten dogs, four snowmobiles and two trailers, six trucks, and supplies and gear. They'd used the first day to inventory supplies, restock food, and give the dogs some exercise, and had spent all of the next day in a snowmobile operations class taught by a Polaris dealer. They'd checked out of the hotel that morning and were on their way to an oil company compound in the oil sands. The compound, a five-hour drive from the airport, was owned and operated by Pétron Oil, a co-funder and supporter of the upcoming wildlife study. Tate estimated that he and Marian were only a couple of hours behind the others.

After Tate stopped to get Marian a coffee and the two of them were back on the road, Marian asked Tate about the two months of training that she'd missed. He told her about the fitness exercises, which included Indian trail runs up mountain roads, sometimes twice a day. The runs involved a single-file line, where the last person sprinted to the front, and so on. Tate told her the group would cover three to six miles at a time. Other days the runs were off-trail through dense forests, so that each member was bushwhacking. He told her not to worry. "You look like you're in pretty good shape," he said.

Then Tate asked Marian how much Lyle had told her, and she admitted that he had told her very little. "He just wanted to know if I'd ever had a DUI," she said.

Tate talked about the orienteer who had been turned away at the border because of a prior DUI. "There aren't always clean lines to human behaviors," Tate said. "But, hey, if it hadn't happened, you wouldn't be here, and that's a good thing, right?"

"I'm so happy to be here," Marian said.

Marian also learned that the teams had participated in a ten-day emergency responder course during those two previous months. Her résumé had included her first responder training, a certificate she had kept current, which had no doubt given her an edge in Lyle's last-minute decision to offer her a position.

As Marian finished her coffee and stared out at the polished white landscape and the endless highway around them, Tate talked about the multiple projects going on at any one time. One job was wrapping up in New Mexico, where a border collie mix was looking for Jemez Mountains salamanders, a candidate for the endangered species list. Tate talked about the incredible ball drive of the dogs. "It's an obsession," he said. "Given the choice between playing with a ball or eating a rib eye steak, they'll choose the ball."

Marian couldn't help but think of Deacon and his poor attempts at searching for Rodney, the stuffed sea turtle. After she'd submitted her application for the job, she'd been determined to turn Deacon into a detection dog so that should she be called for an interview, he would give Marian an advantage. After work each day, Marian would hide the stuffed turtle from the gift shop and praise Deacon enthusiastically and feed him treats when he found the turtle.

During her lunch breaks she would throw a tennis ball for Deacon on the beach and reward him with beef jerky when he ran after the ball and brought it back to her, which he seldom did without her chasing him into the water. She'd envisioned the snow-covered trails she and Deacon would hike, the solitude.

In her caffeinated state and excitement and lack of sleep, as she listened to Tate talk, everything looked beautiful to her: the cold, stark landscape; the long highway; the images of Tate's words; his light brown eyes that shot quick, animated glances toward her as he spoke; the color of his pupils in the sun's reflection like tree sap, amber and transparent.

Marian asked Tate if he had a favorite project, and he told her about the Yellowhead ecosystem along the eastern Canadian Rockies. "Fifty-two hundred square kilometers of pure God's country," he said. The study examined the impacts that recreation, forestry, and oil and gas exploration were having on the grizzly and black bear populations by analyzing scat samples for hormone levels, diet, and DNA.

Before the use of detection dogs, researchers had relied heavily on hair snares, typically consisting of barbed wire around an attractant for the purpose of snagging a tuft of the bear's fur, and radio collars, Tate said. Because the hair snares relied on the use of an attractant, the data could be considered biased. And though radio telemetry data was helpful, it came with risks, as demonstrated by the death of a park employee that previous spring when a bear was released from a culvert. The bear had attacked a young intern before a high-caliber rifle could put the bear down.

Two hours into the drive, Tate pulled off at a truck stop in Boyle to refuel and to get lunch. He and Marian sat across from each other at a booth, and as they ate cheeseburgers and shared a plate of French fries, she told Tate about Deacon and how much she missed him.

After Lyle had offered Marian the job, she'd called her parents to see if they would take Deacon while she was away. "It would just be temporary," Marian told them. And he was very well trained.

And so her parents had agreed. Marian had found a flight on Alaska Airlines that allowed larger dogs to fly as cargo if the dog and kennel didn't weigh more than one hundred and fifty pounds. She slipped a note with instructions for her parents into a plastic sleeve and taped it to the top of Deacon's crate. And after she checked Deacon in, she checked his small bag of toys, as well. Two hours later, she'd boarded the flight on Air Canada.

Maybe it was because of her lack of sleep, but her eyes became teary as she told Tate about Deacon, and she wiped away the wetness and apologized.

And did Tate's eyes become teary also? He didn't want her to apologize. He said he felt terrible for her. He told her about a dog he'd had when he was a boy growing up in Glendive, Montana. Said he'd found the dog after baseball practice one day and the dog had followed him home. "I'd read to him. Honest to God, don't laugh. He'd sit up in bed with me and I'd read him these books I'd get from the library. At first I just called him Dog, but then I named him Arthur because we were reading a story about King Arthur and Guinevere, and I thought my dog was like a king."

"That's so sweet," Marian said.

"Yeah." Tate was smiling and looking away. "He drowned," Tate said.

"What? Oh my God. I'm so sorry. What happened?"

"We had a river behind our house. We got a lot of rain that year. There were these kids who lived down the street. And Arthur, he had Labrador in him. He liked to fetch things, kind of like these dogs we've got with us up here. So these kids came over and threw a stick in the river, and Arthur went in after it. He got the stick, but the river was too powerful for him to turn back."

"Were you there? What did you do?"

"I was running alongside the river and crying and trying to get to him. I'd get close, and he'd try to scramble onto the bank. He'd be looking at me with these big brown eyes, all pleading and frightened, wanting me to save him. But then he'd get washed away again."

"Tate, that's terrible. I'm so sorry."

Tate leaned back in the booth and placed both hands flat on the table. "Well, what are you going to do." He ate another French fry, then took a swallow from his glass of root beer. "I wrote an epitaph for him," he said. "I still have it. Except I wrote it in pencil. It's kind of hard to make out now." Tate finished his drink. "I got this," he said. He picked up the bill from the table and walked up to the cash register.

He was taller than Marian had realized, close to six feet. About an inch of wavy brown hair showed beneath his knit cap and fell over his ears. Marian tried to guess his age. Probably midthirties.

After Tate paid and left a tip on the table, he told Marian he had something for her, and so she followed him out to the truck, where he opened up the back, and Arkansas was again wagging her tail and whining with delight.

"Hey there, girl," Tate said. He let Arkansas out of her crate. She leapt down and pranced beside him, her eyes bright and fixed on his every move. Marian knelt beside the dog and stroked her coat.

"She's beautiful," Marian said.

"I thought maybe you could use some dog medicine," Tate said. "I know how hard that must have been putting Deacon on that plane."

Marian wrapped her arms around the dog and cooed in her ears. Then the dog swiveled around quickly, and Marian noticed that Tate had something in his hand. Next to the parking lot was an open field with windblown eddies of snow. Tate pulled his arm back and threw a blue rubber ball, and Arkansas tore off across the empty parking spaces and into the eighteen inches or more of snow before the ball landed maybe sixty yards from where they stood. The dog's back legs kicked up flakes of the white powder, creating a wraithlike image in her wake.

"She's fast," Marian said. And no sooner had Marian said those words than Arkansas came tearing back to Tate, the ball already covered in frothy saliva. She dropped the ball at Tate's feet, her body tense with anticipation, as if Marian could hear the dog saying, *Again!* This time Tate handed the ball to Marian, who drew her arm back and threw the ball as far as she could, maybe forty yards. And even after Arkansas had sprung after the ball, Marian could feel Tate watching her, and her cheeks burned red from the wind and the cold and her awareness of Tate, who now was saying very little.

She and Tate continued to throw the ball for Arkansas, and Marian continued to love on the dog each time the big, sloppy, beautiful Lab brought the ball back, until Tate said they should get going.

They didn't talk as much on the rest of the drive. Marian felt herself dozing a little and feeling grateful to be where she was. She had loved playing with Arkansas. She couldn't wait to meet the other dogs in the program. And three months would fly by, and she and Deacon would be running on the beaches in Michigan and then driving across the Midwest to Missouri for her next seasonal job. And maybe she smiled as she dozed because she didn't know then that it would be weeks before she would be able to throw her arms around a dog once more, or that in less than a month, she would never see Deacon again.

3
January 2017

Marian
Oil sands, Alberta, Canada

When Marian climbed out of Tate's truck at the Pétron Oil compound, she immediately heard the humming of electricity, like a dull ringing in her ears, from all the buildings and lights and generators and diesel trucks whose engines were plugged into outlets when not in use.

"Welcome home," Tate said.

Marian squinted against the snow and the bright afternoon sun. And when a woman with long brown hair approached them amid the sunlight and the glare from the snow, she almost appeared like an apparition. Tate introduced the woman as Jenness, the other team leader, who then extended her hand toward Marian. The cuff of the woman's down coat pulled up the slightest bit so that when Marian shook Jenness's gloved hand, she noticed the tattoo, a small hawk feather, etched in black, on the underside of the woman's exposed wrist. The woman was no taller than Marian, around five feet four inches, and appeared lean despite her thick snow layers. She said she had Marian's key and room assignment and would show her to the orienteer housing.

"We only beat you here by a few hours," Jenness told Tate. Then she pointed out two trailers at the other end of the parking lot where she and Tate and the six handlers would be staying with the dogs.

Tate and Jenness exchanged banter about logistics and business and the names of people Marian didn't know, and because of Jenness and Tate's easy way with each other, Marian wondered if they might be a couple.

Marian and Jenness each picked up one of the duffel bags. They carried the bags to one of three large modular buildings. There were a couple hundred rooms in the building, Jenness said, and several communal bathrooms. "You'll have your own space, but I have to warn you, it's really small."

The room was about the size of a walk-in closet, with barely enough space for a twin-size bed, a small desk, and a bureau. Marian tried to turn around and bumped the duffel bag into the desk chair and stumbled a bit, and when she did, she grabbed onto Jenness's shoulder. Then Jenness laughed. "Like I warned you. The rooms are small."

"I don't mind," Marian said.

"Trust me. We've stayed in a lot worse."

Because the two women with the large duffel bags were still standing in the small space, the room suddenly felt like the kind of tight quarters where one can hardly breathe, and perhaps Jenness sensed the same thing because she set the bag down and said she'd let Marian get settled in. There was a folder on the desk with maps and instructions and helpful tips about the compound, and another folder with a schedule and information to bring Marian up to speed. "It's a lot to take in," Jenness said. She was now standing in the doorway with one hand on the doorjamb. "Don't worry. I'll walk you through everything. And don't be afraid to ask questions."

Beyond the three long modular barracks that housed seven-hundred-plus oil workers and the conservation group's six orienteers was a building with a TV commons area and an exercise room. Beyond that building was the cafeteria. After Marian organized her small space, she joined the others in the cafeteria for a group meeting with Jenness and Tate.

Six dog handlers had been hired as seasonal employees for the oil sands study. This was their first project. Their employment would end once the study was over. The six orienteers were here as volunteers. Each team would consist of a handler, a dog, and an orienteer. Marian had taken on other jobs as a volunteer, as long as housing was provided, for the experience alone, and this was one of those.

The purpose of the study was to assess the impacts the oil exploration was having on the caribou, moose, and wolf populations living in the oil sands. This would be done by using the dogs to locate scat from these different species. The scat would then be packed in dry ice and shipped back to the lab at the University of Washington, where it would be analyzed for DNA, hormone levels, and diet. Of special concern on this study were the caribou, which would be each team's priority. Wildlife investigators had predicted that the caribou would become extinct in the oil sands within the next two decades.

The handlers were responsible at all times for the dogs. The orienteers were to navigate each team's course of travel, collect the scat, and record the waypoints. This meant that the dogs were off-limits to the orienteers. Jenness and Tate said that now that the dogs were on site, it was important to limit their distractions, and interaction with too many people wasn't a good thing.

Jenness and Tate went on to explain that orienteers were rarely assigned to a study. "When there are two people, usually one of them will be talking, which interrupts the focus of both the handler and the dog," Tate said. But this particular contract had required that each team consist of two people for safety measures, primarily because of the cold.

For the first ten days, the handlers would be running training exercises for the dogs to get them acclimated to the area and to further enhance the scat-ball concept. The orienteers would be working in pairs to assess the roads. The oil company's ice road network varied from year to year. The orienteers would be exploring that network, while making a tracklog with their GPS devices. They would also be determining which roads could handle the weight of the trucks. At the end of each day the orienteers would be downloading their tracklogs onto the program's geological information system, where the data would become road layers that could be added to maps.

Determining which roads were stable proved to be challenging, as the roads were built on top of peat bogs, called muskeg, which was why the terrain was only accessible when the ground was frozen. The general rule was that if there were young trees or shrubs in the nearby landscape, the road most likely was one to be avoided, as the road would be too soft. But the absence of low-growing vegetation wasn't always an indicator, and there would be a loud *thunk* and the truck's tires would fall through the muskeg, which was what happened to Marian on her third day. Jeb, an orienteer from Oregon, was riding with Marian, who was behind the wheel. They'd just turned onto a road that led through dense woods of Canadian spruce and canoe birch, when the truck *thunked* and came to an abrupt halt.

They had brought a shovel for just this reason, and while Jeb dug around the truck's wheels, Marian took a handsaw into the woods to cut branches. They layered the branches around the wheels. Marian again climbed into the driver's seat, started the engine, and slightly accelerated, while Jeb pushed from behind, but the wheels only spun, and so she and Jeb continued their efforts again and again, but to no avail, until finally the two of them decided they'd better call over the radio for help.

While they waited for assistance, Marian

learned that Jeb was twenty-five, just a year younger than she, and after college had held a number of different jobs including working as a deckhand on a fishing boat in the Bering Strait and driving a bulldozer for an excavation crew at construction sites. He said he wanted to go back to school one day and study writing. Marian liked his long blond hair, which he wore in a ponytail. She told him he reminded her of her younger brother who was working as a youth minister at a church in Grand Rapids, where the two of them had grown up in Michigan.

At some point the conversation turned toward the dogs, and Jeb said that most of the program's dogs had been one step away from being euthanized. "Just look at them now."

Marian and Jeb were sitting on the tailgate and were eating from a bag of trail mix when they heard a truck approaching. They retraced their path along the road to the turnoff, where the ground was more solid. Tate pulled up beside them and rolled down his window.

"I got a couple of chains in the back. Each of you grab one. I'm going to back in and get a little closer."

And so Marian and Jeb did as Tate instructed, and Tate parked and got out. He connected the two chains and hooked the ends on the closest axle. Within minutes Marian and Jeb's truck was out of the bog and they were loading the chains back into the bed of Tate's vehicle.

Then Tate asked Marian to ride with him. "You can brief me on the road conditions." And so Marian climbed into the passenger seat next to Tate, and Jeb walked around to the driver's side of the other truck and hoisted himself behind the wheel.

After they got going, Marian told Tate about the grid units to the northwest having the best network, and that there were only a few working roads to the northeast. She gave Tate specifics about the muskeg and the terrain.

Marian had removed her gloves and while she was talking, Tate reached for her hand. "You're cold," he said. "You were out there a long time." Marian said she was fine. Other than that, there was now nothing obvious to say, and her hand remained beneath his until he asked her what she hoped to get out of her time there, and his right hand grabbed hold of the steering wheel again.

Marian hesitated before answering because she did not want to sound presumptuous, and Tate said, "It isn't a difficult question," and Marian told him what she really wanted was to be working with the dogs.

"You want to be a handler," Tate said.

"I wish I'd had the chance to try out."

"We've had a lot of folks over the years who started out as orienteers, Jenness included. What you want isn't out of reach."

The living area of one of the two handler trailers had been converted into the group's workstation. It was late when Marian had finished downloading her GPS tracklog and entering her notes regarding the roads, sometime close to midnight. A dusting of snow blew over her boots as she walked back to the orienteer housing, and snow-flakes collected on her lips and lashes, though the sky was clear. She thought of Deacon and loneliness and other matters that collected in her mind at a day's end when sleep was close. Only three weeks before, Marian had been running down a sand-packed trail with Deacon bounding alongside her. Her life had felt snagged in a trailer and a place too hot to call home. She was fair-skinned with sun-enhanced freckles and too much Irish and Scandinavian blood to be living in Texas.

For the past four years, Marian had gone from job to job. Her family worried that she was chasing happiness and might be better off with a man, even though they typically weren't conventional thinkers. After Marian had started college and still did not have a boyfriend, her father asked her if she was gay. But Marian did not think she was gay. She met a boy her junior year. He had brown hair, and when the sun shone on it, the ends looked like copper. He was friends with Marian's roommate, a tall, strong woman with Chippewa blood. The boy's name was Hawkon, and he told Marian he had Chippewa blood, too, like her roommate. He was an English major who enjoyed writing poetry. Marian liked his name and the poems he wrote, though she did not understand them, and she liked the copper tips of his hair. They talked and read poetry for a month before he kissed her one night underneath a streetlamp in downtown Ann Arbor. They had just left a bar and three empty beer bottles each. And when he kissed her, he slid his right hand beneath the fall of her hair, lifting it slightly from the nape of her neck, and her spine chilled from the warmth of it all. After he walked her back to her dorm, she tried to write a poem for him, but her words felt futile.

Hawkon did not stop by the next day or the next, and a month later when she had not heard from him, she cried. She thought her roommate was asleep, until the covers on her roommate's bed stirred, the mattress springs creaked, and bare feet padded across the vinyl floor. Linda lifted the poly-fill comforter and crawled in beside Marian. She smoothed Marian's hair and breathed warmth against her skin. The next night, Linda slipped beneath the covers with Marian again, and the night after that. Her fingers stroked Marian's arms. She tugged at the neckline of Marian's T-shirt and kissed her freckled shoulders. They became lovers, but Marian never wondered if this was love, and only once after their lovemaking did Linda speak those words, shortly before falling asleep.

Marian had actually only been with one man, when she was twenty-three, a kind man with fleece sheets who would bring her coffee in the morning. But he'd eventually moved on, as had Marian, when their seasonal job together ended.

Marian visited the women's communal bathroom. She was thinking about emailing one of her co-workers from Turtle, Inc. But when she walked out of the bathroom, she was startled by Tate, who was standing just outside the doorway.

"I understand you want to take the sleds out tomorrow," he said.

Marian told Tate about seeing only one road on the grid unit that she and Jeb had been assigned to check and that she wasn't sure what kind of shape the road was in. "After today, I'd feel better taking the snowmobiles."

"Do you know how to handle these machines?" he asked.

And Marian told him she did, that she'd grown up riding snowmobiles in Michigan.

"Do you want me to give you some pointers?"

"I'll be okay," she told him.

Marian moved down the hall and was surprised to find she'd left her room unlocked. She didn't think much of it until she opened the door and removed her boots and began to peel off the layers of her clothes. In that moment she felt certain that a man had been inside her room. There were footprints on the floor that were too large to be hers. She thought of the oil workers. She checked her belongings. Everything was in its place. But when she turned in she knew someone had lain on her bed, because her pillow had the unfamiliar scent of a man that she would later come to recognize, of spruce and sweat and diesel oil and outdoor air.

And when she eventually came to know Tate's body and the comfort of his breathing and the way his skin and clothes smelled, she asked him about the night when she had turned her pillow over and had lain awake for too many hours and had promised herself never to leave her door unlocked again.

"You were in my room," she said.

"That's right."

"Why were you on my bed?"

He told her that her door wasn't locked, that he'd come looking for her to ask her about the sleds. He knew the orienteers had been complaining about their rooms. He'd wanted to get a sense of just how small the rooms were. He was being a responsible team leader.

It all made sense to Marian. It always did.

4
February 2017

Marian
Oil sands, Alberta, Canada
There was a moment when Marian saw Tate differently, when she looked into his amber-and-brown eyes, which were closer than they had ever been before, and she felt her blood move through her and heard a whirring in her ears as if she were on a plane that was either taking off or landing, though she was not sure which. Tate held her gaze as one who is in perfect control, and never before had Marian felt as protected and safe; never before had she felt as vulnerable and exposed.

The moment happened the same week the program lost one of its dogs, and Marian wondered if she might have been responsible. Then her parents told her about Deacon, and she no longer felt sure of herself or anything she had felt sure of before, and her heart was broken; yes, she thought, this great beating muscle felt as severed as a bone.

Marian had been assigned to work with Noah, who was tall and gangly and barely out of college, and Chester, part Labrador and golden retriever, who was new to the program. The group's field schedule included three days on and one day off, and then two days on and one day off to give the dogs a break. But that all depended on the weather. The coldest workable temperature was −10°F. Any colder than that and the air could damage the dogs' lungs.

Each night before going into the field Marian would meet with Jenness to prepare for her team's next assignment. Jenness would provide Marian with a clear-coated paper map of the team's study cell. The map included a geological information system with radio telemetry data of existing caribou that had been collared, and habitat model layers. The habitat model layers estimated where there might be lichen-rich resources, an important staple in the caribou's diet. From the map Marian would determine the best course of travel that her team should take.

Typically teams collected anywhere from fifteen to twenty-five scat samples a day, which included moose, deer, caribou, and wolf. However, often teams would find so much deer and moose scat, particularly if they were in an area where the animals had been feeding on carrion, that they had a special protocol: After collecting one, skip the next five before collecting again. This was just so the team could keep moving and identify more individual species. But caribou, being at risk for extinction, was the study's priority; all scat from that species was collected.

The teams had been conducting fieldwork for almost four weeks now, and in those four weeks, what had first begun as a six-hour day in mid-January, including time en route to and from each team's respective survey area, had now extended to nine hours by the second week in February because of the increase in daylight. The longer days required greater stamina from each of the team members, as well as the dogs. Though the terrain was flat, unlike the steep trails on which the teams had trained in Montana, the snow could be three to four feet deep, which required the handlers and the orienteers to take turns breaking trail for the dogs.

Over those four weeks Marian had grown increasingly frustrated with Noah. He was sullen and moody and difficult to work with. That particular day in February was no exception. Noah had pulled the truck off at kilometer post 10 and unloaded. They would hike the rest of the way along one of the decommissioned roads to their survey area. Marian powered her phone and Bluetooth, then waited for the GPS on her Android device to make a satellite connection. The GPS device would log her position every thirty seconds.

Noah had let Chester out of the back of the truck. The dog ran off a few yards to relieve himself, but within seconds he was jumping on Noah, his front paws pressed against Noah's chest. The dog licked Noah's face and then jumped down and sniffed Noah's hip pack, as if waiting for him to pull out the rubber ball. Chester wore a harness over an insulated vest. Noah strapped a bell to the top of Chester's harness and secured a small GPS tracking device in a pocket on the harness. Chester's GPS device would log his position every second. The dog's tracklog, along with waypoints of where scat had been found, would later be downloaded onto a map.

Marian's job was to navigate her team and to collect and record the scat. Noah's job was to work with Chester, recognizing when

Chester was onto a scent and rewarding him when he'd found a scat sample. Away from the road, the snow level quickly became at least three feet deep and dense. Pushing their way through it was like wading through wet concrete.

By noon, Chester had found five samples, two of which were caribou. Some of the samples were buried three feet beneath the snow. Using a collapsible shovel, Marian cleared the snow away from the scat. She also had tools for chiseling samples loose from the frozen condensation. Then she'd remove her gloves and mittens and, with only a latex layer, pick up the samples and deposit them in Ziploc bags. She'd record the samples and their waypoints on her phone. And sometimes Chester would be onto the next sample before Marian had finished her tasks, especially if they were in a kill zone. If they entered an area where there was a carcass, they could be sure there would be an increase in samples. Too often Marian could be moving from one sample to the next, without having time to pull on her gloves and mittens and warm her hands.

On that particular day the temperature was hovering just barely above –5°F, and by midafternoon they had indeed entered a kill zone. Marian's hands were freezing. The tips of her fingers on her right hand were already turning white. She held them in her mouth to try to warm them while she hurried to the next find.

She knelt in the snow, which came to just over her shoulders. "These are all deer," she said. "I think it's time we follow the deer and moose protocol. You know, skip five for every one." But Noah had already disappeared around the timber. Though she could no longer see them, she could hear Chester's bell.

"Hold on!" she yelled.

She dropped the sample. She could barely maneuver her hands now. "To hell with it." And she moved on to try to catch up. But just as she rounded the corner into an open space, Chester was onto yet another find.

"That-a-boy," Noah said. "Nice job."

Chester stood alert. Snow had frozen to his coat in icicles, and his muzzle was covered in a white dusting like freezer burn. Icicles hung from his mouth where his drool had frozen. As Marian drew closer, Chester's feet pranced in place, creating a crater around where he stood.

Noah threw the ball about ten feet behind them and along the trail. Chester retrieved it in a couple of quick bounds. They were moving again. "Don't skimp on this one.

It's caribou," Noah said.

Marian knelt to collect the scat. Noah was right. The sample was caribou. She was writing the date on the bag when Chester barked.

"Way to go. You got that," Noah said.

They were definitely in a kill zone, Marian thought.

"Hold on, Chester," Marian said.

"What's that?" Noah said.

"I told Chester to hold on." She put the sample in the dry sack attached to her pack.

Noah was walking toward her. "You don't talk to him, you got that? You don't say his name. You don't throw the ball for him. You don't acknowledge him."

"I didn't throw the ball for him."

"Are you listening to me?"

"Back off, Noah!" Marian wasn't looking at him. Her fingers could barely move. The battery on her phone was low. She had an extra one in the breast pocket of her jacket, but to replace the battery would mean more time that her hands would be exposed to the cold.

"You need to step it up," Noah said.

Chester had walked over to Marian. She didn't look at him.

"Let's go, boy. Check over here," Noah said.

Marian went ahead and replaced her battery. The pain in her right hand was almost unbearable. She would try to use her left hand with the next sample. She packed her supplies away and relayered her gloves. She added additional hand warmers. Then she attempted to quicken her pace, to literally jump from one foot to the next as if in a slow jog, along the trail that Noah and Chester had made. She winced as the blood returned to her fingers as if she'd stuck her hand inside a pincushion. And wasn't the temperature dropping, and wouldn't it be too cold for Chester to work? She'd forgotten to check the temperature when she'd had her phone out. She would remember to do so when she collected the next sample. She pulled her neck gaiter over her nose and held it in place. And how far were they now from the truck? She should have looked at the map more closely when she'd stopped.

These were her thoughts when she heard a high-pitched screaming sound, both child-like and animal-like, followed by a rapid series of yelps and barks. Noah and Chester had gotten ahead of her again and were in the thick timber to her left. Running to catch up wasn't possible, though she tried, and on doing so toppled over more than once. She clambered back up each time. A residue of snow coated her clothes, and hardened clumps stuck against the fibers of her hat and in her braid. Chester was in some sort of pain. And amid the barks and yelps and high-pitched cries, Noah was yelling, and the panic in his voice seemed to only exasperate the dog.

She saw Noah hunched over the ground. Chester was lying flat on his side. His back legs kicked frantically. Marian lumbered toward them. She fell on her knees beside Noah. Chester's head was pinned to the ground by the jaws of a conibear trap, used to harvest fishers and martens. The trap was much like an enlarged, two-sided mousetrap, though with the pressure of at least ninety pounds. Chester's gums were torn and bleeding. Blood was trickling out of his right ear, which was also torn badly.

The teams had been warned about the trap lines, the routes along which traps had been set. Though Pétron Oil gave the teams some idea as to where the traps might be, neither the oil company nor the conservation workers had access to precise locations for the simple reason that trappers would not give up this information. Fur trapping was a vital staple in their lives. They were not going to risk their kills being poached.

Jenness had told the orienteers and handlers to watch for snowmobile tracks that were not headed in any particular direction, saying oil workers did not go for joyrides into the wilderness. The trappers, though, headed straight into the woods, as did the conservation teams. For this reason, if Marian saw snowmobile tracks or foot tracks and knew that none of the conservation group's teams had been to that grid yet, she'd avoid moving in that direction. There was also the problem of one of the dogs being lured by the bait of the traps. Marian couldn't help but wonder if in all the haste of the afternoon she had missed some sort of sign. Even though Noah had been breaking trail when this happened, it was Marian's responsibility to navigate her team.

Noah cursed and yelled as he tried to pry apart the trap jaws on the end closest to Chester's muzzle.

"Give me your pack," Marian said.

But Noah ignored her. All of his focus was on trying to pry the trap open.

Marian pulled off her mittens and unzipped Noah's pack while it was still on his back.

"Grab the other side of the trap!" Noah yelled. He was no longer wearing his mittens either. He was down to a thin layer of wool gloves.

"That's not going to work." Marian's hands dug through the pack. She was thinking of the mousetraps she had set over the years in the housing where she'd stayed during some of her jobs. She thought about how she would go about resetting a trap, which was never done by lifting the metal jaw. "Noah, where's the leash?" she asked.

"I don't know!"

Marian continued to dig through the pack until she found the leash toward the bottom, beneath a package of trail mix and a fleece layer. She retrieved the leash and the fleece top. Still on her knees, she moved toward Chester's head. "It's okay, boy," she said. Her voice was as soothing as she could make it sound. His yelps turned into long whimpers and cries. "That-a-boy," Marian said. She stroked his back.

"What are you doing?" Noah pulled again on the trap and grunted in one enormous exhale. The springs did not budge, nor would they, Marian knew.

"Fuck!" Noah pounded his fists against the snow. He then chucked a handful of it as if throwing a baseball at high speed.

Again Chester yelped and barked.

"I need you to move, Noah," Marian said,

and he did. He sat back, and in a quick glance Marian saw the defeat in his body and a sad desperation on his face. "It's going to be okay," she said, and though she had meant those words for Chester, she was sure Noah thought she'd intended them for him. She tied one end of the leash to the top loop of the spring on the trap side that was pressing down along Chester's mouth. She then ran the leash through the bottom spring loop and back through the top. "Hang in there, Chester. You're doing great," she said. She stood and placed her foot on the trap chain so that she could pin the trap to the ground.

"I can do that," Noah said, and so he took her place. Marian hauled up on the leash until both sides of the spring met, which released the tension of the jaws. With one side of the trap reset, Chester's neck and body squirmed from the release of some pressure, though he still was unable to break free. Marian repeated the process on the other side of the trap that had clamped down against Chester's neck. The dog whined loudly and as soon as his head and neck were released, he sprang to his feet, but when he did, his head lolled back toward the ground as if he no longer had the strength to hold it up.

With all of the activity, Marian and Noah had created a clearing of at least a ten-foot radius. Chester moved several feet away from them. His whines became more muted and tentative, like a soft whimpering. He lay on his stomach with his forelegs out in front of him and lowered his head onto his paws. This was the first time Marian noticed that two of his boots were missing. In his struggle, he'd managed to kick them off. She approached him slowly to try to keep him calm.

"Please tell me he's okay," Noah said, and Marian knew instantly that Noah was crying. She looked over her shoulder to see him once more sitting in the snow. His knees were drawn up in front of him, as if he were afraid to get any closer to Chester, as if he were afraid to find out that the dog might not make it.

Marian unzipped the fleece layer she'd pulled from Noah's pack. She laid it over Chester's shoulders and head. She didn't care that Chester was Noah's responsibility. In that moment Chester needed help. She removed her pack and set it on the ground. She retrieved her first-aid kit. "We're going to have to get him back to the truck," she said.

"He's not going to be able to walk," Noah

said. "You saw him."

"We'll take turns carrying him. I just want to get some antibiotic on his wounds."

Marian also had a small wool blanket in her pack. After she applied the antibiotic ointment, she wrapped Chester in the blanket. But when she slipped her arms beneath him to lift him, not only did he squirm free, but she also realized full well how heavy he was.

"We're not going to be able to get him out of here," Noah said. "He's got to weigh close to eighty pounds. I can lift him, but I'm not going to be able to carry him through this snow."

Because there was no cell service in the area, only Wi-Fi back at the compound, Marian brought out her satellite phone from her pack. Once it had powered up and made a connection, she called Jenness and relayed their situation. She described Chester's injuries. "He's in a lot of pain," Marian said. "He's not able to follow us out."

Jenness said she would contact the oil company's emergency responders. Though other teams had taken the conservation group's machines and would still be en route back to the compound, the oil company had rescue workers on call who could assist.

"I can meet them at the vehicle," Marian said. She went on to relay the vehicle's location. And so it was agreed that Noah would stay with Chester, and Marian would meet the responders and lead them to Noah and Chester's location.

When Marian got off the phone, it was already after three, with less than two hours of daylight left. She checked her GPS receiver. She and Noah had hiked about a kilometer to get to their six-by-six-kilometer study cell and somehow were now just outside that cell on its northwestern edge, which put them over four kilometers, approximately two and a half miles, away from their vehicle. Without having to break trail or collect samples, Marian thought she could cut the time in more than half from what it had taken them to get this far.

"I'll have my satellite phone on," Marian said. She told Noah to power his up in case someone needed to reach him.

"How did this happen?" Noah asked, his voice still weak with defeat.

"I don't know." Marian looked away. She needed to get going. "I'll leave you with my pack." She wanted Noah to have whatever extra supplies he might need, including food and liquids. Along with a first-aid kit, there was extra food, a thermos of hot water, and sleeping bags and blankets back at the truck. She wasn't worried about herself.

"At least take one of the thermoses," Noah told her. "You'll need to keep yourself hydrated."

Marian agreed, and she realized how careful they were being with each other. She took one of the thermoses out of her pack. "I'm leaving you my headlamp," she said, though she knew its batteries wouldn't last long.

"Take it. You won't make it to the truck before dark. You'll need it. I've got mine in my pack."

Noah had since removed his pack. "Take your batteries out of your headlamp," she said. "Keep them close to your body."

"I will. I'll put them inside my pants."

"Gross," she said, though she knew what he'd said was a good idea, and they both laughed.

"Okay, I'll be back. Stay warm." She looked at Chester. He was lying still where she had tried to pick him up, but he was breathing steadily.

5
Present: July 2017

Nick Shepard
Sandpoint, Idaho

Nick Shepard walked with a cane to his car. His left leg felt heavier than his right, and each step took the kind of effort that made him perspire beneath his heavy beard and along his lower back. Some days were easier. This wasn't one of those days. He crossed the small parking lot and, despite the effort, felt glad for this moment of independence. There would come a time when the doctors would say he could no longer drive. When that time came he would have to rely more and more on his wife, who would quit her job then and say it was all right, that they didn't need the money anyway. It was true. They lived simply enough, but the medical bills were adding up, and hadn't politics made a mess of the whole health care system, but don't get him started. No, today was a lovely day, and his appointment had gone well. His wife would be glad for the news. They'd pour a glass of wine tonight and celebrate, even though he preferred something stronger, bourbon or scotch, but he wasn't supposed to mix hard liquor with Depakote. Actually, according to the drug's warning labels he wasn't supposed to drink alcohol at all, but a little wine never hurt anyone, his doctor had said. Besides, a man shouldn't have to give up all of his vices. Maybe he'd have that bourbon.

He kept his appointments at 10 a.m. each Monday. This allowed him plenty of time to make the forty-five-minute drive from Bonners Ferry, where he and his wife lived, to Sandpoint. And after his appointments, he'd stop at Connie's Café for a coffee and lunch.

Today the sun was warm. He rolled down the windows and drove to the café and listened to *Blonde on Blonde,* a Bob Dylan recording, on its fifth track, that his son had made for him, not because his son liked Bob Dylan, but because of the concert Nick had taken the boy to see in Coeur d'Alene two years ago when Nick didn't know glio cells had begun dividing and multiplying inside his brain. Peter, his son, thirty-eight and married, had two children of his own, both teenage girls, and though Nick was not religious, he prayed every day that these girls would be safe, that whoever was out there would leave them alone.

At eleven o'clock, the café was quiet. Nick picked up a complimentary copy of the *Statesman* from Boise and sat at the corner table near the window. But when Angie walked over to pour his coffee, he folded the paper and set it in the chair beside him, and after they spoke a few pleasantries, she asked him if he was ready to order.

He said he'd like the roast beef sandwich. He'd have the potato salad. Maybe he'd have dessert. She could come back later and he'd let her know. He blew on the coffee before taking a sip. He liked it black. He was glad for his appetite and that a roast beef sandwich still tasted like roast beef. He'd already been through one round of chemo. The nausea hadn't been too bad. His wife swore he'd put on weight, and since when was that a good thing, he'd told her.

Other patrons arrived and took seats around him and talked to one another, and dishes clattered. He ate his roast beef sandwich and potato salad, and when he finished eating, he pushed his plate aside. He opened the newspaper over the table and read about oil fracking, and why homelessness was more common now than just twenty years ago, and a gubernatorial race that had gone corrupt, and what political race was not corrupt he wanted to know, and he got so pissed off that he ordered another coffee instead of dessert and stared out the window at the mishmash of thoughts in his head, making sure they were still his thoughts, and that his brain still worked despite the golf-ball-size tumor that the surgeons had removed two months ago, and all of the brain cells they had removed with it, and how big was the hole in his frontal lobe, and the small tumor in his temporal lobe that was so close to his spinal cord that it was inoperable, so his doctor had said, and maybe he should find another doctor. But the cancer wasn't growing, and yes, he'd have that bourbon after all. Today he saw his oncologist. Next Monday was physical therapy. He liked the whirlpool. Perhaps he and Cate should put a whirlpool inside their house.

But really what he was thinking about was the young woman who had called. It was true, people contacted him all the time about one case or another. After all, there had been three-hundred-plus victims over thirty years. He ignored most of the people who tried to get in touch with him. He didn't answer his phone, seldom listened to messages, and had no trouble finding the DEL key on his keyboard. It wasn't so much the murders themselves; it was more like being interrupted, an annoyance. He contemplated all of this because he wasn't sure why he had answered the phone that day, and what was her name, Marian, yes, but her last name. He'd written it down. Even run a background check on her. She'd impressed him with her many jobs saving the habitat. There was something innocent about her that was rare these days.

But all of that was after the fact, after he'd reached for the receiver, after she'd rambled on, and he could tell she was nervous. He was intrigued. She had her own personal mission. She knew what she wanted. She didn't feel like an interruption to him. Besides, coincidence was for those who wanted to avoid the deeper meaning in life. There were no coincidences as far as he was concerned.

It was on Friday, after lunch and some reading and a little yard work. He had just walked into the kitchen from his garden, where he had pulled a ripe tomato from one of the three vines, had bitten into the fruit as if eating an apple, and the light red juice had run down his arm. He'd gone inside to tear off a paper towel, to wash off the juice.

The phone had rung, and he'd reached for the receiver, like an old habit, instead of turning on the faucet. And somewhere in the conversation Marian had stopped referring to her boyfriend as "he" and "him" and instead said his name, though her voice sounded tentative when she said it, as if she were giving something away she would want to reclaim as soon as she had let it go. But there it was, out in the air, and now in Nick's consciousness, where so far it had not been consumed by the big C cclls that at the moment were not growing in his brain.

And was it déjà vu or had he heard the name Tate before? It wasn't a common name, and might Nick have jotted it somewhere in his copious notes, which had now all been turned over to a Canadian digital archivist. Nick had befriended the Canadian a couple of years before on the Moyie River. The man was bird-watching. Nick and his wife were bird-watching also, and one thing had led to another. And besides, Nick had recently retired and was looking to downsize his belongings. For a reasonable fee, the Canadian would turn Nick's notes into digital files. That was almost a year ago. The Canadian had said it might take as long for him to complete the project. Nick was all right with that. He knew where everything was. He could retrieve the notes if he wanted, rent out some storage unit where the papers would collect moisture and dust. But what would be the point of that? Getting rid of the evidence of his work had felt cleansing.

Nick knew it wasn't the murders that haunted him so much as the killers, as if they stood in the shadows of his life, always watching him. And there was the one killer in particular who had remained a part of Nick's subconscious. But that was before Nick had stepped down from his work, before he'd crossed any ethical boundaries, before he'd made a young woman afraid. Maybe the disease would rid him of these thoughts, get rid of the killers' faces and names and affect, give him some release from the remaining window of his life that, from what he understood of this disease, was more like a porthole.

Marian wasn't from Montana, but she'd heard about the Stillwater cases: four women who'd disappeared and been murdered over the course of six years: one woman for approximately every eighteen to twenty-four months. Marian wanted to know if her boyfriend had found one of the bodies. A little over two years had passed since the last victim had gone missing. Maybe the murders had stopped, or they'd been taken elsewhere.

Three of the victims' bodies had been disposed of within a couple of miles of each other in the Stillwater State Forest, just over the border in Montana. The other body was found outside Helena. Nick wasn't supposed to have gotten involved with the Stillwater cases, or with any other cases for that matter. Wasn't that why he had moved twenty-five hundred miles or some such distance across the country, to leave his thirty-some-odd years of working with criminals and their acts of violence behind him, to watch birds and study wildlife, to read poetry, to garden a little and get some writing done, and maybe sleep a little better than he had before his move.

Marian said she'd searched archives of local papers, read articles about the missing women, but none of those articles had given the identities or any specifics of the people who had found the victims' remains. Nick knew one body had been discovered by a couple who was doing some backcountry snowshoeing; two of the others were discovered by hunters; another was found by a man and his dog. The man was cutting firewood. Nick asked the woman if her boyfriend ever cut firewood. "I think so," she said.

"Did he ever hunt?" Nick asked.

"No, I don't think he ever did."

Nick didn't recall who had found the remains of the women, and he wasn't sure he would have written the names down in his notes. He wasn't part of law enforcement. He was more interested in the personalities of the victims and of the killer. He'd even gone so far as to type up narratives of what the victims' lives were like before they had disappeared. He'd tried to inhabit their minds, put himself in each one's point of view.

He gave Marian the names of some of the investigators on the cases, but she wanted to be cautious regarding her search. No one could find out. And Nick understood that it wasn't information about the cases that she was really after. She wanted to understand who her boyfriend was psychologically and emotionally. She wanted to know if he could have been responsible for the murders. She didn't say those words precisely. Instead she asked if Nick would profile her boyfriend. Would he do this for her?

And so he'd agreed to help this woman who loved dogs and turtles and a man who'd said he'd found a body in the woods. And after they hung up Nick washed the tomato juice off his arm and thought about the day almost eight years before, when he'd stood at the kitchen counter in this exact spot, the article about the missing woman with the red pickup truck spread out in front of him.

Nick and his wife had chosen Bonners Ferry, Idaho, for a quieter way of life, a different perspective. It was a radical change, Nick's son had told them. Nick had wanted to do something radical. "Why Idaho?" his son had asked him. "Why not Idaho?" Nick had said. It was more affordable and not as popular. After all, whom did the boy know who had packed up house and home in Boston to settle down in Idaho? After Nick and his wife moved, Cate found a job as an office manager for a family dentist in town. Nick left his forensic profile work and went back to counseling, determined to leave his past behind. He opened a private practice in a small space down the street from where his wife worked. He helped couples that were having marital problems. He treated teenagers who were getting into trouble at school. Business was slow for Nick, and he liked the pace. He'd take his time in the mornings, enjoy a second cup of coffee. Then he learned about Natasha Freeman. Nick had just set his coffee cup in the sink. And maybe he was getting ready to turn on the faucet and rinse the cup. The paper was spread out over the counter. Cate had already left for work. He returned to the paper and glanced at a headline about a missing woman in Montana, whose red pickup truck was found alongside Highway 12 outside Helena. The woman's cell phone had a Massachusetts area code. She was originally from Franklin, a town about fifty miles southwest of Boston. Perhaps it was the East Coast area code that caught Nick's attention, or that the woman was from Franklin, Massachusetts, or perhaps it was simply that she had gone missing.

Nick cut out the article. He folded it and put it in his wallet. He saw three clients that day and was glad when his afternoon ended early. After he saw the last client to the door, he removed the article from his wallet, and on the legal pad on his desk, he jotted down facts about the missing woman. He wasn't going to get involved. He would simply do what he'd done in the past, try to piece together the last seventy-two hours of the missing woman's life, pay attention to details that were reported, understand the woman's personality, her dreams, the places where she was the most vulnerable. He was keeping himself sharp, he told himself. That was all. Maybe she'd run off to start another life, to get away from a bad relationship. But then two weeks later, her body was found, and though Nick had given up his work as a forensic profiler upon moving to Idaho, he found himself lured back in. He ended up devoting more than six years of his life to the Stillwater cases before stepping down for good. The whole thing, the hours and minutes and days, had left him fatigued to the bone. But he'd never divulged to anyone, not even Cate, the real reason why he'd quit.

He'd been retired for a year now, and the past three months of that year had been spent in doctors' offices. Sometimes he'd hear from the investigators he'd worked with, but ever since his diagnosis, they seemed to bother him less and less, and when he did happen to run into them, they wanted to talk about sports or politics or misdemeanors, which suited Nick just fine.

Doctors told him the cancer had probably been growing for a couple of years before they'd discovered it, before the day Nick had walked out to get the mail and his left foot wouldn't move the way he'd wanted it to and he'd called his wife and told her he was going to drive to the hospital to get himself checked out, and she'd told him to call an ambulance or to wait five minutes and she'd be home and would take him. But the hospital was close and Nick knew he could get there sooner if he drove himself, and really, what he was worried about was that he might have suffered a stroke.

Nick was glad he didn't know about his disease when he retired, because if he had, maybe he wouldn't have gone on those long walks with Cate, or taken up bird-watching, or made the trip to Michigan where he'd visited the shores of Lake St. Clair in Detroit. He took Cate by his childhood home, or what had remained of it, a small bungalow his parents had rented when his father was working in the auto industry. From Michigan, they'd traveled back to Boston, where they visited their son and their two granddaughters, and Nick fished once more off the John W. Weeks Bridge, as he had done when he was at Harvard.

And since those trips, he'd turned to writing and literature, even composed a handful of poems, and yet not a day went by that he didn't think about the victims, especially the ones from the Stillwater cases: Natasha Freeman, Erin Parker, Lynn-Marie Pontante, Melissa Marsh. And though he'd turned over thirty-plus cartons of notes to the Canadian archivist, sometimes he'd pour a drink of the harder stuff and take out the file from his desk drawer in a small room at his home.

Inside the file were portraits he'd written on the lives of the four women from the Stillwater cases. These cases weren't the only ones Nick had worked on that had never been solved. There were the missing children in the San Francisco Bay Area; there was JonBenet; there were the Connecticut River Valley murders. But the Stillwater cases had been Nick's last assignment. And during his work on these cases, from what the doctors told Nick, is when the cancer began.

With these cases Nick had spent an even more exorbitant amount of time examining the lives of the victims. He'd visited Natasha Freeman's childhood home, tying it in with a visit to see his son; he had interviewed the professors of the courses she had taken at the University of Montana. He'd done something similar with Erin Parker's case, interviewing Erin's mother upon multiple occasions, shopping at the Walmart in Kalispell where Erin had worked. He'd driven the roads that she'd hitchhiked, had sat with his own back against the building of the Stillwater Bar, as she had done.

With each portrait, Nick's writing changed, his intuition sharpened. One portrait had taken on the form of a letter to the killer, another that of a diary. Nick's tumors were in the left hemisphere of his brain. Intuition occurred in the right hemisphere, specifically the cerebral cortex, the ventromedial prefrontal, and some ceruleus or other whose name he couldn't recall. Understanding now that the cancer had already begun its malignancy, Nick wondered if perhaps in the weakening of his frontal and temporal lobes, these other sections of his brain had become more active, had overcompensated for his other deficits.

Nick remembered sitting for hours in Melissa Marsh's apartment, or art studio, as he liked to think of it. She'd captured her life in five distinct images that she'd painted on the walls. The fifth image was left unfinished. He'd spent a similar amount of time in the yurt where Lynn-Marie had been living. He'd held her personal items. He'd spoken to her acquaintances and friends. He'd sat in her pickup truck. He'd petted and held her dog and looked into the dog's eyes because he knew the dog named Tully had seen Lynn-Marie's killer.

The sharper Nick's intuition became, the longer he spent trying to inhabit the past lives of these women, looking for the kinds of clues the crime scenes had omitted.

Some might think of the intuition as something magical. Nick understood otherwise. It all came down to subtle and brief signals in the brain. Einstein called the intuitive mind a sacred gift and "the rational mind a faithful servant. We have created a society that honors the servant and has forgotten the gift," he'd said.

Nick had written the portraits with a typewriter much like the one a teacher had given him when he was in eighth grade. His son said typewriters like these were in vogue. Nick didn't care about vogue. "Buncha crap," he said. He liked the way his fingers felt on the keys, and the way the keys sounded when they snapped and struck the paper. There was a kinesthetic connection that Nick found appeasing, and a nostalgia for those days as a young teenager when he would tap out stories and ideas, when he learned that, aside from disease, the only power anyone or any event had over the quality of his life was what he allowed. This made him think a bit of Viktor Frankl; the Nazis could imprison Frankl, hold possession of his body, cause him great pain, but his mind was his alone. Nick had allowed these women into his life. Marian was a reminder of these women and the killer who'd never been found.

He'd asked her questions. One in particular: When did she first sense something was off about this guy? And like too many other women, she hadn't paid those kinds of moments much attention. And wasn't that usually the case? It was a deadly shame. Nick told Marian he would help her, and he'd made a couple of calls over the weekend. One was to a reporter who owed Nick a favor and had covered the Stillwater cases. Nick said he was getting his files in order, while his mind was still capacitated, and could she help him with some missing information. This wasn't exactly untrue, as lately Nick had been thinking about making such a gesture to one of the universities. The other call was to the man in Canada: Had he digitalized the Stillwater files yet? The reporter had gotten back to Nick that morning. Marian's boyfriend hadn't found one of the bodies. Nick was interested, a feeling, like a slow trickle in his sternum. He, like Marian, wanted to know who this boyfriend was. Maybe it was nothing, and yet already he felt the familiar buzz, a bit dulled, but it was still there. He would follow up with the digital archivist. He would need the details from the cases. Maybe this Tate fellow was worth looking into. Though there'd been persons of interest in the investigations, none had become real suspects.

Cate was worried, Nick knew. Was he sure he wanted to get involved, she'd asked. "What is it about this one?"

"For one, there's the boyfriend's name. I can't place it, but I've heard it before. It's relevant, and I'm not sure why. Then there's the girl. She's young, she's innocent, just like the victims. The clock is ticking, I know. But it's important that I help her."

Cate had given him her reassuring smile. "That's all I need to hear."

6
February 2017

Marian
Oil sands, Alberta, Canada

Though Marian had been tempted to take a more direct route than the path she and Noah and Chester had made, she realized that breaking trail on a new course would actually take longer. It would also require her to use the GPS on her phone, which would deplete the phone's battery. As she got going, she found it easy to follow their earlier tracks and was thankful that though the sky was heavy with clouds, she and Noah hadn't experienced snow.

She wanted to run, but even with the broken trail, there was no way she could. Still, she challenged her pace, and as her legs moved, this was what she heard: the crunching and squealing snow underfoot; the rhythmic travel of air in and out of her lungs; the scruff of nylon against nylon as her arms brushed against her coat; the dull thumping of her heartbeat in her ears. This was what she saw: snowmobile tracks in the timber where the trees' proximity to one another had expanded, allowing Marian to make out the general direction that a sled had taken. How had she missed these tracks earlier? How had Noah missed them, as well, this sure sign that a trapper had been in the area? But then she saw where she had collected the last sample. She would not have even gotten to the place in the timber where the tracks of the snowmobile could be seen before Chester had already triggered the trap. Yet she knew Noah's mistake could have easily been her own. She'd been too focused on her aching hands and her frustration with him.

She made it back to the truck within a couple of hours. Her eyes had adjusted to the growing darkness, and she had not used her headlamp until the last thirty minutes or so. She started the engine and switched the CB radio to channel thirteen for Pétron Oil's emergency response dispatcher. The responders were almost there, she was told, with a trailer loaded with a couple of snowmobiles that were ready to go.

Marian pulled out her satellite phone and sent Noah a text. Help on its way. How are you doing?

After she texted him, she called Jenness to let her know she'd made it back to the vehicle.

"How cold are your hands?" Jenness asked.

"They're okay," Marian told her.

"What about your feet?"

"They're fine," Marian said.

And then Jenness said that Tate had gotten a ride with the responders.

After the call ended, Marian saw that a text had come in from Noah. Still here. We're okay. Glad you made it.

Within a half hour, the responders arrived and Tate was with them. They'd brought three snowmobiles, a large first-aid kit, and two ski stretchers that could be pulled from the back of the sleds. Marian climbed out of the truck. No sooner were her feet on the ground than Tate was jogging toward her. "Are you okay?"

"I'm fine," she said.

He placed a hand on each of her shoulders and was holding her square in front of him. "Are you sure?" he said.

"Yes. I'm fine. I want to help," she said.

The stretchers were secured behind the two responders' sleds. Tate handed Marian an extra snowmobile helmet from the truck. She pulled on the helmet and then climbed onto the third sled to lead the group to the location. Tate straddled the seat behind her. In less than twenty minutes they saw Noah's flashlight.

As Marian had predicted, though he was cold and distressed about Chester, physically, Noah was okay. But Chester had continued to lose blood despite the pressure Noah had applied to the wounds. The responders were ready to load the dog onto one of the stretchers and strap him down. Tate told them to hold on. "He can't afford to lose any more blood."

Tate had taken out his first-aid pack from the back compartment of the sled. Inside the pack was a tactile suture kit. "It's okay, boy," Tate said. He instructed the rest of the group to hold Chester still. With all the calmness in the world, Tate cut back the fur on the wound over the neck, where Chester was losing the most blood. Then he cleaned the wound and rubbed it down with sterile wipes. Tate opened a package with suture thread and a needle attached. He held the needle with a metal instrument. Despite the cold, Tate moved with the deftness of a surgeon. Within a couple of minutes Tate was able to close the wound. "This should hold for now," he said.

And as if speaking through her own shock,

Marian said, "You just saved his life."

But Tate didn't seem to hear her. Already he was helping the responders secure Chester onto the stretcher. "There, there, boy," Tate said. "You're going to be okay."

When they returned to the compound, Jenness was waiting for them in the parking lot. She'd already arranged for a veterinarian to meet Tate and Chester at the animal hospital in Fort McMurray, about a forty-five-minute drive away.

"I'm going with them," Noah said.

Jenness didn't answer, and neither did Tate.

Chester was still in the backseat of the responder vehicle. Jenness leaned in and stroked his head. "How is he?" she asked Tate.

"Sore and weak. His breathing is steady, but I don't think he's going to be working again any time soon."

Jenness had her camera with her and took a few shots of Chester's wounds.

"How are you on fuel?" she asked Marian.

"Over half a tank. We're good."

Jenness and Tate thanked the responders, one of whom only spoke French. Then Tate laid Chester on a blanket in the front seat of the conservation group's truck. But when Noah opened the door to climb in the back,

Tate made it clear Noah wasn't coming along.

"Get a shower," Tate said. "Get something to eat. Both of you."

Later that night, after Marian had eaten and showered and had spent a couple of hours in her room feeling bad about the whole thing, she put on her boots and parka and walked up to the first handler trailer to check in with Jenness.

Jenness's bedroom was a short distance off the workstation. Her door was cracked open enough for Marian to see her sitting on her bed cross-legged. She was holding a mug and looking at some papers in a blue folder that was on her lap. Yeti, a border collie mix, who, like Arkansas, had been brought along as a backup dog, was stretched out on the bed with her head on Jenness's thigh. As Marian looked at the two of them, she thought Jenness was beautiful, in this natural, I-am-exactly-where-I-am-supposed-to-be sort of way, with dark-framed glasses and a knit hat pulled low over her forehead and ears. Marian knocked, which seemed to startle both Jenness and the dog. Jenness quickly closed the folder and set it aside. "Come in," Jenness said.

"Can I talk to you?" Marian said.

"Of course."

And so Marian took a few steps toward the bed. She tugged at the zipper on her parka and pulled the zipper two thirds of the way down. "I just wanted to apologize to you about today," she said. "I'm really sorry."

Jenness held her mug with both hands a few inches from her face. But then without taking a sip, she lowered the mug to her lap. "We want everything to go perfectly. We do the best that we can. But things don't ever go perfectly," she said. "Accidents happen. We make mistakes."

"I should have paid closer attention. I should have seen the tracks. I wasn't keeping up. Noah and Chester got too far ahead."

Jenness set her mug on the nightstand. "Do you think Noah was pushing Chester too hard today?"

"I don't know," Marian said, because she didn't want to be put in that position.

"Maybe I'm not being fair asking you that," Jenness said.

"He loves that dog." And Marian wasn't sure why she was defending Noah. Maybe it had to do with the defeat she'd seen on his face, and because that defeat could have very well been her own.

Yeti had inched herself closer to Jenness, who was now gently massaging her behind the ears. "We're not saying he doesn't love the dog, but right now Chester's out of commission. We're going to bring Arkansas in as his replacement."

Then Jenness said, "What would you think about becoming a handler? It's something Tate and I have talked about. You'd have a learning curve."

And Marian said something about being a fast learner, that becoming a handler was the reason she'd applied for a position on the study. "I'm ready for this."

"Do you think you'll still feel that way in another month?"

"I know I will. It's the work, the outdoors, the dogs. It's everything I could imagine."

Jenness told Marian about two full-time positions that were opening up after the oil sands study. The candidates would need to be ready to make a long-term commitment. "Think about it," Jenness said. "It might be a good fit for you. The pay's not great, but we manage."

"I've spent the last four years managing," Marian said. "It's never been about the money."

"It's not a normal life."

"I don't want normal. I don't even like normal. I'm unhappy with normal." And then Marian said, "I would give anything to be living in these kinds of places and going out and seeing things that others will never see and having a dog by my side. I want the bigger perspective."

Jenness laughed a little. "This is a palace compared to most of the places we've stayed." But then her face became serious. "It's not really a job. It's a lifestyle. There's no pay raise. No ladder. There's not a next step."

"I don't want ladders," Marian said.

"It can destroy your life," Jenness said.

Marian moved over to the foot of the bed and sat down. "Did it destroy yours?"

Jenness looked at the night-black windowpane to her right, or at her own reflection, and was it sadness Marian saw on Jenness's face, or nostalgia? She leaned back against the pillows and pulled her long brown hair over her shoulders. Her eyes turned to Marian. "I was dating someone when I came onto this job," she said. "We were going to do this together. We went through training, got hired on at the same time. Our first project was in California. We were on a fisher study. Then I was in South Africa and Jamie was studying lynx in Maine. We lasted a couple of years. That's pretty good. Most people here can't handle a relationship."

"What happened?"

"Jamie wanted to be a farmer and moved back home to Iowa."

"What about you?" Marian asked. "Why are you still here?"

"I tried to stop once, a couple of years ago. I worked at a vet clinic. I even tried to date again. Let's just say things didn't work out. Besides, this is all I really know how to do."

The news of Deacon snuck up on Marian like a cold draft, and really, if she was honest with herself, she should have seen it coming. Jenness had told everyone to take the day off. The temperatures were too cold for the dogs to be in the field. Marian did laundry, worked up a sweat on a treadmill, hung out with a few of the orienteers. And sometime late in the day she connected with her parents over Skype. They couldn't keep Deacon anymore. Her father had a bad knee; the dog had too much energy; the situation wasn't fair to the dog. Her parents told her about Deacon's new home, about the nice man who lived in the country. They said they were so sorry, and Marian knew they were. She should never have asked her parents to watch after him. They worked full-time jobs. And there was another truth, though Marian didn't say it. What if she became a handler and was asked to stay on? What might have happened to Deacon then? But in that moment she didn't want *what was best;* she wanted Deacon with her.

Marian smelled popcorn and snow and ventilator heat. She lay on the bed, staring at the water stains on the ceiling. God, she missed that dog, that lanky-legged, scraggly-brown-furred, little guy. And her mind filled with lovely memories, funny memories, and the romantic ideas she'd had of the two of them in this place, before she'd understood the job, before she'd known better.

There was a knock at the door. She said, "Come in." And then there was Jeb, standing in the doorway. Everyone was going into Fort McMurray and wouldn't it be good to get out, he said.

And so that was how it began, at a bar in Fort McMurray. Marian had eaten a cheeseburger and had drunk two beers on tap. But because she had been thinking about Deacon, it wasn't until she started on her third beer that she realized Noah wasn't there.

"Haven't you heard?" Jeb said. "He's packing up."

"What do you mean he's packing up?"

"He's going back to North Carolina. He's taking Chester with him."

Liz, the handler with whom Jeb worked, had joined them at the bar. "It's true," she said. "He's adopting Chester."

And Marian was glad for Noah and Chester; she really was. Then Jeb asked Marian to dance, and he said it would be fun and that Marian looked sad and he didn't want her to be sad anymore. That was when she told him about Deacon, and Liz put her arm around Marian's shoulders and said how sorry she was and that Marian was in the right company to be feeling sad over a dog. Jeb grabbed Marian's hand and said they were going to dance. He scooted out of his seat and pulled Marian onto the dance floor, and something from country's top forty was playing and Jeb was smiling with this sweet boyish grin, and so Marian danced and tried not to think about Deacon or anything at all.

When the music changed, Marian continued to dance, and so did Jeb, and others had joined them on the floor also. They drank more beer and danced to more songs, and Marian felt the sweat chill on her skin as if the wind had blown up her spine, because the door kept opening to the outside as more and more locals poured in.

And then one of the men asked Marian to dance, and so she joined the clean-shaven man on the floor, but the music changed to something slow and the man put his arm around Marian's waist and pulled her close, and she was still breathing hard from all her dancing. The man wasn't much taller than Marian. He tucked his chin into the crook of her neck, and she could feel his breath in her ear.

"You're one of those tree huggers, aren't you?" he said.

His hand slid down her back and over her jeans and he squeezed Marian hard. She tried to push him away, but he held on. She felt dizzy from the beer and the scotch that someone had given her. "Stop it!" she yelled. She pushed the man again. He loosened his grip and stumbled a couple of feet backward, and from over his shoulder Marian saw Tate approach the dance floor and move through the crowd of couples. He stepped between Marian and the man whose hands had been too close, and she might have heard the man laugh, but his laughter was moving farther away.

"Are you okay?" Tate said.

"I'm okay," Marian said.

"Do you want to sit this one out?"

But Marian said she wanted to dance.

Tate took her hand and gently held it out to the side and held on to her waist with his other hand. And as he coaxed her body to move with his, she said, "I shouldn't have had so much to drink."

Then Tate said, "Go easy on yourself, will you?"

There was the sound of a steel guitar playing through the speakers and a slow tempo and sweet lyrics, and as the two of them danced, their bodies moved closer to each other, and even when Tate's hand ever so slightly lifted the hem of Marian's sweatshirt so that his fingers were only one layer away from her skin, she could no longer feel the chill blow up her spine. She laid her head against Tate's chest and he wrapped his arms around her. His flannel reminded her of her sheets back home, of places warm and safe and familiar. And then Marian saw Jenness standing at the end of the bar, and though there were people around her, she was alone without a drink in her hand. And in those few seconds that Marian saw her, the two of them made eye contact. Marian wondered if something might be wrong because though Jenness was looking in Marian's direction, she also seemed to be looking somewhere far away. But then the music and Tate and the dancing had turned

Marian around so that she was looking in another direction, and by the time she could see the bar again, Jenness was no longer there.

The last notes to the song played out. Tate led Marian from the dance floor and to a booth off to the side. He asked her if she wanted anything else to drink. She said she'd just have water. Tate ordered a ginger ale. Marian leaned her back against the wall and pulled her legs up onto the bench seat. And as she sat at the booth with her legs stretched out in front of her and her boots crossed at the ankles, and as sweat trickled down her hairline, she could feel Tate watching her.

"Something's wrong," Tate said.

He got up from his side of the booth, and when Marian realized he was going to sit down beside her, she straightened up and set her feet on the floor.

Tate folded his arms over the table and turned his head toward Marian. "What is it?"

With his face so close to hers, and their bodies touching, she told him about Deacon, and Tate leaned back against the booth and lifted his arm over her and wrapped it around her shoulder and pulled her closer to him. "Oh, Marian, I am so sorry."

Marian's eyes teared then as she thought about Deacon. "I shouldn't be crying. It really is the best thing."

"There's nothing wrong with crying," Tate said. "You just lost your best friend."

7
FEBRUARY 2017

Marian
Oil sands, Alberta, Canada

The night Marian danced with Tate and sat beside him in the booth and told him about Deacon, he asked her if she had ever seen the northern lights before and she told him she never had. Tate paid for his ginger ale, and the two of them walked out of the bar. The moon was dark that night and the air cold and clear, perfect for aurora hunting, Tate told her.

As they headed north out of Fort McMurray, the air so cold that their headlights created halos of fog, Tate described the northern lights and their streams of color — white, red, purple, green — which Marian had only seen in pictures. "The first time I saw them I was on a polar bear study in Norway," Tate said. "I was staying in a cabin near one of the nature reserves. I'd set my alarm to wake me up every hour. But it wasn't my alarm that woke me up. I could see the lights through my window. I threw on my parka and boots, afraid I'd miss the whole thing. I've seen them two other times since then, but there's nothing like that first experience."

Tate told Marian about his stay in Norway, about the Svalbard archipelago and the polar bear that had mauled a group of young people, killing one of them. "The boy was only seventeen," Tate said. "The bear came into the camp where the kids were staying. They'd set up trip wires like they were supposed to do, but the trip wire failed." Tate talked about how trip wires that detonated deterrent explosives were always set around the camp areas for protection against the bears. People were encouraged to keep guard dogs with them, as well, and have someone on watch at night.

"Weren't you afraid?" Marian asked.

"I was more afraid for my dogs," Tate said. "I had two of them with me at all times. One was this great big malamute. Another was a husky mix. And I stayed in cabins at night, not in tents like those kids."

"How long were you there?"

"A couple of months."

Marian was mesmerized. "Did you ever see a polar bear?"

"Lots of them. The first one I saw was stretched out on an ice floe like he was the most gentle thing in the world. That was the one study where we were allowed to carry a gun."

Marian thought this was what she could live for, experiences like these. "What about the study?" she asked. "What did you find out?"

"Found out there weren't as many bears as people thought. They're starving for the same reason we've got more fires in California and farmers growing peaches the size of prunes. Glaciers are calving, ice is melting. With global warming, the great polar bear has nowhere left to go."

"This matters to you, doesn't it?"

Marian felt Tate look at her then. "We're not so different, Marian, you and I. The way I see it, we're cut from the same block of wood, like a giant sequoia. You ever see a sequoia before?" And Marian told him she hadn't.

"Well, that's how I see it," Tate said. "We're similar. You feel familiar to me."

"You hardly know me," Marian said.

"I know you," Tate said. "I watch you. I see what matters to you. I see you with the dogs, the way you were with Chester. You and I are drawn to the same kinds of experiences. We care about the same things. There's not a lot of women who'd be putting up with these subzero temperatures like you do."

Then Tate said, "Jenness and I have been talking. We think you'd make a good handler. With Noah and Chester gone, you and I will be working Arkansas. You'll be my orienteer for the next three or four weeks, to give you a chance to observe. That should give you time to unlearn some of the things you may have picked up from Noah. After that, we'll start transitioning you into the position."

And Marian felt triumphant and giddy and thanked Tate so much, and everything appeared strange and new and beautiful.

"Well, all right, then," Tate said. He turned left onto a snow-packed road. And then over the dark horizon, Marian saw a flash of light and her body shot up erect and she leaned forward and placed her hands firmly on the dashboard. "Did you see that? Oh my God, did you see it?" Because just as quickly as the stream of flash had shot across the horizon, it had disappeared.

And Tate was laughing then. He told her that what she was seeing was a substorm. "Sometimes the lights will start and stop like that."

Tate made another turn, and within minutes they were parked in front of an open expanse.

"It's one of the boreal ponds," Tate told her. "We can go out there if you want."

Marian slid out of the truck behind Tate. He tried to hold her hand, and they both laughed because her mittens and his gloves were too thick to hold on to. And so they tromped through a couple of feet of crusty snow, frozen in layers from the wind, and she and Tate bumped into each other because they were walking so close together, and Marian might have fallen, but Tate grabbed her arm and held on to her until she was steady again.

They moved to the center of the pond, a gentle wind playing in the trees behind them. Marian gazed up at the big black sky lit with stars. "What do we do now?" she asked.

"We wait," Tate said. He stepped behind Marian and wrapped his arms around her. And as Marian looked at the sky and thought about how beautiful the cold made everything, Tate said, "It's sad that you're missing Deacon so much. I must tell you, though, I grieve for Arkansas and the other dogs already. Each one of them will stop working one day, just like Chester. They'll get adopted out, go to good homes. But sometimes their leaving feels so in the present. In theory, grieving for them now will ease the pain when it happens. But I want you to know, the quality of how you treated Deacon is a form of grief. You're in pain because of how much you cared for Deacon when you had him. Think of it that way. It should help."

Then Tate turned Marian around so that she was facing him. "Mm, I like this position better," he said. With his teeth, he gently tugged the edge of her scarf down to her chin. He held his lips so close to hers that she could feel the condensation of their breaths upon her skin, and when he kissed her, his lips were cold and his mouth warm, and they kissed until his lips became warm also. He smiled, and she smiled, their faces still close together. He nipped her scarf again with his teeth and pulled it back up so that it covered her nose, and he hugged her until they both began to shiver.

They decided to walk back to the truck because they were cold and it was getting late and Tate wanted to make sure the engine would start. And just as they approached the vehicle, a streak of white light appeared low in the sky. Marian squealed and Tate laughed. Then a soft glow appeared over the dark timber on the far side of the pond, as if the moon were rising, and as the glow rose higher, it turned into several wraithlike images of green, "like ghosts being let out of their graves," Marian said.

Tate told her about an old Inuit myth. "They believe the aurora are the light torches used to guide the new arrivals, all those people who've died a violent death."

"How do you know so much?" Marian's voice was barely above a whisper.

Tate didn't answer right away. Instead Marian listened to the wind and the cold branches somewhere behind them, and the frozen snow beneath their feet as their weight shifted. "I like you, Marian." Tate's voice was as soft as Marian's had been.

While the lights continued to dance, Tate removed one of his gloves, reached inside his coat pocket, and took out his phone. Marian thought he was going to take pictures, and suddenly she couldn't believe that she had left her phone in her room at the compound. But then Marian heard music, the clear sounds of an acoustic guitar and a soothing male voice. Tate returned the phone to his coat pocket while the music continued to play, and slid his hand back into his thick glove.

The lights were dancing, the music was

playing, and Tate said he and Marian should dance, too. Marian wrapped her arms around Tate's shoulders and tilted her head back to the sky, and the two of them rocked from side to side as the acoustic guitar and a banjo played and a male voice sang of stars and a stable and diamonds and coal.

After they could no longer feel their toes, they climbed into the truck and warmed their bodies and watched the lights until they faded, for another half hour or so. And on the way back, Marian leaned her head onto Tate's shoulder and listened to the music that continued to play from his phone, and the static and occasional voices over the broadband radio. And she thought about solar winds and magnetic field lines and the earth's upper atmosphere that created such a display of lights, like a visual orchestra.

When Marian got back to her room she couldn't believe that it was nearly four o'clock in the morning. There was a note on her door: *Text me when you get in. Couldn't find you when I left. Want to make sure you're okay. Also Jenness has been looking for you. Jeb*

But it was so late. She'd text him after she got some sleep. She lay back on the twin mattress, a smile on her face. It was then that she checked her phone, which she'd left charging on her nightstand. There were a number of missed calls and a voice message. A couple of the calls were from Jeb, who had sent several texts as well, wanting to know where she was. The last missed call was from Tate, at 4:06 a.m. Marian thought about calling him back. Had she left something in the truck? But then she saw that the voice message was from him: *"I want you to know I had a really nice time with you tonight. I'm just sending you some good thoughts. Sleep well, and I'll see you in a few hours."*

8
Present:
July 31–August 1, 2017

Marian
The Den, Montana

The Den was located on over sixty acres of sprawling woods and a couple of fields west of Whitefish. All around The Den were thousands of acres of state and national forest land, dotted with a few private parcels. The compound included a heated barn with individual kennels for the dogs, a main house where Lyle stayed and which all the staff made use of, with a living room and television, an eat-in kitchen with two refrigerators, a laundry room, and Lyle's office. The handlers who held full-time positions with the program stayed in individual huts, as did Trainer, a large, beefy man in his early fifties, who managed the property and the kennels. The huts were furnished with a twin bed, a desk, a small bureau, and a two-by-two-foot wood stove. Following the oil sands study, Marian had joined the staff as a full-time handler. Her hut was situated between two limber pine trees about fifty yards up the hill from the bathroom and shower house, and about thirty yards downhill from the hut where Tate had stayed. Marian had spent many nights in Tate's hut, the two of them having become involved six weeks into the oil sands project. Their relationship had begun slowly, deliberately, like an orchestration, two lives unfolding together in that awesome landscape of frozen tundra. She'd believed they could weather anything, including the inevitable distance that would come between them once they left each other for different assignments.

Marian's first project after returning from Alberta had been a bighorn sheep study in Utah, with Arkansas and Yeti. Tate had been assigned to a wolf study in Washington, with Ranger, one of the program's newest adoptees. It was on Saturday, July 15, while Marian was on the sheep study, five months into her and Tate's relationship, that she'd received word of Tate's death. The sun had been setting over an escarpment of sandstone, the remaining daylight glowing a rich garnet and lavender. She'd picked up her phone to take a picture and had seen that she had a missed call from Lyle. Already she feared the worst, because for the past two days Tate had not returned any of her calls.

"Tell me," Marian said, when she called Lyle back. "It's Tate, isn't it?"

It had been all Marian could do to pack up and make the drive back to The Den. And there was Emily Marsh, the summer intern who'd been working with Marian, and the two dogs, and the night wind blowing through the rolled-down windows. Tears spilled down Marian's face as she drove, and Emily offered more than once to take over, but Marian said no, she needed to drive.

There'd been a vigil when Marian had returned, around a bonfire in one of the fields. Trainer played his guitar and sang songs by the Beatles and Bob Dylan and James Taylor and Don McLean: "Mr. Tambourine Man," "American Pie," "Fire and Rain," "Let It Be," "With a Little Help from My Friends," and the handlers pulled up the lyrics on their phones and sang along. Different ones in the group shared stories, and Marian laughed and cried with the others until the sun rose.

But the next day Jenness had knocked on Marian's door and told her Lyle needed to see her and to meet him at the kennels. Lyle had checked on Arkansas and Yeti, as was routine when a handler returned from a study, and he'd found the dogs whimpering and in rough shape. Lyle said he hated to do this to Marian right after she'd learned about Tate, "but did you see this?" He showed Marian the pads on the dogs' paws, raw and cracked and bleeding. And Marian dropped down beside the dogs and took their paws in her hands.

A dog's pads could become raw and cracked if the dog was covering a lot of rough terrain, or running on hot asphalt, or stepping on sharp objects. But Marian had checked both dogs faithfully while in Utah; she was sure of it. She wondered what could have happened between Utah and Montana. It was program policy that should a dog's care be neglected, a handler's contract would either be suspended or terminated.

"Take some time off," Lyle said. "Go home. Go see your parents in Michigan."

Marian was still kneeling beside the dogs. She held one of Arkansas's paws gently in her hands; she stroked the top of the paw. She couldn't go back to Michigan and leave everything that reminded her of Tate. She couldn't leave the others who knew the man she loved. She couldn't leave the dogs.

And maybe Lyle had felt bad for Marian,

because he agreed that she could stay on at The Den, though she'd be suspended for the time being from any new projects. She could help with the dogs, he said. She could assist him in the office.

During the weeks following Tate's death, one by one Marian watched the other handlers leave: Liz and Dudley to new assignments; Jenness on a backpacking trip to Alaska.

Marian's alarm would wake her at six each morning. She'd be at the house before six thirty and would make the coffee. Then she'd spend the next four hours exercising the remaining eight dogs who were not on assignment with Dudley or Liz or the handful of part-time handlers. She'd take the dogs, two at a time, for runs on a circuit of forest trails, or have them run alongside her on a mountain bike through the woods, and sometimes she would double over in a spasm of grief and the dogs would jump on her and lick her face. In the afternoons Marian would work in the office or help Lyle train the dogs. And she was filling in for Jenness while she was away, answering emails from people who had inquired into the program and updating the group's social media.

But the evenings were the hardest. This

was one of those nights. She'd just returned to her hut when Nick Shepard got back to her.

"Is this a bad time?" he asked. And Marian said no, this was fine.

"I'll get to the point," Nick told her. "Your boyfriend didn't find one of the bodies."

Marian was sitting at her desk. Nick had confirmed what she'd already suspected. Still, her uneasiness spread. "Why would he tell me such a thing?"

"To elicit a reaction. To get your attention. I'm not sure."

Then Nick said, "I'm more interested in your reason for doubting him. Someone found the bodies. Why not Tate?"

Eventually Marian would tell Nick everything. "It's complicated," she said. "I wanted to believe him. But he always seemed to have a tragic story to tell. And this time there seemed to be an element of truth missing. He never said the woman's name or who she was. He never said where she was from. And I was too shocked at the time to ask him. Then I read where one of the bodies was found by a man and his dog, and I thought that could be Tate."

"What changed your mind?"

"I was working a job in Utah. I had a summer intern with me. She told me her sister was one of the Stillwater victims. That's when I took another look at the articles. I was curious about the murders; that was all. But then something unsettled me. Tate had gone into great detail when telling me about the body. What he described wasn't possible, given the times the bodies were discovered. They would have been too badly decomposed. Either Tate was there shortly after this particular woman died, or he was making the whole thing up."

"When did Tate first tell you about the body?"

"Back in March, a couple of weeks after we'd become involved."

"How did he describe it?"

Marian propped her elbows on the desk. She remembered every detail of that night, she and Tate lying on his bed, his arms around her, her trying to believe him. "He told me she was unclothed. She was lying on the bank of a stream. Her ankles and feet were still in the water as if she'd been taking a bath. He described her hands, saying she'd bitten her fingernails until they'd bled. And he talked about her eyes. He told me it was as if they were looking right at him. I was a biology major. I'm familiar with the stages of decomposition. And this was a body that had been left in the woods. One of the first things to be scavenged would have been the eyes."

"So Tate tells you he found one of the bodies. You're not sure you believe him, but you're willing to give him the benefit of the doubt. Those doubts escalated when you met the victim's sister. When was this?"

"In July, before I learned of Tate's death."

"At some point you searched for my number. It's not listed. Doesn't matter. You found it. What changed for you? What was the deciding factor that made you call?"

"I'd read about you in the articles. But it wasn't until Tate's sister visited that I decided to call. She came by The Den to collect Tate's things. We ended up spending the day together. It was chilling, really. Her brother suddenly became someone I barely knew. He had lied to me about so much, and I had no idea why. Once Tammy left, I looked up your number. I found it through a paid service online. I waited until I'd scattered Tate's ashes to call you."

"Tate had deceived you. Was the sister aware of this?"

"No, and I didn't say anything. It didn't seem like the right thing to do."

"Tell me about the lies."

Marian leaned back in her chair and pulled her legs up on the seat. "He'd said he was from Glendive, Montana, that his dad was a rancher. But he wasn't from Montana. He was from a small town in Nebraska. And he didn't grow up on a ranch. He never even lived on a farm. There were other things, like his childhood dog. He said the dog drowned in a river and he'd tried to save him. But his dog had run out in the road while Tate was playing one day and had gotten hit by a car. I realized that if Tate had lied about his childhood, maybe he'd lied about other events in his life."

"Aside from the body Tate said he'd found, were any of these other fabrications apparent to you when Tate was alive?"

"He told me his dad had been mayor of Glendive. I couldn't find anything about his dad online. I couldn't find anything about Tate either, which didn't surprise me. Tate wasn't on social media. But I told Tate about not finding any mention of his dad."

"What did Tate say?"

"He said something about me not trusting him, about me accusing him of being dishonest. Then he told me it was his stepfather who had been mayor, and that his biological father had beaten the shit out of him, that he was a raging alcoholic who had left home when Tate was nine. He said it wasn't something he really liked to talk about, but since I'd brought it up, since I'd gone sniffing around in his past, I might as well know the truth. 'There are skeletons in closets,' he told me. 'Sometimes those skeletons are best left alone.' I felt terrible."

"He played the situation to its fullest," Nick said. "He got you to feel sorry for him, and he made you think twice before ever doubting him again."

Marian picked up a pen off her desk and turned it around between her fingers. "Until I met his sister."

"Tell me about the sister."

"She was named after Tate, after his initials. Tate Alexander Mathias. They were four years apart. She lives in Omaha now. She and Tate grew up in the small town of Crete. Neither one knew who their father was. Their mother worked in a pet food factory. It was just the three of them. Their mother never married."

"So there wasn't a father or stepfather. Could have been a boyfriend of the mother who abused Tate. Sometimes a person's lies can be based on half-truths, like the incident with the dog, but we'll get to that later."

"Tammy thought it would be nice to have some of Tate's ashes spread in Montana. She planned to bury the rest of his ashes next to their mother's. She said Tate and their mother were close."

"What happened to the mother?"

"She died of breast cancer."

"How old was Tate?"

"He'd just started college when she'd gotten sick. He quit school to take care of her and pay the bills. Tammy said he worked at a veterinary hospital close to home. I think their mom died a couple of years later. Tate had told me about his mother's passing. For once he was telling the truth."

"Did Tate have any kind of criminal record that you know of?"

"No, that wouldn't be possible. His job took him all over the world. He had to be able to pass through border patrol and customs. Just this year there was an orienteer who got turned away at the Canadian border for a prior DUI. I'm pretty sure Tate had a clean record."

"I can run a background check to be certain. It would be good to have that information."

Then Nick said, "Marian, how long has it been since Tate died? I looked for an obituary. I didn't find one."

"Almost three weeks. Tammy was going to put something in the paper in Crete. Maybe she hasn't gotten around to it. Tate hadn't been back since their mother died."

"When was the last time Tammy saw Tate?"

"She visited him a few years ago when he was working on a project in Illinois. She said she never made it out to Montana, and Tate had only visited her once in Omaha. They didn't speak often, maybe once a month."

"Your grief is still raw. This can't be easy for you."

And Marian thought about the initial qualities she'd come to know Tate by, his kindness and compassion, his intuitiveness and understanding. And then there was the physicality of him; of course there was that. "Like I said, it's complicated," she said. "I miss the man I thought he was. Other times I'm afraid."

"What are you afraid of?"

"I don't trust my thoughts. I remember things. Mostly subtleties. Sometimes those things frighten me."

"Are you thinking Tate might have been involved with the murders?"

The light through the windows had muted. Soon Marian would be sitting in the dark. She hesitated too long. "I loved Tate beyond belief," she said. "I don't think he was involved with the murders. He was never violent. And yet there is a small part of me that wonders if he could have been responsible, and those thoughts are what I'm afraid of. I even tried to find an alibi for Tate. I thought there would be studies he was on when the victims went missing. So far I'm not coming up with anything. But I haven't had much to go on, only the program's social media. I tried to get information from our coordinator. Tate hadn't been in my life a long time. I was trying to fill in the missing pieces. I said something to that effect. But Lyle wasn't much help. He's got handlers coming and going all the time. He talked to me in general, but none of the studies matched the dates the women went missing. I think the information I'm really after is on a network, which I don't have access to, and it's not really something I can ask Lyle to spend his time on." Marian added, "When I called you, I was hopeful. You know, thinking you'd get back with me and it would have been true, what Tate told me, that he'd have found the body exactly as he said he had, and I could turn off all these thoughts. I have to find a way to put this behind me. But right now I don't know how."

"The man in your life has died a violent death. The events are recent. You have a lot of uncertainty about him and your relationship with him, enough that you reached out to me. In moving forward, what are you looking for from me? How can I help?"

The kindness in Nick's voice affected Marian deeply. "I want to know who the man was that I loved. I want to know why he lied to me. I've been looking for signs, something he might have left behind that will give me answers. But I keep coming up empty. And if I'm really honest with myself, I want to know that Tate wasn't capable of killing these women."

"First, I'll support you in whatever way I can," Nick said. "As far as determining who Tate was, what you're asking for is a psychological autopsy. I've done a few over the years, usually involving suicides, or when law enforcement wanted an assessment of a deceased suspect. But without evidence, without detailed information regarding Tate's movements, a psychological autopsy isn't going to tell you whether Tate killed these women. At the very least it will give you insight into the man you were involved with, and it might tell us whether he would have been a person of interest in the murders."

"Am I crazy to think he might have been involved?"

"I don't think you're crazy. I think you're

concerned. You have every right to be." Nick continued, "In keeping an assessment of Tate quiet, I'll be working with a lot less information than I'm accustomed to. I'll be pumping you for every tidbit you can recall, every incident, every odd statement, every email he sent you."

"We never emailed," Marian said. "Tate didn't even own a computer. If he had to send a message or upload data, he used his phone, or else he used one of the program's computers."

"What about any journals or handwritten letters?"

"Not that I'm aware of."

"That's going to make things difficult, but not impossible. I'll be relying almost completely on your recall," Nick said.

And then he asked, "How comfortable are you with the sister?"

"We spent the good part of a day together. She's someone I feel comfortable with."

"I'll want a timeline for Tate. I know you've made some efforts toward that, but maybe there's someone else you can talk to. Perhaps Tate's sister can be of help."

"All right," Marian said.

"At some point we should talk about the cases. I don't know how much you know. There was some information in the papers and not all of it may have been accurate. We'll be discussing sensitive material. It would be best if we could talk in person. I've relied on video calls before and that may be helpful."

Marian wanted answers and was eager to talk to Nick again. "I wouldn't mind making the drive," she said. "I've got time later this week."

Nick hesitated, and Marian hoped she wasn't being too presumptuous. "You're the only one I've spoken to," she said, because she wanted Nick to trust her.

"All right, then," Nick said. They agreed to meet that Friday. Nick gave her his address.

Marian was indeed sitting in the dark when she got off the phone. Her hut felt hot and dry and stifling, and smelled of her sweat and too much pent-up emotion. Despite her extreme gratitude toward Nick and her resolve to work with him, she hated the thought of betraying Tate's sister. She'd felt an affinity for Tammy immediately. They'd promised to stay in touch. She would have to tread carefully.

She gathered her towel and the flannel shorts and T-shirt she slept in and descended the hill toward the shower house.

She'd set something in motion with Nick. *This* was happening. God, she hoped she hadn't made a mistake. Her job was already tenuous. And she wanted this job. None of her other work had felt as meaningful, had brought her the same level of satisfaction. If the others found out about Nick, if they knew what she was up to, she could lose everything she'd worked so hard to attain. Tate had been with the program for ten years. He'd been one of them. She was still the newcomer. Again, she wondered how Arkansas and Yeti could have become injured while in her care. She felt edgy and unsure of herself. She hadn't been sleeping well. She feared this night wouldn't be much better.

Marian ran the water as hot as she could stand it, hoping it would work out the kinks in her body. Trainer had installed motion sensor lights in the shower house and bathrooms. At some point after Marian had shampooed her hair and lathered her body, the lights switched off. She stood in the dark, let the hot water run over her, let her body remain still, memories of Tate, the big things and little things, arranging and rearranging themselves in her mind, the night thickening around her. The water turned lukewarm, then cool. She reached for the lever and shut it off. The room remained dark. She waved her arms. The lights didn't turn back on. Maybe the bulb had burned out. She wrapped her towel around her. Something moved outside the stall, and her body flinched, and she wondered if an animal had gotten in. But then she heard the hinges on the shower house door. "Hello!" Marian called out. "Trainer? Lyle?" She listened as the door swung closed. Her skin prickled with heat despite the water droplets that ran down her arms and legs. She cinched her towel tighter, her breathing tentative and shallow.

In the morning, Marian met Trainer at the barn. She told him about the bulb burning out.

"I'll take care of it," he said.

And then, "Were you up there? Last night? I heard someone when I turned off the shower."

"I got my shower before supper," Trainer said.

"Someone was up there."

"Maybe a bear? I saw some tracks behind the main house."

"Black bear or grizzly?" Marian asked.

"These were a black bear. Looked like a sow. If they can break into a freezer like they've been known to do, I'm sure they can figure out a shower house door. I'll make sure and empty the garbage cans up there. Don't want anything attracting them."

Marian walked through the barn to the last kennel on her left, where Arkansas and Yeti had been staying together. The dogs were prancing in place by the kennel gate, both of them smiling their happy pant. Each kennel was the size of a single horse stall with a dog door on the back side that led to an outdoor run. "Hey, girls," she said. She let herself into the kennel with them, then closed the gate behind her.

Though the dogs' paws had healed, Marian had continued to massage lanolin into their pads each night and check them for abrasions and give the dogs a thorough checkup, and in the mornings, she'd check them again. "Lookin' good," she said. She picked up the pink chenille blanket off the floor that the dogs had been sleeping on. "I'm going to bring this in the house and wash it," she told Trainer. But when she shook out the blanket, a piece of sandpaper fell out of one of the folds. She retrieved the sandpaper, not thinking much of it. One of the dogs might have carried it in. Trainer was always doing odd jobs around the property. It wasn't until she saw the bloodstains and black smudges like the skin on the bottom of the dogs' paws that the idea hit her — someone had hurt these dogs.

"Hey, Trainer, can I show you something?"

Trainer walked over to her and she handed him the sandpaper.

"I wonder if the dogs were chewing on it," he said. "It may have torn up their gums. Did you check their mouths?"

"I check their mouths every morning. I check every inch of these dogs. Their gums are fine. I think someone intentionally hurt them."

"That's crazy thinking, Marian. No one here would do that."

"Trainer, I wasn't negligent. I keep running things through my mind, over and over again. These dogs didn't get injured under my watch."

"Probably not a good idea to be throwing out accusations."

Marian blew the air out of her lungs in one big gust. "You're right. I'm sorry." The last thing she needed right now was to get in trouble with Lyle, and yet in her mind she kept thinking someone had gotten to the dogs, maybe during the vigil for Tate, or early that next morning. Someone wanted her out of the program, and she had no idea why.

9
PRESENT: AUGUST 2017

Marian
Bonners Ferry, Idaho

Nick Shepard lived in a single-story house with light blue siding and a stone chimney. The house abutted heavily forested public lands of evergreens and hardwood. As Marian pulled up the gravel driveway, Nick stepped onto the small side porch. She recognized him from the pictures she'd seen — long silver hair pulled back in a ponytail, a full grayish-white beard. He wore jeans and a red fleece top and a beret-style cap. When he and Marian shook hands, she found him to be warm and approachable, and his eyes much kinder than they'd appeared in the photos, almost sweet. He opened the door for her and invited her in.

"You have a beautiful spot," Marian said. "There are so many trees." And then, "Why Bonners Ferry?"

"Like Garbo, I wanted to be left alone."

Marian might have been taken aback, but Nick brushed the comment off with a wave of his hand. "Do you want something to drink?" he asked.

She said she was fine. Besides, she'd brought a water bottle with her. She followed Nick to a large pedestal table just off the kitchen. Did he have a limp? Yes, she was sure he did. "Are you okay?" she asked.

He seemed a little surprised by her question. "Oh, this." He looked at his left leg. "Arthritis. I've had it for years. It stiffens up on me sometimes."

She set her backpack on the floor beside her and took out a legal pad and a pen.

"The woman is prepared. I like that."

Nick and Marian spent the next fifteen minutes talking about the work she did. Then Nick said, "But that's not why you're here." He leaned back and supported his elbows on the arms of his chair. "When we spoke last, you were concerned by the way Tate misrepresented himself. There's a way we rewrite experiences, a way we change and shape events to conform to a perspective we have of our self and of others. Though some of the things Tate told you or referred to may or may not have been true, it doesn't matter. He incorporated them into his world, his being in the world. Do these stories and claims make him eerie, weird, unique, or do they hint at something darker? Real or not, what he was saying is, 'I am part of all of these events, and they are part of me.' The intent is to elicit a reaction, to reinforce his position," Nick said.

"Tate told you he came from a ranching family. A strong masculine image was probably important to Tate. He presented himself as the product of a male-dominated culture. He may have associated physical strength and independence with a rancher. Let's go a step further. Tate said his father was mayor. That would have been another way of him saying he came from a position of male power. This is all part of Tate's script for how he perceived himself and how he wished to be perceived by others."

"Why wasn't he worried about being caught? He had to know at some point I would find out," Marian said.

"But he *was* caught, at least on one occasion. You questioned him about his father being mayor. Tate had a way of manipulating the situation to make you feel as though you had done something wrong. I'll need more information from you to pursue this line of thinking further, but for now let's just say that Tate wasn't concerned with the consequences of his actions. He was confident that he could spin whatever spiel necessary to maintain his position."

"I was gullible," Marian said. "And weak. I wanted to believe him."

"You weren't weak. You were manipulated. There's a difference." There was a large picture window next to the table that looked out onto a patio and backyard. A hummingbird feeder hung in front of the window. Nick paused for a long minute as if watching the feeder, as if waiting for a bird to appear. "Do you have a picture of Tate on you?" Nick asked.

Marian reached for her phone in her bag. She pulled up a picture of Tate, one she'd taken in the oil sands.

Nick looked at the photo intently. "I've seen him before," he said. "The name sounded familiar. I can't place the face, but I know we met." Nick handed the phone back to Marian. "I told you I would run a background check on Tate. You were right. Tate did not have a criminal record. You may want to ask the sister if Tate was ever in trouble as a young person, if he ever had a juvenile record, but for now we can assume Tate was a law-abiding citizen."

Marian retrieved a business card from her back pocket. "I found this in Tate's room," she said. "It may be nothing." She handed

Nick the card for an attorney in Norfolk, Nebraska. "I'm not sure why I held on to it. Tate had just died. I couldn't sleep. I'd gone to his hut and was looking through his things. At that point I still believed Tate had grown up in Montana and had graduated from the University of Montana like he'd told me."

"What was Tate's connection with Norfolk?" Nick asked.

"According to his sister, that's where he went to school. Northeast Community College."

"How long was he there?"

"A year, I believe. He commuted from home."

"Do you mind if I keep this? It might be worth making some calls." Then Nick told her he'd be discreet. He'd done this sort of thing before.

"Let's change gears," Nick said. "Let's talk about the cases. There were four victims. The first, Natasha Freeman, was twenty-nine. She worked as a teacher's aide at an elementary school in Helena. She disappeared from her vehicle one night, about a half-hour drive from her home. Her body was found two weeks later, just before Christmas, by a couple who had gone snowshoeing. Freeman had been left in the woods about three miles from her vehicle. Her clothes were found near the body. Examiner reports showed that she'd been strangled from behind. There was no evidence that she had been raped. A boot was recovered farther up the hill, and some broken branches were identified. It looked like there'd been a struggle. Authorities believe she was murdered at the site where the couple came upon the remains. There was snow on the ground when she disappeared. By the time her body was discovered, new snowfall had covered any prints that might have been left."

Marian had been jotting down the details of what Nick said. She thought of the pictures she'd seen of Natasha. "She was beautiful," Marian said. "That's what I thought when I saw her picture." Marian looked up and met Nick's eyes.

"The second victim was younger, barely twenty years old," Nick said. "She'd recently moved to the Whitefish area. Erin Parker disappeared in the fall, almost two years after Natasha's murder. Friends said she'd hitchhiked to a trailhead in the forest. She didn't show up for work the next day. A search party was set in motion. Two months later a man was in the woods with his dog. He was cutting firewood and came upon

Erin's remains. We didn't make the connection with Freeman until the examiner's report determined that both the hyoid and the laryngeal bones had been fractured. Parker was killed by forearm strangulation from behind. And, as with Freeman, her clothes had been removed. Interesting thing with this one, though," Nick said. "When her phone was recovered from a ditch along one of the highways, there was a picture of her at the trailhead. Someone else had taken the photo. The phone had been wiped clean of any fingerprints."

Nick asked, "Did you ever notice any scarring from scratches on Tate's body?"

"Not that I recall," Marian said.

"There was a sign of a struggle between Parker and the killer. We have reason to believe she put up a fight. The killer may not have walked away unscathed," Nick said. "With this particular case, there was some dismembering of the body — clean, postmortem cuts to the wrists, made with a sharp-edged instrument, possibly an axe. The victim may have had the killer's DNA under her fingernails. Her hands were never recovered."

Tate kept an axe and a shovel in his truck. Marian had used it to split wood for her stove. Nick had been right. These kinds of details were not in the articles she'd read. The room had suddenly taken on an eerie quality: the gray light that filtered in through the picture window beside them, the ticking of a clock somewhere in the other room. A long-haired cat jumped onto Marian's lap, startling her back against her chair. The cat was purring loudly. His claws snagged Marian's jeans before the cat lay down.

"I should have asked if you were allergic to cats."

"No, it's fine," Marian said. And all the while she was thinking Tate could not have done these things, not the man she'd loved. Her shoulders tensed; her neck felt stiff.

"In the Stillwater murders, the killer took different measures," Nick told her. "As I've said before, not everything that pertains to a crime is released to the media. When I was working cases that appeared to be connected, I'd reconstruct the crimes, look for differences. No two cases are exactly the same. It's in the differences that we find our clues. Just as you can't walk through a room without leaving physical traces — a hair, skin cells — you can't commit a murder without leaving psychological traces. We have to focus on understanding the killer's logic, his style of thinking, why he does the things he does, and the place to begin that inquiry is with an examination of the extant crime: where the body is found, how the victim was treated, whether the crime was committed there or elsewhere, what weapon was used. Serial killers, like most humans, adapt to circumstances; they change, and what is different from one murder to another is far more informative than what remains the same."

Then Nick asked Marian if she'd ever seen Tate with a camper or a small trailer.

She never had.

"The third victim went missing a little over two years after Parker's remains were discovered. Lynn-Marie Pontante was just shy of nineteen years old. She was working at a stable where she was given a place to live and a small income. She was last seen paying for gas at a convenience store. A boyfriend was questioned in her disappearance. He was the one who'd reported her missing. Seven months later her remains were discovered about a mile from where the remains of Erin Parker were found. A father and his son were hunting for turkey when they came upon an abandoned camp trailer. About fifty yards from the trailer they found Lynn-Marie's clothing, and eventually her bones. And like the other two victims, Pontante died from forearm strangulation from behind. But the difference in this case was the condition of the skeletal remains, particularly that of the pubic bone and the coccyx.

"Lynn-Marie had narrow hips, a narrow pelvic region. She'd been told that sex would be painful, that she might need to go through physiotherapy for vaginismus. And her pelvic region was too small to deliver a baby naturally. Though there was no evidence of penile penetration, her pubic bone was separated, and she had a fractured coccyx, or tailbone, most likely from a blunt object or a fist inserted into her vaginal cavity."

Marian had instinctively held her breath as Nick spoke, something horrible lurching inside her.

"The killer took his time with this one. He used the trailer to buy him that time to play out his script. The trailer was old, no doubt a leftover camp of one kind or another used by hunters over the years, maybe some loggers. What matters is that our killer knew these woods. He knew about the trailer. He was taking more risks. There was evidence of the victim — fingerprints, hair, the victim's blood, even though the cause of death was still strangulation. There were other fingerprints also, other DNA samples, but none that we could get a match on. Not everybody is in the CODIS database, and there were no doubt various people who'd used this trailer over the years. But the question is raised regarding the location of the victim's death. The victim's remains were found outside the trailer. In this situation it's prudent to assume she was tortured and killed inside the trailer, and then her remains were disposed of."

At some point Marian had set her pen aside, as if there were something very cold in the act of writing these details down. And there was the humbling effect of it all. Marian was still a living, breathing part of this deeply unbalanced world.

Nick told Marian that if his memory served him correctly, and that wasn't a sure thing these days, Pontante disappeared from the property where she worked and was living. Her vehicle was still at the premises, as was her purse and other personal items.

Nick stared down at the table. His body remained still. Then he sighed loudly and apologized. "I lost my train of thought." He told Marian that earlier that morning he'd been looking over some portraits he'd written on each of the victims and the events surrounding their disappearances. He should probably have those notes in front of him, he said.

Marian stroked the cat's fur while she waited for Nick to continue. She felt the reality of these women's lives and deaths so palpably, her chest ached with an impossibly heavy weight.

"The fourth victim was Melissa Marsh," Nick said.

Marian thought of Melissa's sister, Emily, who had worked with Marian in Utah. Emily had kept a picture of Melissa on her phone screen, and each time Emily would swipe the phone to enter a coordinate and record a sample, Marian would notice the moment of hesitation, and she'd know the young intern was remembering her sister's death all over again. The photo had been taken just days before Melissa's disappearance.

"Marsh worked at a veterinary clinic," Nick said. "She was walking from the clinic back to her apartment. There were people who saw her that day on the road, including a witness who'd seen her accept a ride from someone. Authorities didn't believe the case was connected with the other Stillwater murders. They canvassed the area near her apartment. They dragged the river behind where she lived. I told them they needed to look in the forest, that the body would be found in a similar location to the others. They didn't believe me. They were looking for similarities, and this case was different. A year later a man hunting for black bear came upon her bones. They were scattered in about a fifty-yard radius off a logging road in the Stillwater forest. Dental records confirmed they were the remains of Marsh. Pieces of her clothing were found at the scene as well."

This death felt particularly personal to Marian because she knew the victim's sister. There was a tissue box on the table. Nick handed it to Marian. "Like I said, this is sensitive material."

Nick went on to explain that even in cases such as Melissa's, when there were only skeletal remains to go by, medical examiners were able to determine hyoid and laryngeal fractures. "Forearm strangulation from behind is likely to crush the larynx and fracture the hyoid. It takes about twenty pounds of pressure," Nick said. "There's a point on the neck where the carotid artery extends to the brain. If you put sufficient pressure on the artery, you're looking at about ten seconds to the victim being unconscious, and twenty-four seconds to death. And there's less chance of a struggle when the victim is strangled from behind, less chance for trace evidence under her fingernails."

"What was different about Melissa Marsh's case?" Marian asked.

"Melissa used to warn others about the dangers of hitchhiking. She was picked up on a public road in broad daylight two blocks from her apartment. The witness who saw her get into the vehicle said there wasn't a struggle. She wouldn't have willingly gotten into the vehicle of a man she didn't know. And why would she accept a ride in the first place when she was only two blocks from home? More than likely she'd agreed to go somewhere with the driver. There are two points here that make this case different. First, this time our perp knew his victim. He'd had prior conversations with her, had established a level of trust. The pursuit of the victim is highly seductive for the killer. With each point of contact, the killer's fantasy would have intensified and his anticipation escalated, heightening the climax of the actual attack. Second, with Melissa, our killer was taking risks; he was pushing the limits, as if saying, 'Look what I can get away with.' The more he can get away with, the greater his ego. As Charles Manson said, 'You've got to accept yourself as God. You've got to realize you're just as much the devil as you are God.' And as with Lynn-Marie, the killer may have taken his time with Melissa once he had her under his control. Though we can't know for sure, I assume he did."

Then Nick asked Marian what kind of vehicle Tate drove, and she told him a silver Nissan Xterra. "I have it now," she said. "His sister signed over the title to me. The vehicle has a lot of miles on it."

"He had it for a while, then," Nick said.

"He bought it used. According to the title, he had it for six years. Why?"

"Melissa Marsh was seen getting into a green SUV."

Marian breathed a little more easily. Her shoulders began to relax.

Nick pushed himself up from his chair, and the long-haired cat on Marian's lap raised his head and jumped down. Nick held on to the edge of the table as he walked around it toward the kitchen, and with each step he shifted his weight as if his left foot were asleep.

"Are you sure you're okay?" Marian asked. But again he dismissed her with a wave of his hand and said, "Fine."

A cabinet opened and he set a glass on the counter. She heard him take out a second glass. "You like bourbon?" he asked.

"I'm not a big drinker."

Marian listened to Nick open the refrigerator, scoop up some ice, and drop the cubes into the two glasses. The cubes clinked again when he poured the bourbon.

His legs were moving more fluidly when he reappeared and set one of the glasses on the table in front of Marian. Then he lowered himself back into the chair across from her.

"Despite the differences of each of these cases, the similarities remain the same," Nick said. "The killer terrified his victims; he humiliated them by having them take their clothes off; and he destroyed them."

A gust of wind knocked the bird feeder against the window. The noise startled Marian, though it didn't seem to faze Nick at all. "It's getting ready to rain," he said. "With the dry spell we've had, we can use it."

Marian had wrapped both hands around the glass in front of her. Its condensation collected on her palms. "Why do you think the first victim was found outside Helena?" she asked.

"Could be an area where the killer was living at the time. Could have been a route he frequented often. It may not be any of those things. More than likely the event was inadvertent, not something he planned. We're looking at a person who would have been in a constant process of fantasizing that led up to the initial murder. Maybe he looked in windows. Maybe he walked into homes and moved things around, scaring the shit out of people. All of these things would have been a rehearsal of the process going on in his head. The idea that there has to be some kind of trigger to incite a psychopathic killer is a myth."

Marian said something about Natasha Freeman being in the wrong place at the wrong time, and Nick said, "Correct," and that once a predator has destroyed his prey, he will inevitably kill again. "But between each of these women's murders, this guy would have hunted dozens of times. He may even have gone so far as to establish face validity with a potential victim, in other words get her to trust him, which he would have done in a matter of minutes. The level of excitation he would experience on the hunt or in establishing that validity would be much better than the actual kill."

"Would he ever pursue a relationship with a woman?" Marian asked.

"There may have been girlfriends over the years. He may have been in a relationship when he committed the crimes. Perhaps as a cover-up. More than likely out of convenience. But whatever sincere feelings a woman may have had for the killer would not have been reciprocated."

Marian's stomach dipped, as if Nick were speaking about her. "Your drink's getting warm," he said. She picked up the glass and lifted it to her lips. The room had become full of the kind of shadows that precede a storm. A napkin and a piece of mail blew off the table. Marian reached down to pick them up. The envelope was from Kootenai Health Cancer Services in Sandpoint. She placed it back on the table.

Nick rose from his chair and walked into the living area. He shut the two windows and turned on a lamp. He suggested they move to the other room. Marian gathered her things and joined him, bringing her drink with her. She sat on the sofa in front of the two windows. Nick sat in the recliner. He pushed his weight back in the chair and raised the footrest.

"I've stayed too long," Marian said. "I'm sorry." And she went to put her items in her pack.

Nick said, "If I thought you'd stayed too long, I would have said that."

And so Marian relaxed against the sofa, and when she did, the cat reappeared and jumped up beside her. He purred loudly, dug his claws into the pilled upholstery, and lay down with his back pressed against Marian's thigh.

"His name's Good Fellow. He likes women."

Marian rubbed the cat behind his ears and stroked his fur. She sipped the cold bourbon until it was almost gone. "Melissa Marsh disappeared over two years ago," she said.

"Yes. I believe so."

"So far, no one else has gone missing."

"That we know of," Nick said.

"Does a killer like this ever stop?"

"Theoretically, no. The ideation is there. He'll still carry out the fantasy in his mind. Sometimes a killer might get sloppy, take too many risks. He may feel like authorities are getting too close. He might move on and take the crimes elsewhere."

"The cases are still being investigated," Marian said. "What made you stop?"

Nick pushed himself up from the chair and walked across the living room to the hallway. He returned, holding a framed photograph. He stood next to Marian and showed her the picture.

"This is why I stopped," he said. "That's Cate. My wife."

The photo was taken in front of a bed of

peonies.

"She likes to garden," Nick said. "So do I. We planted those peonies together. We'd like to plant a lot more."

Nick walked over to the recliner and sat down. He set the picture of his wife on the small table beside him.

"Do you take a lot of pictures?" Marian asked.

"I guess I do. Birds, wildlife."

Marian finished her drink. "I should get going," she said. She thanked Nick for his time.

"I'll have more questions for you," Nick said. "We should talk again soon."

Marian excused herself to use the bathroom. And as she was washing her hands, she noticed the two prescription bottles on the vanity. Both had been written for Nick. One was for lorazepam, the other for temozolomide.

When she walked back into the living room, Nick's eyes were closed. His head had dipped toward his right shoulder. He was sleeping soundly. Marian picked up the crocheted afghan that was draped over the back of the sofa. She stepped softly across the room and laid the blanket over him. The cat jumped into Nick's lap. Though Nick's breathing deepened, he didn't stir.

The rain had just begun to fall when Marian left. Once she was in her vehicle, she took out her phone and looked up lorazepam. It was used to treat anxiety symptoms. It was also used to treat seizure disorders. Then she looked up temozolomide: an orally active alkylating agent used in adjuvant chemotherapy for persons diagnosed with glioblastoma multiforme, a stage IV brain tumor. She stared at the words on her phone as if she could hear their foreboding and felt the sharp edge of grief for Nick and his wife, who'd appeared so lovely in the photo, and for Natasha Freeman and Erin Parker and Lynn-Marie Pontante and Melissa Marsh.

10
Present: August 2017

Marian
The Den, Montana

Looking into Tate's past wasn't going to be a simple process. Nick had been right. Marian was searching for two things: Who was this complicated man whom she'd loved? And, could he have been involved with the Stillwater murders? Nick had cautioned her on the latter, saying a psychological autopsy wouldn't tell her whether Tate had killed these women. But Marian knew that a timeline could prove that he didn't. If only she could access the program's network, she was sure she could find a detailed account of Tate's past assignments. She could prove to herself he had never been at the scene of the crimes. For the time being, she would have to rely on other resources. She would talk to Trainer. He'd been with the program since the beginning, looking after the property, taking care of the dogs. He was a big, warmhearted man from Louisiana who could talk for long stretches if someone gave him the opportunity.

The morning after Marian met with Nick, she showed up at the barn earlier than usual.

"Morning, sunshine. You're up early." Trainer was scooping food into the dogs' bowls.

"Thought you could use some help," she said.

"Couldn't sleep?"

She shrugged. The truth was, she couldn't remember the last time she'd slept well. That previous night was no exception.

The morning was cool, the air crisp like a glimpse of fall. Marian attempted her and Trainer's normal banter among the hungry whines from the kennels: What was the weather forecast? What did the day's schedule look like? But mostly they made a fuss over the dogs, sending them cooing affirmations: "Hang on, Winter, your food's coming. I know, you're such a good boy"; and, "Yeti, if you aren't just the sweetest thing," and "I love you, baby girl." Trainer had a soft spot as big as Marian's when it came to the dogs.

Marian began delivering the bowls of food to the different kennels. When she was finished and the dogs were gulping down their breakfasts, which for most of them would take no more than a couple of minutes, she asked Trainer if she could talk to him. "I've been thinking about something Tate told me, about the Stillwater murders. He said they took place not far from here. I was wondering what that was like for the staff. Were the handlers ever afraid?"

The dog food was stored in a metal garbage can. Trainer fastened the lid. He folded his arms against his chest and leaned his back against the wall. "They talked about it, sure," Trainer said. "Only two of the victims were from around here, and I think both of them were hitchhiking."

Marian wanted to correct Trainer. According to Nick, only one of the victims was hitchhiking. Melissa Marsh had gotten into the vehicle of someone she knew.

There was a flicker in Trainer's blue eyes. "A couple years back, Jenness quit the program. Took a job at the vet hospital in Columbia Falls. She worked with one of the women who was killed."

"I heard that," Marian said. "I worked with the woman's sister in Utah. She told me her sister and Jenness were friends." And maybe Marian would have asked Jenness about the situation upon returning to The

Den, but there had been word of Tate's death and then Jenness's impending trip to Alaska. "Did she ever talk about it?" Marian said.

"Well, like I said, she was working at the clinic when it happened. A couple of us were in contact with her. No one knew for sure what had happened. The body wasn't found until a year later, about the same time Jenness asked for her job back. But, no, Jenness kept pretty quiet about the whole thing."

The dogs had finished eating and were starting to play with their bowls. Trainer began making his rounds, gathering the bowls from the kennels. Marian did the same. They stacked the bowls in the storage room. "There's a guy not too far from here that the police were looking into," Trainer said.

Marian looked up sharply, her eyebrows raised.

"You know that old farmhouse on Stage Hill? The big white one? He lives there by himself. Used to live with his mom, but she passed on. His name's Dana Lear. He's a schizophrenic who sometimes forgets to take his meds. You may want to avoid that direction when you're going for a run."

Nick said there had been persons of interest. She'd not realized one of them had lived so close, no more than a few miles from The Den. "Why wasn't this mentioned to me before?"

"It's been a while since his name went through the rumor mill. I think he's fallen off the radar. I don't know the details."

Two days later Marian had gone into town to run errands. It was late in the afternoon, pushing close to six when she was on her way back. But instead of turning into The Den, she kept on going another three miles, until she made a left-hand turn onto Stage Hill Road. The land opened up and the sun shone down as if there once had been farms along that section of clearing. The impulse had been spontaneous, and yet here she was, driving slowly, her neck bent at a precarious angle, as she looked at the two-story farmhouse, painted white, coming up on her right. It was built on top of a hill, and Marian was staring into the sun, and the house loomed above her like an ominous shadow.

Marian slowed to a stop, directly in front of the house, and about fifty feet away from a black pickup truck that was parked in the front lawn with a *For Sale* sign in the window. The pickup was probably an antique, with a beveled bed, and the price on the sign said $8,900.

Marian had not made the turn onto Stage Hill Road with a strategy in mind. Aside from curiosity, she had no idea what she was doing here. Of course there were people of interest, individuals capable of horrible things that she couldn't believe Tate had been capable of. She was trying to get to the root of something, that was what it was, and maybe this place would tell her the things she wanted to know. Maybe it would point her to Tate's innocence.

She parked her vehicle on the edge of the road and the two-foot-wide shoulder of gravel and dirt. She could feign interest in the pickup truck that was for sale, and with that facile plan in mind, she opened her door and climbed out of the vehicle and walked around to the front lawn where the truck was parked. Though there were no trees in the yard and despite the evening sun, the shadow from the house was chilly.

The grass was tall, maybe a foot and a half, and dandelions had gone to seed, and in the ditch alongside the road was Queen Anne's lace that had grown stately. Marian stepped toward the front of the pickup truck and inclined her head forward, as if reading the *For Sale* sign more closely, and after a few seconds she casually looked up the hill toward the house. At first she noticed the front door, painted green, and the first-floor windows with curtains that appeared to be lace, and then she looked up to the second floor. In the window to the far right was a man standing broadside and staring back at her, and she immediately felt more nervous than she'd already been, and she wondered if he could tell, and her face was sweating, and she wondered if he could tell that, too. She skirted her eyes away. She would stick to her plan; she was an interested buyer. She stepped closer to the truck and peered inside just long enough to be convincing, and heard a voice inside her head telling her to go, and though the air was still, even the grass seemed to whisper. Her heart tapped in her ear like something staccato as she walked back to her vehicle, as she felt the man still watching her, and if she were a child, she would swear the house was haunted. She was prejudiced, she knew, because of what Trainer had told her, yet the house was expressionless, and the face on the man was expressionless, too. She started her vehicle and looked up one more time, and yes, the man was still standing there, and Marian was certain even his hands had not moved.

■ ■ ■ ■

Late the next evening, sometime after dark, Marian was sitting at her desk with her laptop in front of her and talking with Nick over Skype. They'd been in contact the past few days by email, ever since she'd visited him at his house. He'd said he had some information for her.

"I made a couple of calls," he told her. "The first was to the attorney in Norfolk. He acknowledged that Tate was a client of his. Due to client confidentiality, that was all he was going to tell me. The second call was to a friendly court clerk in the county office who did some digging for me. During the time Tate was attending classes at the college, he was charged with unlawful intrusion. There'd been a telephone complaint of someone looking in windows. Police caught him, charged him under the statute. The case was turned over to the prosecutor. Tate hired a lawyer, gave some story about taking a shortcut, said he saw a light on and kept moving. His attorney made the argument that Tate was a full-time student, employed, with no prior record or offenses. The charge was dropped."

Marian stared back at the screen, in shock.

"What if he was telling the truth? What if he actually was taking a shortcut through someone's yard?" But really what she was doing was giving herself time to let Nick's words sink in.

Nick's face appeared resolute and calm. He was leaning back in his desk chair.

"What kind of person does that?" Marian asked.

"A predator," Nick said. "Someone with a sexual deviance."

"You think he was a peeping Tom."

"That was the charge."

Marian felt like she was losing another piece of the man she'd loved, and part of her wanted to hold on, even frantically, to the person she'd thought he was. Tate would have still been a teenager, not even twenty. It was a long time ago. She reminded herself that the charges had been dropped. Shouldn't that account for something? But she was disturbed by what Nick had told her; of course she was.

"Your first loyalty right now is still to Tate," Nick said. "That's understandable. But at some point your first loyalty needs to be to yourself. I hope that in our working together, you'll be able to get to that place."

"Is that why you're helping me?"

"That's part of it, yes."

"This is taking up a lot of your time. And you're okay with that?" Marian was thinking of Nick's illness. He had not mentioned it to her, and she did not feel it was her place to bring it up.

"I'll help you as I can," he said.

Marian asked Nick what his other reasons were for getting involved.

"My involvement has to do with the victims. No stone left unturned. Something like that."

Then Nick said, "Let's bring the conversation back to Tate for a minute. I'm wondering if he was ever humiliated by a woman he was close with, particularly when he was a young boy or a young man."

"I don't know," Marian said. "Not that I'm aware of."

"Is this something you could ask the sister?"

Marian was thinking. "Tammy mentioned a girlfriend of Tate's from when he was in college. I found her online. I've thought about reaching out to her. She's married now. Lives in Lincoln. She might know something."

"Reach out to the girlfriend. See what you can find out."

They were about to end the call when Marian asked Nick about Dana Lear.

"There was never an inquest, but yes, he was a person of interest. The guy collects knives. He drives a green SUV, or at least he did at the time. He's creepy as hell. Is he capable of murder? He very well may be. Did he commit the Stillwater murders? I'm not convinced he did."

Nick said, "One woman worked the night shift at a convenience store. Lear invited the woman to his house. He became noticeably upset when she turned him down. When she got off her shift, he was waiting for her at her vehicle. He said if she didn't go out with him, he would have to show her his knives. She made up some excuse, said she had to get home, that she would think about it. Then she called the police and filed a restraining order. Another woman was a waitress at a diner. The guy wrote letters to her explicitly describing his sexual fantasies. Each fantasy involved knives. The police didn't do anything until she looked out her window one night and saw Lear standing across the street from her house."

"Police never questioned him in the Stillwater cases?"

"They asked him to come into the station. He refused. He was a suspicious character who drove a green SUV. That wasn't enough to charge him with a crime."

"But he wasn't *your* person of interest," Marian said.

"He never was. Lear is a schizophrenic. At the same diner where the one woman worked, Lear had been seen having an entire conversation with himself. The Stillwater killer is methodical. He was able to get these women to trust him. I don't think Lear is capable of that same level of manipulation and organized thinking."

"Even if he's taking his meds?" Marian asked.

"I never talked to the guy. I can't know for sure, but it's doubtful."

Marian heard something outside, the breaking of a limb, the crunching of ground cover and debris, the footfall of a large animal. She wondered if she might be hearing the sow whose tracks Trainer had seen.

"What's wrong?" Nick asked.

Marian had been staring out at the blackness through her open window. She turned back to Nick's face on the screen. "I live in the woods," Marian said. "There are a lot of noises outside."

"Do you lock your door?"

"After what you told me about Lear, I'll make sure I do." She wouldn't tell Nick about her stopping at Lear's house. She could already hear Nick's reprimand.

After the call was ended, Marian shut her window. She grabbed the can of pepper spray from the holster on her pack beside her bed, and after she had waited a few minutes to make sure the animal was gone, she picked up the flashlight that she carried with her when she went to the bathhouse at night and stepped outside. She wanted to see if she could find any tracks that would identify the animal. But the ground around her was strewn with pine needles and scrub grass and creeping juniper. She walked up the hill a little ways behind her hut, stepping among the shadows in the woods from a crescent moon, her own shadow looming larger than life like Goliath. A light blinked on from down the hill. The motion sensor bulb on the outside of the shower house had clicked on. Marian stood still, her body jumpy and alert. Within no time, she heard the sound of water splashing onto concrete. The shower house windows were open. Trainer was getting a shower.

She turned back around, her flashlight pointed at Jenness's hut. The west-facing window was open. Weather forecasts predicted rain over the next couple of days. Marian was sure Jenness would not have intentionally left the window open. And so Marian walked toward the hut and saw that the screen had been removed. Each hut had a keypad where a passcode had to be entered to lock or unlock the door. Marian did not know the code, and the door was secure, so she walked back to the window and opened it farther. She set the flashlight on the windowsill and hoisted herself up and into the small quarters.

Marian had never been inside Jenness's hut before, though she wasn't surprised to find it arranged the same as her own. The room was tidy, the bed made. Everything seemed to be in its place, and Marian thought how fitting for Jenness, and yet how unfitting for the window to be open and the screen to be out. She did not want to turn on the overhead fixture or a lamp, for fear the light would draw the attention of Trainer, and so instead she shined the flashlight around the room.

Under the bed were several clear plastic storage bins. One by one Marian pulled out the containers and looked inside. The first was full of clothes, fleece tops and sweaters, all neatly folded. Another contained a smorgasbord of freeze-dried meals and a package of butane lighters. The third bin contained more packages of freeze-dried food and several cans of bear spray. Marian scooted the bins back under the bed.

There were a number of framed photos on top of Jenness's bureau. One was of a woman who looked to be in her fifties, whom Jenness bore a resemblance to — dark hair, dark eyes, dark eyelashes. Another picture looked like a family shot: two parents, three young girls, a white German shepherd. Marian picked up the photo, certain she could recognize Jenness in the face of one of the girls who appeared to be the middle one in age. Evenly taped on the wall above the bureau were photos from different projects, including the recent study in Alberta, and group shots of some of the handlers and orienteers. Next to one of the group pictures was a photo of Marian, a close shot with only a gray sky behind her. She was wearing her multicolored knit cap. She was smiling, and the close-up image was so clear Marian could count the freckles along her nose and across her face, and yet she had no recollection of when the photo had been taken.

There were other pictures as well, some taped above Jenness's desk. Marian pulled open the desk drawer, where she found bills and receipts and a backpacking magazine with a feature on Alaska.

On Jenness's nightstand was a photo with the printed caption *Denali State Park: Ke-*

sugi Ridge that looked as though it had been cut out of a travel magazine. Jenness had left for Alaska almost a week after the vigil for Tate. She'd taken a month's leave from work and two weeks' vacation time with plans to backpack in Wrangell–St. Elias National Park, hike Kesugi Ridge, cross the Arctic Circle all the way to Prudhoe Bay, and camp the entire way. She wouldn't be back until the first weekend in September.

Marian thought about her last conversation with Jenness before she'd left. The group had been worried about Jenness. Marian had been worried as well. Jenness would be driving alone over twenty-four hundred miles each way. She'd wanted to see the countryside of British Columbia and the Yukon Territory. Once in Alaska, she'd be backpacking solo, often for days without cell service. She had a satellite phone, she'd reassured everyone.

"Do you still want to do this?" Marian had asked after the news of Tate's death. "Aren't you afraid?"

Jenness had stopped by Marian's hut to check on her. Marian was lying on the bed, the clumsy mess of grief all over her face. Jenness was sitting beside her.

"I'm not afraid," Jenness had said.

Marian said, "I'm worried. But I'm also

jealous."

Jenness, who had been brushing Marian's hair, paused for a moment and held the brush lightly over Marian's spine, as gentle as sunlight. "I'll be okay," she said.

Marian was touched by Jenness's comfort and the closeness she felt with Jenness now. She rolled over and pushed herself to a sitting position, bent her head forward, and unclasped the silver chain with her St. Francis medallion. "I want you to have this," Marian said, as if this gesture would keep Jenness safe, because the tragedy of Tate's death still felt entirely too close. She held the chain around Jenness's neck, the medallion falling just above the neckline of Jenness's top.

And Jenness asked Marian if she was sure, and Marian said of course, and Jenness said how grateful she was. "You're going to be okay," Jenness said. "You know that. You're going to get through this."

"I know," Marian said.

Within a week, the group had a text message from Jenness. She'd made it safely to Alaska. And she'd continued to check in every few days, as she'd promised.

Beside the framed photo of Kesugi Ridge was a basket filled with different-colored yarns and a variety of knitting needles. Marian sat on the quilted bed covering and thought of Jenness with her long braid and her cup of tea, propped up in her bed with her knitting, or on the sofa in the main house when Lyle and Trainer and Marian and Jenness had watched *The Return of the Jedi.* Marian reached for the basket and brought it closer, and was surprised by the weight of it. She wrapped her fingers around the soft spun wool that reminded her of the scarf Jenness had knitted Marian for her birthday. With Tate now gone, Marian wondered if she and Jenness were friends, and Marian almost felt sorry for herself because she realized how few close friends she had.

While lost in that thought, her hand sank deeper into the brightly colored skeins and touched something hard. Marian wrapped her hand around the stock of a gun and lifted the gun out of the basket, and when she did several needles fell onto the floor and clinked against each other, the noise startling Marian, who still felt jumpy. She held the nine-millimeter pistol in front of her. She'd fired one like this before. She'd grown up around people who owned guns, including her uncle. And yet given her current setting, the handgun felt severe. The

Den was university property. Guns were not allowed on the premises, and only on one study in the Svalbard archipelago had a handler been allowed to carry a firearm. Marian released the magazine and found that it was fully loaded, and immediately felt something cold like shock. She wondered what Jenness had been up to, and whether she'd had the gun because she was afraid, and if she was afraid, should Marian be afraid also? Jenness would not have been able to bring the gun with her over the border on her trip to Alaska, Marian knew. The handlers weren't even allowed to travel into Canada with cans of pepper spray. Instead, they had to purchase bear spray after they'd crossed the border.

Marian reinserted the magazine, pressed her palm against it hard until the magazine snapped into place, and returned the gun to the basket. She picked up the needles from the floor and returned them as well. Then she stood from the bed and smoothed out the quilted comforter.

She had not closed the desk drawer all the way. When she tried to shut it, the drawer jammed. She tugged it open to realign it, shifting the contents inside, and noticed a piece of paper with what appeared to be some sort of login information: *gator,*

K9Con, WU1032. Jenness had added Marian as an administrator to the social media accounts before she'd left. This login key did not match what Marian already had. And Gator was the name of a dog who had worked with Lyle for years before Lyle had been promoted from handler to program coordinator. Marian felt that electric jolt of adrenaline. She memorized the information, hopeful that she had just stumbled upon access to Lyle's computer and the program's network.

11

FROM NICK SHEPARD'S FILE
VICTIM PORTRAIT # 2
Erin Parker

Erin Parker was from Greenwood, Arkansas. She wore glasses and talked with a lisp and a Southern twang. She was a large girl, with a solid build, which she'd inherited from a man whom she'd never known. She had quit high school when she was sixteen to work as a cashier at Walmart, and by the time she was twenty had remained at the same job and still lived at home.

Her mom charged her fifty dollars a week for rent. Erin didn't mind. Her mom had it hard. Hadn't been with a man, as far as the girl knew, since Erin was born. It was the fact that her mom was beautiful that the girl minded the most. Why couldn't Erin have come out looking like her mom? Instead she'd come out with big feet and hands and a freckled face like her dad.

Erin had a picture of her father. He was leaning against a metallic gold Firebird. He had bulky arms that were crossed over his broad chest. His red hair was cut short. His eyes were green. He wore a navy T-shirt and blue jeans, and the kind of steel-toe boots Erin sold at Walmart.

Erin learned that her father's name was Owen and that he'd been visiting from Montana when Erin was conceived, but that was all that Erin knew, and all her mother had chosen to tell her.

Nancy Parker was hard and sad and strong, and if she weren't so beautiful with long brown hair that was almost black and clear blue eyes and lean hips that defied the fact that she'd ever borne a child, the girl might have stood up to her mom and demanded to know more. But all those ingredients, and the kind of sadness that felt like it just might be because she had a daughter in the world, made Erin shy away from her mom, and in some ways want to be just like her.

"Don't get pregnant," her mother would tell her, even though Erin had never been on a date. But she thought about men. She liked the ones in Greenwood who wore working boots and blue jeans and rough flannel shirts, who'd ask her for a pack of Marlboros. When she got off work, she'd think about those men. She'd imagine them at jobs in the woods or on farms, fixing trucks, driving tractors, or cutting up trees with a chain saw. She'd think about running away with one of them, of living on his farm or in his cabin in the woods.

Erin's only friend was a boy named Jeffrey who worked in the garden center. She thought he might have a crush on her, but he was shorter than she was, and he wore skateboard shoes, and sometimes he had acne. They ate lunch together most days, and played video games in the electronics section on their breaks. On her birthday, when she turned nineteen, he gave her a nickel-plated necklace with an opal pendant. On her next birthday he gave her a ring.

They were in the break room when Erin told him she was moving to Montana.

"You'll never find him," Jeffrey said. "You don't even have his last name."

"I know that," she'd said.

"Then why are you going?"

"It's hard to explain." And she thought about words like *hope* and *love.* "Because I want to do something different with my life."

When Erin got off the plane in Kalispell, she took a cab to the Walmart, where she'd already lined up a job, and after work, she pulled her suitcase behind her to a furnished apartment only five blocks away.

A man named Owen worked in the sporting goods section. He'd never been to Arkansas and was too old to be Erin's father. Sometimes Erin would have dinner with the man and his wife in their two-story home. On her breaks, instead of playing video games, she would hang out with Owen. When the two of them weren't busy, he would teach her things about hiking and camping. He showed her how to set up a tent and roll up a sleeping bag into a stuff sack and read a trail map.

By the summer, Erin had gotten good at hitching a ride to places she wanted to go, such as Glacier National Park, or the Flathead County Animal Shelter, where she volunteered twice a week and walked the dogs. Owen would worry about her, but she assured him that she was careful, that she was a good judge of character. Mostly she caught rides with women, or guys who looked more interested in hiking than committing a crime.

It was the third Thursday in July and she had the day off. Owen had told her about a trail along Stryker Ridge, just north of Whitefish. Erin set out that morning from her apartment, as she often did, with her backpack on her shoulders and her thumb in the air. A man driving a truck pulled over. He said he was a fishing guide. He could take her as far as the

Stillwater Bar. Erin said that was far enough. She could get another ride from there.

The man pulled into the empty parking lot of the Stillwater Bar about ten that morning. As Erin was climbing out of the truck, her cell phone rang. She thanked the man for the ride, then went to retrieve her phone. She had a missed call from Jeffrey. They hadn't talked in over a week. Erin walked to the side of the bar and sat down in the dirt. She leaned against the brown siding and called Jeffrey back.

"I was just leaving you a voice message," he said.

They talked about their jobs and employees Erin still knew from the Walmart in Greenwood. They talked about the video games that Erin no longer played.

After almost twenty minutes into the call, Jeffrey said, "You've changed. You seem different."

"I feel different," Erin said.

"Don't you miss it?"

"I miss you and my mom, but no, I don't miss it. I like it here." She went on to tell Jeffrey that she was getting in good shape. "My hips aren't as big, and my legs feel really toned."

"You don't have big hips," Jeffrey said. "And I always liked your legs."

Erin was about to say something else, but

then she paused. "That's strange," she said.

"What?"

Erin spoke again, "Hold on a minute."

A white Jeep Wrangler had just pulled into the parking lot. It turned around as if it were going to head back onto the road in the same direction. But then its brake lights went off, and the driver's-side door opened.

"I'm going to go," she told Jeffrey. "I'll call you later."

A man climbed out of the vehicle. "You okay?" he yelled.

"Yeah, I'm fine." Erin had already stood up and was putting her phone away.

"Do you need a ride somewhere?"

"You wouldn't by chance be heading up toward Stryker?"

"I am if you are," the man said.

The man asked a lot of questions on the ride: Did she hike a lot? Where was she from? "Not often we get a Southern accent all the way out here," he said. He wanted to know what the Ozarks were like and why she had moved. And when she talked he seemed genuinely interested in what she had to say. "You're a courageous woman," he told her. "You should feel proud of yourself for making such an important decision. You've no doubt got an exciting future ahead of you."

The man was older than Erin but not by too

much. He was wearing jeans and a flannel shirt and hiking boots and he wasn't wearing a ring, and Erin felt good about herself as the two of them exchanged banter.

"What about you? Do you hike a lot?" she asked.

The man told Erin he'd just gotten back from a thru-hike.

Erin wasn't familiar with that term, so she asked the man about it.

"It's where you go from one end of the continent to another. I started in Mexico and hiked all the way to Canada. It's called the Continental Divide Trail. You ever hear of it?"

Erin told him she hadn't.

"Have you ever seen the Continental Divide?"

"No," Erin said.

"Well, now, that's something you should see."

The man parked his vehicle at the entry for Stryker Ridge. Erin removed her phone from her pants pocket.

"Why don't I get a picture of you at the trailhead," the man said.

They climbed out of the vehicle and walked over to the trail. Erin handed the man her phone and posed next to a sign that read: *Warning! Grizzly bear habitat!*

"Did you bring bear spray?" the man asked.

"It's in my pack," Erin said. The bear spray had come with a holster that Erin usually attached to her belt or the shoulder strap on her pack. She was about to remove her pack and retrieve the holster and spray when the man asked her if she'd like company on the trail. He didn't have anywhere he had to be, and he'd really enjoyed talking with her. It would be nice to get to know her better. Besides, people weren't supposed to hike alone in bear country, he said. His gear was in the back of his Jeep, and he could bring the bear spray.

He seemed legitimately concerned about Erin hiking alone, and hadn't Owen told her that some of his best friends were those people he'd met on the trail? Any concern she may have had she quickly dismissed.

They hiked for almost a mile and didn't see anyone else. Then the man told her about a hot spring due east of the trail and that it would be a good spot for them to stop for lunch. Though Erin had never thought of herself as attractive, she'd been feeling good about herself lately, and she wondered if the man might be interested in her.

She said the hot spring sounded like a good idea and she followed the man onto a game trail that led through a forested area of western red cedar. She listened to the man tell her stories of his hiking adventures. He told her stories about the trees, too. At one point he picked up a large strip of cedar bark. He took out his knife and scraped the inside layer of the bark until he had roughed up the fibers into what looked like a fuzzy ball of thread.

"Even if it's raining," the man said, "you can start a fire with this. Some of the best tinder around."

Then the man stepped aside and let Erin walk ahead of him. "We don't have much farther," he said. "Just keep following the game trail."

As they continued, the air seemed to change, something electric like the stillness before a storm. The man had become quiet, and Erin began to wonder if something was wrong, and her heart beat funny, as if it were skipping a beat. "Maybe you should take the lead," she said. But in the second she stepped off the trail to let the man pass, he pressed in from behind her and wrapped his left arm across her chest, and the blade of the knife grazed the side of her neck, and Erin's thoughts were reeling and she opened her mouth to scream, but the man's right hand clasped over her face, covering her mouth, and she gagged on the taste of his sweat and the bark resin on the skin of his palm.

"Didn't your mother tell you never to talk to strangers?"

Erin's voice still struggled to get out. Tears stung her eyes.

"You're going to do exactly as I say."

Her head jerked forward in a nod.

He began to loosen his grip. "Easy does it," he said.

Erin leapt forward and ran fast and hard. Her pack pounded on her back. She unclasped the straps, all the while her legs still pumping, moving deftly over debris and limbs. Her pack caught on a branch and jerked her backward momentarily until the pack slid from her arms. She could feel the man closing in on her, could hear his laughter. *No! Oh, God, no!*

And then he was on top of her and her face dug into the ground and her mouth filled with pine needles and dirt. She could not move. The man's arm was braced across the back of her neck.

"Please!" Erin cried.

She rocked her hips back and forth until she was able to free her right arm and reach it over her head. She grabbed hold of the man's neck, dug her fingers into his skin.

He grunted and shoved her that much harder into the ground. Her face began to bleed and burn.

"You're going to do exactly as I tell you," he said.

Erin tried to nod beneath the weight of his arm. The flesh of her face caught on something beneath her and made her wince.

Slowly he climbed off Erin, all the while holding the knife close to her face. "Take off your clothes," he said.

Erin sat up, dirt and blood and tears streaming down her face. She removed her fleece shirt and let the garment fall onto her lap.

"That's it," the man said. "Now, take off the rest."

Erin pulled her T-shirt over her head. She was wearing a sports bra. Its snug elastic cut into the extra flesh that she'd yet to lose. She stood up and began to work the bra over her hips, feeling as though her legs would crumple beneath her.

"Everything," the man said.

She removed her boots and socks. The pine needles felt like hot embers beneath her feet. Then she unbuckled her pants, slid them down her legs, and stepped out of them. Her lip continued to bleed. Her teeth were coated in the gritty mixture of spit and dirt and blood.

"Underwear, too," the man said, because she was still wearing the new boyfriend briefs she had bought herself. She slid them down and stepped out of them also, and when she did, her foot got caught on the elastic. She toppled over and cried that much harder. She curled up into a fetal position and rocked herself back and forth against the ground.

"Get up," the man said.

Erin continued to cry. "I can't."

"Get up!"

She pushed herself onto her hands and knees, and then to a standing position, blood and snot and tears dripping from her chin.

The man stepped toward her slowly. He traced her arm with the fingers of his right hand. He moved behind her. His fingers then traveled over her abdomen. His other arm reached across her collarbone. Using his chin, he moved her hair out of the way. His voice and breath were against her ear. "Like I said, didn't your mother tell you never to talk to strangers?"

In that second Erin held in her mind the image of the beautiful Nancy Parker. Erin's chest rose as she gulped in air, as a sob racked against her rib cage. The man's arm tightened around her neck, and there were Jeffrey and Owen and a father whom she'd never known, and her legs kicked beneath her in a frantic rush, and *oh, God, the pressure in her head. Oh, God, she couldn't breathe.*

12
Present: August 2017

Marian
The Den, Montana

Without remote access on her laptop, the only way Marian could log on to the program's network was from Lyle's desktop. Lyle typically worked for at least a couple of hours each afternoon, training the dogs in the backfield of the property. The day after Marian had come upon the login information in Jenness's hut, and Lyle had gone outside to begin the afternoon training, Marian sat at his desk, slumping low in his chair so as not to be seen through the window. He'd left his computer on and the screen saver was rotating through photos of the program's dogs. When Marian moved the mouse, the login page came up. She entered *gator,* and felt wildly excited when Lyle's desktop appeared. She quickly identified the icon for the program's network on his desktop screen, double-clicked the icon, and was brought to a second login page. She felt a buzz in her fingertips, that jittery feeling she got when she'd drunk too much coffee. Lyle could come back to the house early. Trainer could interrupt her, and here she'd be, surreptitiously trying to access a network that Lyle had not given her access to. The windows in the office were open. She would have to listen carefully for sounds of Lyle or Trainer approaching. She typed in the username and password. The network loaded. She couldn't believe it. She was in. And there, in front of her, was a list of program folders, including one titled Archives.

Marian opened the Archives folder, where she found another folder named Research Projects. The latter contained information on the program's field studies going back more than six years, which would cover the time span when the last three Stillwater victims had gone missing. Marian decided to work backward. She ran a search for studies that took place in May two years ago, when Melissa Marsh had disappeared. Three projects came up. Marian tried to narrow her search by typing in Tate's name. No luck. She began opening documents, reading through reports and summaries from the three projects until her eyes blurred, but was not finding any mention of Tate. She would need to look through the files at large, and there were hundreds of them. She simply didn't have enough time. She would have to copy the files onto a flash drive and go through them at her leisure on her laptop.

From the open window above the desk, she heard Trainer and Lyle talking. She logged out of the network, then went into preferences and locked the computer so that the screen saver would show up instantly. She crouched out of the chair and moved over to the small workstation on the other side of the room, where her laptop was plugged in. She would bring a flash drive with her tomorrow and copy the Archives folder. She wished Lyle had been more specific regarding the projects Tate had worked on. He'd mentioned a moose study in the Adirondacks, the wind farm study in Illinois, and then there was Tanzania, a trip Lyle had made with Tate, for the purpose of studying the effects of poaching on African elephants. But Lyle had given no order or dates to any of the studies. Tate's ten-year history with the program felt like one enormous Hidden Pictures puzzle in a *Highlights* magazine. And yet everything about this search felt urgent. Nick was ill. Marian was unsure how long he'd be available to assist her. Already she felt guilty for taking up his time, though he'd willingly committed himself to helping her as long as he could, had even seemed to enjoy it. And any day Lyle might assign Marian to a project, and she'd enthusiastically jump all in. She would have to work through the files in the evenings. If Tate had an alibi, she was determined to find it.

Lyle would be returning to the office any minute. Marian occupied herself on her laptop. She saw that she had a new message on Facebook. After Marian and Nick's Skype session had ended the night before, Marian had reached out to Holly Fontaine, Tate's college girlfriend. Holly had now written back and said she'd be happy to talk and was glad Marian had contacted her. She'd heard of Tate's death through a mutual friend of hers and Tammy's and said how sorry she was. She couldn't stop thinking about it. She said she'd be available that evening if Marian wanted to give her a call, and included her telephone number.

Instead of eating with Trainer and Lyle that evening, Marian told them she was going to make a sandwich to bring back to her hut because she had some more work to do. She propped her pillows behind her on her bed and gave Holly a call.

"Every day I remember something we did or something he said," Holly told Marian when they spoke. "This must be terrible for you."

Marian asked Holly how long she and Tate had dated, and could she talk about what Tate was like then, because there was so much Marian didn't know. "We didn't have enough time," Marian said.

Holly and Tate had met at orientation their first year of college. They'd dated throughout most of that year. "He was charming and sweet," Holly said. "He hadn't had much experience dating, and he could be a little awkward at times, which I found endearing." She talked about some of their dates, to movies and to a college dance. "He didn't know how to kiss. Like I said, he didn't have much experience. But we worked on that. To be honest, the relationship was mostly platonic. Tate was shy in that way."

"Did he ever talk to you about his childhood?" Marian asked.

"You know, he really didn't talk much about it. He seemed mostly preoccupied with his studies, doing well in school. I remember him saying he was going to be a millionaire by the time he was thirty, that he was going to buy some land and a bunch of cattle and go into business for himself. He could be like that. He had a lot of big dreams."

"How was it when the two of you broke up?" Marian asked.

"I was young. I wanted to date other people."

Marian was surprised. "I didn't realize you were the one who had broken things off. How did Tate take it?"

"I don't think he took it well. There was something strange that happened. I can't believe I'm telling you this. Maybe he was just really upset, but after we'd broken up, there was this night I was in my room. I looked up and I saw him staring at me through the window. It scared the daylights out of me. I was living on the first floor in a dorm, and visiting hours were over, so I opened the window, and Tate said he'd just wanted to talk to me. A few days later I spotted him walking across campus. I think that was the last time I saw him."

And Marian felt the same eerie disturbance as the night before when speaking with Nick, and suddenly she realized that Tate's arrest for looking in someone else's window would have happened before he and

Holly had broken up, but if Holly was aware of the arrest, she didn't mention it.

"Did the two of you ever talk again?" Marian said.

"I sent him a note when I heard about his mom getting sick. But, no, we never talked, and he didn't try to contact me or anything."

Holly and Marian spoke about a half hour more. Holly wanted to know about the work Tate had been doing, the trips he had taken, and isn't it crazy when something like this happens and you feel like you are nineteen again, Holly said. And Marian remembered that Holly was the same age that Tate had been, almost ten years older than Marian was now.

Marian had heard the melancholy of nostalgia in Holly's voice, and yet what stayed with Marian after they got off the phone was the image of Tate in Holly's window, as if Marian were in that exact moment in time, the invisible watcher, and she could see Tate's eyes through the pane of glass, and she felt something heavy in her chest, like depression, like she'd lost the possibility of anything good.

There was still at least an hour of sunlight left in the day, soft and glowing. Marian changed into her running clothes because she did not want to remain alone in her hut. She wasn't sure she felt like running; maybe she would walk. She shook out her arms as she stepped down the hill, and eventually picked up her pace to a jog, and as she turned onto the road, she thought of the morning Tammy had driven out to The Den to collect Tate's things. Marian had finished exercising the dogs, and upon coming out of the barn she had seen Tate's vehicle parked next to the main house. Her hand had instinctively gone to her chest and she'd been filled with the strange sensation that she could walk around the vehicle to the passenger side and open the door and climb in. And Tate would return from a death that had never been and the two of them would pack up the dogs and go back to the fields and the woods and the forests and the mountains. And Marian was thinking of this because her love for Tate had felt sweet on that morning almost four weeks ago, her grief still holding on to what was good.

Tammy and Marian had spent the afternoon together and had stopped for dinner in Whitefish. And over dinner, Tammy had given Marian the title to Tate's vehicle. She wasn't sure the vehicle would make it back to Omaha, she'd said. And she didn't want to turn it over to a dealership. Marian had never owned a car and couldn't believe Tammy's gesture. She drove Tammy to a hotel in Kalispell, about a half-hour drive south of Whitefish. After she pulled into a parking space by the front door, Tammy said, "You really loved my brother, didn't you?"

Marian's eyes glazed over with tears. "I really did."

That was when Tammy asked Marian if she would spread some of Tate's ashes in Montana. "I think he would have liked that."

There was an empty coffee tin in the back of the vehicle, which Tate had used to water the dogs. Marian brought the tin with her up to Tammy's room. Tammy carried the wooden box with Tate's ashes. She unscrewed the bottom of the box using a coin and removed the bag.

Marian took the plastic covering from the hotel's ice bucket and placed it inside the coffee can. Then Tammy carefully poured about a third of the ashes into the container. A cloud of fine dust wafted into Marian's eyes and stuck to the tears on her face. How could this be the man she had loved? How could this be what was left of the body she had held on to?

Marian had chosen a three-mile route and

was approaching the final mile. She pushed back her thoughts and concentrated on her thighs, like slow-moving pistons. The road pitched uphill. Her breathing became shallow. Her sweat turned cool on her skin. She hadn't paid much mind to the three or four vehicles coming or going, until a green SUV passed her from behind, moving at a crawl, and now remained at a slow speed, within fifty feet in front of her. Marian could feel the man watching her from his side-view mirror, though she could no longer see his face, nor could she read his license plate. A clean rush of adrenaline moved through her blood. She slowed her pace, hoping the driver would move on, but he kept creeping in front of her. Then another vehicle approached, again from behind. Marian looked over her shoulder at the light green truck that she recognized as belonging to the Forest Service, and when she turned back around, the SUV had sped on.

13
March 2017

Marian
Oil sands, Alberta, Canada

After Noah had returned to North Carolina, taking Chester with him, Marian had moved into his room, in the same trailer as Jenness. For the next three weeks she had worked alongside Tate and Arkansas, as Tate trained Marian to become a handler. And at the end of each day, she'd lie with Tate on his bed and listen to his stories of dogs and wilderness and danger, and she'd inch herself closer to him, to the smell of fresh air that still clung to his skin and the sweet musk of a Labrador's coat and the piney tang of his sweat. And sometimes they would take Arkansas out of her crate and let her join them on the bed, and Tate would praise Marian for her natural way with dogs and tell her how much Arkansas loved her. "You have the gift," he'd say. "It's like you can look inside their souls. You were born for this." Marian's full name was Marian Whelan Engström, and she told Tate her middle name meant *wolf,* and Tate called her she-wolf and said no wonder she was so good with the dogs. Other times Tate would tell Marian how smart she was. "I think you're brilliant. Seriously brilliant." He'd run his fingers through her long hair and tell her she was beautiful, the most beautiful woman he'd ever seen.

Marian loved the things Tate saw in her and the stories he would tell and the way his body reached for her. He'd given her the kind of admiration no man or woman ever had. He'd described her best self. He'd done more than that; he'd described the kind of woman she wanted herself to be. And after they made love, it would be everything she could do to pull away from him and return to the other trailer, where she and Jenness and two of the other handlers were staying. And did she sense something awkward in the air each night when she returned, the kind of awkwardness that made her feel like she'd done something wrong? None of the others were in relationships together, and Jenness had warned Marian about the difficulty of two people dating in the program. Marian would close the door to the trailer quietly behind her, because the others would have already turned in. She'd remove her boots and walk on the balls of her sock feet to her room. And as she passed by Jenness's room, Marian would notice that there was always a light on, a thin slice of golden yellow beneath the door no matter what time Marian turned in.

On one of those nights, Jenness was just stepping out of a steam-filled bathroom, her body wrapped in a towel, her long wet hair trailing down her back. Jenness stopped and said, "Oh, there you are," and Marian stared at the magnificent falcon tattoo on Jenness's left thigh.

"Let me throw something on," Jenness said. "I want to talk to you."

Jenness disappeared behind her bedroom door and within a few minutes reappeared, now dressed in a pair of sweats and an oversize flannel shirt.

"Are you ready for tomorrow?" Jenness asked.

In less than eight hours, Marian and Tate and Arkansas would be taking a helicopter into some of the most remote territory in the boreal forest of the oil sands. "I can't wait," Marian said.

Jenness pushed her door open wider. "Come on in," she said. "I've got something to show you."

Jenness picked up her camera from the bed. "It's really not very difficult to use. It can be cumbersome, that's all. I line the case with thermal packs when heading into the field, and there are extra batteries." Would Marian mind taking pictures and maybe some video the next day, Jenness wanted to know. And of course Marian wouldn't mind. And so the two of them sat on the bed as Jenness gave Marian a crash course on how to operate the camera. Then she made sure the extra batteries were charged. "Just warm up the packs in the microwave before you head out. The case is insulated. It will keep them warm."

Marian had never flown in a helicopter before, and the next morning when the small utility Airbus floated skyward, she felt her stomach float skyward also. Then the aircraft lurched forward, and Marian clung to the window. Tate laughed amusedly, as if flying in a helicopter were something he did every day. Marian took out the camera and began to snap pictures, and then through the lens she spotted a caribou herd.

"Tate, look!" Marian yelled above the sound of the twin engines and the main rotor.

"That's a small herd," Tate yelled back at her. "There should be more."

Marian turned the camera toward Tate. He was still looking out his side window, and the way the cloud light shone on him, and the pensive look on his face, made her breath catch somewhere deep inside her. *He's beautiful,* she thought. *He's the most beautiful man I have ever seen.*

"They're the only species where the males and females both grow horns," he said. "It's quite remarkable."

Tate and Marian hadn't brought the crate. A nervous Arkansas was wedged between them. The dog jumped up with her back paws still on the floor and stretched her torso across Marian's lap. Marian hugged the warm dog and let her lick her face.

"Should I be jealous?" Tate said. Marian looked at him sideways and smiled.

"If anything ever happens to me, take care of her for me, will you?" Tate said.

"Nothing's going to happen to you," Marian said.

Sometime in the afternoon, after four hours of collecting samples in woods as dense as night, they came upon a clearing, about a hundred-square-foot area that their maps showed to be a pond. And in the moment they stood in the center of that clearing, the white cloud cover dissipated and the sun shone through, and the air felt as clean and crisp as fresh starched sheets.

"Well, I'll be," Tate said. "The heavens are smiling on us." And he laughed at what he said, and Marian laughed, too. They still had a couple more hours before the helicopter would pick them up, and they had additional ground to cover, and so they moved on, stepping into woods again, though the trees seemed to stand farther apart from one another than in the previous areas where they had been.

"It's beautiful," Marian said. "And I'm not even cold."

But then the wind whipped up around them and threw snow debris in their faces, and they raised their arms against the remaining gust. "I didn't see that coming," Marian said. They trudged on, and because Marian was collecting the samples and taking pictures each time she stopped, she fell a little behind Tate, maybe thirty yards or so. The wind sent another microburst through the trees and scattered the snow in eddies that covered their tracks.

"Over here," Tate yelled.

Marian realized she'd gotten somewhat off course, and when she turned to redirect herself, she saw the mound of flesh and snow a few feet from her, the deer's brown eyes half open, as if the animal had literally curled up into itself to stay warm and had frozen to death before falling asleep. She knelt to touch the body, laid her hand against the deer's chest, and found that it was warm, which startled her momentarily because she thought the animal was alive. But its eyes did not move, and the rest of the animal's hide was cold and rigor mortis had indeed set in. Marian knew that the muscles of a large animal could continue to hold warmth even hours after an animal had died. And yet she couldn't shake the feeling that this animal's life had just ended within only an hour or two of Marian getting there.

Tate and Arkansas were still farther ahead. She should get going, but for now she stared at the animal a few seconds longer. She felt that if there was warmth in the animal's body, its spirit was still there, and that by remaining with the animal, Marian could somehow bring it comfort.

She heard a snap in the woods behind her. At first she thought it was Tate. Maybe another animal. Maybe a limb breaking from the wind. She stood and hurried to catch up.

"Everything okay?" Tate said.

"Fine," she said, her breathing heavy. "I

thought I saw something."

"What was it?"

The air felt trapped in her windpipe. She coughed a couple of times. "It was nothing," she told him, because she wanted to keep the moment to herself for a little while longer. And she was tired. She hadn't been sleeping well and every muscle in her legs burned with fatigue. This had been her most difficult transect yet. Tate said, "All right, then." He continued to break trail. Marian followed behind Arkansas, the dog's bell ringing through the cold.

The remaining two hours felt automatic to Marian. Her mind was elsewhere, and her spirit had dampened with the perspective of life and death and a night eight years before when she was a freshman in college. Even if Marian had gotten there earlier, the man would have died, people had assured her — well-intentioned people like her father, who'd brought Marian home that night and had sat up with her when she couldn't sleep, and an overweight policeman who was chewing spearmint gum, and a chaplain from the college. "Yes," Marian had said. She understood that, but at least he wouldn't have died alone.

It was the end of January, the temperature just below freezing, with a couple of inches of fresh snow on the ground. Marian had gone for a run to give her mind a break from studying. She was almost back to her dorm when she found the man lying on the sidewalk in front of First Congregational Church. His belongings were in a plastic bag that he'd used for a pillow. She'd stopped to see if she could help him inside the church. Maybe a door would be open. Maybe there was a place where he could get warm. But when she knelt beside him, she saw the white pallor of his skin. She slipped a hand inside his coat collar to feel for a pulse, and though she could not find one, she was sure his skin felt warm, and so she'd rolled the man over and placed her mouth on his to resuscitate him, his lips as blue as stone. She continued to breathe air into the man's lungs and intermittently give compressions to his chest with her palms stacked on each other, until she felt a gloved hand on her back and heard a voice say, "He's gone."

Tate and Arkansas and Marian had completed their transect and were back at the drop-off location when they heard the loud *thwop thwop thwop* of the helicopter. Tate leashed Arkansas and within minutes Marian felt the gusts of the propellers. They were quiet after they climbed into the aircraft, spent from the long day and the physical exertion. Even Arkansas was tired out, lying on the floor with her head on her paws. The sun was just beginning to set, casting a golden glow over the dark evergreens below, and Marian said how beautiful everything was. "It's a miracle, really," she said, and she told Tate she was thankful for so much, and Tate said, "I've never bowed to anything." And Marian was taken aback, not so much by what Tate said, but by his eyes, wide and empty, as if the air between them had suddenly turned colder. Marian realized how little sleep Tate must be getting. He was tired. That was all. He was in the field most days, and working each night, sometimes even after Marian had left his room. She wouldn't visit him that evening, she decided. She would let him get his rest.

When Tate and Marian got back to the compound, and the sky was becoming dark, Jeb and Liz and their dog, Tucker, were just getting in. They'd taken the sleds into an area a good hour and a half southwest of the oil company.

"I'm going to get her squared away," Tate said about Arkansas, which Marian knew meant not only getting the dog settled and fed but also drying her neoprene jacket and boots, checking and treating her paws and moisturizing her pads, checking the dog's hips and knowing if she needed a day off, brushing the dog's teeth and inspecting her gums, and making sure her coat was brushed and dry.

"I can do that," Marian said.

"No, I got it." Tate turned his back and began walking toward the trailer.

Marian then called out to Jeb, who was unloading the machines.

"How'd it go?" she said when she caught up to him.

"Not bad. How about you? You get a good bird's-eye view?"

"Yeah. Saw some caribou."

"No kidding."

They were standing at the back of the trailer. Tucker and Liz were beside the open cab, where Liz was leaning in to gather the rest of her things.

"You need a hand?" Jeb asked her.

"All set," she said. She leashed Tucker, threw her pack over her right shoulder, and walked over to join them. "How was the flight?"

Marian told them about the small herd and the caribou samples they'd found.

"God, what I'd give to have a day like that. Maybe before we pack out of here, Jeb and I will have a go on the helicopter. What do you say, Tucker?" And Liz reached down and gave Tucker a rowdy pat. He was a high-strung blue heeler who, like all blue heelers, loved to work.

Then Liz walked away, the air punctuated by the crunching and squeaking of her boots against the frozen parking lot.

"You got a minute?" Jeb asked.

"Of course." Marian walked with Jeb back to the orienteer housing. They left their boots on the drying rack and then headed down the hall to his room. They unloaded their packs, took off their coats, and sat on Jeb's bed, which was pushed up against the wall.

Jeb grabbed one of his pillows, scrunched it up, and wedged it between his back and the headboard. He tossed Marian the extra pillow. "I got turned down," he said.

She held the pillow in her lap and leaned against the wall. "From Pacific?" Marian knew Jeb had been applying to graduate schools to study creative writing, and she knew Pacific University was his first choice.

He stared past her and nodded.

"It's just one school. There are other programs." Jeb's applications required writing samples. Marian said she'd look over his essays if he wanted, and Jeb said he wouldn't mind taking her up on the offer.

"So tell me more about seeing the caribou herd," Jeb said.

"It was a really small herd. No more than ten. There should be more. But that's why we're here, right? To find out what's going on."

And then Marian told Jeb about the deer she'd found that afternoon. "He was still warm," she said. "I knew he was dead, but I didn't want to leave him. Tate was getting farther ahead. I couldn't stay there long." Marian became quiet. Jeb was quiet also.

Marian continued. "When I found the deer, I thought about this night when I was in college. It was my freshman year. I'd gone for a run and had come up on this homeless man lying on the sidewalk. He wasn't breathing. It was really cold. There was snow on the ground. The man had frozen to death. I tried to save him. And you know what I thought after that night? This is going to sound really weird, and I know it's weird, but I thought he was the first guy I'd kissed. He was this old, homeless guy. I tried to resuscitate him. I gave him mouth-to-mouth. And that night I thought, *This is what a man's lips feel like.*"

"That's not so weird," Jeb said. "And I think it's really cool, you trying to save him. That sounds exactly like something you would do. You would have saved that deer, too, if you could have. Just imagine giving a deer mouth-to-mouth."

And Marian smiled then. "I'm really sorry about Pacific."

"Yeah, well, like you said, there are other programs."

Later that night, after Marian and Jeb had grabbed dinner at the cafeteria and she was walking back to her trailer, she wondered why she had told Jeb about the deer and not Tate. And she was surprised about what she'd shared with Jeb about the homeless man.

She set her pack on the floor in her room and took out her phone from her pack's top-load compartment. The battery had died hours ago. She plugged the phone into the charger. She and Tate wouldn't be going into the field the next day. They would be giving Arkansas a break. Marian could wait until the morning to download her data.

As soon as her phone had enough juice, she saw that she had a text from Tate: I was looking forward to seeing you tonight. I thought you would have stopped by. I had something to tell you. I miss you. I know it's silly, but I sorta do.

The walls in Marian's room were a thin panel. Hanging across from her bed was a painting of a deer beside a lake, the kind of painting with bright colors and cheap acrylic that amateurs sell along roadsides. Until that night, Marian hadn't paid much attention to the painting. But as she looked at the deer, for the first time she noticed its dull black eyes, more like two gaping holes.

Are you still up? Marian texted Tate back.

Sleep is for the fainthearted, he replied.

Marian put her parka and hat back on and walked over to the other trailer.

"You came," Tate said. He was lying in bed with the lights out.

"You told me you were still up," Marian said.

"I am."

Tate rose, wearing only a T-shirt and blue boxer briefs. He hugged her and pulled off her fleece hat and kissed the top of her head. He reached behind her and shut the door the rest of the way and Marian heard the metal turn of the lock.

"I'm glad you're here." He unzipped her parka and slid it off her shoulders. Then he took her hand and led her to the bed. "Climb in with me," he said. And so Marian climbed into the bed with Tate, and he pulled the covers over them and held her close. "Talk to me," he said.

"What do you want me to talk to you about?"

"Anything."

And Marian asked him what it was he wanted to tell her.

"I have a lot of things I want to tell you," he said. "I have it all planned out. I can talk to you in general now, about the images that keep playing in my mind, from when we first met at the airport to that day you got stuck in the muskeg, and lots of other images, and they all feel surreal. I've had this image, this feeling almost my whole life of what it would be like with the woman I loved, what it would feel like, how she would look, how we would be together, how it should be. When you've been sort of looking for it all this time, all these years, and then after all these years it happens, it feels surreal. Like déjà vu. Do you understand what I'm saying? It also makes me mad in a way, because of all the years I didn't know you."

It was a lot to take in, and Marian couldn't help but wonder if this was love, and if Tate was telling her he loved her, did she feel the same way about him?

"Marian?"

"Yeah?"

"You still with me here?"

"I'm here."

"You can say something, you know. That was kind of a nice thing I just told you."

She slid her hand over Tate's T-shirt. She could feel his heartbeat beneath her palm. "What you said was really beautiful."

"Tell me something, Matilda," he whispered into her ear. "Tell me why you got so quiet today."

"Why did you just call me Matilda?" she asked.

"Because Matilda means *mighty.* It means strength in battle. You're a very kind person. Being kind can require a fearless quality."

Marian settled in closer to Tate. "There was a deer in the woods. A young buck." She went on to describe the deer she'd found.

Marian and Tate were lying on their right sides. He lifted his left hand and rubbed her shoulder. He kissed her ear. He stroked her hair.

"There was something about his eyes," Marian said. "Like he knew."

"Animals do that. I think people do that, too," Tate said.

"Have you ever seen an animal die?" And just as soon as the words were out of her mouth, she said, "Oh, God, I'm so sorry. I forgot. Tate, I'm so sorry."

"Shh, it's all right."

"I meant because of you growing up on a ranch."

"I know what you meant," he said.

And then Marian asked him if he would tell her about his childhood, because she wanted to picture Tate as a little boy. He told her about the ranch and calving and the eastern Montana winds. He talked about the time he and his sister as primary school kids had dug a path to the barn when fifty head of cattle had gotten stuck in the snow, and he told Marian about the night when he was barely thirteen and had pulled a full-term stillborn from the uterus of an Angus cow.

When Marian had almost drifted to sleep, he said, "I found a body once."

"A deer?"

"No. A woman."

Marian rolled onto her back.

"Her body was naked like a newborn's. She was laid out beside this stream. Her ankles and feet were still in the water as if she were taking a bath."

"How old were you? What did you do?"

Tate shifted onto his back and stared up at the ceiling. "It wasn't so long ago. Did you ever hear about the Stillwater murders?"

Marian told him she hadn't.

"It was back in Montana."

"Was Arkansas with you?"

"No, this happened before Arkansas. I was working with another dog, this little German shepherd named Tillie." Tate laughed then. "Kind of like Matilda," he said. "She was a brave thing, too. I was scouting out this new area for some training ground, and there this woman was. I told Tillie to stay and I went up to the body. Her clothes were lying in a pile beside her. Her head was tilted and her eyes were looking right at me. As I got closer I saw the woman's hands. They were large hands and she'd bitten her nails so short they'd bled."

Tate went on to tell Marian about the four murders, and that three of the bodies were found in the state forest, less than an hour from the group's camp.

"It made national news," Tate said. "I thought you might have heard."

"This is so sad," Marian said.

"It *is* sad. And the worst part is the killer was never found."

"He's still out there? That's horrible. Those poor families."

Tate pulled Marian in closer and encircled her with his arms. "I don't know what I'd do if anything ever happened to you. I worry about that. I know how independent you think you are. I know you think you can take care of yourself. But the truth is, a woman is never safe."

It was two in the morning when Marian awoke with Tate's arms still around her. She tried to slip away without waking him, but as she stirred, she felt his hold tighten. "Don't leave," he said, his voice groggy.

"I have to," she said.

She rolled over and kissed him on the cheek. "I'll see you later." But when she began to push herself off the bed, Tate tugged her hand and she fell back into his arms and he burrowed his beard into her neck.

"You're so warm," she said. "You're like this big bear."

"Come hibernate with me."

"I can't. I really have to go." And so she pulled away again.

"I'll buy you breakfast," Tate said. "Cafeteria special."

Marian laughed and said okay.

"Call me when you're up," he told her.

And then he mumbled something, and it sounded like "love," but Marian wasn't sure.

As with previous nights, Jenness's light

was still on when Marian returned to the trailer. Marian tapped lightly on Jenness's door.

"Come in." She was on her bed with a pile of knitting in her lap.

"You're still up. Do you ever sleep?" Marian asked.

"I had some work to do. Now I'm just trying to turn my mind off. Everything okay?"

"Yeah. Would it be all right if I get you the camera tomorrow? I want to take a look at the pictures I shot."

Jenness hesitated for a couple of seconds. She said that would be fine. And then, "Marian, remember what I told you about relationships. They never work out in this line of work. Just be careful."

There was a pause between the two women. Marian acknowledged Jenness with a nod. "I'll return your camera in the morning," she said.

Marian felt fully awake when she got back to her room. She was thinking about Tate and was curious about the murders and the body he'd said he found. She wasn't sure she completely believed him. He seemed to be full of tall stories and there had already been so much tragedy in his life. She set her laptop in front of her on the bed. Once it had booted, she ran a search on the Stillwater murders. She found articles going back over seven years. She pored through them, looking for something that might indicate Tate, that might confirm that what he'd told her was true. But none of the articles mentioned who had discovered the bodies, other than generalizations. Then she read where one of the bodies was found by a man and his dog, and she knew that must be Tate, and she felt guilty for having doubted him and a strange sense of relief at the same time.

She thought of the day they'd just spent together, the beautiful scenery, the image she'd captured when Tate was looking out the window at the caribou herd. She'd planned on downloading the pictures she'd taken that day to her computer when they'd returned, but she had gotten distracted. And so she retrieved the camera from her pack and discharged the memory card. She climbed back onto her bed, rebooted her laptop, and inserted the memory card.

Hundreds of images began to load from that past year. A number of minutes passed before she saw the pictures she'd taken earlier that day: Tate kneeling in the snow to attach the bell to the harness Arkansas was wearing; Tate walking ahead of Marian with Arkansas bounding behind him and kicking up flecks of snow; that moment on the pond when the world went still and the sky went blue and the sun felt warm. There were other pictures, including the one of Tate looking out the side window at the caribou, and she knew no one like him would ever come her way again and tell her that she was a beautiful path and that he fucking adored her and that he never doubted wanting to be with her. And there were pictures of their girl, Arkansas, her face so happy when she alerted them to a find.

Marian checked off the pictures she'd taken and saved them to her laptop. Then she went to delete the pictures she'd taken of Tate from the memory card. She scrolled through the photos, and except for a couple where Tate was working with Arkansas, she selected them and hit delete. But then she continued to scroll through other photos, months and months' worth, one picture after another, and her fingers began to tremble. In addition to photos of the dogs and the other handlers, there were hundreds of pictures of Tate — Tate walking to his truck, Tate sitting on the steps of a small building, Tate brushing Arkansas. There were too many to count. And in none of the pictures was Tate looking directly at the camera, as if he never knew the photos were being taken. But perhaps what Marian found even more disturbing were the pictures she saw of herself, as if this whole time Jenness had been watching her. Marian leaned in closer to the computer, her eyes so wide and dry they burned. She went back and forth through the pictures. She downloaded each one.

14
Present: August 2017

Nick Shepard
Bonners Ferry, Idaho

It was a Saturday, the temperatures remaining in the upper seventies, and not a cloud in the sky. Nick had just finished picking the last of the ripe tomatoes from the vines and placing them in a brown paper sack to bring inside. Cate was working in the rock garden about twenty yards away. Nick stood on the patio with the sack braced between his torso and his arms, just stood there looking at the woman he loved. There were rosebushes in the garden and Cate was fertilizing them with compost.

Nick opened and closed the back door quietly. He wanted to retrieve his camera and capture some candid images of Cate while she was still in the garden. When he returned with his Nikon, he set it on the patio table and positioned himself on the wrought-iron chair behind the camera, because the table would keep the camera steady in a way that his hands and arms could not these days. And there she was. Why was it that he could see her so much better with the aid of a camera? But he knew it had nothing to do with the camera lens. It had to do with his entire attention being on the subject on which his camera was focused, and what a lovely subject it was today: Cate wiping the perspiration from her brow with the back of her hand, the soft smile of her lips, the flecks of dirt on her lightly freckled complexion.

After he'd let the shutter fly a half-dozen times, he leaned back against the porch chair and turned his face to the sky and let the sun warm his body. *I am the observer,* he thought, because he felt like he was observing a lot of life lately, rather than participating in it the way he had before. For a killer it was the same thing, like watching life through a lens, always the camera between him and his subject matter, never a real participant in the life going on around him.

Marian was right, Nick thought. He hadn't seen the Stillwater cases all the way through. He'd backed out before his work had been done. He'd told Marian he'd wanted to spend more time with Cate. That part was true. He also wanted to sleep better at night. Over the years the dreams had gotten to him. They'd become especially troublesome during the Stillwater killings. In trying to inhabit the killer's mind, Nick had stepped over to the other side. He hadn't told anyone about that night, not even Cate. Maybe that was why he wasn't terribly shocked when he was diagnosed with glioblastoma multiforme. He had invited the darkness to take up residence. But in the end he had betrayed himself. He'd not kept himself safe, and he'd been reminded of how vulnerable and weak the mind can be. *Don't be surprised one day if the darkness turns on its host.*

The incident had happened after Melissa Marsh had gone missing. Though Nick had driven around in his vehicle for months after each homicide, even stopped at the Stillwater Bar and sat in the parking lot, imagined Erin Parker talking on her phone, imagined himself offering her a ride, as the killer had done, this time Nick had gone too far. He'd cruised the roads, stopped by certain locations that seemed ripe — a convenience store here and there, a pizza hangout. He'd offered a girl a ride. He'd looked at the girl the way the killer might have. He'd made her afraid. He'd driven the girl where she'd wanted to go, the mall. He'd gotten onto her for accepting a ride with a stranger, as if now he were the good guy. But there was still that look of fear in the girl's eyes that had stayed with him. All those years he had pursued the beast. That night the beast lived in him, and the whole thing terrified him.

The recurring dream Nick had had while working on the Stillwater cases had continued to haunt him: a killer chasing him into the woods, Nick stumbling and falling, then turning over to see the face of Danny Rolling, the Gainesville Ripper, who'd been responsible for the gruesome murder of five female students in Florida and who'd confessed to the murder of three other people. Nick had exhausted himself on the Florida cases, had spent countless hours interviewing Rolling.

But after he gave a ride to the young woman, the face of the perpetrator in the dream changed. No longer was it the face of Danny Rolling. From that night forward it was always the face of one of the victims. That was when Nick began writing the portraits. With each one he'd felt closer to the women who'd been killed; he'd taken on their respective voices. He was no longer looking through the lens of the killer; he was looking through the lenses of the women whose lives the killer had taken, drawing himself closer and closer to their worlds. Each of the victims was different, and yet there was that one trait that they each possessed: the assumption that sincerity would be met with sincerity.

And now there was Marian. He'd let her in, and she was leading him back to a place he'd sworn he'd never return to.

Upon first glance, Tate's childhood had appeared normal, and aside from a girlfriend breaking up with him, Marian wasn't finding anything in Tate's life that pointed to humiliation from a female. And yet, after learning of the peeping-Tom charge and of a similar incident with the girlfriend, Nick was curious. He wanted a longitudinal study on this guy and had spent the past week making additional calls. He'd cited his credentials, said he was Tate's therapist and was seeking information to help him better understand his late client and close Tate's file. Bending a few ethical rules wasn't a concern of his. He needed information. Crete was a small town. People know a lot in a small town. And people love to talk.

Nick reached out to Tate's high school. He spoke with a guidance counselor, who pulled up Tate's records. Tate was an above-average student. Mostly Bs, some As. He'd been suspended his sophomore year. A girl said he'd touched her inappropriately. He worked at the granary, didn't play sports, wasn't involved in any extracurricular activities. Nick asked if there were any teachers still around who would remember Tate. Nick was given a couple of names.

Nick made a call to the granary. He wanted to know what kind of worker Tate had been. The owner remembered Tate. "When he worked, he worked hard. Nice guy, mostly a loner."

One of the teachers remembered an incident where Tate had run away from home. "Wasn't gone long," she said. "Maybe thirty-six hours. No apparent triggers, no conflicts. Never really said where he went. Mother was beside herself."

"How old was he?" Nick asked.

"Middle teens, fifteen or sixteen."

Another teacher said Nick should contact the elementary school.

"Anyone in particular?"

"Yes. Naomi Bartlett. She's retired now. Used to teach sixth grade. Let me get you her number."

So far what Nick was hearing was an assortment of minor events and details that on their own were innocuous enough but collectively pointed to unpredictable behavior.

Then he called the sixth-grade teacher.

"It may have been almost thirty years ago, but I'll never forget that child. Such a shame."

"What happened?" Nick asked.

"His fifth-grade teacher molested him. He was in my class the year after. I was supposed to keep an eye on him, let the school counselor know how he was adjusting. He was a quiet child. I never had any trouble from him."

"His teacher was female?" Nick asked.

"Yes. At first they were just friendly. She would ask him to stay after school. She would help him with his homework. Then she started taking him places, to movies in other towns. She'd buy him gifts. She bought gifts for his family. Teachers were getting suspicious. In the investigation she admitted to touching the boy inappropriately and having him fondle her breasts. She said he made her feel beautiful. Can you believe it?"

"These incidents occurred in the classroom?" Nick asked.

"In the classroom and at her house when her husband wasn't home."

"Jesus," Nick said.

"She went to prison. The school tried to keep things quiet for the boy's sake, but you know how things go. At least it never went to trial. The case was settled out of court. She served five years."

"Not long enough."

"I couldn't agree more."

When Nick was working on the Stillwater cases, he'd told authorities that the killer was in his twenties or thirties with above-average intelligence and possibly some postsecondary education. He had a job that took him into secluded, forested areas. His vehicle was very important to him, and he spent hours cruising back roads, giving himself a keen sense of the lay of the land.

Nick also believed the killer had been humiliated sexually at some point as a child, by a female who was close to him, most likely a mother or older sister or an aunt. This deep shame would have created some kind of sexual dysfunction for the killer, making him incapable of any real intimacy. Sex would have been seen as an act of dominance but also an act in which the killer experienced confusion between that dominance and his hostile feelings toward women. But Nick said that the humiliation would not really be a question of what had happened as much as how the killer chose to process it and what he chose to believe. For every killer who had been abused, there were tens of thousands of other persons, maybe more, who had been abused also, but had not grown up to be killers.

In the Stillwater murders, the perpetrator did not need to have intercourse with his victims for the murders to be considered sexual homicides. The sexual component was defined in terms of power. He took ownership of each of the women, he terrorized them, he humiliated them by having them take off their clothes, and he destroyed them. The attacks were sexual because of the killer's predatory nature, and they were hostile acts of aggression and violence against women.

As a child, the killer had learned to survive in a world he could not trust by dissociating from his feelings, and as a result he could come across as having a calm and in-control demeanor. But beneath the surface the killer would be harboring fantasies of revenge in which he would reverse the roles of what had been done to him.

Nick had even gone a step further to say that the killer would blame the victim for her own fate as another means of establishing his power over her, of degrading and humiliating her. Ultimately, in the killer's mind, the woman was at fault for being the weaker sex, for being vulnerable, for putting herself in a dangerous situation.

Additionally, Nick had said that the killer would have been close to his mother growing up but would have resented his dependency on her and her inability to protect him from the humiliation he had experienced. He possessed some voyeuristic tendencies such as viewing pornography, stalking women, and looking in windows.

Tate fit Nick's profile of the Stillwater killer, without question. Nick reminded himself that no profiler and no profile ever caught a killer. Bundy was stopped for erratic driving. Joel Rifkin was stopped because he had a taillight out and there was a body in the bed of his pickup. The profiler's goal was to narrow the field, to provide a focus for the investigation. And yet, were Tate still alive, Nick believed Tate would have been a person of interest.

■ ■ ■ ■

Part Two

■ ■ ■ ■

I wanted to destroy her because of what she represented . . . a pretty girl, a threat to me, to my masculinity, and she was a child of God, God's creation.

— DAVID BERKOWITZ, "SON OF SAM"

15
April 2017

Marian
The Den, Montana

The group's work in Alberta had wrapped up at the end of March. The staff had been back at The Den for two weeks now, cutting and stacking firewood for the huts, exercising the dogs, restocking supplies, and training the dogs on their next target samples. Marian found it remarkable that a dog could be trained on a new species in as little as three days.

Tate would be leaving in three weeks for the wolf project, which would continue until the end of July and would take him into some of the densest forest terrain in the Colville and Kaniksu National Forests, where most of Washington's wolf population — approximately seventy in number — lived, as well as into parts of southeastern British Columbia. The purpose of the study was to determine the impact wolves were having on other species, particularly deer and elk and the endangered woodland caribou. Tate would be working with Ranger, a three-year-old shepherd mix who was new to the program and who was in need of reinforcement from a veteran handler.

The bighorn sheep study that Marian had been assigned to would run from the first of July and into August. She would be working with both Arkansas and Yeti, rotating the dogs each day because of the desert heat. As with the wolf study, her work in Utah would involve one team. During the interim, as was customary for handlers between projects, she would work with the dogs, help with communications, and perform odd jobs around The Den.

It was the fourteenth of April, Marian's twenty-seventh birthday. Marian had spent the afternoon with Liz, who had also been offered a full-time position. They'd taken Lyle's truck into the forest to look for deadfall in groves of aspen and birch and had cut firewood for the huts. They'd brought a plastic sled with them, the kind hunters use, to carry the wood to the truck. Liz talked to Marian about her boyfriend, who was working on his doctoral degree in biophysics at the University of Washington, and Marian felt encouraged that her relationship with Tate could work out, despite the distance that would soon come between them.

That night, Marian had plans with Tate to go out to dinner. As she was getting ready she had a text message from Jeb: Happy birthday! Hope it is a good one. California is better than muskeg. Drop me a line when you have time or come visit.

At the end of the study, Jeb had left the cold and the rest of the orienteers and handlers and moved to Riverside, California. He was currently living with four other guys and working as a bartender, but in the fall he would start classes at UC Riverside as a fully funded graduate student. "They liked my life experiences," Jeb told her. "They said I have a lot to write about." The two of them had celebrated over a game of pool and an upside-down cake the consistency of pudding, which Marian had attempted to make in the kitchen of the trailer where she'd been staying.

Marian texted Jeb back. She was happy for him, she said, and maybe one day he'd write about a bunch of dogs in the tundra, and they should catch up soon, and she would give him a call.

In the small closet in Marian's hut was a pair of Laredo cowboy boots with turquoise threading that she'd bought when she was working in Texas. She'd never worn the cowboy boots. The weather had been too warm on South Padre Island, and the weather had been too cold in the oil sands in Alberta. But now it was April in northwestern Montana, where lawns were turning green and sidewalks were clear, and the snow had all but melted in the hills surrounding Whitefish, and Marian wanted to wear something other than hiking boots or gum boots on her night out with Tate. Hanging in Marian's closet, aside from jeans and a fleece vest and a Thinsulate jacket, was a white silk blouse that Marian's mother had given her for Christmas that still had the tags from Kohl's in Grand Rapids.

Marian dressed in a pair of stretch jeans and her cowboy boots and her silk shirt, then brushed out her long hair and swept it over her shoulders. She didn't have makeup, so she dabbed Vaseline onto her lips. Then she grabbed her black fleece jacket from the back of her door and left her hut. The sky had that end-of-the-day glow to it, the remaining light fending off the cold for now.

Tate was leaning against the passenger

side of his vehicle when she got to the parking area, or the gravel pit, as the handlers called it, and the first thing she noticed was his black leather jacket, and then his long legs in what looked like new jeans, crossed at the ankles. He was smiling demurely, and his beard had been trimmed, and as Marian stepped closer he stood away from the vehicle and took her hand and kissed it. "You look beautiful," he said. Marian blushed, and he let go of her hand and hugged her, and she wrapped her arms tightly around his waist. He didn't smell of diesel oil and sweat, or of Arkansas or Ranger or any of the dogs, but of leather and wood smoke and the faint scent of soap, making the cool spring air taste sweet.

Tate opened the door for her. Any loose gear had been moved to the back. The cup holders were empty and had been wiped clean; the floors and seats had been vacuumed; the dashboard was free of dust. He had made reservations at The Lodge at Whitefish Lake, and he hoped she was hungry, and she said she was.

They were seated by a fire and had a nice view of the lake, and Marian would occasionally look out the window at the lake, which had only recently thawed, until the sun dropped over the mountains, and the lake and the sky became indistinguishable in the dark, and all that was visible was her own reflection and the twinkle of lights from properties across the water, but mostly Marian looked at Tate. They ate jumbo shrimp and bread and salad and sirloin steaks and drank a bottle of Shiraz. They talked about their jobs and their upcoming assignments and soon moved on to bigger things like the ISIS attack in Kabul and the conservative dissent in the Vatican, and though Tate said he wasn't Catholic, for the most part, he liked the pope.

Marian was lulled by the candlelight and the fire and the live acoustic music that had begun to play. She ordered the crème brûlée and Tate ordered the chocolate decadence, and before their desserts were served he moved his chair closer to her so that he was now sitting to her left, with only the table's corner between them. He put his right hand on her leg, with his fingers against the inside of her thigh. "You're beautiful, you're intelligent, you're exceptional," he told her. "And I know you keep working every day to be that." And then with his left hand, he traced the front of her neck to just past her collarbone, until the weight of his fingers tugged lightly against the first fastened button, and he told her that his relationship with her was the fullest he had ever known. "You're the whole package, Marian. I truly adore you and love you," he said. "You are my *all.* A-L-L, all."

Marian was about to respond, but the server was now standing beside them with their desserts, and the young man set the dishes in front of them, and would they like anything else, coffee or tea, and Marian shook her head and Tate said they were good, and Marian brought her hand to her face, and her freckles felt hot, and the server walked away, and Marian said, "I love you, too."

After dinner they sat in Tate's vehicle outside the restaurant. Tate held Marian's hand and said he hoped it would fit. And Marian said, "What?" And he said, her birthday present. Then he brought his other hand out of his coat pocket and slid a gold signet ring onto Marian's third finger. The ring was too large, so Marian switched it to her index finger and held it up to her face, where she saw the image of a compass. She told him it was beautiful, and he said it was so she could find her way back to him when their work took them apart.

The stones along the path to the huts glowed white and the ground was soft, and

Marian was trying not to trip from her own giddiness and the wine, and she and Tate walked with their arms wrapped around each other tightly and their hips squeezed against each other, which only made their going along the path even more cumbersome. She tried hard not to laugh, because she did not want to draw attention from the others, but Tate told her they were all down at the main house, she had nothing to worry about, and he was laughing and calling her funny girl. And once they were far enough up the hill, away from the reach of any lights, Tate grabbed Marian by the hips and swung her around and kissed her with more fervor than he had ever kissed her before, teeth and lips against each other, and a groan in the back of Marian's throat, Tate's fingers sliding underneath her blouse, callused and cool against her skin, Marian hooking a leg around Tate's thigh to pull him closer, her hands grabbing onto the back pockets of his jeans, and his legs so firmly planted on the ground that she knew she would have fallen over if it weren't for him. "I love you, Tate. I love you," she said. And he picked her up and carried her over his shoulder and walked the remaining distance to her hut.

She told him the combination from her

perch. He punched in the number and ducked when he carried her inside, then shut the door. Tate slid Marian down his chest and before her feet had touched the floor, she and Tate were at it again, mouths and hips and limbs, and the full length of their bodies strained and pressed together. Tate fumbled for the light switch, because he wanted to see her, he said, and when the light came on, he stared at her, looked at her shirt that was two buttons undone to the south and her cowboy boots, and her jeans, which were slippery with desire. He laid her on the bed, slowing their lovemaking to a deliberate pace, and began to undress her. He pulled off her boots and her socks and set them on the floor and unfastened her jeans and removed them as well. And then Tate asked Marian to take off her shirt and the rest of her clothing, and when she did, he took the shirt from her and held it to his face and gazed upon her body.

Perhaps after this night their lovemaking would go back to the way it had been, like that of two people who'd known each other for a hundred years, whose bodies by rote had become ever familiar, the two of them finding each other in the dark on his small bed, him on top, and the quiet noises they made, Tate lighting the candle for her when she would get up to dress or to relieve herself outside before climbing back in his bed. And Marian had understood all of this as tenderness, because really, she had never known anything else.

But this night, with the light on, Tate's breathing had sounded hungry, and his orgasm wild, and when they were finished and their bodies were slick with sweat and began to chill in the cool room, Tate said he would build a fire and Marian saw him naked in front of the stove, his body supple and muscular and taut. He climbed into bed and sat against the headboard, and asked Marian to sit between his legs and lean her back on his chest. He stroked her hair and her shoulders. He ran his hands down the front of her neck and over her rib cage and breasts. Then he laid his arm across her, just beneath her chin, and Marian could feel the thudding of his heartbeat against her skin.

Tate's clothes were next to the bed. He leaned over and reached for his coat, searched through the pockets, and pulled out his phone. Marian still had her back against Tate's chest and her hands on top of his legs. Tate called his voice mail. Then he followed a set of prompts and held the phone out in front of Marian as he entered the four digits for her birthday. He talked about the miles that would soon come between them. "I want you to know you can always trust me. You can check my voice mail anytime." Tate then set the passcode on his phone to her birthday as well. "I swear to you, Marian, I have nothing to hide."

16
PRESENT: AUGUST 2017

Marian
The Den, Montana

Every night for the past week, Marian had sat propped in her bed with her laptop, drinking from a quart-size thermos of coffee and combing through every file from the program's Archives folder, rarely falling asleep before three or four. And each time she heard a branch snap or the wind tousle a leaf or the boards in her hut moan or an animal skitter up a tree, her body flinched and her heart beat crazy. She was running on too much adrenaline and too much caffeine, ingesting multiple cups of coffee during the day as well, just to keep going. She'd practically memorized six years' worth of the program's studies, identifying Tate as a handler on multiple projects, and yet none of those studies involving Tate coincided with any of the dates the Stillwater victims went missing. "Tate, where were you? Talk to me," she'd pleaded out loud. And she'd prayed to God for answers, literally gotten on her knees.

And then there was her most recent call from Nick, where he'd told her Tate had been sexually molested by his fifth-grade teacher, and Marian had literally been aghast and had hardly slept at all that night. And all of this was made worse by the fact that piece by terrible piece Tate was beginning to fit Nick's profile of the killer. And then there was this: Marian had loved this deeply flawed man, had believed they might have a future together. And now every part of that was disintegrating in front of her. Sure, she'd been naïve and blind and all those pithy things a wise person could tell her, but there were minutes during that past week when she didn't care about any of those pithy things; she just wanted to crawl back in time and into Tate's arms before any of *this* had happened. She wanted to live her moments with Tate all over again, because most of those moments had been supremely good, intoxicating, really, like nothing she'd ever known before.

And perhaps it was all of the craziness brewing in her mind and her sleep deprivation and her diet of caffeine and energy bars that was standing in the way of sound decision making. On the morning that she was supposed to take one of the dogs into the Whitefish Range and look for fresh deer and bear scat for training purposes, she'd decided to drive a little farther north and explore the woods around Stryker Ridge, where three of the Stillwater victims' remains had been found. She'd brought Winter, a husky mix whom Marian swore was a wolf hybrid, with her. And she'd justified her decision, telling herself there were bear and deer in those parts, too. The sky was a sharp blue, and the temperatures were to reach eighty by the afternoon. She took a right off the highway and drove as deep into the forest as she could, taking one of the old logging roads.

Two things happened that day, and Marian would never be able to erase them from her mind, and she would severely wish that she could, because the memory of them would haunt her each time she stepped into the woods. The first happened midmorning, after she and Winter had canvassed the area for a couple of hours. She'd just stopped to get Winter some water, when she looked up and saw a strip of leftover crime tape tied around the trunk of a western larch, maybe ten feet in front of her, and God help her if her skin didn't turn cold and her feet tremble. The instant had happened so unexpectedly, and all she could think of was that one of the victims may very well have lost her life in this exact spot where Marian was standing. She had this horrible sensation that she'd been traipsing over sacred ground, like a burial site. But she didn't walk away. Instead she knelt and wrapped her arm around Winter and told him to stay. He was a young dog, and yet in that moment he was remarkably calm.

Over the past few weeks, Marian had experienced a growing sensation of having known the victims. As much as she'd thought about Tate, she'd thought about them, too, had memorized their images, the details of their lives. The air was as still as Marian's breathing — not an insect buzzing in her ear, or an animal skittering about. Even the birds were silent. And Marian wondered which of the victims had died in this spot. She held all four of the women in her mind, prayerlike, one at a time. She felt nauseous and hollow. Her hands quivered.

"Let's go, Winter," she said. The place made her whisper. She stood and stepped slowly, softly, as if afraid to disturb the area any more than she already had.

She and Winter would circle back to the vehicle, taking a different but more direct route. The terrain was steep, and as Marian hiked, her legs felt weak. She drank water but had lost her appetite. And then she realized there were minutes she had not kept track of, like driving someplace and having no idea how you'd gotten there. She brought out her phone, checked her path. She'd ventured off course, nothing too significant. She'd keep her phone out and follow the route more closely.

The sun was directly overhead, filling the forest with wraithlike streams of sunlight. Marian's skin glowed with sweat. There was something white or gray among the thick patch of trees ahead of them. Marian drew closer, stepped carefully. Winter's ears were alert, his body rigid. And Marian said, "Oh my God," her voice not even a whisper, because she knew she was looking at the same kind of nondescript trailer Nick had told her about. And though her mind froze, her body continued to edge closer. The hitch of the camper was set on two cinder blocks. The metal siding was mostly gray, though painted with patches of white primer where the metal had no doubt been repaired. The door was wooden and splintered at the bottom. A gold curtain covered the small window. Marian grabbed onto Winter's harness and held him back. "Stay," she said. And in that fraction of a second a large dog lunged at the window from inside with a stream of ferocious barks, the gold curtain parting, and Marian felt her heart flip in her chest, and Winter was barking and trying to break free of Marian's grasp, his hackles raised all the way down his spine, and Marian stumbled backward, still holding on to Winter's harness. Every part of her was shaking. She turned and led Winter away from the camper. And maybe this wasn't the spot where Lynn-Marie had been taken, and yet given its proximity to the crime scene where she had just been, every molecule in Marian's body believed that it was. And someone was using it now, despite the memory of what had happened there, which made Marian believe that whoever it was didn't have a soul.

She was still carrying her phone in her left hand. She followed the GPS course exactly this time, her legs moving on pure adrenaline. Winter stayed close, as if he were afraid, and Marian felt certain that he was. And she cursed herself and her madness in these woods that felt so unutterably strange and haunting. And she told Winter she was sorry. What had she been thinking? She began to panic and was sure she couldn't breathe. She'd become obsessed with her search for Tate's innocence, or guilt, or whatever it was. She'd become obsessed with the killings. She was out of her depth. And she told God she was sorry, she really was, but she didn't know how to stop this quest that she was on, and she asked for help, and she tried to slow her breathing, and the sweat dripping off her chin felt as cold as ice water.

By the next morning, Marian had finished going through the last of the files in the program's archives, and again she hadn't slept more than three or four hours. She still had nothing positive to show for her efforts. She was beyond exhausted and discouraged, and her life was crawling around her with all of its details to take care of — laundry and groceries and responsibilities at work and her mother's birthday to remember, and emails to answer for the program. And so she'd set aside a day to take care of some of the noise.

The brakes on the Xterra were making a grinding sound. She'd put off having them checked for too long, so she made an appointment in Kalispell where she knew Tate had brought the vehicle in the past.

The rear brake pads needed to be replaced, she was told after the inspection, and the service department could replace the pads that afternoon. The whole thing would take a couple of hours, and did she want to wait or did she need a loaner vehicle. She said that she would wait. And she relished having those couple of hours where she could close her eyes and sleep.

She sat in the waiting area with magazines and leather chairs and a big-screen TV, and she got distracted by the news that was covering the recent hurricane along the Gulf Coast. And then she thought about something Tate had said, and she'd been shocked when he had said it, about people who built their homes in natural disaster zones, and what did those people expect but to get hit with a natural disaster. They lacked good common sense, he told her. And Marian said he was cruel, and he said people's mistakes were costly. Only minutes before, they'd been washing the dishes together in the main house and being silly, and Marian had felt so completely happy, and how had they even gotten onto the topic of natural disasters, but then she remembered; it had to do with an assignment in Louisiana that the program had put in a bid for, and one thing in the conversation had led to another, and now the giddy atmosphere had completely dissipated.

Marian was staring blankly at the TV screen suspended on the wall, when the thought came to her like a flicker. She approached the service desk. She had a question, she said. Would the service history for her vehicle show whether the previous owner had ever taken out a loaner? The man behind the service counter said the service invoices would give her that information. Marian asked if it would be possible for her to get a copy of those records. And the man said perhaps what she was looking for was the Carfax report. But Marian said, no, the invoices would be more helpful because they would show how much money had been spent on the vehicle, and that would be good knowledge to have, didn't he agree? Then she said the previous owner was deceased and had been a close friend of hers, as if that might make a difference. And maybe it did, because the man said how sorry he was for her loss, and yes, he could pull up those invoices. He'd try to have them for her by the time her vehicle was ready. And Marian said if it would make it easier, she only needed them from the past three years.

Marian was back in the waiting area with her head tilted over the seat and her eyes closed, when the service man said,

"Ma'am?" And Marian opened her eyes and sat up, and the man was holding a stack of papers, not too thick, and Marian thanked him, and he said, "Not a problem."

Marian laid the papers in her lap. She began thumbing through the dates, and really, she did not expect to find anything. But then she came across several invoices from a couple of years ago, and God help her if her heart didn't stop in her chest. On May 18, the day before Melissa Marsh went missing, Tate had brought the vehicle in to have a couple of gaskets replaced and a brake line repaired. He'd taken out a green Nissan Rogue, and had returned the loaner two days later. Marian felt numb. She continued to stare at the invoice. Someone called her name. Her vehicle was ready. She put the papers in her backpack. She walked to the service desk. She paid. She collected her keys, and perhaps she said thank you, but everything she did felt automatic.

She stepped outside. She climbed into her vehicle. Tate was driving a green SUV the day Melissa went missing. There it was. And Marian wondered how many other people were driving a green SUV on May 19, over two years ago. And surely there were hundreds of people in the Kalispell area whose vehicle matched that description. And how reliable was the witness anyway? In one of Marian's conversations with Nick, he'd said that the witness had been home from work sick. She'd gotten up to use the bathroom and had looked out her bathroom window. She did not have her glasses on, and she'd seen the vehicle from at least a couple hundred feet away. And Marian thought perhaps the vehicle the woman had seen was charcoal gray, or dark blue, or even black, and that it had only looked green because of the glare of the sun. And maybe the person getting into the vehicle wasn't Melissa Marsh, because how sure could the woman be from that distance without her glasses on? Any of these things were possible, Marian thought, as she drove down the highway and made the appropriate turns until she was back at The Den, and she felt like she was hyperventilating, because her fingers and legs still had that numb and tingling feeling.

She had just shut off the engine and was reaching over to the passenger seat for her backpack, when Trainer slammed his hand down on her hood and startled her to no end, and she flew back in her seat, and he apologized to her through her rolled-down window, because he didn't mean to scare her, and how was she doing, he asked.

Marian said, aside from being three hundred dollars poorer, she guessed she was doing all right.

"Take a ride with me," Trainer said.

"Where to?"

"The farmer's market. There'll be food there. About time you started eating again."

"I'm eating," Marian said.

"Energy bars don't count."

And Marian said she supposed she could go with him, but she wanted to drop her backpack off at her hut first.

Marian felt light-headed as she climbed the hill toward her hut, and Trainer was right, she knew. She needed to start eating better. She needed to cut back on the coffee and get some proper sleep. She took the invoices out of her backpack and placed them in her desk drawer, but before she closed the drawer all the way, she stopped. Something was off. Her desk chair was pulled out. Not a big deal. She usually sat in the chair when putting on her shoes. But she had this thing about chairs. Even as a kid she'd make sure all the kitchen chairs were scooted back in around the table after her family had eaten. Call it obsessive-compulsive or just quirky; it was her thing, and something didn't feel right. She set her backpack on the floor. She sat at her desk and opened her laptop. She wanted to send Nick an email. Her desktop screen came up. *What the heck,* she thought. She was sure she'd turned off her computer after she'd used it that morning. Maybe she'd just thought she'd turned it off. Maybe she'd hit the wrong key, and had closed the laptop instead and put it to sleep.

She opened her email account. She had a message from Ryan Schulman, a reporter for the *Daily Inter Lake News* out of Kalispell. He'd been in contact with her lately about the program, and more specifically about the role of the handler. She'd been taking care of these kinds of communications while Jenness was away. She'd get back with him later, and hurriedly pulled up a new message to Nick:

> Tate was driving a green loaner vehicle the day Melissa went missing. I have the records. She hit send. Then she shut down her computer, and she waited until it had completely powered off before closing it.

Marian and Trainer were on their way back from the farmer's market in Whitefish when Trainer bypassed their usual route to The Den, and when Marian said, "Where are you going?" he'd said he had something to show her. They drove a couple more miles to Stage Hill Road.

As they came up on Dana Lear's house, Trainer told Marian to take a close look.

"What am I looking for?" Marian asked.

"Notice anything different? Look closely."

The black truck was still parked in the front lawn beside the road, but the *For Sale* sign was gone. Then Marian noticed a *Keep Out, No Trespassing* sign on the front door that she hadn't remembered seeing the day she'd pulled off the road and gotten out of her vehicle. The other thing she noticed was the detached garage. The garage door was open, and inside the garage was a green SUV, just like the one that had been coasting in front of Marian on her run the week before.

Trainer drove past the house and said, "It seems to me the guy doesn't want people coming around. You were asking a lot of questions the other day. You don't want to be messing with this guy."

"Why are you telling me this?" Marian asked.

"Because he called this afternoon. Wanted to speak with the lady of the house. Identified himself as King Lear. When I told him there was no lady of the house, he said he was sure Lady Cordelia lived there and that she'd stopped by his place the other day."

"What makes you think he was looking for me?"

"Described her as having long, flowing black hair. A little creepy, if you ask me."

"My hair's brown."

"You're splitting atoms with me, Marian. You know the gist of what I'm saying. You ever read *King Lear*?"

"Maybe in high school."

"Well I've read a little Shakespeare. Was an English major back in the day. If I'm not mistaken, Cordelia doesn't make it."

"And the purpose of completely freaking me out is?"

"It wouldn't hurt you to be a little more careful. Don't go looking into those murders you were asking me about. Best to leave things alone."

17

FROM NICK SHEPARD'S FILE VICTIM PORTRAIT #3 Lynn-Marie Pontante

I was eighteen when my father left my mother. I had already graduated from high school and had spent the summer at an equine training camp in Idaho. The day I returned my father was sitting in a chair across from the sofa, in a small room we referred to as the library. He'd called a family meeting with me and my mom and my two older brothers. The air was hot from the sun's glare through the windows and my own apprehension and the other emotions and bodies in the room. The smell of the barn and horses from the camp where I had been was still on my skin and clothes. Horsehair stuck to my arms. I picked off a single short strand and pressed it between my fingers.

I didn't go to college that fall, despite my

parents' and my original plans. I needed to look into the eyes of horses and a sweet old Lab that had always been mine. I needed to feel the mountains and the larch and the tall western pines.

I came upon the ad on a Sunday afternoon while I was reading the paper. *Wanted: Caretaker of senior horses. Housing provided.* I didn't tell my family that I had applied, and they were surprised when I said I was going. I cried the first two hours of the drive from Spokane to Libby, with my dog, Tully, sitting beside me. I could still smell my mother's perfume and sadness on my face.

I moved into a yurt on a large piece of tangled property with six fenced-in paddocks and a barn that housed eight horses. Most of the horses were lame, and though they could no longer be ridden, they seemed to enjoy themselves and came right up to me when I called them.

There was a picnic table outside the barn. Between chores, I would sit on top of it and play my guitar. I would write songs about love and Jesus and kindness. I would sing to the horses and to Tully stretched out on the picnic table beside me, the sun warming her black coat and the white hairs on her belly.

Jason pulled up to the barn one day when I was singing. He stepped out of his truck with his long, lanky legs. He wore jeans and cowboy boots, a long-sleeve shirt, and a cowboy hat. He carried a toolbox and said he was the farrier. The owner of Greener Pastures had told me the farrier would be stopping by. But I hadn't expected someone like Jason, boyish and almost shy though he was in his midtwenties, with eyes as green as a meadow and wavy brown hair the color of the bark on an alder. Two of the horses had hoof rot, or thrush as Jason called it. He showed me how to apply the antiseptic and gave me boots to keep their feet dry. I liked the way he talked to the horses, and I liked the way he talked to me, patient and gentle in that simple way of his, as if nothing in his world were ever in a hurry.

Jason checked on the horses each week after that, and on his third visit he asked me if I would play him a song and when I did he said I sang pretty and asked me if I would like to go to church with him. Jason and I started spending more time together. We'd go to church on Sunday mornings, and on Wednesday evenings I'd play my guitar for a small gathering of people that met in a classroom at the church. Jason and I would eat dinner together after the fellowship, and on other days we'd take walks together on the property where I lived. He'd help me feed the horses and put them in for the night. Sometimes we'd sit together at the picnic table and talk till midnight. I was falling in love with Jason. And though we'd never said the words to each other, we talked about it once. We were sitting in a couple of chairs outside my yurt. The air had the chill of autumn and we were holding hands. "I think love should mean something," he said. "When I say it, it's going to mean a whole lot." I knew then Jason was the one I wanted to marry. I knew he was the kind of person I could go on loving for the rest of my life.

It was a late Wednesday afternoon when I first saw you. I'd already finished my chores and had showered and dressed in some clean clothes for that evening's fellowship service. I'd driven to town to pick up some beet pulp for the horses. Then I stopped to get gas before driving back to the barn. Because I used cash, I went inside to pay. You were paying with cash, also. You'd pulled out your wallet and removed some bills to cover a beverage you had on the counter. That's when your license fell out. I was standing behind you and saw your name etched on the plastic. You stepped on the card, slid it toward you, and reached down and picked it up.

After I paid for my gas, I drove the five miles to Greener Pastures. I carried the bag of beet pulp into the feed room. Then I walked the fifty yards or so to the yurt to wash my hands and freshen up. Jason would be coming by before long to give me a ride. When I stepped out of the bathroom, you were standing in my small living area, next to a table where I'd dropped my mail. "I'm looking for Lynn-Marie," you said.

It wasn't unusual for people to stop by with questions about Greener Pastures or to want to have a look around.

"I'm Lynn-Marie," I said.

You told me you lived up the road a short distance and had a couple of horses you needed someone to look after because you had to go away. I was happy to help you out. "I could stop by tomorrow," I said.

But you told me it was urgent, that you were leaving shortly, that your only sister had been in a car accident and she might not make it. I remembered seeing you at the convenience store and you dropping your card. I wondered if you had known about the accident then and that perhaps you had dropped the card because you had been upset by what you had just learned.

You went into great detail about the car crash, about the drunk driver who'd swerved into your sister, Jay-Jay, and thank God your nephew and niece weren't in the car with her, and you could give me a quick ride up to your place, it would only take a minute. You'd known the owners of Greener Pastures for as long as you could remember. They'd spoken highly of me when you'd called them, and they'd told you to stop by, that they were sure I'd be able to help you out.

Of course I would help you. I still had a half hour before Jason would be there. "I can just follow you," I said. "My truck is by the barn." But your vehicle was right there and it would be faster, and finding my way to your property could be tricky, you said.

Tully was smelling your jeans and wagging her tail. I may have even said, "Tully likes you. She's worried about you." You said what a funny name for a female dog, and I told you it was a variation of the Hebrew word that meant *the dew of God.* I left Tully inside the yurt and told her to stay. I told her I loved her and I would be right back. She whined a little and stopped wagging her tail.

You told me about your sister as you drove. You told me about her two kids. You cried as you talked about them. I told you how sorry I was. I tried to assure you that she'd be okay. I asked you if you believed in God. You told me that you did. "We should pray for her," I said. I closed my eyes and prayed out loud, and while I prayed, you said, "Yes, Jesus," and

"Yes, dear Lord," and "Thank you, Father."

When I opened my eyes I knew something was wrong, because you were looking straight at me with those empty eyes, and I said, "Shouldn't you be watching the road?" You turned your eyes back to the road then, and I asked you how much farther.

"We're almost there," you said.

Ten minutes later, we were still driving. "You're not taking me to your property, are you?" I said.

You said no, that you were taking me to see your sister, because you wanted me to pray over her.

I didn't say anything then, but I knew we weren't going to see your sister, just as I knew you didn't have any horses. I moved my hand onto the door handle, preparing myself to jump out. You saw my hand and locked the doors.

"I wouldn't do that if I were you," you told me. You whipped out a knife from a sheath on your belt, and in no more than a second your right arm had me pinned against my seat, the knife so close to my neck, I was sure I could feel the heat of the blade.

"I'm not afraid to die," I said. "There's nothing you can do to me."

You laughed and said we'd see about that.

After a couple of hours you turned onto a

logging road that switch-backed up a mountain. All the while I prayed that God would deliver me. I worried about my mother and my father and my brothers. I worried about Jason and Tully.

You pulled up to a camping trailer, the kind that hitches onto the back of a truck. The hitch on the trailer was sitting on top of a couple of cinder blocks. You turned off your truck's engine. Again I went for the door. You grabbed a handful of my hair with your left hand. Your right arm wrapped around my neck, the blade of the knife nicking my lip. And as I kicked and screamed, you pulled me toward you over the console, my hip catching momentarily. You dragged me out of the truck and toward the trailer, your arm choking me tighter, making it difficult for me to breathe. Then you reached behind you, pushed the door open, and shoved me inside.

The trailer smelled like old cigarette smoke and dirty ashtrays. I remember a rust-stained sink built into cheap kitchen cabinets, and green cushions with yellow stains against a paneled wall. A single mattress lay on the floor at the other end of the trailer. The sheets on the mattress had a maroon and black geometric pattern. There was blood on the sheets, like the kind an animal might leave on the ground if it were wounded and being dragged across the dirt.

I don't remember everything you did to me that night. There are hours that I don't recall anything at all. You asked me to take off my clothes. I unbuttoned the silk shirt I had worn for Jason. I balanced my weight on my right foot and removed my left boot. Then I removed the other boot also.

"Take off everything," you said.

I unbuckled my jeans. I tried to pull the belt free from the belt loops. The buckle was large, like the kind someone might win at a rodeo, like the kind I could use to hurt you. But you were faster. You shoved me against the wall, held the knife to my throat. "Don't get smart with me," you said.

Once I had removed the rest of my clothes you told me to turn around slowly. My body was trembling. I said your name. "You don't want to do this." I told you God loved you. My voice was calm, perhaps calmer than it had ever been, as if someone else were speaking for me. "Give me the knife," I said.

You handed me the knife, like you were in some kind of trance. But as soon as it was in my hand, I panicked, if only for a second. I threw the knife across the room. It fell somewhere behind the green cushions.

Without a beat you told me to get it.

I retrieved the knife. I handed it to you, and I

began to pray, “Dear Lord, please help this man.”

You grabbed me by the throat and shoved me onto the mattress. You pinned me with your right arm and raped me with your left fist. And was there gurgling; was there blood I heard from somewhere in my body? I thought of my family, especially my mother. *Please, dear Lord, look after her, I pray.*

18
May 2017

Marian
Cabinet Mountains, Montana

Marian had not had much time with Tate since the two of them had celebrated her birthday, and she was beginning to feel their upcoming separation. Tate would be leaving for the wolf study in a couple of weeks. With the longer daylight hours and warmer temperatures, the staff often didn't stop to eat dinner and shower until eight or nine o'clock. In addition, the upcoming projects had involved planning, such as locating housing for the handlers and dogs at the different job sites, even if that meant finding a garage with a plug-in freezer. These types of operational tasks were almost always taken care of late into the evenings.

"Let's take a day and go somewhere," Marian had said when she and Tate were working with the dogs in the field behind the barn and the sky was full of a late-spring drizzle.

As Tate talked over different destinations, he came up with the idea of a mock wolverine study. Marian was still a novice handler. The extra training would do her good. She would work with Ranger, who would be more of a challenge for Marian than Arkansas. Tate would be there to observe and offer guidance. It would be an instructional day for Marian, as well as time the two of them could spend together, Tate said. And because Marian had not seen much of Montana, Tate decided they'd spend the day in the Cabinet Mountain range, and said that the Selkirks, where he would be that summer, and the Cabinets were the two wildest mountain regions remaining in the contiguous states.

He created an eight-by-eight-kilometer cell and went ahead and designed four transects that he wanted Marian to follow. They'd be working an area between the Clark Fork River and the boundaries of the Cabinet Mountains Wilderness. Each transect would take anywhere from one to two hours, depending on the terrain and how many samples Ranger found.

They'd set their alarms for three that morning. Already there was a heavy fog and a cold drizzle, but weather forecasts predicted the fog would lift. Marian made coffee to bring with her. Everything else she needed — snacks, layers of clothing, lunch, field supplies — she'd packed the night before. Then she let Ranger out and fed him, while Tate hid several samples of wolverine scat around the barn for the purpose of reintroducing Ranger to the scent.

Because Tate was eager to get going, he led Ranger on the sample odors, which Ranger found right away. And each time Tate threw the ball, Ranger retrieved it, brought the ball back, and dropped it within a few feet of where Tate stood.

They left The Den by three thirty. They'd be driving west toward the Idaho panhandle and into the Kootenai National Forest. They didn't play music. Tate's radio didn't work. There was just the intermittent sweep and *thwump* of the windshield wipers, the tires on the road, Marian sipping from a thermos-size cup of coffee, and every now and then Ranger's heavy sigh or his nails scraping against the hard plastic of the crate in the back of the vehicle, and Tate's silence.

Ever since meeting Tate, Marian had thought of Arkansas as *his* dog, and she wondered how Tate felt about being assigned to a different one. "Will you miss her?" she asked him on the drive over. It was Lyle's philosophy that the handlers should be prepared to work with any of the dogs. Each dog had its own personality, its unique way of communicating, its own skill set, its individual flaws. One might have a high play drive that could be difficult to control on a study; another might communicate too many finds that were outside the target species; one dog might like to eat scat or roll in it; another, presumably like Ranger, might not want to give the ball back. Handlers had to be prepared for all of that. No dog was perfect for all studies. Or a dog could become injured, as had been the case with Chester. And each dog would eventually retire. Lyle believed that to limit a handler's exposure to one dog would greatly handicap that handler and the program.

But still, Marian thought. There was the human-to-animal bond. Surely there was that.

"What are you going to do? They're just dogs," Tate said.

Ranger's tail thumped against the crate. Marian said something about the whole man's-best-friend thing.

"You disappoint me, Engström. You really do. If you're looking for a best friend, you're in the wrong line of work." Tate returned to his silence, but after they'd passed another mile marker and the motor of the windshield wipers had whirred and Ranger had settled down again, Tate said, "A handler can't be looking to bond with anything."

And Tate was referring to dogs, Marian knew, and besides she didn't believe him; he loved Arkansas. And so she reached over and held Tate's hand because she thought she understood.

Tate parked the vehicle along a Forest Service road south of Bull Lake. They would be hiking into a wooded area in the Cabinet Mountains, just to the west of the wilderness boundaries. Marian got Ranger out of his crate. "Take care of business," she told him, and at that command he ran off about ten feet, sniffed around, and relieved himself, then was back by her side, his tail wagging, his feet prancing. She fastened an orange vest around Ranger and layered his harness over the vest. Then she attached a bell to the back of the harness and inserted his GPS tracker in the pocket. Marian had already powered her GPS tracker and paired it with her phone.

"All set?" Tate asked. And Marian said she was.

Marian wore her daypack, along with a large canvas hip pouch. She reached inside the pouch and took out the blue rubber ball. "Hey, Ranger, you ready to find it?"

Though the fog had lifted once they'd crossed the Kootenai River, the air was raw with freezing drizzle, and no doubt snow in some of the higher elevations. Marian didn't mind the cold. The smell of swelling fern and damp earth and cedar was intoxicating. The woods were more dense here than around The Den, and everywhere was the sound of rushing water from so many streams and creeks, hidden in the forest, running high with frigid snowmelt.

Marian tried to pick up the direction of the wind, but detecting it was difficult among so many trees, and the air was mostly calm that day. They'd started on a narrow game trail that switchbacked up the side of a mountain. Then Marian, looking at her map, began to hike northeast. Ranger caught on and, following her lead, moved several feet ahead of her, but after a few minutes, Tate said, "You're too close. Give him more space."

And so Marian slowed and let Ranger open the gap between them. After a few minutes Ranger began loping back and forth in front of her in almost a zigzag pattern.

"His direction has changed. What's he telling you?" Tate asked.

But Marian didn't think Ranger's direction had changed. "He's onto something?" Marian said.

"Are you sure?"

Ranger had now headed off course to Marian's left. And though he was still moving in a cursory pattern, his gait had slowed.

"You're sure he's onto something?" Tate said.

"I think so."

"You can't just *think so.* You have to be sure. How would you interpret him? What is he telling you?"

Ranger had definitely slowed his pace. His hackles were up. His head was to the ground.

"There's a lot to distract a young dog out here," Tate told her. "This isn't the tundra. Think about what you're doing."

A big part of being a handler was knowing how to effectively read and understand the way the dog communicated: Was he onto something? Had he found a scent item? Was he looking to the handler for guidance? Marian knew she'd made a mistake.

"Ranger, NO! Come back."

"You can't talk to him that way," Tate said.

And Tate was right. Ranger wasn't paying her any mind. He was venturing deeper into the forest, almost in a stalking pattern.

"He smells something dead," Tate said. "You have to pick up on this sort of thing. You have to call him back. You have to give him direction in a positive way. You can't scold him."

"Over here!" Marian called to Ranger, and already she could hear the waver in her voice.

"Are you serious?" Tate said.

Ranger turned his head back once but then continued on his way.

"Over *HERE*!" Marian tried again.

Though Ranger stopped this time, he didn't come back.

"What is wrong with you?" Tate said. "I thought you knew this stuff."

Marian felt paralyzed with frustration. This was supposed to be fun. This wasn't fun. She could hardly hear Ranger's bell from the sound of the water, and the fern was so tall and the woods so dense, she was afraid that if Ranger got much farther away she wouldn't be able to see him either. She hoped Tate would soften. *God, please let him soften.*

"You have to be commanding, but not harsh," Tate said. "And your voice can't waver."

Marian began walking toward Ranger.

"Make him come to you," Tate told her.

Despite the cool weather, perspiration was running down Marian's sides from under her arms. She stopped, wet understories of ferns and mosses and shrubs up to her calves; her pants legs were already soaked and dappled with droplets.

"Lead him in the direction where you want him to work," Tate said.

Marian moved back in the direction of her assigned transect. "Come on, boy! Let's have some FUN! Let's check over *HERE*!" And Marian cringed at the high-pitched sound of her voice even before Tate corrected her again.

"Stop! Please stop. I can't listen to this anymore. Where is Marian?"

"I was trying."

"That's just it. You're trying. You're trying too hard. You've got to be yourself. What's happened to you?"

Marian's frustration and disappointment escalated. She turned her face away.

"You're going to do this, Matilda. I'm not going to do this for you."

Tate's voice had sounded kinder this time.

Marian was able to relax enough to pull it together. And she wondered why everything had seemed so much easier in Alberta, despite the knee-deep snow. "What do I do?" she asked, her voice as calm as she could make it sound.

"You can't come in with so much force. It's not going to work. You have to find your middle ground. If you're too dominant, he's not going to come to you. If you're too excited, he's not going to trust you. You have to find your confident voice."

And fortunately, Ranger had lost interest in whatever odor he'd picked up on and was back at their feet, ready to get going again.

"Go ahead," Tate said. "Lead him where you want him to go."

As Marian walked, with Tate following close behind her, she breathed in and out slowly; she watched Ranger closely. In what seemed like no time at all, Ranger had changed direction dramatically. He was onto something again. Marian thought his pace had slowed once more, as if he were being careful; she thought he was showing signs of curiosity instead of the kind of excitement Arkansas would show when she was on a target species. His head was up and then down and then up again. This time Marian didn't wait for Tate. "There's something cool over HERE," Marian said. "Check over HERE."

"Don't call him off. He's actually on a target. You're interpreting him incorrectly." But this time Tate's voice was barely above a whisper, as if not wanting to distract the dog.

Ranger fishtailed back and forth. Tate had been right. The dog was funneling in on a target scent. His tail was wagging. He was becoming excited.

"Look at his nostrils. Watch the way he moves his head, the way his breathing has changed. He's processing the odor. The farther he is away from the scent, the more he raises his head. Watch him. Now he's turning back into the scent. See his head lowering to the ground. He's getting closer."

Marian stepped in Ranger's direction.

"Follow him, but don't get too close," Tate said. "Don't distract him. Let him do his thing."

Though Ranger had not found a wolverine sample, he'd located a pile of black bear scat, a species odor Tate had recently trained Ranger to identify. The scat was no more than a few hours old and would provide a good layering sample when working with the dogs.

Marian said, "You DID that. You're awesome," to Ranger, while concentrating on the tone of her voice and hoping she wasn't sounding too excited. She threw the ball behind her about ten feet. Then, using two sticks, like chopsticks, because she did not want to waste a pair of latex gloves, she collected a portion of the sample and bagged it.

"Should we be concerned?" she asked Tate, since the scat was fresh.

"They're coming out of their dens, all right," Tate said. "And they're hungry. But that bear's already miles away from us." Tate went on to tell her that the bears' appetites were still waking up and that they'd be on the move and feeding mostly on sedges and grasses and insects for a while.

Marian packed the sample and was ready to go but then realized Ranger had never brought the ball back. He was lying on a patch of moss and chewing contentedly on the thick rubber ball.

"Bring it back," Marian said. "Come ON. Let's search over HERE."

But the dog would have no part of it. When she approached Ranger, he ran away from her, with the ball still in his mouth.

"Drop it!" she said. That didn't work either.

And so Marian looked to Tate. "What am

I doing wrong now?"

"You have to visualize him bringing it to you and dropping it," Tate told her. "You have to remain positive and know at all times that you are going to get what you want."

And so she visualized, and she visualized some more, but none of these visions were coming true. She tried to send positive energy out to the universe, but what she was sending was really just her *WHEN IS HE GOING TO DROP THE BALL* energy. She tried to pretend her frustration away. That did not work either. She knew Ranger could feel all of this, like when someone is waiting for a person to get ready, and the person waiting is discreetly tapping his foot, or staring at his watch — Marian knew that was how tense the energy between Ranger and her had become.

"You're unsure of yourself," Tate told her. "He knows that. Think about it. Before you even asked him to bring the ball back, you were already anticipating a negative reaction. If you're unsure, he's going to be unsure of you."

Marian told Tate that was exactly what she had been thinking, and how did he know so much.

And he laughed then, almost smug. "Let's

just say I've had a lot of experience."

Despite the rain, Marian lowered herself onto the wet ground. She wasn't liking Tate very much in that moment. She wanted time to figure out on her own how to make things work with Ranger, to understand what she needed to modify. She wanted the experience to feel intuitive, because she knew she could never find that magical middle ground when she was trying so hard to please the man she loved.

She leaned the rest of the way back until she was lying down. She let the thin drops fall onto her face, run over her cheeks. She closed her eyes and listened to the rain dripping from branches and to the rushing of a stream nearby. She smelled the redwood cedar and Douglas fir. And from somewhere in the distance she heard the long, haunting, high-pitched note of a male thrush. And then she smelled Ranger's wet coat; heard his bell and his happy pant; felt him brush up against her. She opened her eyes. He was standing beside her. He dropped the ball next to her shoulder.

"We should get going," Tate said. He was standing about three feet away from her with his arms crossed over his chest, and she had the feeling he'd been watching her the whole time. "I think you got this now."

The rest of the morning and the early afternoon went much better, with fewer interruptions from Tate. Marian's commands felt more natural. If Ranger circled back to a target sample, Marian would casually say, "Hey, you got that. Good job. Let's keep going." Or when she needed to bring him back in the game, she'd tell him, "Something is really cool over *here,*" again keeping her voice casual and calm.

And Marian had been able to notice the white-flowered trillium that dotted the forest floor, and in the areas where the snow had only recently melted, the spikes of pink shooting stars and wide patches of glacier lily. When the forest opened up and became less dense, Ranger began locking onto target scents more frequently, and led Marian to at least five wolverine samples by the end of their second transect. Each scat sample was full of bones and feather and fur.

Tate had knelt beside Marian while she was picking up one of the samples. "Imagine the jaws on these guys. They'll eat anything," he told her. "They'll snap a deer's femur in half. They can chase away a cougar or a grizzly if they have a mind to. And the amazing thing is, no one ever sees them. They could be all over these woods, and you'd never even know they were watching you."

Marian asked Tate if he'd ever seen a wolverine.

"Once," he said. "Feeding off some corpse in an avalanche path."

Though they took a couple of short breaks at the end of each transect, the hiking had been long and arduous and covered much of the Berray Mountain area, thickly forested terrain with ponderosa pine and western larch and Douglas fir and darkly canopied footpaths that for brief moments left Marian without sight of Ranger.

But by late afternoon during the final transect, he was loping through moist alpine meadows, his coat shiny from the day's rain. The Bull River was close, its current a loud rush. They made their way through another patch of forest land that descended sharply to the river's bank, thick with reed grass and willow and black hawthorn, and from there, a rocky outcrop collected into a small peninsula that jutted into the river, creating a twist and funnel in the water that pulled floating debris, loose bark, and clumps of river grass and branches beneath the surface, only to propel the debris upward farther downstream.

Ranger was waiting for them on the rocky pier. He lapped water, then cast his eyes back at them and wagged his tail.

"How would you interpret him now?" Tate asked. Even though he'd been less critical and commanding since earlier that morning, he'd still continued to ask her this question.

"He wants to know if he should cross the river," Marian said.

Marian was becoming comfortable with her new mind-set, as if she had learned how to put herself in the canine's place, to see how the world looked and felt through his eyes, to feel his anticipation of playtime upon a successful find, or the excitement upon distinguishing a scent in the air, or the coolness of water lapped up against his tongue. The whole approach felt seductive and sure and continued to send a thrilling twinge down her spine and no doubt a confident light to her green eyes.

Tate was standing behind Marian. "Nice work," he said.

Marian removed her cap and shook the droplets from its brim before placing it back on her head. "Hold on, Ranger," she called. "We're not going swimming today."

She and Tate walked onto the rocky point. The dog wanted to play and was leaping off his hind feet with his front paws reaching toward the sky. "Settle down," Marian told him. He stopped jumping but ran a tight circle around her instead, brushing his wet coat against her legs, and all the while panting and taking in excited gulps of air.

Marian put the ball away in her side pouch and zipped the pouch closed. She and Tate then removed their packs and sat on the cool rocks. Though they'd taken short breaks between her transects, they hadn't eaten lunch and she felt starved. She pulled out a couple of slices of beef jerky. Tate broke a Clif Bar in half. And so they shared each other's food and drank from their water bottles, with Ranger stretched out in front of them, his head on his front paws, his eyelids now struggling to stay open.

"You did really well today," Tate said.

"Yeah?" Marian turned her head toward him, her elbows on her knees, which were pulled up in front of her.

"You should give yourself more credit," he said.

"You were hard on me," she said. "Why?"

"You needed to learn a lesson. This isn't easy work. You know that."

"It wasn't like this in Alberta," she said.

"Things were different in Alberta. There weren't as many distractions. We were breaking trail for the dogs. In this country, the dog breaks trail. It'll be the same in Utah."

"You made me really nervous," Marian said.

"You made yourself nervous," Tate told her. "Think about it."

"Why do you say that?"

"You're reactionary. You feel too much. If you didn't care about me one way or the other, if you didn't care about what I thought, you would have been fine. It was only when you stopped giving a damn about what I thought that you were able to tune me out."

"It sounds cruel," Marian said.

Tate said, "Cruel but necessary. You can't react under stress. You can't get frustrated with the dog, no matter what is going on. I needed to see how you would react. I needed to know what you would do when the stakes are high."

Marian felt Tate's hands on her back. He squeezed her braid, and when he did she could feel the water drip down the back of her shirt.

"I should have brought a rain shell," Marian said. Tate had not worn one either. Weather forecasts had predicted a break in the clouds with afternoon sun, but even now, the cloud cover was a dull white and the temperatures had remained in the forties, and the rain had continued to fall at a light but steady pace.

"You cold?" Tate asked her.

"Chilly," she said. As she spoke her legs and body shivered. She thought back to that morning and the complete blunder she'd made of things. But she also remembered the moments when everything seemed to come together, when she stopped focusing so hard on herself and became aware of the world around her. And so she told Tate about that moment, when it all came together, about the water dripping through the conifer branches and the call of the thrush.

"You became the observer," Tate said. "I get that. I've been doing that all my life."

Tate took a bruised apple out of the side pocket of his backpack. He offered it to Marian but she shook her head. "Animals, people, what's the difference?" he said. "It's all the same. You watch something long enough, you become that thing you're watching. You understand its every move. When it hurts. When it's afraid. You learn how to respond to that." Tate nudged Ranger with his foot. "Isn't that right? You know what I'm saying."

Tate took another bite from his apple,

then offered Ranger a bite, too. Afterward, he pulled his arm back and, like a sidearm pitcher, threw the apple across the river. Ranger was quick to his feet and ready to leap in the water.

Marian grabbed him by his harness. "NO!"

"Good reflexes," Tate said.

And Marian asked if that was part of the training.

Tate laughed. "No, seriously, I wasn't thinking."

But then Tate wasn't laughing and Marian sensed his seriousness again.

"This is a nice spot," he said. He picked up a rock, turned it over and over. "Give me your hand," he said. And so she did.

He placed the rock in her open palm and folded her fingers across the rock's smooth surface. He cupped both of his hands over hers and clasped his fingers together.

"I want you to keep this," he told her.

"What do you want me to do with it?" she asked.

Tate let go slowly, as if balancing the rock and her upturned fist on the pinnacle of her knee. "I want you to remember," he said.

When he didn't say anything else, Marian asked him, "What do you want me to remember?"

"I want you to remember this spot. When I die, this is where I want my ashes to end up. It seems fitting, don't you think? The whole river-of-life thing."

And of course Marian was taken aback because she didn't know why he was talking about dying. "Why are you telling me this?" she asked.

"We're all going to go sometime," Tate said.

Marian had not moved her hand.

"At some point," Marian said.

"That's right," Tate said. He picked up a different rock and pulled his arm back. Ranger was already in a sitting position and wagging his tail. Marian grabbed him by the collar with one hand and wrapped her other arm around his chest.

Tate let the rock fly. It sailed downriver and skipped along the water's surface four or five times before disappearing. "Just like that rock," Tate said. He stood, then lifted his pack onto his shoulders and buckled his sternum strap. Marian zipped her pack shut and stood next to him. She slipped the rock he had given her into her pocket.

Tate called for Ranger, and by the time Marian had lifted her pack onto her shoulders, Tate and the dog were already climbing through the thick brush on the riverbank.

The day had shifted, as if even the air were different. And perhaps it was the fatigue from the early morning, the work, the day's hike. Ranger was tired. Marian was tired. She never finished her final transect. Instead, she followed Tate, even struggled a little to keep up against his long strides. And as they climbed the pitch, as they moved against gravity, her muscles warmed, her body was no longer cold, and she was certain that the sun was burning brighter and the clouds were lifting, despite the heavy mood between her and Tate. He was right. She felt too much. She felt everything.

The western larch needles were a fulsome green, and from all around, Marian heard the birds, their flutter of wings from up high in the branches, their occasional calls: robins and mountain bluebirds and wrens and warblers. She caught flashes of bright yellow from low-growing violet, and in those damp woods she found her first morel mushrooms. She stopped to gather some, and when she looked up, she could no longer see Tate, nor could she hear Ranger's bell over the sounds of the river that was now behind her, or the nearby creeks and the natural drainage ditches.

She was irritated that Tate had not waited for her. She was irritated that she had fallen behind. She took out her phone from her hip pouch so that she could navigate her way back to the vehicle. And then she realized she did not hear the birds anymore. She did not hear the squirrels in the trees. Despite the sounds of water, the air was still, and for the first time that day she felt afraid, as if something were watching her. The muscles across her shoulders wound tight. Slowly, she looked all around her for some kind of movement, her heartbeat drumming loudly in her ears. She was not alone. Something was out there, electricity moving down her spine and her legs. She had been quiet while she'd been picking the mushrooms, and now Tate and Ranger weren't around. The first rule in bear country was to make noise.

"Hey, bear!" Marian called out, the protocol when hiking alone. She moved slowly ahead and looked around her. The ground was too thick with vegetation for her to notice tracks, and the woods too dense for her to see very far in front of her. "Hey, bear!" she called again.

But then she came to the alpine they had crossed earlier and she breathed a little more easily because she had better visibility and because the area felt familiar. The sky had opened up to a magnificent cerulean blue. The sun glared down, creating steam off the ground, and the clearing was wide enough for Marian to view the peaks to the east, still draped in snow.

As she stepped into the woods on the far side of the alpine, she thought she heard Ranger's bell, from somewhere off to her right. And then she heard Tate calling for her.

"Over here!" she yelled.

He'd come back for her, she thought. And when she saw him he was carrying something out in front of him in the palm of his right hand.

They caught up to each other, and he kissed her and showed her what he'd found for her — a thrush nest, the outer layer made of fir and hemlock twigs, the inside a hardened cavity of mud and decomposing grass and downy bird feathers. "Kind of apropos, don't you think?" he said. And his eyes were glistening and he was smiling.

She had never seen a thrush nest before. She reached inside the nest and rubbed the down feathers between her fingers. "They're so soft," she said.

Tate took the bear spray out of her hand and slipped it back into her harness. "Did you see a bear?" he said.

"No. But there might have been one."

Marian removed her pack and set it on the ground. She'd brought a wool hat in case the weather had turned colder. She took out the hat and fit it around the small nest — about four inches in diameter and a couple of inches deep. Then she laid the nest on top of the other items in her pack.

Tate lifted her pack, and Marian slid her arms through the shoulder straps and fastened the hip belt.

As they walked on, Ranger trotted ahead of them a short ways, and Tate told Marian about a girl he once knew who could draw like no one he had ever known. "She'd draw birds: hawks, ravens, falcons, hummingbirds, boreal owls. The detail was extraordinary. She was one of those Audubon supporters. She could spend an entire day observing birds. I swear she was some kind of raptor in a previous life. I called her the artist girl, but I guess *the bird girl* would have been more apt."

Marian wondered if Tate was talking about someone he'd been involved with, and she hated the way that thought made her feel. Nothing about this day had gone as she'd planned, and because she was feeling jealous, her thoughts turned to Jenness, and all she could think about in that moment were the pictures she'd found on Jenness's camera. Marian said she wished she could draw, or was as adept with a camera as someone else they knew. And then, "She has a thing for you, you know," Marian said.

"Who does?"

"Jenness."

"What makes you say that?"

Marian told Tate about the photos Jenness had taken of him. "I saw them when I had her camera."

"She takes photos of everyone. That's her job." Marian could hear the irritation in Tate's voice, and she could have stopped. She could have gone back to the way things had been, to the two of them having a nice walk through the woods to the vehicle.

But Marian continued. "She's got pictures going back two years or more. Hundreds of pictures." And then Marian said, "I think she's jealous. I saw photos of the two of us together."

Marian told Tate about the picture of her getting out of the truck the night they'd gone to see the northern lights. "It's like she's watching us. It's like she's always checking up on where we've been. She's probably wondering where we are now."

"That's quite an assumption you're making. It's a stretch, even for you. You should be real careful about what you're saying. I can only hope you haven't said this to one of the others."

"Tate, it was four in the morning when we got back. Why would she be up so late?"

And then Tate stopped and turned to Marian. "Do you have any idea the kind of hours Jenness and I were putting in? Do you have any idea what it takes to be a crew leader? You think it's all just about going off with the dogs and tromping through snow and bagging all kinds of shit. Or hanging out in the woods and picking mushrooms like Hansel and Gretel. You don't get it. The two of us were lucky if we got any sleep at all. You didn't decide which cells the teams would visit each day. You didn't keep track of where the teams had already been, or which roads were actually open, or where the oil company was focusing their seismic activity. It wasn't your responsibility to make sure everyone knew where the trappers or traps were in the area, or where the oil company's machinery might be in the field that day. You weren't the one who had to shadow incompetent handlers or novice beginners, or do routine checkups on the dogs, or take the dogs out at four in the morning because one of them had gotten sick. You don't know what you're talking about, Marian. And besides, if Jenness were jealous of you, why would she want you in the picture? Think about it," Tate said.

If it was Tate's intention to make Marian feel bad, he had succeeded. She couldn't undo what she had already done. She couldn't take back her presumptuousness, or the fact that it was *she* who had been jealous of Jenness. Of course Tate would come to Jenness's defense. Why wouldn't he protect someone with whom he'd worked side by side and whom he'd known for almost six years longer than he'd known Marian. And then Marian got it. Jenness probably knew Tate better than anyone else ever had. Maybe Marian had it all wrong. Maybe Jenness had been looking out for Tate. The other handlers would come and go. Jenness had said so herself. She and Tate were the only two who'd remained constants.

Marian and Tate continued to follow a course back to the truck, him walking in front of her again. The stretch ahead would be easier now that they were moving downhill. She hated the silence between them. If only she could salvage the day. And then she heard the birds, slow at first, and she realized how quickly the hours had passed, how imminent the long drive back to The Den was. And she heard the hooting of a great horned owl, barely audible with the sound of their footsteps and Ranger's bell and the steady sounds of running water. And she thought about the bird girl. And because Marian so badly wanted Tate and her to be talking again, to go back to the way the two of them had been, she asked him if he, too, had heard the owl, and he said that he had. And she told him about an irruption of snowy owls that had been showing up in Michigan. "Once they make it across Lake Superior they're really weak," she said. "We have a place that rehabilitates them. Still, a lot of them don't make it." And when Tate didn't say anything, she asked him about the bird girl. "Is she someone you dated?"

But Tate was still quiet. Not angry or impatient, just subdued, as if his thoughts were very far away. "I'd rather not talk about it" was all he said.

Marian was tired. She knew Tate must be tired, too, and she wondered why it was taking them so long to get back to the vehicle. Tate seemed to be slipping deeper into his thoughts, and she noticed that once again he was moving farther ahead. She opened her hip pouch to take out her phone and check her navigation, and when she did she saw the morel mushrooms that she'd stored in there earlier, and how did Tate know she had stopped to pick mushrooms when he and Ranger had been out of sight. She stood still to check her phone more closely, and yes, she was sure, they were moving in the wrong direction. And there was something amiss that she could not name, a persistent uneasiness like a cool compress against her skin, and she felt suddenly afraid, and she turned to her left in the direction of the truck, and she stepped onto a game trail that switchbacked down the hill, and she quickened her pace, deep shadows rubbing against her, the air swabbing her arms and legs. She reached in her pocket and took the river rock that Tate had placed in her palm and chucked it as far as she could, her fear as pure as anger.

And how did he and Ranger make it there before her, she would never know, but there they were, and Tate was grinning and said she wasn't putting that ring he'd given her to much use if she was going to keep falling so far behind. And then Tate told her she was suffering and he was sorry for his part in that. "Sometimes my words can be harsh. I don't mean them to come across that way. I talk openly with you because I feel safe with you. I share things with you because I feel I can do so."

And Tate's words softened her anger and fear, and she said she was sorry, that maybe she'd been selfish, because, really, she regretted what she'd told him about Jenness, but mostly she wanted to put this day behind her.

And Tate said, "Be that of what you are, Miss *She-Wolf* Engström, I adore all the levels of you."

And yet on the drive back, as Marian feigned sleep, she thought about the swift-moving Bull River, and the debris that the high runoff had swept from the banks and that its current had pulled under, and she thought of the apple core Tate had thrown to the other side, and the rock he had thrown later, and a black dog named Arthur who, when Tate was a boy, had drowned in a river somewhere in Montana.

19
PRESENT: AUGUST 2017

Nick Shepard
Bonners Ferry, Idaho

Nick wasn't afraid of dying; after all, it was the one thing he had in common with every other living creature in the world. But he was afraid of other things, like not being able to go for a walk, or wipe his own ass, or smoke some good tobacco, or make love to his wife. And he was afraid of the things he would no longer remember, like the name of his son, or a single line from a T. S. Eliot poem, or the first time he saw his wife cry when she witnessed a homeless child begging for food on the streets of San Francisco.

But on that particular Thursday, Nick's body and mind were still in good enough working order. He patted the breast pocket of his big flannel shirt to make sure he had his pipe and his pouch of Larsen Signature tobacco that his son had brought back for him from Amsterdam. Then, with the help of two ski poles, Nick made his way across the yard to the back of his property and onto a trail that cut through the woods.

The deeper he ventured into the two-hundred-some acres of hemlock and aspen and larch, the greater his exertion became, and he felt the rush of anxiety come over him, but not because of the pain in his body, which he cursed with each breath, but because walking in these woods reminded him of so many of the crime scenes he had visited. In over ninety percent of the cases he had worked, that was where the bodies of the victims had been found, among trees and leaves and detritus. But he was one of the privileged. He was a man, and a good size at that, over six feet before the last couple of years, when, he swore, he had shrunk at least an inch, and still weighed more than two hundred pounds. With a younger body, or even a healthier one, he could walk these woods any time he liked. He could run along neighborhood roads or walk across parking lots. He could enjoy the kind of solitude that put women at risk. Then there were the statistics: Ninety-five percent of stranger-to-stranger homicides were committed by men against women. Maybe he'd get his wife a Rottweiler before he died, or a Doberman pinscher. His wife liked dogs. They'd once had a cocker spaniel they'd adopted from the pound. They'd had cats over the years also, a couple of which were still hanging around.

Nick's wife didn't think women should carry guns. Nick wasn't so sure about that. His wife carried pepper spray. She'd never had to use it. More than likely the pepper spray had expired. He'd have to remember to order her some more. He'd order her a box of the stuff and place it on automatic reorder for every couple of years after he was gone. Not the most romantic of gestures.

The walk was becoming more difficult. He stopped to catch his breath, and then goddamn it if his leg didn't spasm, and he yelled out in pain and dropped the ski poles and grabbed his left leg, which crumpled beneath him and sent him to the ground. The doctor called these episodes seizures. Nick was supposed to place a white pill under his tongue, but he didn't know where he had put those little white pills, probably someplace convenient back at the house, which was the farthest thing from convenient right now. And besides, those little white pills put him to sleep, and wouldn't that be something, him falling asleep in these woods and his wife sending out an entire search posse for him. He continued to yell and curse his leg and curse the cancer, and by the time the seizure subsided he was drenched in sweat and his body fatigued.

He grabbed hold of the ski poles, but it was useless to try to stand. He simply didn't have enough strength left in him. And so he scooted off the trail and propped himself against the trunk of a hemlock. The dry wind began to chill his damp skin. He took out his pipe and his pouch of tobacco. His wife wouldn't be home from work for a couple more hours. He didn't have a cell phone with him, didn't even own one, swore they were a nuisance to humanity. But maybe having a cell phone right now wouldn't be such a nuisance if he knew how to use the damn thing. He took a pinch of tobacco and packed it down in the bowl of his pipe. Then he packed down a couple more pinches and struck a match. With the bit in his mouth, he puffed gently and lit the tobacco. After a half-dozen more puffs, he tamped down the ash residue and lit the tobacco again. There was something about smoking a pipe in the woods that was intensely satisfying — the rich aroma of the tobacco mixed with the scents of late summer.

He could get used to this, he thought, spending more time outdoors, smoking in the woods. He wouldn't be here in six months. He probably wouldn't be here in three months either. His wife didn't like to talk about that, but it was true. And how much time did he have before he lost his independence, before the cancer decided to grow again and take over the infrastructure of his brain?

Nick brought his attention to Marian. He'd felt an urgency to help her and to learn all that he could about Tate. Nick and Marian had been in regular contact over the past couple of weeks, including a number of video calls and emails. He'd told her, "Tate was the orchestra leader. He was the center of his world. From what you've described so far, this guy would not have been capable of a long-term, committed relationship." Nick's impression was that Tate had a tendency toward objectification. Marian had been an object to Tate, something he could use to his benefit, until he began to experience boredom with his newfound toy.

Instead of loving Marian, Tate had projected upon her traits that he'd believed were worthy. Very simply, she'd become an extension of himself. "You bring a lot of qualities to me," he'd told her. She was brilliant; she was the most beautiful woman he had ever seen; she was God's gift to the dogs; she was courageous and strong and sure and kind. What more could he ask for? He spoke of her being gifted to him and how fated they were to be together, and in the words of a true narcissist he told her how similar they were, that they were cut from the same block of wood.

In the beginning of Marian's relationship with Tate, he had seemed too good to be true. He praised her often. He was charming and confident. He told her no one compared to her. If she felt bad about something, such as missing her dog or getting stuck in the ice, he made her feel better. Tate had performed well, and she'd fallen hard for him. They'd danced beneath the northern lights, watched endangered caribou from a helicopter, hiked in some of the most beautiful landscape known to humankind. He'd given her the perfect birthday: a candlelight dinner, exchanges of endearment, passionate lovemaking, romance at its finest. Tate had her, and he knew it. The prize had been won. And like a high-potency drug, Marian had become addicted. The best cocktail she'd ever had. But just at the moment when he'd had her complete trust, his façade had begun to crack — an insult here, a glib comment there, a cold shoulder, a rude edge, the withdrawal of emotional intimacy. And a bewildered Marian had been left trying to make sense of the man she had loved.

Marian had told Nick about a conversation she'd had with Tate on the phone when they'd been on separate assignments. "Early on he'd said we shouldn't talk about past relationships. That couples got themselves in trouble when they went down that road. But that night he started asking me questions. He wanted to know how many men I had been with. I told him I had been with one other man, but it had been wrong, that I didn't feel toward the man the way I felt about Tate. 'Then why did it happen?' Tate wanted to know. Why had I lowered myself to that standard?"

Nick pointed out to Marian what he was sure she already knew, that Tate had set her up for the insult.

"How did you move past that?" Nick asked.

"I don't think we ever did," she said.

And then there was the deception. It was true what Nick had told Marian, that each person is the author of his or her own storybook. We start that book early on. We shade a little here and there, until we start to believe it. But most of it is accurate. Tate was writing what he wanted to present to the world, and most of it was bullshit. He wasn't boastful about it. He'd usually wait until he was asked and then present things as matter-of-fact. This was who he was by his creation: the savior, the rescuer, the center of his universe, the guy who pulled people out of muskeg and saved dogs' lives by stitching their wounds. Getting Marian to believe his lies was a way for him to indulge in his fantasies, while laughing the whole time at her gullibility. From the way Marian had described Tate, if he were the killer, he would be like a predatory Paul Bunyan. He was bright. He was smart. Sex wouldn't have been a necessary component of his crimes.

Without an exact timeline and hard evidence, Nick had cautioned Marian regarding connecting Tate with the murders. Yet now with the green loaner vehicle and Marian's investigation into the program's records, which suggested Tate may very well have been in the area when the homicides occurred, he was looking more interesting all the time as a possible candidate. The

Stillwater Forest was Tate's territory. He knew those roads and woods intimately, instinctively, like a hound on a hot scent. Nick also believed that if the killer had been involved with someone, the relationship would have played itself out in much the same way as Marian's had played out with Tate.

Nick thought about Cate and how fortunate he had been. All these years cemented between them. Had he ever really deserved her? They'd been two kids in college listening to Leonard Cohen at a coffee shop on Boylston Street, sitting among friends, and Nick had said if he was drafted he would travel to Canada. Cate said she liked colder weather and she would go, too. She was a Buddhist; he was an atheist. They got along just fine.

He'd finished smoking his pipe. He emptied the bowl and returned the pipe to his pocket, and wasn't that Cate he heard calling for him?

"Over here!" he yelled, but his voice was as weak as the rest of his body, and the very strain of it set him into a coughing fit. He could use some water. He could use something stronger. Cate would find him. She always did.

He continued to cough. She continued to

call for him. Her voice was getting closer. And then he saw her, about fifty yards away on the trail, walking toward him, the sun shining behind her through the branches, and if he believed in God and all that celestial afterlife, he'd swear she was an angel. She was his angel. He had grown sentimental over the years.

And he was her Saint Nicholas. He liked that.

"Over here!" he called again. This time his coughing subsided and she spotted him.

"I'm okay," he called out to her.

"What am I going to do with you, old man?" She had a bottle of water in one hand, and his pills in another.

He took the water bottle but swatted the pills away. "Don't need them," he said.

"Too late?"

"Yeah."

She sat beside him and laid her head on his shoulder. "I'm sorry," she said. "Was it a bad one?"

"I guess it was."

"Are you in pain?"

"Not anymore. Just tired."

"Want to sit here a little longer?"

"That would be nice."

And then, "Cate?"

"Hmm?"

"I'm going to miss you."

She was quiet and he hoped she wasn't crying.

"Say something," he said.

She sniffed and rubbed her nose. Her breathing deepened. "I'm going to miss you, Saint Nicholas."

He laid his right hand against the side of her face and stroked her skin, still smooth and soft after all these years.

"I was thinking about something today," Nick said. "And I need to talk to you about this. I need you to be okay with me talking to you. I was thinking about all of the victims, the hundreds and hundreds of victims."

And then Nick started to cry, and goddamn it if he didn't cry like a baby, and he dropped his hand from Cate's face, and she wrapped her arm around him.

"I'm going to die, Cate. And I'm okay with that. I really am. Because you're going to be there with me. When I go, it will be your face I'll see. Your voice I'll hear. I'm one of the lucky ones. But these girls, these women, all these victims, they left this world, they left their lives, with the face of a monster, a killer. His face was the last they saw. It was his voice that they heard. They died humiliated and terrified."

Cate sat forward. She turned toward Nick and cupped her hands over his bearded cheeks. "I want you to hear me. I want you to listen to me. You have to know you did everything you could. You're one of the good ones, Nick. You were always one of the good ones. You need to make peace with this."

And he knew, as he had known before, it wasn't just he who had given his life to these victims and families. It was Cate also. It was she who had been by his side in the night when the dreams came. Who had supported him through the hours and hours of work. Who had eaten alone and gone to bed alone when he'd been visiting crime scenes and working with detectives. It was she who had awoken by his side when he'd answered the phone at all hours of the night. And the phone still rang. Sometimes a reporter, a blogger, a curious bystander, family members and friends of the loved ones who'd been killed. Just that morning, there had been another call, a message from a young man named Jeffrey. He said he'd been a friend of Erin Parker. Maybe Nick would run a background check on him, like he'd done on Marian. Maybe he'd call the guy in the morning. Tonight he wanted to have that bourbon, cook a steak on the grill, and make love to his wife.

20
Present: August 2017

Marian
The Den, Montana

A little over five weeks had passed since Tate's death. It was the third Sunday in August. Trainer had cooked barbecue chicken and zucchini and baked potatoes on the grill. Marian had made a cheesecake and picked up a couple of bottles of chardonnay. It was just the three of them: Marian and Lyle and Trainer. Jenness wouldn't be back from Alaska for a couple more weeks. Liz and Dudley were still away on assignments. And the next day, Lyle would be catching a six a.m. flight to Seattle. He would be making one of his semiannual trips to the university, where he'd be in planning meetings the rest of the week.

They sat at the round glass table on the patio off the kitchen. The windows to the house were open and music was playing, an indie alternative band that Trainer had chosen. After Marian had finished eating and was on her second glass of wine, and the music had switched from soft rock to something acoustical, Lyle mentioned the northern spotted owl project in Oregon that would resume in four weeks. "I could use another handler," he said. "Might be time we put you back on an assignment." And he wanted to know what Marian thought about that, and she said that was the best idea she'd heard in a long time.

Ever since Marian's fitful run and the strange phone call Trainer had received from Dana Lear, she'd been keeping Yeti and Arkansas with her at night. She hadn't asked permission. She'd collect them from the barn after Trainer had let all the dogs out one last time, and return them in the morning before Trainer made his rounds. But that night after the dishes were done, Trainer said, "Go on and get your girls. I'm sure they're waiting for you."

Marian was surprised that Trainer knew, and her look said as much, and she asked if Lyle would mind.

"Lyle's got bigger things to worry about than you and a couple of dogs taking pleasure in each other's company."

Marian stopped by the barn and retrieved

Arkansas and Yeti. She was enjoying a good buzz and felt light-footed on the path up the hill, swinging the remaining half bottle of wine in her hand, the dogs trotting ahead of her toward her hut.

She punched in her key code, then let the dogs in and flicked on the light. She'd left her phone on her desk and saw an incoming call from Jeb.

"I was just checking in," he said, which he'd been faithfully doing each week ever since Tate had died.

And after small talk, and Jeb saying that Marian seemed to be in a good mood, and Marian saying she was, and her telling him about the northern spotted owl project, and wasn't that reason to celebrate, she poured wine into a mug and told Jeb to have a drink with her. And she asked him to read her something, because that was how their conversations always went, Jeb reading to her from an essay he'd written. The arrangement had begun a couple of weeks after Tate's death, when Marian was too sad to talk and wanted only to have someone else carry the conversation and bring her mind someplace new.

After Jeb had finished reading to her about agricultural runoff in an estuary along the central California coast, and he and Marian had discussed the contamination of flounder and sand crabs and other aquatic organisms, a text came in from Tammy: Are you still up? Can we talk? Marian texted Tammy back and said she would give her a call. And so she wrapped up her conversation with Jeb, who knew nothing about Marian's suspicions of Tate, and when she called Tammy she asked if everything was all right.

Tammy said she was doing okay, that she was just having a bad night of missing her brother.

"Tell me about the dogs," Tammy said. "Talk to me about the projects." And so Marian told her about Arkansas and Yeti, who were lying beside her on the bed, and about her upcoming assignment in Oregon. And then she told her about the other handlers and the projects they were on, because she understood Tammy's need to be distracted with the lives of people other than herself. After they'd been on the phone about a half hour or more, Tammy said, "Did I ever tell you about the night our mother died?"

Marian listened as Tammy talked about her mother's illness and her final days in hospice. "Tate was kind," Tammy said. "I remember thinking my brother is the kindest man I will ever know. And he had so much to take care of. He met with the social workers and the funeral home. He took care of the bills. And when our mother passed, we were sitting by her side, each of us holding one of her hands. I lost it," Tammy said. "Tate walked around the bed and took me in his arms. I must have cried for hours. He sat there and held me and told me we were going to be all right. I was a teenager, and he was just barely twenty, but he was the one looking after me. And that night, he helped one of the nurses bathe our mother's body, to prepare her for the crematorium. The hospice said it was custom to include the family, if there was a person close to the deceased who would like to help. Tate was so loving throughout everything, Marian. I don't know what I would have done without him."

Marian emailed Nick that night before turning in, and she told him about the things Tammy had said, because, despite her having learned of the green loaner vehicle, she did not see how the person whom Tammy had described could have taken the life of another. And these things were on her mind, because in her last video call with Nick, he'd said he didn't believe Tate had been capable of love. And he'd suggested that Marian had loved the way

Tate made her feel. "He would have made a good actor," Nick said. And yet Marian believed there had been glimpses of Tate that had been real, and might she have loved the man in those moments of truth, and might his behavior the night his mother died be another expression of that truth?

Marian awoke a little after five and couldn't fall back to sleep. Sometime in the night, she must have kicked the dogs off the bed, because they were curled up next to each other on the floor, watching her, and no doubt waiting to see if she was really awake. She rose and dressed quickly in a pair of jeans, a men's V-neck T-shirt, her canvas shoes, and her fleece jacket. Then she grabbed her laundry bag of dirty clothes. She headed down the hill, the dogs wagging their tails and running ahead of her, her feet slapping against the dry needle duff in the pre-twilight silence. She had a dull headache from the wine the night before, and her neck and shoulders were wound tight with a painful kink below her right ear.

After she brought the dogs back to their kennel in the barn, she headed over to the main house and set her clothes in the laundry room. She'd get to them later. She filled a glass of water at the kitchen sink and took a couple of Advil. Then she made enough coffee for her and Trainer to each have several cups. While she waited on the coffee, she stepped into the office off the kitchen and turned on the lamp. Lyle said he'd left her a file on the northern spotted owl project on his desk.

She looked through stacks of papers and reports and several metal file stands until she found the information on the owl project squeezed tight among other folders in one of the stands. Tucked behind the owl project material was a manila folder with large black lettering written across the body of the folder: *Add to Archives.* Inside the folder was a purple flash drive. Up until that moment it had not occurred to Marian that the Archives folder on the network wasn't complete, that files were still being uploaded. Did she dare get her hopes up? And yet she felt that jolt of adrenaline. One study, that was all she needed, to place Tate somewhere other than one of the scenes of the crimes, to give him an alibi. She booted Lyle's computer and entered his password. The desktop came up. Marian inserted the flash drive, double-clicked the icon, and waited for the files to appear. And there it was, the Yellowhead grizzly and black bear study. Tate was on that project. He'd said it was his favorite. "Pure God's country," he'd told her. The detection dogs had been part of a comprehensive monitoring program to examine the impacts of human disturbance on grizzly and black bear populations in the Yellowhead ecosystem. The project was conducted in two separate time periods, or tiers. The first began over six years ago in late spring. Three separate dog teams sampled a fifty-two-hundred-square-kilometer area between mid-May, the approximate time the bears would emerge from their dens, and July 31.

Erin Parker had disappeared that same year on July 21. Even if the job had ended a couple of weeks early, Marian had seen firsthand the amount of time and detail involved in closing a work site and packing up. She didn't see any way Tate could have made it to Stryker Ridge where Erin went missing, on the twenty-first. Marian found a yellow legal pad on Lyle's desk and flipped the pages over to a clean sheet. She picked up a pen. She couldn't jot the dates and information down fast enough.

And then there was the second tier of the study, two years after the first. Samples were collected from the same area during the bears' hyperphagia season, between the first of August and mid-October, the same year

Lynn-Marie Pontante had been killed, the young woman from Libby, Montana, who'd disappeared on September 18.

Marian felt euphoric. She raced through each word in the paper, searching for proof that Tate had been on those studies. There were five dog teams, and, as with the project in the oil sands, each team included a handler and an orienteer. And after she'd read through the paper's results and discussion, there it was, in the fine print under the acknowledgments, at the end of a long list of names, such as Evergreen Pet Supply for providing food, and Alaska Horizon Air, and Parks Canada, and the Wolf Education and Research Center for providing scat samples for dog training — there was the list of names of those who had assisted in all aspects of scat collection using detection dogs: M. Freeman, H. Smith, J. Hartman, S. Marlow, J. Ubigau, P. Coppolillo, A. Hurt, M. Parker, and among others, there was Tate — T. Mathias.

She leaned back in her chair, her heart pounding. "He didn't do this. My God, he didn't kill these women." She began scrolling through the rest of the files for the Yellowhead project. She stopped when she came to a folder titled Study Photos. Her body leaned forward again.

Three photos in, there he was, kneeling beside a chocolate Lab, a cap pulled down low over his forehead, brown hair in wavy tufts over his ears. The picture had been taken six years ago — the first year of the study. The photo had a descriptor tag, as did all the images. The dog's name was Cavalier. There were a few other pictures also: Tate and another man, whom the descriptor identified only as Tate's orienteer. They were walking down a rocky trail. A third photo showed Tate loading Cavalier into the back of his silver Xterra.

The gallery of photos from the follow-up study, two years later, also included images of Tate. He was with the same dog. Only this time he was working with a female orienteer: Jenness Cattet. Marian leaned in closer to the screen, her elbow next to the track pad, her chin on her fist. Jenness in olive green cargo pants, a man's flannel shirt, a blue knit cap, her long hair banded at the nape of her neck, her face tilted toward Tate, her smile broad. Tate laughing, his eyes almost closed. The dog between them.

In additional photos of Jenness, she was with another orienteer, Jamie Gabbey, a woman who looked to be in her mid-twenties. The woman was taller than Jenness, maybe around five feet, eight inches, with round, high cheeks and curly, shoulder-length hair the color of hewn pine. Marian remembered something Jenness had said, about she and the person she'd been involved with joining the program at the same time, but Jamie had wanted to farm and had moved to Iowa. It had not occurred to Marian that Jamie was a woman, that Jenness wasn't heterosexual. Jenness's sexuality wasn't something anyone had mentioned; why would they? Marian had been wrong, she realized, to think Jenness had been involved with Tate or was interested in him romantically, and she felt foolish for her petty jealousy.

The soft golden glow of dawn was coming in through the office window above the desk, and the motion light on the barn was on; she could see it if she leaned in over the desk and looked to the left through the window. Trainer would be in soon.

As if on a whim, Marian pulled up the Finder on Lyle's computer. She was thinking of other projects Tate had told her about, including the polar bear study in Norway when he'd first seen the northern lights. She'd not found anything about that study on the program's network, and the flash drive she'd just explored had only contained files on the grizzly and black bear project. She typed in *Norway* in the Finder's search option, thinking maybe she would find something on Lyle's hard drive. Several documents on the polar bear study in the Svalbard archipelago came up. Everything Tate had told her was true: the detonation wires, the guard dogs, the requirement that he carry a gun. The study had taken place from the first of December through February, over seven years ago. The network had only covered projects going back six years, and even those years hadn't been complete. Marian wrote down the specific dates of the project. Here it was, right in front of her. Natasha Freeman had disappeared outside Helena on December 9, the same year Tate would have been studying polar bears in the Arctic. On the night she was killed, Tate had been over four thousand miles away.

Marian closed the files. She ejected the flash drive and shut down Lyle's computer. She leaned back in the chair and folded her arms over herself as if she were cold. She stared at the notes she had written down. Her history with Tate was intact. Not perfect by miles and miles. He was not perfect. She was not perfect. They were both flawed, but they had made something.

The door to the mudroom opened and

closed. Marian heard the grunt and exhale of air as Trainer pulled off his boots, then his footsteps as he padded across the kitchen on his thick-socked feet.

He stood in the doorway to the office. "Morning, sunshine," he said. He asked her if she'd like a cup of coffee and she said that would be nice.

Most mornings after Trainer had finished taking care of the dogs, he would make something for breakfast, usually scrambled eggs and bacon, or French toast — some sort of meal that required more effort than pouring cereal into a bowl. Trainer didn't make breakfast right away that morning. Instead he pulled up a chair in the office and drank coffee with Marian and told her that the nights were getting colder and that there would be frost soon.

And Marian asked Trainer about a woman named Jamie Gabbey, and Trainer said that was one of Jenness's friends. "She stayed on for a while, then ended up moving someplace in the Midwest."

"Iowa," Marian said.

"That sounds about right."

Trainer asked Marian if she'd been following Jenness's posts, and Marian said she had, and he said, "That's some beautiful country." And Marian agreed and said she'd like to visit Alaska sometime.

The conversation lulled, and because Marian was still thinking about Tate, she said, “He was a good guy, wasn’t he?”

And Trainer said he supposed he was, and that some men were hard to get to know, and that he was glad Tate and Marian had gotten to know each other.

Then he went into the kitchen and got the pot of coffee, and brought it into the office and poured them each another cup. “There was this one Christmas,” Trainer said. “Lyle was away on a study. It was just Tate and me holding down the fort, and he goes off in the woods, calls me from somewhere up in the forest. Tells me he’s cut some tree down the size of Mount Kinney. Wants me to come help him bring it back to The Den. So I go driving up this road to find him. I’ve never been to Mount Kinney, but I swear this tree was that big. So that’s what we called it. And every Christmas after I’d ask him if we were going to put up another Mount Kinney.”

And Marian imagined the whole thing and asked if Tate and Trainer had decorated the tree.

“Naw, Tate had to take off, was going back to visit his sister. But the two of us, we made our own stand. Cut up some two-by-fours.

Sawed the trunk down until we could get the tree to stand up in the barn. Tate said it was really for the dogs anyway. Wanted them to have a nice Christmas."

Trainer told Marian he'd make her some breakfast, but she said she needed to exercise the dogs and would eat later. And by the way, she said, because she'd been meaning to bring it up, had Trainer been up to the huts on the hill lately, because she'd noticed Jenness's window was open and the screen was out. He said he'd look into it.

Marian tore out the piece of paper she'd been writing on, and flipped the other pages back over the pad, and that was when she saw the notes for the first time, in Trainer's handwriting. There was an address for the cabin where Tate had been staying in Cusick, Washington, a small town at the foothills of the Selkirk Mountains, along with a contact name and telephone number. There was also the address for the lab back in Seattle.

Marian held up the legal pad. "Trainer, what's this?"

He rubbed a hand over his fleshy face. "That's just something Lyle asked me to do."

"Asked you to do what?"

"Wants me to make a trip to Washington.

Says we still got samples in a freezer over there. Needs me to ship them out to the lab. Needs me to clear out some of Tate's things."

"I thought Tammy did that."

"We still got a crate up there and dog food. Things that belong to the program. Got a hunter who's going to be wanting his cabin back soon."

"I'm going," Marian said. "I'm making the trip. I can do all of that."

"Marian —"

"I'm going, Trainer. Besides, you need to stay here with the dogs."

"Now, Marian, that's just not happening."

"Why not?"

" 'Cause Lyle would have my ass over a pit of flaming coals, that's why."

"Lyle doesn't have to know. I can be back by tomorrow. I need to do this, Trainer. You know I need to do this."

And Trainer spent more time saying no and telling Marian that making that trip wasn't emotionally good for her. And Marian asked Trainer if he'd ever lost someone he'd loved, and he said he'd lost a friend or two, lost a cousin also. And Marian said, "I have to do this."

Trainer finally acquiesced and said, "Don't go getting any crazy ideas. You're just packing up some shit and shipping it out to the lab."

"That's right," Marian said. "I'm just going over there to pack up some shit and send it to Seattle." And then she tore off the piece of paper with the notes Trainer had scribbled down and put it in her back pocket with the other piece of paper.

Trainer told her there was an extra cooler and duct tape in the storage room in the barn. She'd need it for the samples. Then he shook his head and said he hoped he wasn't making a mistake. He reached for some papers on the edge of Lyle's desk and said, "You're going to need these." Marian tried to take the shipping form, along with the correct codes and packaging requirements from Trainer, and when she did, he held on to them a second longer. "Call me. I'll be right here," he said.

Marian knew it would take her almost five hours to get to the cabin in Cusick, which, if she hurried and got on the road, would put her there by early afternoon. It was crazy, when she thought about it, how many days she'd been in Tate's old vehicle, taking the dogs on a swim, or out for an afternoon of training, or even heading into town to run errands, and she'd get the impulse to head west on Highway 2 and cross over the Idaho Panhandle into Washington. Or nights when she couldn't sleep and she'd imagined leaving right then and arriving at first light. She'd known she'd eventually make the trip, hike to the place where Tate had last been.

Authorities had recovered Tate's phone and turned it over to Lyle. Marian had given him the passcode so that he could download Tate's final tracklog. Using the GIS, Lyle had created a map that showed Tate's transect his last day. Marian had printed a copy of the map, had tried to imagine his course, imagine the things Tate had seen. She retrieved the map from her desk drawer and put it into the small hip pack she always wore into the field. She'd already made up her mind that she would hike to the location where Tate's body had been found, and part of her wanted to camp there, unroll her sleeping bag, and lie beneath that same sky, as if in some way it would make her feel closer to Tate, and the night wind in those mountains would whisper in her ear and give her the answers to everything she wanted to know about Tate and that fateful day.

She would bring her camping supplies just in case and would make the decision once she got there. She brought her backcountry pack out of her closet and began loading it with gear: tent, headlamp, sleeping bag, hydration pack and water filter, stove, white fuel, first-aid kit, bear spray, and the only two dehydrated meals she had left: scrambled eggs and beef stroganoff. Last, she packed a few toiletries and an extra layer of clothing. She grabbed her wallet and keys and was preparing to leave when she thought of Jenness's gun. Trainer would be checking the window and screen. Perhaps he had access to Jenness's hut, as he'd had access to Marian's, and she couldn't remember if she had concealed the Glock in the heavy skeins of yarn, as it had been when she'd first found it. If Trainer saw the gun and reported it to Lyle, Jenness could at the very least be suspended from the program. The Den was university property. The same rules as those on any of the campuses applied.

Marian left her pack and climbed the hill to Jenness's hut. Trainer was right. The mornings were turning cold, despite the hot afternoons, and would be colder in the Selkirks. She hoped she'd packed enough layers for the colder temperatures.

She raised the window on the west side of Jenness's hut, and even before she was all the way inside, she glimpsed the black stock of the pistol in the basket. The yarn had gotten caught around the gun's trigger and the trigger guard. Marian untangled the yarn; she fitted the pistol in the pocket of her fleece jacket and zipped the pocket closed.

Knowing that the gun was in her pocket, in the process of climbing through the window opening, she rolled her body onto its other side and pulled herself forward, and when she did, her foot knocked against something on the table. Marian turned her head just in time to see the picture frame falling apart on the floor.

She slid into the hut once more and knelt on the floor to put everything back together, and after she'd reassembled the frame with the Alaskan image of Kesugi Ridge, she glanced up and her eyes caught something taped on the bottom of Jenness's desk. Marian placed the picture frame on the nightstand. Then she crouched lower and looked underneath the desk. Jenness had created a pocket out of duct tape and thin cardboard, and tucked inside that pocket was a blue file folder.

Marian pulled out the folder. It was full of newspaper articles from the Stillwater murders, and pages and pages of tracklogs, and notes written on the back of an envelope that looked like some kind of cryptic shorthand, and several photographs. Marian felt an ugly hollow in the pit of her stomach, and so much silence, she could hear the air traveling in and out of her lungs. She sank against the floor, the folder open in front of her. She picked up one of the photos, a picture of Jenness with another woman. Marian recognized the woman. Melissa Marsh. Marian had memorized each of the Stillwater victims' faces. She studied the photo: Jenness with her long braid along the side of her face, her threadbare jeans that cut below her hips, a snug tank top, her face tilted just enough that Marian could see in her eyes something tender and thoughtful and complicated and fragile. The two women were standing arm's length apart. Jenness's wrists hung loosely over Melissa's shoulders, her hands in a relaxed clasp behind the nape of Melissa's neck, her thumbs tucked into Melissa's short, messy, straight hair, deep brown, almost black. Melissa's hands held on to Jenness's small hips, her thumbs lifting the hem of Jenness's shirt enough for her fingers to spread over the dimpled curves at the base of Jenness's back. Trainer had said that Jenness had known one of the victims, and Marian had understood that he'd been referring to

Melissa Marsh, but he'd not said that the two women had been involved romantically.

In another photo, Melissa was facing forward, her chin tilted over her clavicle, her full lips pressed together, almost smiling, and those deep brown eyes looking back at the person behind the camera, with what — longing, hope.

The third photo — and this was the one that got to Marian, like a cold wind crawling over her skin and settling somewhere deep in her chest — was of Jenness and Melissa and Tate. Jenness and Melissa had their arms thrown over each other's shoulders. Tate was sitting next to Jenness, looking somewhere off to the side. The three of them appeared to be at a restaurant, sitting together at a long table. Tate knew her, Marian thought. Tate knew Melissa Marsh. But then she reminded herself that Tate hadn't been anywhere near the crime scenes when these women had disappeared. Still, she wondered why when she had told Tate about the pictures on Jenness's camera, he hadn't said anything about Jenness being a lesbian.

Marian set the photos aside and picked up one of the articles, published the year after Melissa had gone missing: *Bones identified as Melissa Marsh, third unsolved murder victim.* The article had been written by Ryan Schulman, the same reporter who'd been emailing Marian about the program. Marian had read all the articles on the Stillwater cases, but up until now she had not paid attention to any of the bylines. She picked up another article: Melissa's obituary.

And then the quiet changed and Marian was aware of noises from outside the hut — birds, small animals, a squirrel jumping from one branch to another and snapping a limb, perhaps — sounds that could be Trainer on his way to check on the window. Marian quickly collected the items and closed the folder. She picked it up and carried it with her to the window. Jenness had hidden these materials for a reason, and Marian wanted to know why. As long as Trainer didn't lock the window, Marian could return the folder before Jenness was back from Alaska. It all made sense to Marian in the moment. She climbed through the window, holding on to the folder in her right hand. And with the images from the photos fresh in her mind, she thought of Utah and Melissa's sister, Emily, and the final conversation she'd had with Tate on the phone.

21
July 2017

Marian
Nokai Dome Wilderness Unit, Utah

When Marian drove out of Whitefish, Montana, in a white, full-size Ford pickup with a cap over the bed that the program had rented, Emily Marsh, a recent graduate from Montana State University, was riding with her. And in the back were two dog crates with Arkansas and Yeti, a month's worth of dehydrated dog food, camping supplies and personal food and items, scat collection materials, and plenty of five-gallon containers of water. Not only had Lyle assigned Marian to the bighorn sheep study, he'd also wanted her to mentor Emily, who would be serving as Marian's orienteer. Emily, who had grown up in Columbia Falls, had been assisting another conservation group out of Bozeman while finishing her degree in animal science. She'd come to Lyle looking for a summer internship.

Marian and Emily would be car camping throughout the Nokai Dome Bureau of Land Management area, over one hundred thousand acres of some of the most remote and primitive land in Utah. Except for a few short backpacking trips, they would hike into their study cells each day from the vehicle to collect scat samples from desert bighorn sheep. The contract was through Utah's Division of Wildlife Resources for the purpose of studying the population and health of the Nokai Dome herd.

The two women drove a thousand miles over two days, and during that time they talked about everything from their majors in college to the geocaching club Marian had belonged to in high school, to favorite movies and favorite foods, and pets they'd had growing up, and the summer Emily had worked at a gift shop in the Grand Canyon. And somewhere outside Pocatello, Idaho, Marian asked Emily if she had any siblings.

Emily asked Marian if she'd ever heard of the Stillwater murders. And Marian said she had.

"One of the victims was my sister," Emily said. "She and Jenness were friends. That's how I first learned about the program."

Marian said how truly sorry she was, and she stared ahead at the blue car in front of them with the Ontario license plate, and at the irrigated field that ran along the right side of the interstate, transfixed and deeply sad by what Emily had told her.

When they stopped for a bite to eat, Emily showed Marian the picture of Melissa on her phone screen. "It's the last picture that was taken of her." Emily went on to tell Marian that she'd just gotten home from college for the summer. She'd spent the night at Melissa's apartment. That next morning Emily took the picture while her sister was in the kitchen making coffee.

"I don't know why I did that," she said. "But that morning was the last time I saw her."

"Your sister was really beautiful," Marian said, and she told Emily how sorry she was for her loss.

The Nokai Dome was divided into three units. Marian's team would be focusing on unit three, full of steep-walled canyons, mesas, and the Red House Cliffs escarpment.

But Marian wouldn't see any of this when they arrived because it had long been dark when they set up camp at the base of the

Red House Cliffs. They fed and watered the dogs, pitched their tents, and unrolled their camping mattresses and sleeping bags, the temperatures hovering around forty degrees, which was typical at this elevation in the desert, over six thousand feet, after the sun went down.

It was dark when they awoke, as it would be every morning; both women were slow to crawl out of their warm sleeping bags. Marian started a fire; they made coffee, ate oatmeal, and packed what they would need for their assignment. They would be working Arkansas that first day and would have to bring enough water for both them and the dog. The handlers didn't let the dogs carry their own food and water on a job; the work already demanded enough from the animals, and this rocky terrain with its steep pitches was no exception. Marian would also want to cover as much of the day's transects as they could before the hottest part of the afternoon, when temperatures were expected to rise to the low eighties. Without shade, not only would Arkansas be fully exposed to the sun, but the ground could also scorch her pads.

Marian and Emily extended a tarp from the back of the truck to provide shade for Yeti and left her with plenty of water. And as they headed out of camp for their first study cell and the sun started to rise, Marian felt a fresh awareness of the light and the burnt orange and deep salmon landscape, and the shades of blue and garnet and lavender, and as much as Marian enjoyed being alone, as much as she enjoyed pure solitude, she was glad to have someone witness what she was seeing for the first time.

Their study area that day would bc on the lowest shelf of the escarpment, which they would get to by scrambling up loose sandstone and rocky drainages. The shelf, or bench, was a perfect habitat for bighorn sheep, with its boulders and gnarly juniper and Mormon tea and sage. There was plenty of vegetation with the different grasses and sedges, and enough rocky interfaces to allow the sheep to remain hidden from predators, including cougar and coyotes and hunters. The width of this bench, which extended like a never-ending band, varied from about a hundred yards to a half mile or more, and in other places even up to a mile. It wasn't until three hours into the morning that they began to see some fresh sign, and Arkansas, who had almost lost interest, became excited once more.

By the afternoon they'd only found four

fresh samples. Marian and Emily each climbed onto separate boulders to take a break and eat a light lunch, and Arkansas, after lapping up her water from a collapsible bowl Marian had carried on her pack, stretched out beneath the branches of a juniper. And when Marian checked her phone to make sure it was still pairing with her GPS receiver, she switched it to cellular to see if she could get a signal and noticed she had a bar, and if she climbed higher, she thought, she might get a stronger reception. So she left Arkansas with Emily and climbed higher up the escarpment until two bars showed up on her phone, and then she sat amid the crumbling sandstone, and after sliding a foot or two and digging her heels in for leverage, she tried to reach Tate, who was on the study in the Selkirk Mountains of Washington, knowing she could at least leave a message.

She was surprised when he answered, not having realized this was his and Ranger's day off. He'd just gotten back from the small grocery, where he'd picked up a steak and some fresh corn.

Marian told him about the boulders and cliffs and the incredible colors, which, though he had seen this part of Utah before, she said maybe one day they could see together. And in the sun and dust, with Emily and Arkansas in sight, she told him about Emily's sister, careful that her voice would not carry. "I like her," Marian said about Emily. "It's nice having her with me."

Tate didn't respond, and Marian heard noise in the background as if he was moving things around, unpacking his groceries perhaps. She was disturbed by his reticence and asked him why he wasn't saying anything.

"I'm listening," was all he said. And so Marian continued, "I've been thinking about the victims and what you told me. You never said the name of the woman you found."

Tate said he didn't see why that mattered. And Marian said, "I was just wondering if you were the one who found Melissa." But Tate said he wasn't sure. And Marian said, how could he not be sure? And she heard the alarm in her voice and hoped Emily had not been in earshot.

Then Tate said, "Maybe these women had it coming to them. Did you ever think about that? Every day there are women making poor choices, putting themselves in danger. You two should be careful out there."

"I can't believe you're saying this." Marian's voice had risen a decibel. She said she had to go, in fact, maybe they shouldn't talk for a while. And Tate said, "Well, all right, then," and told her not to get eaten by any lions.

After those first few days, Marian and Emily traveled deeper into the Nokai, where the only vehicular access was by way of narrow, often washed-out roads of desert dirt and rocky debris. These deeply gullied roads led to old drill holes and drill pads, and if not navigated carefully, a vehicle might roll into one of the many arroyos or worse yet one of the steep canyons. There was no cell service, and though Marian carried a satellite phone that belonged to the program, handlers were only supposed to use the satphones for emergencies or to check in with Lyle each day and give him an idea of their next day's transect.

About a week into the study, after they had returned to camp and the dogs had been put to bed and the stars were as magnificent as any the two women had ever seen, Marian built a fire and laid a tarp on the ground, and she and Emily stretched out beside the fire as it hissed and popped, and they watched the night sky, and there were shooting stars, at least three that they saw.

Marian sat up and put more wood on the fire and stoked the flame.

Then Emily said, "She had this thing she used to say, my sister, about letting a place talk to you. About understanding a place and the qualities that make it what it is."

The new wood caught; the smoke changed directions as if the wind had shifted. Marian asked, "What was she like?"

Emily told Marian about her sister's way with animals, and her love for the mountains and glaciers. "She loved growing up where we did. She loved the summers she spent working in the park. She could cut down a tree and clear a trail and she wasn't any bigger than you are." And Emily told Marian about the way her sister would study a place and take it all in — the trees and rocks and streams and clouds.

"She was a really good artist," Emily went on to say. "She could draw anything. Especially birds. She did a lot of work with the Audubon Society in Kalispell. Snow geese were one of her favorites. She liked peregrine falcons, too. Really, any kind of bird. She would sit quiet in a place and study them. Then she would draw them for hours, over and over again, until she got every detail right."

Emily said her sister had been saving

money to buy some land she could put a small trailer on. "She just wanted to live around nature."

And in listening to Emily, Marian wrapped herself around the story of this young woman's sister, felt the words that Melissa had spoken, in the sky and the shadows and the colors that Marian knew awaited her come morning, listened to the qualities of this big, lonely space where she'd felt her bones warm from the dry desert sun, a warmth that agreed with her in ways humid places never had. Even now she felt the heat from the day still on her skin and in the ground beneath her, despite the cool night, and she felt a purpose in this simple and complex and beautiful moment that left Marian both hungry and full.

"Thank you for telling me about your sister," Marian said.

After nearly two weeks since arriving in Utah, and their water and food supply almost gone, Marian and Emily drove the sixty-five miles of mostly slow, graded-road travel to the small town of Blanding. They checked into a hotel and went out for a real dinner and bathed the dogs and returned calls and answered email. Marian had a text message from Tate: I guess the thrill is gone.

But there were no voice messages, so she would not have known if or when he had tried to call. And she didn't call him right away. Instead she waited until everything was done for the night and the truck had been packed, and then she went down to the lobby. But her call to Tate went to voice mail and because he had not left a message, she did not leave one either, and her irritation made her fully awake, so she sat at a desktop computer in the lobby's small business center and, out of curiosity, ran a search on Emily's sister.

Marian read through the articles on the Stillwater murders, including one that was written after the skeletal remains of Melissa's body had been found, by a man bear hunting, the article said, and she read posts online about Emily's sister, and a copy of the obituary that had appeared in the *Daily Inter Lake News* out of Kalispell, and another copy in the *Flathead Beacon.* And she felt completely unsettled, and suddenly worried that Emily might come down to the lobby and realize what Marian had been doing all of this time. And so Marian quit the browser and tried Tate again, and when he didn't answer, she kept trying to call, until she finally left a message: "Pick up your goddamn phone."

22
Present:
August 2017

Marian
U.S. Department of Fish and Wildlife, Idaho

As Marian drove to the cabin in Cusick, Washington, where Tate had stayed, and sipped black coffee from a travel mug, the elation she'd felt earlier that morning muted. And perhaps she was still thinking of red rocks and desert sheep, of Emily and Melissa Marsh, and of the last time she and Tate had spoken. Her grief was changing, she realized, and despite her fatigue from too many nights with little sleep, she felt stronger, as if she were no longer the victim of her own nostalgia.

On the drive, Marian had tried to reach Nick to tell him about the studies she'd found, to say Tate couldn't have been involved in the Stillwater murders. Nick hadn't answered, and she'd decided to call him again later, rather than leave a message.

She was crossing the Idaho panhandle when she saw a sign for Coeur d'Alene. She thought of Rick Waller, the coordinator for the Grizzly Bear Recovery Program and one of the wildlife managers who had investigated Tate's death. Waller worked out of Coeur d'Alene at the U.S. Fish and Wildlife office. Marian hadn't set out that morning as early as she'd hoped. Already she was going to have to wait and ship the samples out the next day; another delay wasn't going to matter. Waller's number was programmed into her phone. Marian gave him a call. His voice message said he was in the field but should be back in the office by two.

The first two weeks after Tate's death Marian had called Waller several times, as well as Mike Blais and Heidi Tevis, who worked for the Washington Department of Fish and Wildlife and had also worked on Tate's case. And yet with each call she'd been told these investigations take time, and that the bear responsible for Tate's attack had not been caught and identified.

Within a day or two after Tammy had signed the necessary paperwork to have Tate's body released, the DNA analysis of hair and saliva found on Tate's body and clothing came back from a lab in Bozeman, and yet there were no matches with any of the collared bears in the recovery program, nor did the DNA match that of the three grizzly bears the biologists had caught in snares that had been set near the fatality site. Within those first weeks after Tate's death, the wildlife investigators were still undecided regarding what had transpired that day. Had Tate surprised the grizzly, had the dog triggered a defensive response from the bear, or had the bear's behaviors been purely aggressive and predatory?

"You need to be patient," Lyle had told her. "And at some point you may have to accept the fact that we can never really know what happened." And Lyle had talked with all of the handlers, reminding them to take precautions when working in bear country. "Continue to make noise. Talk to the dogs. Be aware of your surroundings. Keep your bear spray within easy reach." But he also reminded handlers that this was an isolated incident, and that lightning was by far a greater threat to them.

When Marian arrived at Waller's office, she told him she was on her way to Cusick to pack up the samples Tate and Ranger had found, and did Waller have any new information; had they identified the bear?

Before Marian could say anything else,

Waller asked her how much she wanted to know, and she told him she wanted to know everything.

"You two were friends," he said.

"We were."

"You two were more than friends."

And Marian nodded.

He led her to a small conference room. He told her she could have a seat and that he needed to collect a few things.

When Waller returned he was carrying a file full of papers and a large brown paper bag, like a leaf bag, that had been folded over and sealed with packaging tape. He said he had a box in his office with reams of notes and paperwork from the investigation that had been assimilated into a twenty-two-page case review that the team had recently completed. Waller laid the folder on the table. "I'm going to ask your permission before I show you anything," he said.

"Okay."

Did she want to see the drawing of the crime scene? And so this was how it began, and every so often Waller would ask Marian if she wanted to continue, or he would ask her how she was doing. And Marian would reassure him that she had prepared herself, and that she wanted him to tell her everything he knew.

He set the drawing on the table and slid it toward her. The drawing was done by hand. Waller had constructed the diagram on three separate visits to the scene. The first thing Marian's eyes went to was the drawing of the body, face up. The right arm was bent and raised above the head. The left arm along with the torso had been partially covered with soil and debris, indicating that the bear had cached the body to continue feeding on it later. The torso had been opened ventrally. The left leg was bent slightly out to the side. The drawing noted that Tate was still wearing his daypack, which was beneath his torso. His hip pack, though not on him, had been cached with the body. Much of Tate's clothing had been torn from him. Different pieces had been found around the site and were identified in the drawing, as well as a water bottle that was about a third full, a can of bear spray that had been partially discharged, and Tate's phone.

The drawing also noted matted grass and broken branches in a path leading up to twelve meters from where the corpse was found. And despite the heavy rain the night before, the team identified two hind prints along that path, and a partial front print next to the body. All of these findings suggested that the body might have been dragged from where the attack occurred to the cache site.

The diagram was alarming and terrifying and made everything real, and it was all Marian could do to keep her composure. "What do you think happened?" she asked.

"We found Tate's prints and the dog's. I think they were working the area. I'd like to think it was a defensive attack, that they startled the bear."

Marian mentioned the noise that handlers and their dogs were always making. And Marian had examined the map of the area until her eyes had burned dry. There were no streams near the attack site. She'd checked the weather. There was no wind that day. The storm had not moved in until sometime after dark. There was nothing that would have absorbed the noise Tate and Ranger would have been making.

"I'd *like* to think it was a defensive attack," Waller said again. But he also acknowledged the disturbing fact that the body had been both eaten and cached, and that they had not found any carrion that the bear might have been protecting within two hundred meters of the site. These were indicators of a predatory attack. If the attack were defensive, meaning if the bear had been reacting to a perceived threat to either him or a carcass, the bear would have walked away without consuming the body.

He said at first they thought it could have been a fatal defensive attack by one bear, and a second bear may have scavenged the remains, but the DNA evidence only showed one individual bear species. Because the bear spray had been at least partially discharged and because there were bite marks to the right arm, along with bruising, the investigators believed Tate was conscious before the attack and had tried to defend himself. There was a knot on the back of Tate's head, confirmed by the coroner's report to be subcutaneous bleeding, which led the team to believe the bear had charged Tate, knocking him to the ground, where Tate had landed on his back and hit his head.

However, investigators were unable to determine at what point the body was consumed. Tate had been dead for at least twenty-four hours before the two game wardens found his remains. It was possible the bear had attacked and killed Tate and then returned later to consume the body.

"Could Ranger have incited the bear?" Marian asked.

Waller said anything was possible. "Without a witness, there's no way to know at what point the bear's behaviors became predatory," he said.

"And there was no sign of the dog."

"No." Waller went on to say that though a lot of dogs might bark at a bear, once the bear attacks, particularly a grizzly, most dogs will run in fear, and often back to the owner, which can get the human in trouble. Whether that happened, there was simply no way to know.

"Ranger could be anywhere."

"That's correct. There was no evidence at the scene that the dog had been attacked."

Marian realized that everyone back at The Den had just assumed Ranger had died in the attack also. They could at least hope now that the dog had gotten to safety. And yet Marian also knew that the bear wasn't Ranger's only threat. If wolves and cougars could reduce the caribou population down to near single digits, a dog could easily become prey without a human by its side. All of the dogs in the program had been microchipped. If Ranger had been found and taken to a shelter or a veterinary hospital, the program would have been notified.

Marian asked if the review was public record.

When Waller said it was, she asked if she could have a copy.

He was leaning back in his chair with his hand held to his chin. He watched Marian for a few seconds. She remained calm and looked at him straight on. He said he would make her a copy. Then he stood and walked out of the room.

About five minutes later he returned. He set the copy in front of her.

"How confident are you that you'll find the bear?" Marian asked.

"It's hard to say. We set snares around the area immediately following the attack. Out of the five bears we captured, three were grizzlies and none of them were a match. We also canvassed the area by helicopter but didn't have any sightings. We've notified conservation officers in British Columbia. Most likely our suspect got spooked with all of the smells and commotion and took off. By now that bear could be four hundred miles into Canada or Montana. Still, we'll keep the area closed a couple more weeks."

Marian knew that Waller and the others had worked hard to protect the bears and to bring the grizzly back. She was familiar with the Grizzly Bear Recovery Program. And yet in most incidents of a fatal bear attack, the animal was identified and euthanized, especially if the attack had been predatory.

Marian had done her research. She was aware of the increasing number of predatory attacks by both black and grizzly bears in recent years, as well as attacks in which the bodies had been consumed. A couple of them had taken place in Alaska. There were others that had occurred in Yellowstone. A woman in British Columbia had been attacked and killed in her yard by a black bear. DNA evidence showed that multiple bears had fed on her corpse. Conservation officers had set traps to identify all of the bears involved in the feeding and emphasized the threat bears posed to people once those bears had become habituated to human flesh.

The situation was similar with a case in Yellowstone in which a man was killed and cached by a grizzly. In that case investigators believed a sow and two cubs had collectively fed on the body, though there had been no clear indication whether the sow had been responsible for the fatal attack. The sow, already responsible for a defensive yet fatal attack on another person in the park within the same month, was captured and euthanized and her two cubs were relocated to a zoo. And there were other cases in which bears had acted as predators and fed on a human body, including an incident with a man camping outside the Yellowstone park boundaries. Marian knew that bears had a keener sense of smell than any other animal, three hundred times that of a bloodhound. A bear could detect its prey up to a mile away, and some scientists believed a bear could detect a carcass upwind from twenty miles away.

Wildlife managers were divisive when it came to the reasons behind this increase in predatory incidents. Some believed these behaviors were the result of declining food sources due to global warming. Waller didn't agree with that. He said, "These animals can adapt. If one food source is removed, they'll adapt to another in the wild, such as elk calves."

But Waller also acknowledged that "this isn't the parks" and said there were an estimated seven hundred to eight hundred grizzlies in Yellowstone alone. The grizzly population in the Selkirk recovery area, a twenty-two-hundred-square-mile ecosystem between British Columbia and parts of the three separate states, was around sixty, with that number equally divided between Canada and the United States. "They have plenty of habitat. Unless we're talking about a defensive attack, these bears would most likely walk away from something unknown to them."

"But not always," Marian said.

"Just as with people, we can't always predict a bear's behaviors," Waller said.

Waller went on to tell Marian that he believed the problem had a lot to do with information not getting out to people, or people not following the recommendations or taking those recommendations seriously. In each of the attacks, people knew they were in bear country. "And in the park fatalities," he said, "none of those people were carrying bear spray."

"What about Tate?" Marian asked.

"Only a third of the can had been expelled. Visibility was poor in the area. Either he surprised the bear or the bear surprised him. We believe he was knocked down by blunt force. He may not have even seen it coming. He could have tried to use the spray after the bear was already on him. And, aside from having the dog with him, he was hiking alone. In two of the recent park fatalities, like Tate, both men were hiking by themselves."

For a moment Marian thought about Jenness hiking and camping alone in Alaska. "The bear is still out there," Marian said.

"I know."

"He could be a threat to someone else."

Waller didn't say anything.

And then Marian asked, "Were you scared? When you and Blais and Tevis went in there?" Marian understood that a bear's instinct was to protect its cached kill.

"We brought a couple of game wardens with us. But yes, I was scared," Waller said. He and the others hadn't had a lot of time when they'd come upon the kill site — only a couple hours of daylight left that first day, and they were approaching prime feeding time for bears. Whichever bear had killed Tate would be returning to feed on its cached food supply. "We had to get in and out and get the body out of there as quickly as we could." Waller said they returned to the area over the next couple of days to finish collecting evidence and survey the scene.

Marian asked if there were pictures.

But Waller didn't think that was a good idea. "The body was at least forty percent consumed by the time we got there. It was an awful scene, Marian. It's not something you'd want to see."

"What about the bag?" Marian looked at the large paper bag next to Waller's chair.

Waller's eyes remained on Marian. "Tate's belongings," he said. "The items we found at the scene."

"May I see them?"

He reached for the bag that was on the floor beside him.

"I can release the items to you," he said. "The sister doesn't want them."

"You've closed the case."

"We brought the snares in a couple of weeks ago. As long as there are no other encounters, we'll open the area back up in a few more weeks. But a case like this is never really closed," he said. "We have the DNA. If there are any other incidents, we'll see if there's a match."

Marian thanked Waller for everything he and the others had done. She appreciated their work. She appreciated them putting their lives on the line. "I know you all are doing a good thing," she said.

She signed a release form for the items.

"You need to prepare yourself," he told her. "Make sure you want to do this. Don't look through the items until you're ready."

Marian put the report in her pack. The large paper bag was heavier than she'd realized.

"Do you need some help?"

"No. I got it." She picked it up and held it against her chest. She thanked Waller for talking with her. She carried the items out to the vehicle that Tate had driven on the day of his attack.

23
Present: August 2017

Marian
Cusick, Washington

Marian had arrived at the cabin in Cusick around five, having stopped in the town of Newport to pick up the key from the owner and to purchase dry ice for shipping the samples. Back in June, Marian had borrowed Trainer's truck and visited Tate at this same cabin before she'd left for Utah. Everything was just as she'd remembered it: the full-size bed in the corner, piled high with army blankets; the checkered sofa with torn cushions; the two-person dinette table next to the window; the wood stove and stack of firewood and five-gallon bucket of kindling; the small kitchenette; Ranger's crate and container of food in the corner next to the stove, and Marian felt that familiar aching lump in her chest when she saw Ranger's belongings. Though the miniature refrigerator had been cleaned out, there were still nonperishable food items in the cupboards, including tea and coffee.

Marian's grief felt smaller here. The cabin was cold, and Marian was alone, and everything seemed surreal, as if none of it — Tate, and Ranger, and her work in Alberta, and a handful of huts in a forest in Montana — had ever happened. Marian started a fire to take the chill out of the air. She made a cup of Earl Grey tea and then removed the report from her backpack and laid the document on the table. The report's heading read: *Fatality of Tate Mathias on July 14 from a bear attack in the Salmo-Priest Wilderness of the Colville National Forest.* The document, prepared by both federal and state personnel, provided a summary of the incident, the investigation, and the response. The report also presented photographs and detailed drawings of the area after the body had been removed. Much of the material Marian already knew: the call that Lyle made to the Pend Oreille county sheriff's office at 0600 hours the morning after Tate had failed to check in; the two game wardens from the Washington Department of Fish and Wildlife who responded to the call and began searching the area where Tate had planned to be working the day he'd failed to check in, as provided by Lyle; the discovery of Tate's remains at 1430 hours, including his belongings and identification; the subsequent investigation by three wildlife personnel who were dropped off by helicopter that same day, just south of the area of the fatality.

The review included a description of the body from the investigators, as well as the findings from the county coroner. Tate's clothing had been mostly removed; his face had been mauled, as had his right shoulder and left leg. There was some swelling on the back of his head, consistent with that of someone who had fallen backward. An estimated forty percent of his body had been consumed. His remaining flesh showed both puncture wounds and claw marks. There were areas of significant bruising on his right arm and hand and neck, indicative of wounds suffered while he was still alive. The coroner's conclusion was that Tate had died of severe injuries received during the attack. The additional wounds, including open fractures to his ribs, were made upon the bear's consumption of the body after Tate had died.

But there was also information in the review that Marian had not been familiar with, including two hikers on the Pacific Northwest Trail, which abutted the area

Tate had been working that week, who had seen Tate and a dog at approximately 0800 hours the morning of the attack. And on the following day, when the investigators revisited the scene, additional grizzly tracks were found, as well as scat, suggesting that the bear had returned to the cache site after the body had been removed.

For DNA purposes, bear hair and saliva were collected from Tate's body and pieces of his clothing. The DNA from the hair, saliva, and scat was all from the same male grizzly. And though no carrion was found in the area, the scat showed traces of not only human consumption but also that of an elk.

The amount of water and food found in Tate's daypack led investigators to believe that the attack had occurred sometime that morning. Further, a GPS receiver was also found in the top compartment of the pack. After the receiver's battery was charged, investigators were able to download the tracklog, which had recorded Tate's position every thirty seconds from 0630 hours till 1120 hours, at which time the receiver either stopped working or was not able to make a satellite connection due to the backpack being underneath Tate's body. Ranger's datatracker was never recovered.

The review went on to discuss the thirty-day trappings that took place following the attack, and the fifteen-day aerial reconnaissance. During the flights, there had been five grizzly bear sightings, and each of those bears was collared and did not have the same DNA as the bear responsible for the attack.

Marian had been looking over the report for the past couple of hours. Except for the small wall sconce that pivoted over the table, the light in the cabin had grown dim. She picked up the bag of Tate's belongings, which she had set in the chair across from her at the table, and carried it with her to the sofa. She turned on a floor lamp and sat on the worn-out cushions. Then she pulled her legs up onto the sofa and began removing the tape from the bag.

She turned the bag on its side and emptied the contents, including Tate's daypack, onto the floor. The royal blue pack had tears down the fabric and patches of crimson stains. Ranger's water dish was still attached to the outside by a silver carabiner. Marian unzipped the pack and went through its contents: Tate's first-aid kit; two water bottles, one still completely full; a plastic bag with energy bars; the plastic container that Marian knew had held Tate's uneaten lunch; another container of water, half full, which Tate had carried for Ranger; Tate's GPS receiver; a solar charger. Everything Marian could think of was there, except for his wallet, which the authorities had given to Tammy.

Tate's hip pack, a khaki color, had also been recovered. The clasp was still attached. The belt had been torn all the way through. The plastic bags and vials and samples Tate had collected that day were all there. The ball was not, and Marian imagined Tate having thrown the ball for Ranger, and Tate standing in the woods and entering data into his phone. The phone had been found on the ground and had no doubt been knocked from Tate's hands, or else he had dropped it when he'd gone for his bear spray. He was preoccupied, Marian thought. He never saw the bear coming.

The only other items were Tate's hiking shoes, a pair of wool socks, and Tate's brown leather belt. Marian set the recyclable items aside — the first-aid kit, water bottles, GPS, and charger. She did not want to hold on to the other items. She understood why Tammy had not wanted them either. She held the daypack upside down and shook it to make sure she had not missed anything. A bell jangled and fell onto the floor.

Marian picked up the small bell with the Velcro fastener and set it aside with the other items she would return to Lyle. The handlers usually carried extra bells for the dogs, should a bell come off while a dog was in the field, so she did not think anything of it. Marian put the bloodied items back into the bag, then carried the bag outside to the garbage bin. She gathered the other articles and put them in the front panel of her pack.

The bathroom to the cabin was in a separate building and was equipped with two showers and toilets and sinks and a washer and dryer, for hunters who would pay rent to pitch their tents on the cabin's property. The freezer where Tate had stored the samples was in a storage closet accessed from the outside of the bathhouse.

Marian grabbed her toiletries from her backpack and a clean set of clothes. She walked the fifty or so feet to the separate building, stripped out of her clothes, and stepped into the shower. There was a bottle of scent eliminator soap and shampoo that hunters used. The bottle had not been there when she'd visited in June, and Marian wondered how many other people had stayed at the cabin since Tate's attack.

After Marian dried off and dressed, she

went to set her towel on the washer. On the shelf above the washer and dryer was a container of scent-free detergent and dryer sheets. She remembered some of the literature Lyle had passed out following Tate's death. A number of bear behavior biologists believed people should avoid scented detergents, deodorants, soaps, and shampoos, even toothpaste and chewing gum, when heading into bear country. Marian had known to store her toiletries and food in a bear canister or hang those items out of reach of a bear should she be camping in bear habitat. But she had not thought about the effect the scent of her soap or toothpaste would have.

Marian turned on the second wall lamp by the kitchen sink and looked through the cabinets for something to eat. She tried not to think of Tate or the pasta they had prepared when she had visited, or the steak he said he'd bought, when she'd called him from the Nokai in Utah. She found a can of vegetable soup. She heated it on one of the two burners and ate it from the pan while standing at the counter. Marian washed the pan and spoon and put them away.

She put another log in the stove and stoked the flame. Then she pulled the file folder that she'd found in Jenness's hut from her pack. She opened it on the table. She set the photographs aside and picked up what felt like a small ream's worth of tracklogs. She looked over the data. It was collected four years ago, between August 2 and October 16. Waypoints had been recorded every thirty seconds, which meant Marian was looking at the tracklog of either an orienteer or a handler, as the dogs' waypoints were recorded every three seconds. The dates matched those for the grizzly and black bear study in the Yellowhead ecosystem of Alberta. Likewise, the waypoints matched those for the Rocky Mountains and foothills in southwestern Alberta. The data entries were becoming a blur. "What am I looking for?" she said.

She made a cup of coffee and then brought a pad of paper and a pen that she'd found in one of the kitchen drawers with her back to the table. She blew on the coffee, sipped it, and stared at the data. She had to make sense of this. Then she wrote down the individual dates for each section of data, and she realized that what she had in front of her was the schedule for one of the dog teams: three days on, one day off; four days on, two days off. The terrain was steep and difficult. The dogs were being given downtime to recuperate.

The silence in the cabin made the room feel enormous, cavernous — just Marian sipping her coffee, staring at data and dates, flipping over pages. And beneath those pages were the articles from the Stillwater murders. There was something important here, and she wasn't seeing it. Marian leaned back in her chair, the caffeine slowly taking effect. She continued to stare at the dates she'd written down. And then it hit her, a sudden jolt that made her sit up straighter. September 18, the date Lynn-Marie Pontante went missing. Whichever team this data belonged to had not worked on that day. Nor had that team worked the following day.

Marian picked up her phone. She looked up the distance between Banff, in southwestern Alberta, which would have been close to where the teams were staying, and Libby, Montana, and came up with a five-and-a-half-hour drive. Someone could have made the drive to Libby, could have abducted Lynn-Marie. Jenness had worked as Tate's orienteer on the study. These records had to belong to either Jenness or Tate. But Marian had already ruled Tate out; he could not have committed these crimes, she tried to reassure herself.

Despite the coffee, Marian felt unable to concentrate, as if she could no longer lock onto anything specific and clear. She set the tracklog aside. She laid the articles out in front of her. She picked them up one at a time and read through them. The last article she read was Melissa's obituary. She was twenty-seven years old. She had grown up in Columbia Falls, had spent five summers working on trail crews in Glacier National Park. She volunteered with Dawn of the Wild, a wildlife rehabilitation center for birds, and the Audubon Society out of Kalispell, and was working as a veterinary technician with Timber Line Animal Hospital. She was survived by her parents, a brother, a sister, grandparents, and aunts and uncles and cousins.

Marian picked up the photo of Melissa and Jenness and Tate. She thought back to the day she'd spent with Tate on the mock wolverine study in the Cabinet Mountains, when they'd been walking in the woods and he'd told her about the artist girl, but had said *the bird girl* would have been more apt. She'd volunteered for the Audubon Society, Tate had said. And the air in Marian's lungs suddenly felt solid, as if she couldn't breathe, because she felt certain that Tate had been referring to Melissa. She remembered Emily talking about her sister and how much she had loved birds and what a remarkable artist she was. Tate had said the same thing about the artist girl. And yet Tate hadn't mentioned that she was one of the Stillwater victims, and Marian wondered why he had withheld that information. Nor had he said anything about knowing Melissa when Marian had called him from Utah and told him about Emily, Melissa's younger sister, or when Marian had specifically asked Tate if Melissa's body was the one he had found. Again Marian looked at the photo of Melissa with Jenness and Tate. "What were you hiding from me?" she said.

Marian sifted the envelope out from among the articles and data-log. On the back of the envelope were notes in Jenness's handwriting. The number *18* had been written down and underlined. Below that was *5/19,* the date Melissa had gone missing. A telephone number was also written on the envelope, along with the initials *R. S.* The notes appeared to Marian as if they'd been jotted down while Jenness had been talking with someone on the phone. Marian ran a reverse telephone number search. The number belonged to a cellular device in Montana. She hesitated for a couple of seconds, then dialed the number. The call went to voice mail: *You've reached Ryan Schulman, reporter for the* Daily Inter Lake News. *Leave your name and the nature of your call, and I'll get back with you.* Marian had been holding her breath. Quickly, she ended the call. She set the phone down and picked up the article about the search for Erin Parker with Ryan Schulman's byline, and another article about Melissa Marsh's disappearance.

Marian collected the materials back into the folder. She felt unsettled and something akin to fear, and maybe it was because nighttime was upon her, and the cold dark outside the window had muted her spirit and reminded her of shadows. She used the bathroom at the bathhouse one last time, and even the gritty sound of her footsteps in the hard-packed gravel unnerved her.

The cabin was almost too warm when she returned. She would let the fire burn down. She unrolled her sleeping bag on the bed and crawled in. She felt wide awake and wished she had something to read other than the case report. She also wished one of the dogs were with her. As she lay there, she thought about her visit that past June, the last time she'd seen Tate, her memories bittersweet.

In one of her conversations with Nick, he

had asked her if she was ever afraid of Tate. She'd told him about the afternoon in the Cabinet Mountains, though she had also acknowledged that upon looking back she was sure she'd overreacted. There was something mysterious and almost haunting when standing alone in a place as wild as the Cabinets, when all visibility is lost in the dense woods and you realize how truly vulnerable you are. But she had not told Nick about her second night at this cabin, the last night she would ever spend with Tate, and even now she wasn't sure if he was dreaming or he was awake, because he'd seemed to be suspended in another level of consciousness.

Marian had gotten up at some point in the night to use the bathroom, and when Arkansas had seen her, she, too, had stirred as if she needed to go out, and so Marian brought her along. When she returned, Tate was sitting up in the bed. He wasn't propped up on his pillows. He wasn't leaning against the headboard; he was just sitting up staring straight ahead. Marian had used the flashlight on her phone when she'd gotten up, and though she was not shining the light directly on Tate, she could see his face, smooth and empty, and that glazed-over look in his eyes, as if his picture had just been taken and a flash had gone off in front of him and he hadn't been expecting it. She asked him if something was wrong, and he'd asked her why she would think something was wrong.

And she said, "Because you have a different look on your face. Are you sure you're okay?"

He seemed agitated then. His voice became pressured. "Different and weird are the same. It must have been a weird look. Is weird normal?" he asked.

And Marian said, "No, I guess not."

"If it's different, then it's not normal, not the normal look, so weird and normal must be the same."

Tate lay back down. He turned his back to Marian. "Sometimes it's hard to struggle. It's hard not to struggle," he said.

And the rest of the night, though they lay side by side, their bodies didn't touch, as if Marian could feel a draft wedged between them.

The morning after Marian had gone through Tate's belongings, she woke early, the cabin still dark. More than anything she missed Arkansas and Yeti and Winter. She even missed Trainer. She rolled up her sleeping bag, fit it in the bottom compartment of her pack, and set the pack in the vehicle. She loaded the crate and dog food and a box of miscellaneous supplies — marking tape, an extra halter for Ranger, dog treats. Then she took out the cooler with the dry ice and unlocked the outside storage closet so that she could access the freezer. Tammy had already returned the vials to Lyle, who had sent them to the lab. Marian was simply here to pack up the frozen samples, golf-ball-size sections of the scat, each mushed together and somewhat flattened to mix the hormones.

Marian was surprised by the amount of meat in the freezer, in addition to the scat samples, and almost laughed at the idea of it, of food being stored with a bunch of crap. There were all kinds of elk and deer meat that had been processed and packaged, and Marian wondered if Tate had helped himself to any of it while he'd been there.

Marian packed up a couple hundred samples of elk, deer, wolf, and some caribou. Tate had definitely done his work on the study. She taped up the cooler and attached the necessary paperwork in a clear plastic envelope, along with the address label. She then locked up the cabin and left the key beneath the geranium pot along the side of the structure, per the owner's instructions, and drove the hour north to the post office in Metaline Falls. She picked up breakfast and a coffee and ate in the vehicle, while waiting for the post office to open. And while she waited, she checked her emails. There was another message from Ryan Schulman. His questions were becoming increasingly personal. In his last email he'd wanted to know how people in her line of work managed a relationship and if she, herself, had a boyfriend. She'd hesitated briefly, thinking his question was intrusive, but then she told herself he was only doing his job, and so she answered, letting him know that her boyfriend had been killed by a grizzly, that maybe Schulman had heard about the incident, and that relationships could be hard. This time the reporter wanted to know what her grief looked like. *Are you lonely?* he asked, and *How do you spend your days and nights now that your boyfriend is gone?* And this time Marian was indeed uncomfortable by the personal nature of his questions and found it odd that he had not offered her his condolences. She was also curious about Schulman's contact with Jenness. Sure, he could have been communicating with Jenness about the program, in the same way that he'd been emailing Marian, but why had Jenness kept his number in a folder that seemed dedicated to the Stillwater cases?

The post office had just opened and Marian was in a hurry. She'd deal with Schulman later. She carried the cooler inside and shipped it off. Then she took Forest Service roads to the Crowell Ridge trailhead along the western edge of the Salmo-Priest Wilderness.

24
Present: August 2017

Nick Shepard
Bonners Ferry, Idaho

Nick was scheduled for his three-month MRI, followed by a checkup with his oncologist. Cate would take time off from work and drive him on these days, and Nick would try and act like it wasn't a big deal.

But this time the oncologist wasn't all smiles when he walked into the examining room. He sat at the desk and pulled up the images on a monitor. He pointed to pictures of Nick's brain matter, even though it all looked the same to Nick. Bottom line, the cancer was growing. It would soon metastasize to different parts of the brain. How aggressively the cancer would spread, the doctor couldn't say, nor could he say how much time Nick had left. Six weeks, three months. And the doctor was sorry, so very sorry, he said.

"It's okay, Doc. I've had a good run of it."

Cate held Nick's hand and rubbed her thumb back and forth over his fingers. "What about another surgery?" Cate asked the doctor.

Nick already knew the answer, and he was sure Cate did as well. Surgery was too risky. It would leave him a quadriplegic at best, and that was if he pulled through.

The doctor mentioned palliative care. He said steroids could be provided to reduce inflammation. He would give them a prescription for morphine should Nick experience pain.

Then the doctor asked if they had considered hospice. And Cate said they had not. She would take a leave from work. She could take care of Nick at home. There were visiting nurses who could help. She would make sure he was comfortable, but he needed to be able to see the trees, and the deer that would feed in the field in front of their house, and hear the birds outside their window.

"And Nick, there's one more thing," the doctor said. "You shouldn't be driving anymore. Your peripheral vision won't be the same and you'll be at a greater risk for seizures."

When they left the doctor's office, a harpist was taking song requests in the waiting area. Nick turned to Cate. "I wonder if she's ever heard of the Bee Gees. We should ask her to play 'Staying Alive.' "

That night, after they'd called their son and spoken to their granddaughters, and eaten very little for dinner, and held each other, and Cate had cried, they lay in bed and played a word game, to keep Nick's existing brain cells sharp and to take their minds off Nick's prognosis. This particular game carried them through the alphabet, where they took turns coming up with a country that began with whichever letter they were on: Argentina, Belgium, Canada, Denmark, and so on. And, as with the nights before, Cate began to sound drowsy, and neither she nor Nick could come up with a country for *X,* so they skipped to *Y.* Cate said, "Yemen." Nick said, "Zimbabwe." After a couple of minutes he heard Cate's heavy breathing. "Are you asleep?" he asked her, but she didn't respond.

Nick went back to the beginning of the alphabet. This time he changed the game. For each letter, instead of a country, he spoke a victim's name: "Amber, Bearnice, Christina, Dawn, Erin, Frances, Gael, Heidi, Ilene, JonBenet, Kathy, Lynn-Marie." Then he got to the letter *M,* and instead of

Michaela or Mary or Maura or Melissa, Nick said, "Marian."

He'd developed an affection for the girl these past few weeks but was also becoming increasingly troubled, his sleep more disturbed. Marian possessed the same traits as the Stillwater victims; there was no question about it. She was trusting and loyal. She was benevolent and kind. Natasha Freeman worked with children; Erin Parker volunteered at an animal shelter; Lynn-Marie took care of geriatric horses; Melissa Marsh rehabilitated injured birds; Marian worked with shelter dogs in an effort to protect endangered or threatened wildlife. And there was something about the innocence of each of these women that had remained intact, as well as a belief each held in the good of others.

The women were also primarily loners. They'd built lives outside the mainstream. And each possessed a streak of bravery. At eighteen years old, Natasha had left everything familiar to her and driven across the country to meet a cowboy and make a new life. Erin Parker had ventured out west with the remote hope of meeting a father she had never known. Lynn-Marie had left her family and her plans for college to live alone in a yurt surrounded by pastures. Melissa had cleared trails in some of the steepest mountain terrain in this country. Marian's life had taken the shape of a conservation gypsy. With the Stillwater victims, Nick believed the young women's bravery mixed with their trusting nature had been a deadly combination. Nick was certain that none of these women had exhibited fear initially when the killer had come in contact with her. Natasha had no doubt appeared grateful and empathic, afraid of turning the killer down or hurting his feelings. Lynn-Marie and Melissa would have demonstrated empathy, as well. Nick had spent hours imagining the spiel the killer had put over on Melissa — he had an injured dog at home; a mutual friend of theirs was in danger. Any number of scenarios would have worked with her. Nick remembered one case where a ten-year-old girl was home alone shooting baskets in her driveway. A stranger pulled into the driveway and told the girl her mother had been in a car accident and he'd come to take the girl to her. The girl's lifeless body was found behind an abandoned property three weeks later. In that case, the killer was apprehended and confessed to the crime.

As with the ten-year-old girl, the Stillwater victims were transparent. The killer would have easily interpreted their body language, the inflection in their voices. Marian was no different. Tate had read her like a traffic sign.

A growing amount of evidence was beginning to stack against Tate in regard to the Stillwater murders. Granted, some of that evidence was soft, but lately the very mention of Tate's name was sending Nick's body temperature down a few notches. Working from memory, Nick reviewed what he had so far. First, Tate fit Nick's profile of the killer. It was uncanny, really. Then there was the green loaner vehicle that Tate had been driving the day Melissa Marsh disappeared.

Tate's treatment of his mother's body had also caught Nick's attention. Nick thought of an earlier case he had worked in which he had been called to the scene of the crime. Nick had been struck by the postmortem treatment of the body. It was something so minor police had overlooked it. Nick was taken with the way the twigs and branches had been laid over the corpse. Police thought the debris was for the purpose of concealing the body. Nick saw a pattern that reminded him of the Russian Orthodox cross. Police had been able to home in on a suspect of Polish descent who belonged to the Russian Orthodox Church.

In each of the Stillwater murders, the victims' bodies had been found unclothed and beside a stream. Tate's mother had died in a hospice. She'd had stage four breast cancer. A practice of the hospice was to bathe the body of the deceased before it was picked up for embalming or cremation, a ritual that was performed by the nurses and often a family member. Tate had been his mother's next of kin and had assisted the nurses in bathing his mother's body. Because the bodies of each of the Stillwater victims were found unclothed and by a stream, Nick believed the killer may have performed a similar ritual.

Then there was the call from Jeffrey Garrett, who had been a friend of Erin Parker's. He'd wanted to know if there were any new leads on the case. He'd reached out to Nick because the detectives had not gotten back to him. Six years had passed since Erin's death, but her murder was still fresh on this young man's mind. He'd given a ring to Erin before she had moved away from Arkansas and was curious if the ring had ever been found. And in that second of the conversation, an idea had hit Nick as if it had been dropped down from the clouds. "Can you recall if Erin was a nail biter?" Nick had asked. And Jeffrey had said, yes, she was, and that she was terribly self-conscious of her hands.

Erin's hands had been severed at the wrists. No one, to Nick's knowledge, in the course of the investigation had mentioned that Erin had been a nail biter. And yet Tate had included that detail in his description of the body he'd presumably found.

After speaking with Jeffrey, Nick had revisited his notes. He'd believed there had been a struggle between Erin Parker and her assailant. And maybe there *was* a struggle. Erin was a good size, five-nine or five-ten. Nick had determined that she'd scratched her killer and in doing so had trapped the killer's DNA beneath her fingernails. But with this new information Nick was drawing an even more startling conclusion: Erin's hands weren't severed because of the perp's DNA; they were severed because her killer was repulsed by the sight of her fingers. Cutting off her hands had brought him some kind of twisted pleasure. And it had given him power over the victim. He'd been able to punish her for what he saw as a weakness.

And yet, despite all of these things, there was something Nick couldn't get out of his mind. He'd asked Marian if she could recall any times when Tate had seemed cold, indifferent. She told him about a couple of comments Tate had made, one in which Tate had shown disregard for the victims of natural disasters. In another comment, Nick was reminded of his profile of the killer. He'd said that the killer would go so far as to blame the victim for her own fate. The killer would be of the mind-set that if this person weren't a woman, these things wouldn't be happening to her. In one of Tate's conversations with Marian, he'd implied that the Stillwater victims were responsible for what had happened to them because of their poor choices.

As Nick lay in bed next to his wife, though the cancer had no doubt dulled his mind, he felt a sickening clarity. Tate had been able to hold it together most of the time, to deliver a grand performance, to pull off his lies and deceit. Nick was convinced that Tate's supposed empathy was nothing more than a charade, a tool he'd developed by closely observing others and mimicking their behaviors. But there were those few glimpses Tate had given Marian where his walls had come down. Nick shivered against the warmth from his wife's body, against the down of the comforter that lay over them. *My God,* he thought. Tate was a fucking psychopath. No longer was Tate simply a person of interest or a likely candidate in Nick's mind. He'd become Nick's number one suspect. And Nick couldn't shake the feeling, the god-awful knowing that if Tate were still alive, Marian would have been his next victim.

25
Present: August 2017

Marian
Selkirk Mountains, Washington

Marian had brought her GPS receiver and paired it with her phone, where she'd entered the waypoints for the site where Tate's body had been found. She'd already hiked over seven miles through rich forests of hemlock, cedar, larch, and subalpine fir. At times her visibility was almost zero, particularly as she began the hike through dense pockets of virgin alder. In some ways the area felt wilder to her than the Cabinets, but she was also aware that she was bringing a different experience to these parts. She was bringing with her the knowledge of what had happened to Tate, and unlike her day with Tate, this time she was truly alone. She ascended about three thousand feet in elevation where thousand-year-old cedars pierced a clear azure sky. And as she stood on the northeast-to-southwest ridge on the

Idaho side of the wilderness and the wind kicked up around her, tossing the mountain air in her face, she felt a sense of the wildlife: the cougars and bobcats and gray wolves and coyotes; the elk and deer and martens and lynx; the black bear and grizzly bear; and the only woodland caribou herd in the lower forty-eight.

It wasn't until she reached the Pacific Northwest Trail, which crossed the wilderness, that she saw her first group of hikers, three thru-hikers whom she walked with for about a mile before she turned south from the trail and came across her first posting: *Warning! Due to Bear Danger, Area Beyond This Sign Closed.*

Marian had met with Waller; she'd read the review of the attack, which had included the autopsy report; she'd held Tate's bloody belongings in her hands; and yet, it was as if none of it had really sunk in until she saw this sign, this warning, as a result of Tate's death. He had been here, in this area, and his presence felt palpable and so different from whatever presence he'd left behind at the cabin. All the knowledge she now held of his passing seemed to coat her airways like sand. She'd just emerged from the lush areas of forest that received over fifty inches of precipitation a year, where a person was lucky if she could see three feet in front of her, much less be aware of a grizzly.

Make noise, she reminded herself. A holster of bear spray hung from each hip. She removed one of the canisters, slid its safety valve lever to the side, and held it in her right hand. As when working a study, she'd brought her GPS receiver and paired it with her phone, which was opened to the app that showed Tate's last route. And she sang off-key to a bunch of Beach Boys songs that she'd grown up listening to her dad play over his turntable and speakers.

Three more miles and she was in the thick of the southern portion of the wilderness, the forest floor a mosaic of green hues, and all around her towering trees of dark evergreen. There was plenty of moose sign and some elk and the occasional deer, and she wondered if any of these droppings were targets Ranger had come upon. Though she saw bear scat, it did not look fresh. Even so, she sang louder.

Marian had considered the dangers before making this hike. But the snares had been removed. The signs were going to come down. There had not been any other bear encounters. Never before had there been an attack by a black bear or grizzly in this wilderness. Marian absorbed the scenery around her and thought about the contrast between Washington's northeastern rain forest, where she was now, and the vast rocky spaces of Utah's desert: the forest's lush blueberry and huckleberry shrubs and lichen and grand fir, and the desert's stonecrop and evening primrose and cacti and yucca and Indian ricegrass.

But she wasn't in Utah. She was here, in this wild space, lured by fear and mystery in a similar way to how her grief had lured her deeper into Tate's world. And yet was it really the loss of Tate that had anchored her back to him, or was it all the things she could never know? Even when he had been loving her, his love had felt elusive, his arms a ghost at times, and perhaps that elusiveness had drawn her closer to him, like a hunger for something that wasn't there, and if she kept digging deeper, if she loved him more she would find it. And how real is something that is always just out of reach, a mirage that one never gets to, a distance one travels until she is so far gone she doesn't know how to find her way back to the person she was or to a world that exists without him, to a place that is all her own.

And because she was looking at the different plant species and thinking so many thoughts, maybe she had forgotten to keep singing. A branch broke and then another. There he was, standing so regal, parallel to her, about fifty feet away, his coat light gray, almost brown, like velvet; his chest white; his face and legs as dark as chocolate; his massive rack curved backward. He had to weigh at least six hundred pounds. And Marian stood so still, and when she finally breathed, she let the air out slowly so as not to make a sound. She was looking at one of the twelve remaining woodland mountain caribou in the lower states, and one of the forty woodland mountain caribou in the world. In that very moment Marian was witnessing one of the gray ghosts, powerful and fragile and beautiful, an ecosystem species that within a few years might no longer be around.

He turned toward her, a second of eye contact that felt like eternity, and then with all the grace in the world, he walked away, disappearing into the old-growth forest. Marian remained where she was, her body still, her feet rooted to the ground, and for the first time since arriving in Washington, she cried.

Marian did not travel the remaining mile to the scene of Tate's attack. She returned to the trail in the direction from which she had come, and continued to follow it to the western edge of the wilderness, where the trail eventually looped around to a trailhead on Mill Pond. Marian had hiked sixteen miles. The sun would be setting in a couple of hours. And there were other hikers returning to their vehicles, and one of them asked her if she'd seen any bear, and Marian said she hadn't. Another hiker talked about the warning signs that had been posted and that someone had died from a grizzly attack sometime in July, and Marian said, yes, and what a terrible thing. There were two female hikers who were getting into an SUV with an Idaho license plate. Marian asked them if they would mind giving her a lift to the Crowell trailhead, and they said they'd be happy to give her a ride.

26
Present: August 2017

Marian
Libby, Montana

It was after nine o'clock when Marian pulled into Libby, Montana, and stopped at a convenience store to refuel. After she put gas in the vehicle, she parked in front of the store and went inside to buy coffee. She sipped on the coffee while she waited in line to pay, and on the wall beside the checkout counter was a bulletin board with community announcements and business cards and a pair of lost-and-found mittens that looked small enough to have belonged to a child. As her eyes lingered on the bulletin board, she caught the upper-third edge of one of the flyers because it bore the name of Lynn-Marie Pontante, the third victim in the Stillwater murders.

Marian paid for the coffee and walked over to the bulletin board. She repositioned a couple of the business cards and an advertisement for a potluck dinner so that she could see the notice better. The shoulders-up picture of the young woman holding on to the halter of a horse had faded. Lynn-Marie had dark blond hair pulled back in a ponytail. She was last seen wearing a long-sleeve white shirt with blue jeans and cowboy boots. The flyer asked for any leads into Lynn-Marie's disappearance, and Marian realized the notice had been placed almost four years ago, before Lynn-Marie's body had been found.

Marian walked outside, the night laced with the chill of fall. She got back into her vehicle. She checked her phone before leaving and saw that she had another email from Ryan Schulman. This time he wanted to know what her schedule looked like the following day. Would she be taking the dogs on a run, and if so, perhaps he could observe her. And he reminded her that all of this was to help him build a picture of a day in the life of a handler at The Den. Marian emailed him that she might be taking the dogs for a run, and that she should probably clear his request with Lyle.

Once Marian was back on the highway, she thought about horses and a girl she had known in Michigan who'd been thrown from a young gelding and who had not walked the same since. And then Marian thought about other things, such as the cost of feeding a horse versus feeding a dog, and she tried to come up with a ratio of an animal's weight per its helping of food, because she did not want to keep thinking of the image of Lynn-Marie Pontante.

She was about twenty minutes outside Libby, the road ahead as dark and bleak as one of the great lakes, when a deer jumped in front of her, and Marian slammed on her brakes and instantly made impact. Marian pulled the SUV onto the wide right shoulder and turned on her hazard lights. She shut off the engine and switched on the flashlight on her phone. She then climbed out of her vehicle and with the small beam of light discovered some blood and fur from a deer on her left fender, though she did not see a carcass. Marian worried about the animal's injuries, and then in the silence of the highway, she heard movement in the woods and the braying of a deer, and thrashing.

Marian left her vehicle and ventured up the embankment and through the trees toward the sound, and upon shining the flashlight on the ground she was able to pick up the deer's blood trail. As Marian continued to follow the blood trail, the thrashing ceased and the deer became quiet. Then, about a hundred feet from the vehicle, the woods opened up to a small clearing and some old fencing, and caught in the barbed wire was the injured deer, whose eyes were wide and staring back at Marian.

"It's okay," Marian said. "I'm here to help you." Marian would need to report the accident, she knew. She would contact the Lincoln County sheriff's department, and from there someone would most likely reach out to Montana's Department of Fish, Wildlife and Parks. The deer's injuries from the vehicle did not appear serious, but the more afraid the deer became, the more danger she would cause herself by lashing about, and what if the deer had suffered internal bleeding?

Marian continued to speak softly as she backed away. "You're going to be okay. I'm going to get you help." She then walked the rest of the way to the vehicle and around to the driver's side. When she opened the door and the overhead light came on, she noticed the passport that had no doubt slid out from underneath the seat when she'd slammed on her brakes. She thought about the days Tate had spent going back and forth across the border on the caribou and wolf study that had spanned all of the Selkirk range in Washington as well as into British Columbia and parts of northwestern Idaho.

She set the passport aside. She would look at it later. She first needed to contact someone about the deer and hoped she could get a signal. She opened her phone and was glad to see she had a couple of bars. She contacted the sheriff's department and estimated her location, as she did not have an exact mile marker. The dispatcher let her know that a deputy would be there shortly. Marian said she would wait so that she could lead the deputy to the injured animal.

She sat back in her seat and picked up the passport. She opened it to Tate's picture. She did not recall ever having seen a picture of him without his beard. The picture was almost ten years old, as the passport was just shy of being expired. She thumbed through the rest of the pages and looked at the stamps: Nepal, Zambia, Cambodia. She was familiar with the studies from these countries. Nepal involved a pangolin habitat study. With the Zambia project, the dogs had searched for poaching contraband along roads and in villages. Cambodia was the Indochinese tiger project through the World Wildlife Fund. And yet, as she got to the last stamped page for Brazil, where Tate and Dudley had studied the health and population of the maned wolf, a wild canid found in the grasslands of central South America, she felt unsettled by a nagging sensation that something was amiss. She went back to the first few pages of the passport, to a trip Tate had made to Patagonia. This time she turned each page carefully, to make sure she hadn't missed something, and what she didn't find was a stamp from Norway. She picked up her phone and ran a quick search to see if Norway did in fact require that passports be stamped. Maybe it was just an oversight, but deep down something was taking hold of Marian: Tate was never in Norway; he never studied polar bears. Marian realized that none of the materials she'd read on the Svalbard archipelago project gave the name of the handler. And if Tate wasn't on the study, then he wasn't out of the country when Natasha Freeman, the first Stillwater victim, went missing.

Trainer's number was programmed into Marian's phone. When she called him, he picked up on the second ring. He was glad to hear from her. He'd left her dinner. "It's on a plate in the refrigerator," he said.

Marian thanked him for thinking of her, and could she ask him a question, because it had been on her mind. "Who went on the Svalbard archipelago study?"

"That would be Lyle," Trainer said.
"Tate didn't go?"
"We only had enough money to send one team over. We were a small operation back then. That was the year Tate drove to Omaha to spend Christmas with his sister."
Marian was quiet. Trainer asked her how she was doing. "I was getting worried," he said. "Tried to call you a couple of times, but your phone was turned off."
"I know. I'm sorry. I was trying to save the battery." Marian told him not to worry, that she was in one piece.
Trainer tried to convince her to drive on back to The Den. He assured her the authorities would be able to find the deer. "I'm not too keen on you staying out there by yourself."
"The doors are locked. I'll be fine," she said.
"In case we miss each other in the morning, is there anything you need me to pick up for you at the store?" Trainer did the grocery shopping on Wednesdays.
Marian said she was good. And when they ended the call she was aware of a continuing shift in her perspective of Tate and her involvement with him, as if the whole thing were surreal, and she wondered if she might be as crazy as Tate now seemed to have

been, because everything — her being on the side of this road, Tate not having been in Norway, women disappearing, people getting mauled by bears, the woodland caribou being reduced to near extinction — felt very wrong.

Marian thought of Lynn-Marie with her deep-set brown eyes, her high cheekbones, her blond hair, almost brown. And Marian tried to hold on to some hope that Tate wasn't the killer, and if he hadn't taken these women's lives, then someone was still out there, in these woods, along these highways. She opened the glove compartment and took out the gun, and as she did so, the receipt on which she had written Nick's telephone number fell like an autumn leaf onto the floor.

Marian picked up the receipt, and she'd forgotten how late it was, because if she'd realized it was close to ten she wouldn't have made the call. Instead of searching through her phone contacts, she entered Nick's number from the receipt. Nick's wife answered. Yes, he was still awake. And Marian said she was sorry to call so late, that time had gotten away from her, and she could call the next day if that would be better. But then Nick was already on the phone. His voice was weak. He sounded tired. "I can call back tomorrow," Marian told him.

"Nonsense," Nick said. "I was playing with the cat. I've got plenty of time to sleep."

And maybe it was because of the cell reception or because of the sound of a truck that had just passed Marian on the highway, but Nick said, "Marian, where are you?"

She told him about the deer and her waiting for the authorities to arrive. And Nick said, "Do you want me to stay on the phone with you until they get there?" And Marian said, "That would be nice."

Then Marian said, "Nick, I think I've made a mistake."

And Nick said, "What's wrong?"

She went on to tell Nick about the files she'd discovered, that she thought she'd finally found an alibi for Tate for at least three of the murders. "I thought Tate had been in Norway when Natasha Freeman went missing. There was a study in Svalbard archipelago. I was sure he'd been on the study. But I was wrong. He wasn't on the study. He was driving to Omaha to see his sister. Helena is between Whitefish and Omaha. It's not a direct route, but Tate liked to drive. Taking a longer route is something he would have done."

And she said, "Nick, there's more. There

was a grizzly and black bear study in Alberta. The first tier took place between mid-May and the end of July. Tate was there and I have nothing to suggest he left the study and picked up Erin Parker. But he was just over the border and it's possible. Where it gets interesting is with the second tier of the study that took place from the first of August to mid-October, four years ago when Lynn-Marie disappeared. Tate was on that second leg of the study. I have a copy of his team's tracklog. But according to the data, he wasn't working the day Lynn-Marie went missing, or the day after. Libby would have been about a five-hour drive for Tate. With that two-day window, he could have made the trip."

As Marian was speaking, the words rolling off her tongue like thunder, she was staring at the receipt with Nick's number, which she now held in her left hand. And then she stopped abruptly, the air catching in her lungs.

"Marian, are you still there?"

"I'm here," she said, her voice wary, almost quiet, because she could not believe what she was seeing. She held the phone in the crook of her neck and picked up the receipt for the coffee she'd purchased back at the convenience store. She compared it to the receipt that had been in the glove compartment, the same one she'd written Nick's number on two months earlier, just after Tammy had left. Marian had been running errands in Kalispell. And after one of those errands she was sitting in the parking lot of Cabela's, and, using her phone, she'd entered her credit card on an online site in exchange for Nick's number.

As Marian looked at the two receipts, she felt as if the night were closing in on her, cornering her in a very tight space. "Lynn-Marie was last seen at a convenience store in Libby. My God, Nick, Tate was there. He was at that same store the day Lynn-Marie went missing. I have the receipt. I'm looking at it right now. All this time it was in the glove compartment. I was just there, at the store. The receipts are the same. He stood in the exact same spot where I stood, at the counter. He bought a beverage, I don't know, a Gatorade or something. Do you realize what this means? Tate could have killed these women." Marian said all of these things because up until that very moment she had not believed, not really and truly believed Tate could have been guilty. But now there was the receipt she held in her left hand. And there was the passport and the green loaner vehicle and Tate had looked in windows when he was in college. And how could someone Marian loved do something like this?

Nick asked Marian if there was a time on the receipt. And Marian said there was: 5:23 p.m. Nick said he could make some calls. He could find out if the time on the receipt matched the time Lynn-Marie had been at the store. There had been video surveillance footage, Nick said. He'd always believed the perpetrator would be on that footage, even though the images weren't clear and the killer would not have shown his face. Nick told Marian that the detectives hadn't agreed with him on that point. They'd thought Lynn-Marie's killer had been someone who had been a client of Greener Pastures, someone who would have been familiar with the place. But Nick had believed the killer may have followed Lynn-Marie from either the convenience store or one of her earlier destinations, such as the feed store, then remained out of sight just long enough to pull the whole thing off. He was capable of performing any number of scenarios to gain Lynn-Marie's trust, Nick said. This was a killer who played his victims, and he played them well.

Nick went on to tell Marian that he'd had a call from a friend of Erin Parker's. "I've been mulling over the conversation, and I have to tell you, it's not sitting right with me. This friend confirmed that Erin was a nail biter. He said she was terribly self-conscious of her hands."

The dark corner Marian felt trapped in suddenly became a whole lot tighter. "When Tate described the body, he said the woman had bitten her nails until they'd bled."

"Erin's hands had been severed at the wrists," Nick reminded Marian. "I'm convinced the killer cut off her hands because he couldn't stand the sight of them."

Marian felt the pressure in her eyes building, her throat constricting with the horror of it all.

Nick continued. "There's something else. It may mean nothing to you, but Jeffrey, the young man I'm referencing, gave Erin a ring. He wanted to know if the ring was ever found. To my recollection, it never was."

The shadows on the highway from trees as tall as the sky suddenly loomed giant and portentous. "What did it look like?" Marian asked, her voice barely audible. *Please, God,* Marian thought. *Tell me it isn't the same ring.*

"It was fourteen-karat gold plated. The face of the ring looked like a compass."

And God help Marian if she didn't gasp, and she shook her head slowly, and she was no longer holding the receipts, having already set them aside on the console, and her left hand went instinctively to the ring on the index finger on her right hand, and her eyes went wide like someone who is about to be hit and sees the punch coming, and tears ran down her face — hot, angry tears. Marian tried to pull the ring off, but her hands were still swollen from a day spent hiking at almost seven thousand feet elevation, so that it wouldn't budge past her knuckle.

"Marian, what is it?" Nick asked.

"The ring," Marian said. "I have it. Tate gave it to me for my birthday. Oh my God, Nick, it has to be the same one. It was too big for my ring finger. I switched it to my index finger instead. You said Erin was a large woman. Her hands would have been bigger than mine. Do you realize what you're telling me?" And Marian continued to pull at the ring, the metal digging into the flesh of her finger.

"Send me a picture when you get back tonight. I'll see if the young man can identify it."

And Marian said, "Hold on. I can take a picture right now." Marian held her hand over the center of the steering wheel and took a photo of the ring. Then she emailed the picture to Nick. "You should have it now," she said. Nick told her he would check his email when they got off the phone.

And he said, "Marian, I'm sorry. I know things aren't stacking up the way you had wanted. There's nothing that could have prepared you for this."

"You believe Tate killed these women," Marian said, still in disbelief, her emotions trying to catch up with her thoughts, her senses as raw as a gaping wound. "Nick, how did this happen? How could I have been in love with a killer? This is a man I made love to. This is someone I trusted."

"The psychopath is a master of manipulation. He mimics the behaviors of others. He studies his victims, and once he chooses that victim, she may have little choice, he is that good. You're blaming yourself for your vulnerability. That's exactly what Tate would have wanted you to do. Guys like this have a way of increasing their control by making their targets question themselves. We can be quite effective at punishing ourselves for our perceived sins when what we really need to do is get in touch with our own anger. Your personal world is stacked against you. The culture is stacked against you. Your gender becomes a target you wear on your back. Are you at fault for any of this? Of course not. Maybe it's past time to be totally pissed off."

An idea came to Marian, slowly at first. "I think someone else has been on to Tate," she said. She told Nick about Jenness. "I found the tracklog, the one that showed the dates coinciding with Lynn-Marie's disappearance, in Jenness's hut. She was Tate's orienteer on the study." Marian went on to tell Nick about the articles and the pictures on Jenness's camera. "At first I thought she was jealous, that she had a thing for Tate. She wasn't jealous. Jenness had been involved with Melissa Marsh. She wasn't interested in a heterosexual relationship. If anything, she was looking out for me. I'm convinced of it."

"Jenness was involved with Melissa?"

"I don't think the others knew, but yeah, I found pictures of them. Trainer said Jenness had known one of the victims, that they'd been friends. Emily Marsh said her sister and Jenness had been friends also. But I'm not sure anyone at The Den knew of the romantic connection. Except —"

"I spoke with Jenness," Nick said. "I talked with her at great length. She was introduced to me as Jen. I didn't know she was connected with your program. If we're talking about the same person, she was working at the same clinic as Melissa."

"She took a break from the program for a while. That's when she worked at the clinic. She started back with the program about a year ago, around the same time Melissa's body was found."

"You were going to say something before I cut you off."

"I was saying I'm not sure any of the others knew that Jenness and Melissa were romantically involved, except for Tate. He may have known." And Marian told Nick about the picture that had been taken of Tate with Jenness and Melissa. "It was in the same folder as the articles," Marian said.

"That's it," Nick said. "I knew I had seen Tate before. I was speaking with Jenness at her apartment. Tate stopped in to check on her." Nick explained, "Because each of the Stillwater murders began as a missing-person report, one of the detectives got in touch with me right away, on the off chance these cases were related. I wanted to get a sense of the victim and began talking with the people she'd worked with. When speaking with Jen, or Jenness, I got the sense that she and Melissa were more than friends. I told her that their relationship would eventually come out in the investigation. She admitted then that they'd been involved.

They'd only been together a short time, three months at most. They'd been discreet about their involvement because of a rule at the clinic that prohibited employee relationships. We were wrapping up our conversation when Tate stopped by. He was checking in on Jenness, swooped down on her like a knight in shining armor. I shook the guy's hand and introduced myself, glad the poor girl had someone to look after her."

Nick continued, "If Tate was the one who stopped to give Melissa a ride the day she disappeared, he had any number of tactics at his disposal. He could have said one of the dogs was in trouble, or Jenness needed to see her. How long has Jenness worked with your group?"

"At least six years, not counting the year she worked at the clinic."

"Let's back up for a minute," Nick said. "I told you not everything about a case is leaked to the public. For example, the green SUV that the witness saw wasn't leaked for a reason. If the killer found out we had a witness, he'd drive to Timbuktu and trade in his vehicle, or get a paint job. But the family knew, and it wouldn't surprise me if Jenness found out, as well," Nick said.

"Let's play this out. Tate stopped by to check on Jenness; the two of them talked for a while. She thanked him for coming to see her, walked him out to his vehicle, saw the green loaner. He told her his vehicle was in the shop. She wouldn't have thought anything of it at the time. Tate was a friend. But something stuck in her craw. Maybe she wondered how he had already heard about Melissa just two days into the search. Maybe other things came to her mind. You mentioned Jenness had been Tate's orienteer on the bear study. According to the tracklog, he had a window of opportunity. Jenness could have gone looking for him during that window. When he got back, she may have asked him where he'd been and he'd given her some glib answer. Over the years, Jenness could have picked up on the same odd traits you picked up on — things Tate said, moments that felt off, maybe an empty look on his face where he didn't seem to be all there. She tried to capture those looks on her camera, analyze his expressions, take pictures of him when he was unaware. A serial killer doesn't want his photo taken. He might turn up for a group shot, then at the last moment face away from the camera. My take on that is that he not only wants to avoid someone recognizing him, but he wants to prevent someone getting a glimpse of his reptilian eyes — that vacant, vague, nobody's-home gaze that shows itself from time to time when he isn't performing."

Marian knew the look. She hadn't seen it often on Tate, but it had been there.

"Have you talked to Jenness about any of this?" Nick asked.

Marian said she hadn't talked to anyone about this except for Nick and that Jenness was in Alaska and was backpacking off the grid.

"When does she get back?"

"The first weekend in September."

"I think it's time the two of you talked," Nick said.

And then Marian said, "There's something else. I think Jenness was talking with a reporter about the cases." Marian told Nick about the notes she'd found in Jenness's folder, along with the number for Ryan Schulman.

Nick was familiar with Schulman. "There were a couple of reporters the detectives worked with. Schulman was one of them," Nick said.

"And this Schulman, he's a good guy?" Marian asked. "He's been emailing me about the program."

"From what I know of him, he seems to be a good guy." Nick said, "Let's take this good guy Schulman and play out our scenario a step further. Let's say this reporter talked to Jenness when Melissa went missing, same as I did. Maybe she'd felt an affinity for him. He could have been kind to her, brought her coffee, withheld personal information she shared with him about her and Melissa's relationship. Schulman gained Jenness's trust. Over time, Jenness's suspicions about Tate escalated. She reached out to Schulman for information, for details about the other cases. He could give her the kind of anonymity the detectives wouldn't be able to guarantee. And she wanted to be sure of her facts before she contacted authorities. She was building up nerve. She may have told Schulman about a person of interest, but even with him she would have been careful. I doubt she would have given away Tate's name. All the while, she continued to watch Tate closely. She became concerned when the two of you started dating. She'd not wanted to believe that Tate could be the killer, but what if he was? When she'd finally built up enough nerve to go to the authorities, the unthinkable happened. Tate was killed. Given the feelings she'd had for Melissa, she probably thought she should still go to the authorities. But now she had time. She'd make her trip to

Alaska and decide on her return. You were no longer in harm's way."

The nighttime temperatures were dropping. Cold drafts filtered in through the windows. Marian sat with one arm pressed snugly below her rib cage as if trying to contain her emotion — anger and fear so thick, she felt like she couldn't breathe. Everything Nick said made sense. She wished Jenness were back from her trip. She wanted desperately to talk to her.

Then Marian gathered her words in one deliberate thought; she needed to know. "When I was at your house, you said a serial killer might be in a relationship as a cover-up or as a matter of convenience. If Tate really was the killer, why do you think he pursued a relationship with me?"

Nick exhaled into the phone, followed by a slow pause. "I'm not going to mince words," he said. "No matter which way I look at this, I'm convinced you're one of the lucky ones. The bear that attacked and killed Tate did you a service. I have every reason to believe that if Tate were still alive, you would have been his next victim. He was upping the ante, taking more risks. It was only a matter of time until he acted."

Marian's body hunched forward until her forehead was pressed against the steering wheel. Her left arm dug into her stomach. She was folding like a tent. Big, silent tears ran down her face. "I need you to tell me," Marian said. "At what point did he decide he was going to kill me?"

"If I were to profile the victims, you would fit that profile. They were admirable young women, Marian. They were brave and trusting and kind. I have no doubt Tate considered you his next victim from the moment he met you."

Marian's emotions were seething. She bit down hard to gain control. "Then why did he wait so long?" she asked.

"Like I said, he was upping the ante. With each murder he was taking more risks. And if Tate was the killer, he would have been extending the foreplay, carefully selecting the precise place and circumstances for his next crime, enjoying the fantasy, no doubt having his way with you a thousand times over in his mind."

Marian lifted her left hand, raked her fingers through her hair, and sat back in her seat.

"Marian, are you there?"

"I'm here," she said, her voice hoarse and hollow. Her body ached. She gave herself a few seconds. Then she said, "What do we do now? Where do we go from here?"

"If Jeffrey gives us a positive identification of the ring, at some point we should be in contact with the authorities. There are a couple of detectives I still stay in touch with from time to time. I can reach out to one of them when you're ready. A dead suspect isn't someone they're going to spend a lot of resources on, but if they have enough evidence, they can certainly let the families know. Giving the families a name can go a long way toward closure."

The night seemed to stretch on forever. Surely a deputy would be there shortly. And Nick had stayed on the phone with Marian the whole time, had talked her through this big web of a mess, despite his illness, despite being tired, which she could hear in his voice. And Marian said, "Nick, how long?"

He didn't grasp what she was asking.

"I know about the cancer," she said, because she no longer wanted this piece of knowledge to come between them.

"Not long," Nick said.

27

FROM NICK SHEPARD'S FILE
VICTIM PORTRAIT # 4
Melissa Marsh

Last night after work I drove into Kalispell to the used bookstore. I can spend hours there, especially when J is working the evening shift and I know we won't be seeing each other. I've never written poetry, but I find myself gravitating toward it more and more as I seek inspiration for my drawings. Today was one of those days, and I felt oddly compelled to pull out a collection of poems by Billy Collins, whose work I'd never read before. I didn't realize Billy Collins had been a poet laureate, which I found out when I opened the book and read this inscription: "For Fred, my choice for poet laureate. Love, Jeanne."

I was compelled by the questions the inscription raised: Some woman named Jeanne had loved a man named Fred, who wrote poetry.

Was her love unrequited? Is that why Fred had released the book to this used bookstore, because the book held no sentimental value for him? And then I wondered if perhaps Fred had died, and upon the closing of his estate, his books had been donated.

I was so perplexed by these questions as to the nature of Fred and Jeanne's relationship that I purchased the collection and asked the owner at the counter if he recalled obtaining this book that, because of its inscription, made me feel incredibly sad. But with the over fifty thousand books in his store's inventory, he said he did not.

So I brought the book home, and because I wouldn't be seeing J that night, I heated up leftover lasagna. I poured a glass of red wine from a bottle J and I had opened the night before. I turned on an Eva Cassidy recording. I'm the one who introduced J to Eva Cassidy's music. J says there is something melancholy in the young woman's voice that J finds soothing. While I ate and drank red wine and listened to the music, I read poems randomly from the Billy Collins collection, all the while wondering if Fred had read these poems as well.

I think this is why I enjoy used books so much. They have previous lives, like old houses, like people. Tonight I felt inspired by the poetry collection, and not because of the poems I read, though I enjoyed them very much, but by the inscription and my curiosity about these two people's lives.

These thoughts, along with a second glass of wine, and the fact that I was not going to be seeing J, left me thinking about Polebridge and the hood of a Honda Civic, and growing up in a small town.

Ally was my first love, though she didn't know it at the time. I wonder if she knows it now, as if in getting older and looking back on one's life, we gain the perspective we were too naïve to understand then. She's moved on from here, as I always knew she would. Though I'd thought she'd end up running a large business in a city like New York or Atlanta or LA, she married a surgeon instead and last year had her second baby. We keep in touch here and there, mostly on birthdays. She lives in Baltimore now.

Ally and I played basketball together and were competitive to a fault: Which of us would score the most points? Who would make the most rebounds? Who would get the most play time? But when the season was over our senior year, sometime in the spring, and the snow had melted from the roads, one day after school Ally said, "Come on, let's go for a ride." We took her Honda Civic, which had seen better days, and drove northwest to Polebridge on that dirt-and-gravel road. We bought huckleberry bread at the mercantile. Then we drove six miles more to Bowman Lake. We sat on the hood of Ally's car and ate from the loaf of bread, tearing off chunks until the loaf was gone. And we stared out at the lake, the cloud cover so thick it looked like snow. Ally had a scholarship to New York University for the next year. She said she'd wanted to drive to Polebridge and buy huckleberry bread and look out at the lake to remember what she was leaving behind. That's how it went. Every couple of days we'd drive up to Polebridge, far enough away from town so that Ally could become quiet and remember.

Ally had a boyfriend then, a pole vaulter and a point guard, but on those late afternoons on the hood of her car, she didn't talk about Shaun, who'd been captain of the boys' basketball team for the past two years. After we finished the bread we'd light a cigarette, not because either of us smoked — we didn't except on those days — but perhaps because we could pretend to be someone other than ourselves. Eventually we'd lie back on the hood, which would sometimes buckle beneath us. We'd talk about life as if anything were possible. I wasn't college bound like Ally but said maybe I'd go to art school one day and show my paintings in a gallery. The truth was, I wanted to work for a while first, and had applied for a job doing trail work through the U.S. Park Services. As we talked I'd think of kissing Ally. I'd think of running my hand up and down her spine, even though I'd never kissed a girl or a boy before. But Ally wasn't like me, and I wondered if that difference had created the heat between us on the basketball court.

Then one day sometime in May, I told Ally I'd been offered a position on the trail crew at Glacier National Park. I would start as soon as school was out. I would be living with the other seasonal employees and would be working three weeks on, one week off. "You'll be ripped," Ally told me. She said she was happy for me. Then she said she and Polebridge would miss me, and I told her I would miss her, too. At some point in the conversation while I was still talking, Ally rolled toward me onto her side and pushed herself up on one elbow. I'd finished my cigarette and stopped talking and looked at her. Both of us were smiling as if we were nervous all of a sudden. Ally leaned over and kissed me on the lips. But then she didn't pull away, and as her lips hovered over mine for that second, I lifted my mouth toward hers and kissed her again, this time tasting the sharpness from her cigarette. She leaned back against the hood of the car. The two of us started laughing, but despite our laughter, Ally reached for my hand and she didn't let go when we talked of places we'd like to travel to one day, like Paris or Italy or Montreal. We kept holding hands until sometime later when we decided to leave and we climbed off the car.

Years later in my apartment, on the large wall beside my bed, I painted a mural with the Polebridge Mercantile, and a light gray Honda Civic, and two high school girls lying with their backs against the hood and their knees drawn up. The two girls are holding hands and staring up at the sky. There are stars in the sky, as they appeared the last time Ally and I drove to Polebridge, two nights before I started my job at the park.

I didn't paint the mural because of any feelings I still had for Ally. She and I had long since moved on. I painted it because I wanted to remember the first time I felt like it was okay to be different, that it was okay to want to work on a trail instead of going to college, to want to live in a small town and not feel like I had to go far away to be somebody, to want to kiss a beautiful woman instead of a beautiful man. I asked J once if the mural bothered her. "Why would it bother me?" she said. "It's a part of who you are," and I loved her more.

There are other murals on my walls. Beside my kitchen is a mural of my mother in her red pickup truck with her window down. She is waving from the truck window, and in the back of the truck are my brother and my sister and me. Though I did not draw my father in that mural, he's the one she is waving to, and her smile, with her lips pressed together and the corners of her mouth turned up just a little like there is something mischievous behind her thoughts, reminds me of the way my parents still look at each other even to this day.

My father is a tall man. I learned how to shoot a basketball from his shoulders when I was just three years old. And it is he who taught me about birds — about hawks and eagles and egrets and blue herons. He works as the butcher at Safeway in Whitefish. My mother works at the same grocery store as a pharmacy tech. On their days off we would load up my mother's pickup truck with tents and sleeping bags and bear-proof containers full of food and go hiking and camping in the park. From an early age, I swore I never wanted to live away from my family or from the park with its glaciers and alpine forests and deer that would walk right up to us, and grizzlies and elk and bighorn sheep and mountain goats.

On the wall space above my headboard is a

painting of my father. He is lumbering through the snow, pulling a freshly cut Douglas fir tree behind him that we will decorate for Christmas, with me and my little sister, Emily, trudging through the snow behind him.

There are two other murals on my walls. In my living room there is a large painting of Avalanche Lake from the park, and the image of me at twenty years old with a young woman named Katie. In the mural, we are working to clear a fallen cedar from the trail. Katie is holding a bow saw and I am holding an axe. The sun is hot on our skin, and Katie is wiping the sweat from her brow with a red bandana that she kept in her pocket. This was my third year working in the park as part of the trail crew. Katie was my senior. She'd worked trail crew at Yellowstone and Yosemite, and three years at Glacier. She taught me how to wield an axe more effectively, throwing the strength of my whole body into it.

Katie and I didn't date right away, but eventually we became a couple, and I grew confident in my body as both a lover and a trail crew-member. Though I am not a large woman, only five foot five with a lean frame, Ally was right. I had grown strong and felt proud of what my body could accomplish in a day's work.

■ ■ ■ ■

There is another mural in the living area, which I painted a couple of months after J and I met. She is standing tall, with her arms outstretched to her sides. She is wearing a purple knit cap and the autumn leaves are blowing around her feet, and a peregrine falcon is perched on her left arm. This mural might be my favorite. I will never forget that day, when I took J to Dawn of the Wild, a wildlife rehabilitation center for birds, where I volunteer. Dawn of the Wild, staffed with two full-time biologists and the rest volunteers, rehabilitates birds and releases them back into the wild, but sometimes the center provides birds a permanent home should a bird's injuries be too severe for the bird to be fully restored.

That was the case with Astor, the peregrine falcon. He was found by an engineer at the Hungry Horse Dam on the South Fork Flathead River and brought to the center with a broken right wing. Treatment of the bird's injury required amputation. The day I brought J to see the birds, I entered Astor's netted cage and, wearing a thick leather glove, held my hand up to his chest and told him to step up, which he did. I then brought the bird over to J and told her to hold out her arm. She held both arms out to her sides, as if instinctively for balance. At first her face winced in fear, with the falcon being so close, but eventually she relaxed and I was sure I'd never seen J smile so big. There is a sadness in J's eyes that seems to always be with her, but that day when I kissed her with the falcon perched on her arm, for that moment her sadness seemed to disappear. J visits the birds regularly with me now. She says they teach her things, like how to maintain one's wildness while living in captivity.

Last night I put the last piece of lasagna in a container to bring with me to work, and this morning I made a thermos of chai tea. I'll see J today and that will be good. She doesn't work tonight, so maybe she'll come over and we'll think up something to cook for dinner. Maybe I'll invite Emily to join us. She is just recently home from college. The other night she stayed over. We stayed up and talked till sometime after two. She said I look really happy, and I told her I am happier than I have ever been.

■ ■ ■ ■

Part Three

■ ■ ■ ■

In America, murder is a more honest expression of feeling than making love.

— JOHN PHILPIN

28
PRESENT: AUGUST 2017

Marian
The Den, Montana

When the deputy finally arrived, he said he'd been delayed by another call and thanked Marian for waiting. She felt catatonic, given everything Nick had told her and the ring she was still wearing and the things she now believed.

"Are you all right?" the deputy asked her. And she told him she was fine. She led him to where the deer had been ensnared, but by the time they got there, the deer had already broken free, and Marian hoped the doe's injuries hadn't been too severe.

"I'm sure you're ready to get back on the road," the deputy said, and he told her she'd done the right thing in reporting the incident.

Wind crept up through the mountains as she drove back to The Den. She slammed her fists, one and then the other, against the steering wheel. She sped along the curves of the dark highway, around the base of Fritz Mountain and McGregor Peak, through the Kootenai National Forest and the Salish Mountains, as the spin of one memory to another, one lie to the next, all the static over these past months pressed in on her.

She parked behind the barn — parked this vehicle that for all she knew might contain traces of DNA going back the past six years, from Melissa Marsh, or Lynn-Marie Pontante, or Erin Parker, women whose lives now felt irrevocably intertwined with Marian's own.

The lights were out in the house. The lights in Trainer's hut were out as well. She grabbed her pack and slung it over one shoulder. As she approached the entrance to the barn, the motion light came on. Once inside, she used the flashlight from her phone, not wanting to get the dogs any more excited than they already were. Yeti and Arkansas greeted Marian at their kennel gate. After she let them out, she stopped by the storage room and looked in the cabinets for the dogs' prescriptions: heartworm preventive, ear wash, antibiotics, and the tranquilizers administered to the dogs when they traveled. Marian opened the bottle of acepromazine. She tapped two tablets into her palm, collected enough spit in her mouth, and washed them down.

She consoled the other dogs that had stirred, and led Arkansas and Yeti out of the barn with her. Gusts of wind tensed up around them as Marian brought the dogs back to her hut. She got them settled on her bed; she cried into their fur; she let them lick her face. Marian then rose. She told the dogs to stay. She grabbed an extra bar of soap, a towel, and a bottle of shampoo and put them in her shower bag. She stripped out of her fleece jacket, hiking boots, and socks and slipped on her pair of flip-flops. And as she stood in front of her closet, she saw her white silk shirt, her designer blue jeans, and the turquoise-threaded cowboy boots she'd bought in Texas. She thought about the night Tate had taken her to dinner for her birthday, remembered the moment he'd given her the ring and how he'd admired it on her finger — the same ring that had no doubt belonged to Erin Parker. Marian and Tate's lovemaking had been particularly passionate that night. He'd wanted the lights on; he'd wanted to watch her undress. And then Marian remembered the flyer she'd seen at the convenience store earlier that night, with Lynn-Marie's picture: She was last seen wearing jeans, a white blouse, and cowboy boots.

Marian gathered her jeans and silk shirt in one angry sweep and shoved them into the stove. She grabbed kindling and aspen bark and layered them over the clothes. She picked up her butane lighter from her desk and lit the kindling and bark and closed the stove door, all the while convinced that Tate's arousal the night of her birthday had to do with his memory of Erin Parker and Lynn-Marie. It was their deaths that had incited his passion. The horror of that thought crawled over every part of her like a disease. She tried again to remove the ring, but it wouldn't budge beyond her knuckle. She imagined Tate's thrill each time he'd seen the ring on her finger, as if he were reliving Erin Parker's death all over again. And Marian remembered Nick saying that if Tate were the perpetrator, he would have thought of killing Marian a thousand times over. Marian picked up the cowboy boots and heaved them across the room. "Damn you, Tate!"

The dogs' ears went back and Yeti tucked her head into a fold on the bed, and Marian felt terrible and said she was sorry. She turned on her flashlight and walked back down the hill toward the showers, the wind rattling the branches, debris collecting between the soles of her feet and her shoes, shadows dancing across the path in front of her.

The light blinked out when Marian stepped into the shower, and she thought it was because of the wind. She cursed the wind and the bulb and the electricity and Trainer, who was supposed to have checked on the light while she was away.

Marian lathered her hands until she could work the ring off her finger. She threw the ring against the shower wall, listened to it hit the concrete and clink against the drain cover, metal against metal as the ring wobbled until it was still and the only thing left was Marian's rapid breathing and the water running over her. She lathered her hands again, lathered her arms and legs and breasts, scrubbed herself so hard that her skin burned raw. "No," she cried. "Please God, no." She let the soapy water run between her legs, let the shower rinse the soap from her skin.

The door to the shower house opened and closed.

"Trainer? Is that you?" Her voice was hoarse. "Who's there?" Marian yelled. She turned off the shower, wrapped her towel around her. She picked up the ring. Her change of clothes — a pair of sweats and a long-sleeve T-shirt — were hanging outside the shower stall. She dried herself off quickly and dressed. She slid the ring into the front pocket of the T-shirt. Maybe she hadn't closed the door tight behind her. The wind could have swung it open and closed. That was all it was, Marian told herself. Using her flashlight, she stepped over to the sink to brush her teeth and rinse her mouth. And as she brushed her teeth and stared into the mirror, she swore she could see the shower curtain from the stall adjacent to the one she had used moving, as if someone were standing behind it, and all the while Marian told herself she was going crazy. She stared wildly back at her reflection in the mirror. She'd been exhausted, sleeping very little, and the tranquilizers were kicking in, and her mind wasn't working right.

Carrying her shower bag, she walked back to her hut. She shut off the light and burrowed into bed between the wall and the two dogs. She wrapped her arm around Yeti, whose back was pressed against her, and as her eyes adjusted to the dark, she could make out the thrush nest Tate had found for her, on the shelf above her bureau. She scooted out from beneath the covers and crawled over the dogs. She picked up the nest and carried it to the stove, opened the door, and set it inside with the ashes from her clothes. She sank onto the floor and watched the nest catch and go up in flames. She thought of the day she'd spent in the Cabinets with Tate, remembered their conversation in the woods after he'd brought her the nest. When Tate had told her about the artist girl, whom Marian now was convinced was Melissa Marsh, Marian had thought he'd been referring to a girlfriend because of the way he had spoken about her. She could draw hawks, ravens, falcons, any kind of bird, and the detail was extraordinary, Tate had said. Marian remembered the feather tattooed on Jenness's wrist and the peregrine falcon tattooed on her left thigh. She felt certain Jenness had gotten the tattoos after knowing Melissa Marsh, that the designs were replicas of Melissa's work. And in that moment Marian knew Tate's guilt all over again.

Marian closed the door to the stove and crawled back in bed. She concentrated on the dogs' breathing, their intake of air and exhalations that were remarkably in sync. Her phone was on her nightstand. The screen lit up. She had an email from Nick. He wasn't sleeping either, she realized. She read the email message. Jeffrey had already gotten back to Nick. He'd identified the ring. Marian felt a flare of anger in her chest, but she was so exhausted, and she knew sleep was coming fast.

29
Present: August 2017

Nick Shepard
Bonners Ferry, Idaho

Cate answered the phone call from the North Carolina area code. "Hello," and "Yes," and, "Yes, he is." And, "That's good news." And then, "Yes, we can." She picked up a pen. She jotted down information on a pad of paper while she continued her dialogue exchange.

It was seven o'clock in the morning. For the past few weeks, knowing the time would come when Nick's cancer would begin to spread, Cate had been researching clinical trials and operating on three different time zones. At first it looked as if Nick could have his pick, like choosing a second honeymoon destination: Santa Barbara, California; Las Vegas, Nevada; New York City; Denver, Colorado. And then there were the studies themselves: TPI 287 and Ativastin; CC-486 and Vidaza; and a feasibility study of the

Nativis Voyager system, which sounded to Nick like the name of a car. "Let's choose that one," he'd said. "Maybe we'll get more mileage."

But they quickly learned that qualifying for a clinical trial wasn't that easy, and there were a limited number of openings in each of the studies. Then Cate found a Phase I expansion study for recurring glioblastoma out of Duke University Hospital. The purpose of the study was to determine the most effective dose of a genetically engineered poliovirus that would be directed into the tumor via a catheter. The virus would attack that portion of the brain, causing inflammation. The patient's immune system would then respond by attacking the inflammation, hence the tumor.

After Nick's most recent MRI, Cate had completed the necessary paperwork. She'd arranged for Nick's medical records and images to be sent overnight to Duke.

Nick was a match. That was what the person on the other end of the call was telling Cate. And just that morning, a place in the trial had opened up. One of the patients had dropped out. How soon could Nick get there, because the study was getting ready to close.

Why did the person drop out, Nick wanted

to know. But Cate shook her head. She was trying to hear what the other person was saying. Cate had already opened her laptop and was typing at the same time she was listening and nodding her head and answering questions, and Nick had always marveled at the way she could multitask. And then the call ended, and Cate said to Nick, "We don't have much time."

"Tell me something I don't know."

Cate said, "There's a flight out of Spokane this afternoon. If we hurry we can make it."

Nick smiled for the first time that day. "They want me."

"They want you, Saint Nick. We're going to do this."

"Are you sure?" he asked.

"It can buy us more time. I want more time with you."

Nick went to the hall closet and took down two suitcases. He noticed that he was walking with a little more ease. A healthy dose of endorphins, no doubt. Cate was still on the computer buying their tickets. She would arrange for a wheelchair to and from their gates, he knew. Probably not a bad idea. She'd sounded positive when she'd spoken to the nurse from the clinical trial on the phone. "Yes, he is mobile. Yes, he can handle the procedure."

■ ■ ■ ■

People talk fast when they have a lot to say and they're afraid they will lose the attention of their audience, or when that window of time is smaller than all the things the person wishes to express. Cate was talking fast that day as they made the two-hour drive to Spokane International Airport. At first it was the mundane things that had to do with their attempt at an orderly escape from the house: Did he make sure the cats had enough food and water? Should she call the post office and ask the clerk to hold their mail? She hoped Leonard, the teenage boy down the street, would remember to check on the cats. She was sure the key to the back door was under the lawn cushion. She told Nick other things, like the ballet teacher she'd had when she was small who'd developed lung cancer and who had survived and whose lung had grown back. Nick thought, *This is what hope looks like,* and yet he reminded Cate that brain tissue didn't work that way. He wasn't growing a new brain; he'd have a couple of holes in his head if the tumors weren't there. Then he asked Cate to describe the procedure to him.

She used words like *stereotactic* and *convection-enhanced delivery.* She said the catheter would be threaded into the center of the tumors.

"There are a lot of connections between my skull and the center of my tumors," Nick said. "What if they miss?"

"They're not going to miss."

"Why did the one candidate drop out?"

"She experienced a lot of swelling."

"She was paralyzed."

"Yes."

Nick thought of everything that could go wrong, as if checking it off his list. "Aside from paralysis, what are the risks?" he said.

"You could experience a brain bleed."

"I could die."

And Cate said, "You still have time to change your mind. I don't want to force you to do something you don't want to do."

"Since when has anyone forced me to do anything?"

Cate reached over and laid her hand on his thigh. "I'm serious, Nick. I don't want you to do this on account of me."

"I'm doing this for both of us," he said. "Hell, I'm going to end up in a wheelchair anyway. Might as well go out swinging." And with the warmth of her hand on his thigh, Nick felt the pain of nostalgia.

"You're forgetting the other side of the equation," Cate said. "What if you live?"

Nick squeezed her hand. "Well now, that would be something."

Other conversation passed between them: Did Cate call Peter and what did he say, and how were the girls?

"He's catching a red-eye tonight. He's going to meet us at the hospital in the morning. The girls and Elizabeth are fine."

"Did you buy the return tickets?"

"Of course." And Cate looked at him and smiled.

"When are we coming back?"

"They'll want to keep you for observation. We'll be home in about a week. You'll return for a checkup in another three months."

"That's good," Nick said. And then, "I should call Marian."

"Did you bring your phone?" Cate asked. After his episode in the woods, she'd purchased a phone for Nick. She'd had him call her a few times for practice.

"What kind of question is that?" Nick said.

"Do you want to use mine?"

"I don't know her number."

"What about calling the place where she works?"

Cate reached in her bag that was on the

console between them. She handed Nick her phone. "It'll go to Bluetooth," Cate said.

Nick dialed information. *"A text message has been sent and your call is being connected."*

The phone rang several times. A male voice answered.

Nick asked to speak with Marian.

"Sorry, but she's not here."

"Is this Trainer?" Nick asked.

"Speaking."

Nick identified himself, and then said, "I need to get a message to her."

"I know who you are. You're the shrink Marian's been talking to."

Nick wasn't interested in making conversation. "Do you have something to write with?" he said.

"Whoa, not so fast, Doc. It's not every day I get a profiler on the phone. I'm curious. Do you actually talk to the killers? What's that like for you?"

Nick continued. "Look, I'd like to make sure Marian has this number. It's critical that she get this message."

Nick gave Trainer his wife's cell phone number. "I'm going to be out of commission for the next few days, maybe longer. I need her to know that," Nick said.

"You going under the knife or something?"

Trainer asked.

"Something like that."

"Well, hey, what are you going to do."

Nick asked Trainer if he'd written down the number.

"Got it," Trainer said.

The call ended. Nick returned the phone to Cate's purse.

"Do you feel better?" Cate asked.

"A little," Nick said.

But Nick didn't feel better. If Marian was so concerned about keeping her inquiry quiet, why had she told this guy? The conversation he'd just had wasn't sitting right.

30
Present: August 2017

Marian
Flathead County, Montana

Marian awoke to sunlight and dust motes and two restless dogs that were climbing on top of her and licking her face. She picked up her phone and couldn't believe the dogs had let her sleep in till almost nine o'clock. Trainer would have already left, she knew. Wednesdays were his day to run errands in Kalispell and do the weekly grocery shopping. He'd be out of the house by seven and usually wouldn't return until sometime around noon.

Marian sat on the edge of the bed and put on her running shoes. She still felt somewhat groggy from the tranquilizers. The night before felt surreal. She thought about emailing Nick, but the dogs were eager to be let out, so she opened the door and walked them back to their kennel in the barn. She fed them breakfast and told them she'd take them for a run, and because the sun was warm, maybe she'd bring them for a swim. She was determined to push herself through this day, and spending time with the dogs was the only way she knew how to make it from one hour to the next.

She walked over to the main house for coffee. Inside the kitchen she found a thermos on the counter, which Trainer had left for her with a note: *Morning, Sunshine.* Marian drank the coffee. She ate a protein bar. She remembered her wash and went into the laundry room to start a load, but her clothes had already been cleaned and folded. She appreciated Trainer's gesture, even though she wasn't entirely comfortable with him folding her personal things. She dressed in a pair of running tights, a pair of socks. She looked for her running tank, but it wasn't there, so she grabbed a clean T-shirt instead.

She brought Arkansas and Yeti out to her vehicle and loaded them into two travel crates in the back. Then she drove a couple of miles to a clearing along one of the forest roads. She had mapped out a five-mile course along forest trails and roads that, three miles in, cut along the north shores of Gilman Lake, where she could let the dogs swim.

The air was sun-soaked and the sky clear,

a welcome change from the cooler temperatures the night before. Marian attached bells to each of the dogs' harnesses. As she took off on the trail and the dogs' bells jangled alongside her, she was glad for the noise, knowing that the three of them were making enough of a clamor to alarm any bears. She thought about the report she'd read on Tate's death, the images that she'd seen. Something small and wrenching was nagging at her. She kept going over the report in her mind, reexamining each detail: the blow to the back of the head, which the coroner believed was the result of Tate having been knocked to the ground; the bruising on Tate's right arm and hand, which were also consistent with a bear charging Tate and him trying to block the bear. According to the coroner, Tate had died from injuries received during the attack. But there was the irony of it all: Tate's larynx had been crushed, the same as each of the Stillwater victims. Marian couldn't help but wonder if the pressure to his larynx had been the cause of his death.

Marian tackled one incline and then another, until she was on a more even stretch, and as she moved through timber of spruce and larch, the peculiar realization hit her that she'd never liked not knowing where Tate was when they were in the woods together. There had always been something about him that had seemed elusive to her, even dangerous. And yet, if she was honest with herself, hadn't it been that element of intrigue that had made Tate all the more enticing? She'd asked Nick once, "At what point do we know when to walk away?" And Nick had said, "The point at which something doesn't feel right. That's when you walk away, or run if you have to."

Nick had said that if Jeffrey identified the ring, then she and Nick should go to the authorities. Lyle and the other handlers and Tate's sister would find out. For an incredibly brief moment, Marian wondered if she and Nick were wrong, as if none of this had happened at all when in fact all of it had. If anything, she needed to hold on to her moments of clarity like armor. Anything less would make her ineffectual.

Again she thought of the bear attack. Again she went over the report. Forty percent of Tate's body had been consumed. His face had been mauled, as had his right shoulder and left leg. Tate had experienced bruising on his right arm, which was positioned over his head when the body was found. She had not seen any mention of bruising on his left arm. But Tate was left-handed. If a bear were charging him, wouldn't he have instinctively raised his left arm, rather than his right? And if he had raised both arms, wouldn't his left arm have been bruised as well? She picked up the pace of her running until the trail met up with yet another forest road that curved around to Gilman Lake on her left. The dogs saw the lake as soon as she did, and they went running ahead of her and splashed along the shore and picked up sticks that Marian could throw for them and they could retrieve in the water.

The summer had been especially dry and hot, and the lake level was much lower than it had been only a couple of weeks before, and was that something out in the water, about fifty feet from the shore, and Marian was sure that it was, a large, dark rectangle reflecting the sunlight. She tossed one of the sticks toward it. Both dogs took off in the water before the stick landed, but when it did land there was the thud of wood against metal, like that of the roof of a car. Marian removed her shoes and socks. She waded into the mountain-fed lake, numbing despite her warm muscles from the run. About fifteen feet from the shore, she plunged the rest of the way in and began to swim until her fingers were touching what was indeed the roof of a vehicle. Marian quickly dove underwater. The vehicle had completely filled with water, and there was no one inside it that she could see. She swam to the surface to take a breath, and then dove under again to have another look, all the while thinking the black SUV looked familiar. She grabbed onto one of the door handles and pulled herself along to the back, looking in all the windows to be sure no one was trapped inside, and that was when she saw the vanity license plate, JCAT49, and why was Jenness's vehicle not in Alaska where Jenness had been all this time and was supposed to still be? And Marian's voice, though muffled, yelled out Jenness's name, even though Marian knew that Jenness wasn't there.

31
Present: August 2017

Nick Shepard
Spokane, Washington

Nick and Cate had made the two-hour drive to the airport in Spokane and were sitting at their gate. He'd declined the help of a wheelchair. The airport was small. Their plane would be boarding in another half hour. In six hours they would arrive in Raleigh-Durham. As Cate drank a coffee and said they should go out for barbecue that night, and wasn't North Carolina known to have good barbecue, Nick was watching CNN News from a suspended television and thinking about the conversation he'd had on the phone with the guy at the facility where Marian worked. Something wasn't right about the whole thing, something the guy said, his provocative demeanor. Nothing about the call made Nick think he'd been talking to some good ole boy from Louisiana, as Marian had described Trainer. Nick played the conversation over in his mind. And what was that line? Then Nick asked Cate, "Did you find that guy odd on the phone?" But Nick wasn't even sure Cate had been paying attention to the conversation. She'd had her own things on her mind, which mostly had to do with getting Nick to his appointment that next morning with the oncologist at the Preston Robert Tisch Brain Tumor Center, part of Duke University Hospital.

"A little odd, yes. But I wasn't really listening."

"There was something about him," Nick said. "A supreme indifference. 'Well, what are you going to do.' That was it. Sounded like something Danny Rolling would have said. There was no 'Good luck,' or 'I'll be sure to get the message to Marian.' Hell, I don't even think the guy wrote down the number I gave him. Something's not right about this. And since when did a guy from Louisiana lose his Southern accent? I need to get in touch with Marian. If that guy wasn't Trainer, then who the hell was he?"

"You can log into your email account from my phone," Cate said. "You can send her a message."

"That might work," Nick said. And then he remembered that Marian had emailed him her cell phone number after they'd first been in contact.

Nick asked Cate if she would log into his account for him, and so she did. She pulled up his emails and was able to run a search for messages that included *Marian.*

"Here it is," she said. "Do you want me to call it?"

"Yes."

But the call went to voice mail. Cate handed Nick the phone. "Marian, it's Nick. It's important that you call me. You can reach me at this number. You need to stay away from The Den. You're not safe. Get someplace safe and call me."

When he ended the call, Cate said, "If she's anything like Peter, she'll never check her messages. She'll see a missed call and will hopefully call it back, and when she does, we won't be able to answer."

"She'd get a text," Nick said. And because Nick had never sent a text message in his life, Cate entered the number for him. "What do you want the text to say?" she asked.

" 'You are in danger. Stay away from The Den. Get out of there. Go someplace safe.' " Then Nick said, "And let her know the text message is from me. Tell her to call us when she gets to a safe place. We'll be in the air, but we can call her back when we land."

Cate hit send. "Is there anyone else you can call?" she asked. "Do you want to call the authorities?"

"And tell them what, that some guy was rude to me on the phone, that he didn't send me his well-wishes. It's just a hunch," Nick said. "And not something the authorities are going to pay any attention to."

"I've always trusted your intuition."

"That's good," Nick said. "I need you to trust it now."

Their plane was beginning to board. Cate said, "What does your intuition say about the cancer study?"

"I haven't had time to think about it," Nick said. "I'll trust your intuition on this one."

Nick picked up the paper Cate was reading. The two of them got in line.

"If you had a wheelchair we could board sooner," Cate said.

But Nick said zone four was fine. "I like to think I'm still one of the masses." He opened the paper and thumbed through most of the news that he'd already heard, all the while feeling anxious. He asked Cate if she'd checked her phone. "Don't turn it off till after we board," he said.

Toward the back of the paper was an

article about a hiker on the Pacific Northwest Trail who was still missing — a young Irishman who'd spent the summer backpacking alone. He was supposed to meet up with friends in the town of Ozette, Washington, on the Olympic Peninsula, at the end of the trail. He'd been sending them text messages and pictures. The friends became alarmed when the young man by the name of Elias didn't show. And Nick was fairly certain that the Pacific Northwest Trail cut across the same area of Washington where Tate had been attacked by the bear.

32
Present: August 2017

Marian
Flathead County, Montana

Marian had to get back to her vehicle, where she'd left her phone. She had to call for help. She could cut through the woods and pick up another trail that would take a couple of miles off her route back to the truck. The dogs were prancing and wanting her to play. Marian sat on the bank of the lake and put on her running shoes, both dogs shaking their coats beside her and Arkansas dropping the wet stick onto Marian's lap. "Let's go," she called to the dogs. And she took off running onto the forest road, and then veered off into the woods to catch up to the trail she could take for a shortcut to her vehicle. She tried to keep her steps measured so as not to stumble in the woods, branches catching her hair and snagging her clothes, and she continued to move with haste, and the dogs leapt and ran alongside her and then ran farther ahead, and stopped occasionally to look back at her.

Eventually she found the trail and turned right, the dogs now a good fifteen to twenty feet or more in front of her, and Marian began to sprint, and the dogs picked up their speed, as well. She slowed her pace only once to catch her breath, then sprinted again. She knew this trail, knew its curves and inclines and descents. She felt as though a fist were pushing up from her sternum, a mixture of panic and fright. She gauged that she was about a half mile from her vehicle now, and she would get her phone, and she would call the police. But then Yeti veered off the trail and began running due north. "Yeti, no!" Marian called to her, but Yeti didn't stop. And once off trail, there was deadfall and dense thicket, the kind that covers a bog, and the ground was marshy. Marian could no longer see Yeti. She was now walking briskly, pushing the overgrowth aside, straining to listen for the dog's bell, which was hard to hear with Arkansas making noise beside her. They were moving parallel to the banks of Logan Creek. Marian finally caught sight of Yeti, whose nose was to the ground, and Yeti's bell was ringing, and she was whining nervously, and Marian called to her to stay. Yeti continued to whine, never raising her head, until Marian and Arkansas had caught up to her, and Marian saw the badly decomposed body, lying on its side, along the creek bed.

She screamed when she saw it, and backed away from the body, and called the dogs to her, and Yeti was still whining, and now Arkansas began jumping on Marian and was barking. Marian's hands and legs and arms were shaking. She told Arkansas to get down. She grabbed hold of both dogs' collars and got a closer look. And there was the beautiful long braid of dark hair, and oh, God, it couldn't be, please God, no, and then on the naked corpse Marian saw the St. Francis medallion that she had known so well, the one Marian's grandfather had given her when she was just ten years old.

Marian was now crying, and did not know when the tears had come, and she did not want to disturb the area, and yet here she and the dogs were. She had to get to her vehicle. She had to get to her phone. And so she pulled the dogs with her and backed away from Jenness's body until they were on the trail and she was sure the dogs would stay with her this time, and she kept talking to them. She told them she was going to get help, she told Yeti she was a good girl, she told them how sorry she was, and she continued to cry and talk to the dogs in gasping breaths as she ran the rest of the way on the trail and to the forest road, and up ahead she saw the front of her vehicle.

Her keys were in the hip pocket of her running tights. She reached for them and unlocked the doors. Then she loaded the dogs in the cargo area inside their travel crates. They continued to whine and Yeti was now barking and both dogs were moving about and scratching at the inside of their kennels. Marian tried to reassure them, but her voice was shaking as much as the rest of her. She told them to stay, even though they were now confined, and she jogged around to the driver's side and opened the door with haste, and there was her phone. As soon as she picked it up from the console, the screen lit up and she saw that she had two text messages. One was from Trainer, telling her he'd be back around two, and the other was from an unknown number with an Idaho area code. The message was from Nick, who she thought didn't own a cell phone, but here he was telling her she was in danger, to stay away from The Den, to go someplace safe.

Marian's hands were trembling. She

opened the glove compartment and took out the gun. She checked to make sure it was still loaded. She needed to call the authorities. She needed to report the location of Jenness's body. She would then drive to the police department in Whitefish. She would do as Nick said. She would make sure the dogs were safe, as well. *Breathe,* she told herself. Just breathe, because her hands were still trembling and she wanted to be able to use the gun if she had to. She dialed 911. She was about to hit send. She looked around her vehicle, then across the clearing and along the woods. Jenness was dead; her body was beside the creek bed. Four other women were dead, also. The Stillwater killer was still out there. Oh, God, she thought, Jenness was dead.

And again she reminded herself that Tate was left-handed. The bruises were on his right arm. His face had been mauled. Marian had hiked part of the Pacific Northwest Trail that abutted the area where the bear attack had occurred. Two hikers had seen Tate the morning of his death. And oh, God, it couldn't be, she thought. Tate had killed the four Stillwater victims; she was sure of it. The boy Jeffrey had identified the ring. Tate had described one of the victims' bodies to Marian. He had never been in

Norway. He was at the same convenience store as Lynn-Marie Pontante the day she went missing. He'd driven a green loaner vehicle. Melissa Marsh was picked up by a guy in a green SUV. And now Jenness was dead. And something cold and dark sank into Marian's body, and into her arms, her legs, her hands that held on to the gun. The killer was still out there. There was the message from Nick. She was in danger. And there was the victim of the bear attack, whose larynx had been crushed, and Marian realized what had been nagging her all morning, and she held the gun tighter. Tate might still be alive. She continued to slow her breathing. Her body became calm. She knew how to use the gun.

Once more she looked across the clearing and into the woods. There was movement, perhaps a deer, somewhere off in the trees. She heard the breaking and stirring of branches. Then she saw him, Ranger, emerging from the spruce and western larch, his tail wagging, his muzzle in the air. And could it be that he had traveled this far, that he had found his way back and he had not been killed by the grizzly bear?

Ranger stopped, maybe twenty feet in front of Marian, his haunches barely touching the ground. He lifted his head and looked behind him, and she knew. She steadied her right hand around the grip of the gun. She stood behind the driver's door, which was still open. She stared ahead at the woods. Ranger trotted the rest of the way to her, his head toward the ground, his tail wagging. Arkansas and Yeti were still whining in their crates. Yeti began to bark, high-pitched and rhythmic. And there was Ranger, now sitting beside Marian, and yet she did not take her eyes off the tree line. She pressed her thumb against the safety and switched it to off.

Mere seconds passed before he appeared, and she almost didn't recognize him. His hair was cut short above his ears, and his beard was gone. He wore a green brimmed cap and a long-sleeve camouflage shirt.

"Matilda," he called to her. "We've been looking all over for you." In his left hand was a neon green item of clothing, the same color as Marian's running tank. And there was Ranger at Marian's feet, and he was wagging his tail and looking back at Tate.

"Good boy, Ranger. You found me," Marian said, her voice flat and as steady as her body had become. She grabbed Ranger by the harness, all the while keeping her eyes on Tate. She patted the driver's seat and commanded Ranger to jump up, and thankfully, he followed her lead and jumped into the vehicle. Marian closed the door, stepped away from the vehicle, and planted her feet shoulder width apart. She held the gun in her right hand down by her side. All she needed to do was raise the gun, support it with her left hand, and align the gun's sights, her finger on the trigger. It was all so easy, really. Tate had killed Jenness. He had killed four innocent women whose bodies had been found beside a stream.

Tate glanced down quickly at the gun in Marian's hand, then looked back up and met her eyes. And he was smiling, as if the whole thing amused him. "What's this?" Tate said. "I thought you'd be happy to see me."

"Tell me, Tate. Why did you do it? Why did you kill those women?"

"Now hold on just a second, Marian. I don't know what that crazy shrink has told you, but you've got it all wrong."

"How do you know about Nick?" Marian asked.

"Are we really going to do this? Is this what you want? Is this what you need in order to feel okay about yourself? If that's what it takes, sure, I'll go down that road with you."

Marian held on to the gun tighter. The

dogs were whining from the vehicle. She stared straight back at Tate. "Answer the question."

"Let's just say I know all about you and that psychologist friend of yours. In fact, I had a little chat with him this morning. Nice guy. A little hasty, though. But it's a shame, Marian, it really is, how easy it was for you to betray me. I was testing you, watching you. I messed with the dogs a little bit. Nothing too serious. Just enough to keep you around."

"The sandpaper," Marian said. "That was you?"

"Like I said, it was nothing serious. And sure, you could have quit, run back to Michigan. But that wasn't like you. I should know. I trained you. I just needed to be sure of your feelings for me. You had me fooled, Marian. Here I'd thought you were a woman of your word. I thought I was the love of your life. But I was wrong, wasn't I? I was coming back to you all this time, thinking we'd have some glorious run of it, that we'd make a life together, so convinced the two of us were unstoppable. I tried to come for you, crept right up to your hut, and there you were talking to some shrink on your computer, spinning off all sorts of lies about me. What kind of fool did you play me for?" Tate said. "Look, it's not too late for us, Marian. Everyone makes mistakes. I've made my share of them. I'm willing to put this all behind us."

"Why did you do it?" Marian asked, because he still had not given her an answer. "And Jenness . . ." Here Marian's chin trembled and she was sure Tate saw her weakness. "Why did you have to kill Jenness?"

"Whoa, her blood's on your hands, not mine," Tate said.

"What are you talking about?"

"Don't play innocent with me. You're just as guilty as anyone, telling me about all the photos Jenness had taken, like she was watching me, isn't that what you said? I was framed, Marian. I thought you'd be smart enough to see that. This Schulman reporter starts hanging around, asking me questions one day. I knew someone close to me was talking to him, trying to blame me for what happened to those women. But I hadn't figured out who. For all I knew it could have been Lyle or Trainer or Dudley. But no, you went and made that easy for me. I set up a fake email address. Used Ryan Schulman's name. Told Jenness I was emailing her from my personal account. Just like that, she fell for the whole thing. I asked her to lay it all out for me again. And she did. Said she was ready to go to authorities, said she owed it to Melissa. That's not something you know a whole lot about, now is it? *Devotion* isn't really a word in your vocabulary. I asked Jenness to hold off for the time being, said I was pulling together some additional information for her. I was in Washington then. I even sent Ryan Schulman an email, pretending to be Jenness. Told him not to contact me until he heard from me. And like Jenness, he fell for the bait. When I got back, I emailed Jenness again as Ryan, asked her if we could meet. It worked out beautifully. She told me all about her trip. She suggested we get together on her way out of town. We could grab coffee. You know I don't like coffee. I chose a remote location. I told her I had something to show her that she would want to see. I swear to God, she was just like the others. Women will fall for anything."

Tears filled Marian's eyes. She had to be stronger. Tate was getting to her. All she could think of was Jenness, and that she'd played a part in her death. And then it hit Marian. "How did you do it?" she asked. "Once you were back, how did you send an email to Jenness when you didn't even have your phone?"

"Well, now, that's the easy part. I used the phone of the sorry bastard up in Washington. I unlocked his phone with his thumbprint. Then I changed the settings."

"You killed that man," Marian said. "I saw the images of the attack. I read the report. Was it really worth it, Tate? All these people that you killed? Their whole lives in front of them? For what?"

"You give me too much credit."

"What are you saying?"

"I can't change your mind if you want to think of me as a cold-blooded killer. But it's not going to do you or me any good. You saw the images. A bear got to that guy. It happens," Tate said.

And Marian realized Tate must have used Jenness's phone in the same way he'd used the device of the man he'd killed, posting messages and sending emails to the group.

"All this time it was you," Marian said, "emailing me, pretending to be the reporter."

"Just another way of seeing what you were up to," Tate said. "There really was no harm in it. I was biding my time. Waiting for a new identity to come through. I even used your computer to surf the dark web. Checked out all your emails with ole Nick Shepard while I was at it."

"You couldn't have. My computer has a password."

"Really, Marian? The password *Deacon* wasn't hard to figure out."

Tate took a step closer. "But like I said, that's all behind us now. You were afraid. I get that. You were confused. We can make everything right. Jenness is gone. It's just the two of us. We're meant to be together, Marian. Everything changed for me once I met you. You had that kind of effect on me. You're all I've been able to think about." Tate took another step toward her.

Marian raised the gun. "Don't come any closer," she said. She searched his eyes, looked for that one glimmer of truth, something to make him human, to resemble the man she thought she'd loved. And for a second his eyes appeared full of emotion.

"You weren't just my girlfriend. You were my friend," Tate said. "How could you turn on me?"

But Marian knew it was all a charade. She felt the knowledge of his lies like concrete. And in that moment, something in Tate's eyes shifted, and she saw the absolute emptiness, as vast and cold as outer space. And she heard Nick's words again, that Tate would have killed her a thousand times over in his mind. She had been Tate's perfect target. She had been his special one. She'd fallen for all of his lies. She couldn't undo what she'd already done. God, how she wanted to, though. She'd made a mistake. She'd loved the wrong man. The weight of her shame entered her bones, gave her strength. She wouldn't make a mistake this time.

Her finger was on the trigger. Her hand was steady, her body and legs sturdy. And maybe Tate saw the anger in her eyes, because his tone changed.

"You're not going to kill me. You couldn't pull that trigger."

He stepped closer still. "You can't do it, can you?"

Marian waited until he was no more than ten feet away. Tate reached out his hand. Marian fired, and she kept firing until Tate's body hit the ground and she knew he had to be dead.

Marian was not sure how many bullets she had shot. Tate's shirt was saturated with blood; the ground had turned crimson beneath him. His eyes stared off in the distance from the angle where he lay, and the three dogs were barking from the truck, and Marian was shaking uncontrollably. She was afraid that if she moved, her legs might buckle beneath her. She could still hear the gunfire in her head, and her heart was thudding wildly in her ears. Jenness was dead. Marian had to call for help. She turned back to the truck, opened the door. And there was Ranger, ready to leap down, and Marian wrapped both her arms around him and told him to stay, and she held him against her, his body thrashing about, trying to be free. She set the gun on the dashboard and swooped Ranger into her arms and carried him around to the back of the truck. Ranger was not a large dog, no more than thirty-five to forty pounds. Marian put him in the crate with Yeti. She talked to the dogs. She tried to calm them down, and their barking turned into whimpers. "It's okay. Everything's okay now," she said, but it wasn't okay. Jenness was dead; four other women had been murdered as well; and someone's son or brother or father had been killed and fed to a bear off the Pacific Northwest Trail.

Marian walked back to the driver's side of her vehicle, her legs still quivering. She climbed into the vehicle and reached for her phone, which at some point had fallen onto the floor. And the first thing she did was call the number Nick had texted her from. Her call went to voice mail. "Nick, it's Marian. I'm safe now. Tate is dead, Nick. This time he's really dead."

33
September 2017 Through May 2018

Marian

Lyle had insisted Marian take a leave from the program. "I'll handle the reporters. Go home. Take some time for yourself. The job will be waiting for you when you come back." And Marian had assured Lyle she still wanted her job. She'd never been happier than when she'd been working in the field with the dogs, and she hated the fact that she would not be making the trip to Oregon for the northern spotted owl project. "There will be other projects," Lyle had told her.

Marian traveled to Michigan a week after the incident. Her parents took time off from work to be with her. They said they could arrange for her to talk with someone, but she said she wasn't ready. Instead, she slept in and tried to eat the breakfasts her mother would prepare for her. She and her parents took a kayak trip along the shores of Lake

Superior and camped overnight like they did when she was young. Marian visited her brother also and went shopping with her sister-in-law. More than anything, Marian wanted only to be in the company of others.

When Marian returned to The Den a month after being away, Lyle offered her one of the extra rooms in the main house to ease her back into things. She helped Trainer fix meals. She watched movies at night. During the days she worked in the office and exercised the dogs. As the holidays approached, she made another trip to Michigan. She showered her family with Montana jams and salsa and cured beef. By January she was back at The Den.

Lyle was busy preparing the permits and paperwork for a three-month pangolin study in south-central Vietnam. The study would begin in February and would require three teams. "Are you up for this?" Lyle had asked Marian, and she'd assured him she was. She would be working with Yeti and would be accompanying Dudley and Liz and two of the other dogs in creating genetic maps of the pangolin population. The maps would serve as a tool to help law enforcement in determining high trafficking areas. The group would be staying in village housing and working in community forests.

And so Marian made the trip to Vietnam, where she and the others stayed in thatch-roof houses. Vietnamese guides assisted the teams in the field. At night the handlers gathered and drank wine and cooked with coconut milk and fresh herbs. The three of them made sticky rice with mango, and spring rolls, and rice paper rolls with sprouts and chicken and pork. They each talked about their day and books they had read and politics and their families and shared stories about the dogs. And sometimes one of them would remember something Jenness had said or done, and they'd talk about that, too.

In the mornings they rose between three and four a.m. and took turns brewing the coffee. On their days off they caught up on paperwork and restocked their food supplies and helped each other look after the dogs. And on one of those days, Marian came up with the idea to visit Alaska and hike the Kesugi Ridge in honor of Jenness. "When?" Dudley had asked, and Marian said they should go at the end of the study, sometime during May. But Dudley would be returning to a moose project in upstate New York shortly after they returned, and Liz had been assigned to a killer whale study in Puget Sound with a new adoptee. The dog had been trained to detect floating scat from the bow of a boat. "Or else I would go," Dudley and Liz had both said. "And won't there be too much snow then?"

The trail was in Alaska's interior between Anchorage and Fairbanks. Marian had read accounts from other hikers, and from what she had learned the trail would be open in May. Marian was already scheduled to return to Utah in June to finish the bighorn sheep project, so May really was the only time. Marian had also run the idea by Jeb, even though she knew he had school. "It's actually our semester break," he'd said. And, "You shouldn't go alone. This is a big thing you're doing, commemorating someone's life. I want to be there."

Marian flew to Anchorage the last week in May, where she met Jeb. They spent their first night at a Super 8. They didn't mention Jenness that night, or Tate. "This is your trip," Jeb had told her before they'd left. "You make the rules. I'm here to support you," he'd said. And that first night Marian told him she needed to listen to him tell her about his writing and the people he'd met in California. "Just talk to me," she said, "like you did all those weeks before when I needed you to," and she almost said, *the first time Tate died.*

The next morning they rode a shuttle to Denali State Park, and were dropped off at the Little Coal Creek trailhead at the north end of the ridge. They arrived at the trailhead a little after noon, and with sunset a good ten hours away they had more than enough time to make it to the first pass. As they started out, the cloud cover was low, as dense as fog, and much of the trail was either muddy or covered in melting snow. They were consistently post-holing it up to their knees, as the snow was too soft to hold their weight, and they quickly accepted the fact that their boots might never dry out over the course of the four days that they'd planned to spend on the ridge.

The trail switchbacked up thirty-five hundred feet to the first pass, and within the first few hours of that ascent, the sky emptied of clouds, the sun baked down on them with temperatures in the seventies, and all to their right were magnificent views of Denali peak and the Alaska Range. They decided to set up camp just over the pass, where before them lay wide-open tundra, parceled with snow and spongy terrain.

They'd each brought tents and bear canisters and other personal gear. Though they wouldn't be able to build a fire, as there was no dry wood in sight, they found a comfortable spot among some boulders that felt private from the handful of other hikers they'd seen. Jeb made them each a cup of tea from his stove, and Marian had packed ginger cookies and vanilla wafers, and Jeb said, "Food fit for a king."

And because the sun was so warm, they took off their wet boots and soggy wool socks and laid them on the rocks to dry. They leaned back against the boulders, let the sun drench their damp clothes and skin, and at some point as they stared out at the white-laden Denali and the rocky points around it, Marian asked Jeb if what she'd been through with Tate would always define her. It was the first time she had mentioned Tate's name since arriving in Alaska.

"I don't think it will define you. It will make you stronger," he said.

"Tate told me once that because we live and breathe and survive things doesn't necessarily make us strong; it just makes us alive."

"Yeah, and Tate was full of bullshit," Jeb said. "The things that go wrong in life allow us to create new life," Jeb told her. "It takes a lot of strength to do that."

And then Marian said, "Can I tell you

about what happened?" because really she had not told anyone other than the authorities and Nick, not even the reporters or her family, about the details from that day.

"Of course," Jeb said. "You can tell me whatever you want."

And the first thing she said was there was so much blood, because she couldn't get the image of Tate out of her mind. And Marian told Jeb how Tate's eyes had held a look of surprise. "He didn't think I would kill him. Even when he saw the gun, he didn't think I could do it."

Marian walked Jeb through the rest of the details, how she'd had to keep Ranger from jumping out of the vehicle and running over to Tate. She told him about Arkansas and Yeti whining and barking in the back, and that even now there were times when she was sure she could still smell the smoke from the gun mixed with the sweet metallic scent of Tate's blood.

She told Jeb about her call to 911. The dispatcher had asked Marian if she had been physically harmed. She asked Marian if she was in a safe place. The sheriff would be there shortly, and would Marian be all right staying with the body.

It was too much, and the dogs were still whimpering, making it difficult for Marian to hear the dispatcher. Marian needed to get the dogs out of there. She needed to get herself out of there also. And yet this was now a crime scene, and Marian knew she was no longer in danger. She told the dispatcher she would stay. She would wait for the sheriff and the deputy whom the dispatcher had also called to the scene. All the while Marian felt as if she were existing outside her body. Even her words sounded hollow. Dissociation, Nick would have called it. Nick, whose text message had prompted her to take the gun from her glove compartment, whose warning Marian was convinced had saved her life.

After the call ended, Marian had the disturbing realization that what Tate said had been true: that she'd had a hand in Jenness's death. Marian had alerted Tate to Jenness's behaviors. And how ironic, Marian thought, that if it had not been for Jenness's gun, Marian would be dead. Not only had Nick saved Marian's life, but Jenness had saved it, too. That thought brought the kind of intense pain that was unbearable, and the tears came, and her body shook with uncontrollable grief.

The authorities had ruled Marian's actions as self-defense, even though it was not until after Tate lay on the ground with six rounds to his chest and torso that she'd seen the knife he had held in his right hand. Though the United States does not allow posthumous trials or convictions, there was no doubt in the investigators' minds that Tate had killed Jenness. Within a mile from the huts, a campsite was found. Beneath a green tarp was Jenness's backpack, including her cell phone, from which Tate had been sending messages as if he were Jenness. He'd used the magazine from Jenness's hut to post the Alaska pictures.

As with the other victims, Jenness's body was unclothed and found beside a creek bed. Yet, unlike the other victims, her clothes were not discovered beside her remains but instead back at Tate's camp, where they had been neatly folded, as if Tate had held on to the items as some kind of souvenir.

Just as Tate had staged his entire relationship with Marian, so had he also staged his death. Tate's project in the Selkirk Mountains put him in direct contact with the Pacific Northwest Trail. It was speculated that Tate had appraised the handfuls of hikers each day, carefully selecting the young man with the Irish accent who was hiking alone, who bore a resemblance to Tate in size and coloring, and who trustingly would have divulged his plans to Tate, of meeting up with friends at the end of the trail. Tate would have befriended this man in much the same way Tate had befriended the Stillwater victims.

The medical examiner had reported that the victim had sustained a blow to the head, which was consistent with a person being charged by a bear and knocked to the ground. Now investigators believed Tate had struck the man from behind, or else had knocked him down. The victim's larynx was subsequently crushed, which could have been from the weight of the bear, or from the pressure of Tate's arm, or even from a blunt object Tate might have used.

Unless a victim's identity is in question, the victim's DNA isn't analyzed, authorities explained. Upon the initial investigation there had been no question that the victim was Tate. His belongings, including his pack and phone, were found near the body, and Lyle had reported that Tate was missing in that area. With the new information, the wildlife investigators were able to match the DNA collected from evidence at the crime scene to that of the missing hiker, Elias Hutchins. Further, a more detailed DNA analysis had identified the additional animal species as belonging to an elk. According to lab analyses, Tate had washed a set of his clothes in scent-free detergent and had sprayed down his boots with a scent-free product as well. He'd even gone so far as to use the spray product on the corpse for the purpose of reducing his chances of the bear being deterred by the human scent. Tate had switched out the clothes he'd prepared, and also his boots and personal belongings, with those of Hutchins. Then he'd used elk meat to lure the bear to the corpse. Traces of elk were found on the shirt of the victim, as well as on the victim's trousers. Tate very well could have rubbed elk meat all over the victim's body, Waller said. "As far as the bear was concerned, the body was carrion, and it was fair game. It's an elaborate scheme. But it's doable," he said. Waller reminded authorities of a bear's olfactory system, saying it was possible that a bear could smell carrion up to twenty miles away. Tate's scheme really wasn't all that different than luring a bear to a snare, Waller explained, and his team had been able to do that within a matter of hours using only a single slab of meat.

And in the same way Tate had posted messages and sent texts from Jenness's phone, he'd done the same with the phone of the missing hiker. On both phones Tate had disabled location services, and authorities had not been contacted to track either phone using additional technology, as there was no reason to believe anything was wrong. Both Jenness and Elias Hutchins were not in areas where they would have a strong cell phone reception. They'd made these trips to get away. Neither had been expected to answer or return phone calls during the weeks they'd been gone.

Authorities believed Tate had then posed as a hiker and used an alias to target people for rides, choosing individuals who, like Elias Hutchins, were just passing through, who wouldn't have been tuning into the daily news of a bear attack, with Tate's picture posted along with the story. And Tate had changed his looks; without his beard and longish hair, to the unsuspecting eye, he would have barely been recognizable. Already since the story had been reported, one woman came forward saying she had given Tate and Ranger a ride from Metaline Falls, Washington, to Priest River, Idaho. She'd even stopped for Tate to pick up a bag of dog food. She said the man had called himself Matt.

Once on state forest land and within a mile of The Den, Tate was able to make a camp for himself using both Elias's and Jenness's provisions. Investigators speculated that Tate had restocked his food supply those past six weeks by taking from Jenness's reserves in her hut and from items in the main house when he was sure no one was around. And he'd no doubt used the shower house as well, unscrewing the lightbulb so that he wouldn't be seen. In reflecting on the past couple of months, Marian felt certain there were times Tate had been in the shower house when she was there, and she realized the very thin and fragile lining between life and death.

At Tate's campsite, authorities had found several de-scent products, from sprays to soaps and shampoos. Detectives with the sheriff's department had also discovered several thousand dollars in cash at the campsite, which Tate had withdrawn from his checking account before leaving for Washington. This action alone would not have raised suspicions. Tate had always paid in cash and had frequently withdrawn large amounts. And they'd found a Texas driver's license, passport, and social security number for Mark Edward Preston. Tate had used Marian's computer to download specialized software that allowed him to surf the dark web. He'd used Marian's bank information to set up a digital currency account for purchasing the fake identity. He'd had the items shipped to a nearby summer cabin that had been vacated. Tate had even gone so far as to delete the online bank statement from Marian's email that showed his transaction, before Marian had seen it.

As difficult as the call was to make, Marian had reached out to Tammy. She told Tammy she was sorry. She offered to sell Tate's vehicle for her. She would do anything, Marian had said.

But Tammy didn't want the money. "I can't do this," she said. "You killed my brother. I can't talk to you." As far as Marian knew, Tammy still believed her brother was innocent.

The night of the shooting, Nick got back to Marian. She learned about the clinical trial for the first time. Nick would be evaluated by a doctor in the morning, and if all went well he would receive the poliovirus three days later on Friday.

"So he's really dead," Nick said.

"Yes." And Marian filled him in on the details.

"The journey's not over for you," Nick told her. "I'll be there for you in whatever way I can."

"Which means your journey's not over either," Marian said.

And Nick said, "Let's hope so."

Cate kept in touch with Marian over the course of the next few days. "He's groggy from the anesthesia," she said, "but he's doing well." The next call was from Nick. He was home.

"How are you holding up?" Marian asked him.

"The worst part is over," Nick said. "Did I mention they make good barbecue in North Carolina?" But then he turned serious. "How are you?"

"The worst part right now is the media," Marian told him.

"They're just doing their jobs. Besides, the coverage might do some good for the families. Stay off the Internet. Turn off the TV. Things will get better."

And Marian asked Nick what were the odds of him calling The Den the day Tate answered. "Why do you think he picked up the phone?" she said.

"First, Tate was in the house. He may have even enjoyed a nice breakfast. He knew Trainer was off doing his own thing on Wednesdays. Lyle was gone until the following week. Tate knew you had taken the dogs in his old vehicle, and as you found out, he had a good sense of where you were taking them. Maybe he'd gone snooping around the place. The phone rang; caller ID came up. Tate would have recognized the Idaho area code, and who else would have been calling from Idaho on his lucky day? What did he have to lose? He was unstoppable, invulnerable, and dead men don't answer phones. Seeing that call come in would have been irresistible for Tate. And he was going to do and say whatever he damn well pleased. I was the one helping you figure Tate out. Having the chance to mess with my head was just frosting on his cake. If the call turned out to be business, so be it; he could say *wrong number* and hang up," Nick said.

"And my head wasn't the only one Tate was messing with," Nick continued. "Hanging around those past five or six weeks while he put together his final exit strategy would have been both necessary and great fun. Necessary from a details standpoint in assuming his new identity. And great fun in taunting you this whole time, getting in your personal space, watching you like some phantom, all the while rehearsing the final act in his head —"

And Marian finished Nick's sentence, "To

take my life."

"Yes."

"Why did he wait so long?" Marian asked.

"Ah, but you're trying to understand Tate with your own logic. Throw that out the window," Nick said. "That's the only way you can even begin to understand the mind of a psychopath. First, his reward system is practically nil. He doesn't have the same dopamine levels running around in his head as you and I. So where does he get his kicks? From deceiving others and from the twisted crimes he designs in his head. Bundy once said that the fantasy that generates the anticipation is always more stimulating than the crime itself. With each murder, Tate was upping the ante, taking greater risks, heightening the foreplay of his crime, the deception. Tate had great fun seducing you into a relationship with him, luring you deeper into his world. And just when he was getting close to the attack, you laid one on him. You told him about Jenness's photos. Tate became wary then and paranoid that he was on someone's radar. He couldn't have this person hanging around. He became obsessed with what Jenness had on him. Perhaps he lurked around her hut. Maybe he watched Jenness through her window with binoculars. Maybe he listened in on a conversation she had on the phone with this reporter fellow who, according to what Tate said, had come around asking questions. Tate had to be able to come and go as he pleased. He could not be under anyone's microscope — not the reporter's, not Jenness's, not anyone's. He needed latitude to continue killing, to plot out his next ruse."

"What do you think prompted him in the end?" Marian asked.

"The unthinkable happened. You met Emily Marsh. You started questioning things Tate told you. You, his perfect victim, so trusting and naïve. He'd waited too long. And now you had the ring. He'd been foolish giving it to you, taking too many chances, and yet he would have felt tremendous excitation each time he gazed upon the ring on your finger. Still, he'd gone too far this time. It was only a matter of time before you and Jenness corroborated. He felt hemmed in by his mistakes; yet the buildup was too great. He had to fulfill his fantasy. And at the same time, he had to ensure his freedom. And my God, the thrill of pulling off a scheme that big, of faking his death and watching the woman he was about to kill grieve for him. What immense satisfaction that would have brought him.

"You see, Marian, a man like Tate seeks

only power and control over the people in his life, and those people are no more than objects to him. He's superficial, showering others with praise and platitudes, charm and wit, because these are avenues to dominate and manipulate whomever he chooses. He doesn't feel guilt or remorse. He sees himself as invulnerable, a veritable Superman walking the planet and playing the game. He is the whole show — the actor, the director, the scriptwriter, the stage manager, the makeup artist. How much more power he can acquire by having the world believe him dead."

And Marian said, "He had to know we were getting close. We had the ring, the loaner vehicle. We had all the clues that pointed to him as the killer."

"I'm convinced that when Tate discovered that the two of us were in contact, he had an insatiable need to know what clues he may have left behind, where he might have gotten sloppy. And when we were closing in on him, he would have waited just long enough for the perfect opportunity to pull off his final act. He knew Lyle made this trip every year. He knew Trainer's routines. He knew your schedule. The other handlers were away. Tate wanted to see his victory on your face. He wanted you to know how greatly you had been deceived, not only by your falling in love with a man who turned out to be a cold-blooded killer, but by the fact that the person you thought was dead was still alive, and you were going to be his next victim. And he almost got away with it."

On Jeb and Marian's second night camping along the ridge, with another clear sky all around them and the sun casting a purple glow over the horizon, Marian decided it was the perfect time and place to honor Jenness. Marian knew from the others that Jenness had held out hope for years that she'd one day be assigned to a study in the forty-ninth state. When that didn't happen, she saved her money and was prepared to take a leave without pay. And she'd no doubt had hopes at one time of sharing that experience with Melissa. "It's crazy when you think about it," Marian said. "Jenness traveled the world, and yet she never made it to Alaska."

Marian had brought a picture of Yeti, and the St. Francis medallion that the authorities had released to Marian. She'd also brought copies of some of the photos in Jenness's hut — pictures of Jenness's family, and the picture of Jenness with Melissa. Using a small shovel, Marian carved out a divot in the ground and placed the items into the small space. "They loved you, Jenness. I wish I'd gotten to know you better. I'm so sorry for everything that went wrong." Jeb knelt beside Marian. He rubbed her back. He laid his hand over her shoulders. "It's going to be okay," he said. Then Marian scooped up handfuls of the moist soil and covered the items. She and Jeb set a pile of stones over the items also, including smaller stones they'd each picked up along the trail.

Marian had brought a passage by Rachel Carson, and asked Jeb if he would read it: *Those who dwell as scientists or laymen among the beauties and mysteries of the earth are never alone or weary of life.* And Marian remembered everything, the first time she'd met Jenness in Alberta, the feather tattoo on Jenness's wrist, the conversations in Jenness's room, the competence with which she'd led the teams in the oil sands, the gentle way Jenness had brushed Marian's hair, Jenness's ease with the dogs and the way she had loved Yeti. "Jenness, I am so sorry. I am so very sorry."

34
June 2018

Marian
Nokai Dome Wilderness Unit, Utah

A little over nine months after that fateful day in Montana, Marian had returned to the Nokai Dome wilderness to finish what she had started the year before, to complete the big-horn sheep study. She'd insisted to Lyle that she'd wanted to return to Utah alone, that she needed to face the solitude, that the trip would be good for her. She no longer wanted him to think of her with a handicap because of what she'd been through with Tate. "At some point I have to get back to the way things were," she'd said.

This time, Marian only had one dog with her. She was here in June, when the temperatures were still relatively mild for the high desert, rarely reaching above eighty. She would be working Yeti three days on, one day off, with most of their field hours taking place before midafternoon.

She'd done well at first, but with each passing day and night, she'd felt more alone, and her anxiety had gotten the best of her. She'd have fitful sleeps and long for the company of others, and sometimes at night, she was certain she'd called out in her sleep, because she'd awaken to Yeti sitting alert or licking her face.

Marian had asked Nick why the dogs, with their keen sense, didn't know something wasn't right with Tate. "They liked him," Marian had said. "I don't get that."

Nick said it wasn't uncommon for psychopaths to have a relationship with dogs, or cats for that matter. "Animals pick up on the stress levels of individuals," he said. "The psychopath typically carries himself with great ease. The only real emotion he is capable of is externalized anger, which is short-lived, or the excitation of a crime. The average person experiences a variety of emotions in any given day. For an animal, the psychopath might be a welcome reprieve."

It was the eighth day of the study. The morning's transect had been difficult, and the sun was too hot for Marian or Yeti to find comfort. Marian stopped for lunch beneath the shade of a couple of juniper trees. She removed her pack and set it on a slab of sandstone, then removed her hip pack also. She looked over her shoulder at Yeti, who had stopped a couple of yards away. Marian heard the snake before she saw its diamond-shaped head, its body coiled in a loose loop, and there was Yeti standing in front of the snake, her head toward the ground.

Marian told Yeti to stay, because she knew if the dog moved, the snake would strike. She took a stick and banged it against the slab of rock to get the snake's attention, to take its focus off Yeti, not knowing if her strategy would work. At first the snake's rattle grew louder, and it seemed to raise its head higher as if it were ready for attack, but then ever so slowly, it lowered its head toward the ground and slithered away until it was beneath another ledge of rock to Marian's left. Marian ran to Yeti and told her what a good girl she was, and loved on her profusely because what would she do if she were without the dog.

In all of this emotion, Marian's phone rang, when she didn't even know she had a signal, and she sprang toward her hip pack to answer this call from civilization, to hear the voice of another, and by the time she got to her phone, she saw that she had a missed call from Jeb. She picked up both packs and led Yeti away to another couple of trees about twenty yards or so from where she had last seen the snake. She dropped the packs to the ground and tried to call Jeb back, but she'd lost the one bar on her phone, and even when she tried other locations, she couldn't get a signal.

She felt desperate to return Jeb's call. She removed her satellite phone from her pack, turned it on, and waited for it to lock onto a satellite. And when Jeb answered, she couldn't believe it, as if she hadn't spoken to him in a couple hundred years.

"Marian, what's wrong?" he said, as soon as he heard her voice.

"I thought this is what I wanted. To be here, in places like this. I begged for it. And yet I can't do it, Jeb. Why can't I do this? What's wrong with me?"

"Marian, it's okay, you've been through a lot. Maybe it's just too much for you right now."

"It's everything I imagined and it's none of it. Does that even make sense? What if I don't want to do this anymore? What if I can't?"

"First off, your desires aren't a life sentence, Marian. People change. Experiences change."

"I'm so alone, Jeb. I'm so fucking alone. I don't know what's wrong with me."

"You're not alone, Marian. I'm right here." And then he said, "I've always been right here."

Marian's breathing slowed. She sat on the ground. Yeti stepped on her lap and licked her face. And Marian heard what Jeb said, and he was right; he had always been there.

"You're close to Edward Abbey country," Jeb said. "Abbey wrote that the only thing better than solitude was the society of a friend."

And then Jeb told her the real reason he'd called. Though his program ran through the summer, he had a midterm break coming up in a couple of weeks. "I don't know how you feel about this, but I was thinking you could use an orienteer. I ran it by Lyle, and he had no problem with it. I could fly into Salt Lake or Grand Junction. I could rent a car. I could come meet you."

"Are you serious? I mean, yes. I'll help you with the cost. I still have money from Tate's vehicle. I sold his vehicle. Did I tell you that? Tammy told me she didn't want the money. The program rented a truck for me. I can come pick you up. I'll pick you up. Don't rent a car."

And Jeb laughed and said, "I can't wait to

see you." And Marian said, "Jeb, this is the best news I've heard in a long time. I miss you so much."

That night amid the stoic shadows of the cliffs and beneath the desert sky, Marian didn't feel the pains of loneliness, but rather the company of anticipation. She didn't know where her relationship with Jeb would go, and yet she looked forward to seeing him again with the notion of all possibility. And with that possibility she felt something larger than the guilt and shame she'd carried with her that past year. She felt the plenitude of hope, the abundance of gratitude.

Marian thought of the society of a friend, to be heard, to be seen, to be touched, to hear and see and touch another. She closed one eye. She reached a hand to the sky, positioned her fingers just so to create the image of holding one of the stars in her palm. And she entertained the thought of Jeb lying on his back in a park or on the campus green and positioning his hand in much the same way, so that he would be holding the same star as she. It was a romantic gesture, she knew, and yet as she thought of the great connectivity of the earth and sky, there was an exhilarating feeling that really, neither she nor Jeb were very far away from the other.

Marian found the Big Dipper and Scorpio and Cassiopeia, the only constellations she knew, and maybe she would study the stars one day, buy a large telescope and look at the galaxies, but for now, Marian felt content, truly content, something she had not felt in a very long time. As she continued to stare at the sky, she found other impressions, and one that reminded her of the woodland caribou, and she thought of the gray ghost whom she had witnessed in the forest, tenuously balanced in an endangered ecosystem. And in that moment she felt such great empathy it hurt to breathe, as if she were one with everything.

AUTHOR'S NOTE

When I was eighteen years old, a man whom I knew and trusted locked me in a trailer and, at knifepoint, assaulted me for twelve hours. A number of years later, that same man shot his wife before turning the gun on himself. I was one of the lucky ones; I got out of there alive. After this incident, my mom shared with me her own story. When she was five months pregnant with me, a man broke into her home while my father was away and my two brothers were asleep in another room. She, too, had been asleep, only to awake to the face of a stranger. John Philpin, the criminal psychologist and author, who assisted me with my research on this novel, says that ninety-five percent of stranger-to-stranger homicides are committed by men against women. Regardless of whether rape is involved, these crimes are sexual homicides, as they involve men exerting their power over women. Too often women fail to trust their intuition when something doesn't feel right. Too often they blame themselves for their vulnerability. And too often, for the rest of their lives, they carry the burden of shame for having been violated. John addressed these points in an email to me: "We can be quite effective at punishing ourselves for our perceived sins when what we really need to do is get in touch with our own anger. Your personal world was stacked against you; the culture was/is stacked against you; your gender becomes a target you wear on your back. Are you at fault for any of this? Of course not. Maybe it's past time to be totally pissed off." This novel is my attempt to address the fear and vulnerability too many women live with every day, and to encourage women in those incidences when they still have a choice, to pay attention when something doesn't feel right, to heed that small voice inside themselves.

ACKNOWLEDGMENTS

The Last Woman in the Forest has been an absorbing, at times personal, and immensely rewarding journey. I am ever so grateful for the people who have contributed to the research and supported the writing process along the way. As I prepare to acknowledge individuals, I am reminded of the moment at which the first hint of this novel caught my attention.

Over ten years ago I began dating a forester, Shaun Hathaway. He told me about the Connecticut River Valley killer who murdered at least six women during the nineteen eighties along the corridor of the Vermont and New Hampshire border. The killer was never apprehended. Having moved to New Hampshire from Colorado, I had not been familiar with these murders. A little over a year into my relationship with Shaun, he was diagnosed with stage four glioblastoma multiforme, a terminal brain cancer. He and I married, and eventually we hired a young, male home health care worker. One day I asked the home health care worker if he had any siblings, and he told me that his sister had been one of the Connecticut River victims.

After Shaun's death, I felt compelled by these murders and the stories of these young women's lives. I turned to a book Shaun had told me about: *Shadow of Death* by Philip E. Ginsburg. Upon reading the book, I learned of one of our nation's first independent criminal profilers, John Philpin, internationally renowned for his work, who assisted law enforcement on the Connecticut River cases. John, who is mostly retired now, has worked on over two hundred cases and authored eight books. It felt imperative that I connect with him. A new novel idea was taking hold, and John was the person with whom I wanted to explore the idea further. After John ran a background check on me, he returned my call. We began talking over Skype, corresponded via email, discussed plot points at length over the phone, and spent an entire day together speculating on the minds of my characters. We discovered we shared a love for Bob Dylan's music, and literature, and nature, and when I'd become overwhelmed with the writing, he'd reboot my mind with a dose of Bob Dylan recordings. His generosity and the wealth of information and insight he provided me is beyond anything I could have imagined. It is to John whom this book is dedicated, but it is not solely for my appreciation of the help he has provided me, or for the inspiration I've found from his writing, but also because of the more than thirty years of his life that he has committed to assisting law enforcement with identifying the victims' killers. John, you became my confidante throughout the course of this novel. You are a dear friend and I cannot thank you enough.

I also owe a tremendous amount of gratitude to the wildlife biologists and conservationists who have assisted me along the way. As Wallace Stegner so eloquently captured in his "Wilderness Letter," the wild country is a part of the "geography of hope," and these scientists and laypeople live that hope every day. In determining the framework for the novel and my protagonist, I was fortunate enough to cross paths with Mark Freeman, a student at the time in the graduate program where I was teaching. Mark's love for the wilderness resonated with my own. He spoke to me of his time as an orienteer and conservation canine handler while working as a wildlife biologist. Lightning went off in my mind. That was it. Mark provided me with endless resources and contacts and pointed me to the densest grizzly bear population in the lower forty-eight. And so I boarded a plane and was on my way to Montana, Idaho, and northeastern Washington.

Scat detection and collection — which is covered in the novel — and its analysis provide a vital tool in studying wildlife and recommending practices that will preserve threatened and endangered species. The technique was developed by Sam Wasser, director of the Center for Conservation Biology at the University of Washington (conservationbiology.uw.edu) and director of Conservation Canines. Thank you, Heath Smith, lead instructor and director of operations for Conservation Canines (conservation canines.org), for the hours upon hours of conversation, article links, photos, and emails. Thank you for inviting me to join your team of handlers in the Selkirk Mountains. I get sentimental when I think of this group. For your warmth, work, generosity of spirit, and for showing me the ropes, thank you, Suzie Marlow, handler and social media and outreach specialist; Julie Ubigau, handler and outreach and education coordinator; Jennifer Hartman, handler and communications coordinator; and, of course, your four-legged team members. Suzie, thank you for that cross-country interview by phone, and for you and Heath joining me in Seattle. And Jennifer, what can I say? You've been my constant *go-to* for everything handler and dog related in the book. Your patience is remarkable. You were my eyes and ears. Thank you for proofreading those earliest pages. Any errors are my own. My thanks to you and Suzie for that special time in the Adirondacks when I needed to come up for air. As I've told you before: You all are welcome at my hearth anytime.

I am also indebted to Working Dogs for Conservation in Bozeman, Montana (WorkingDogsForConservation.org). Thank you, Peter Coppolillo, executive director, for providing me with background information and for inviting me to observe some of your newest rescue dogs being trained. Thank you, Megan Parker, cofounder and director of research, for answering my questions and allowing me to observe you working with the dogs. And a special thank-you to the amazing Aimee Hurt, cofounder and director of operations, for inviting me to accompany you at your assignment post at the

United States–Canada border, and for graciously sharing your life and work experiences with me as I tried to wrap my head around the character of my protagonist and better understand the work of both handler and dog.

I've taken liberties with some of the facts in this novel. For example, the original conservation canine group, Conservation Canines, is housed in Eatonville, Washington, not Whitefish, Montana. And though most of the geographical landmarks and settings are true to form, there are places such as Gilman Lake, Stage Hill Road, and others that are products of my imagination.

Grizzly bears are beautiful and powerful, and can be frightening. Thank you, Richard Marsh (now retired), grizzly expert and wildlife biologist with Montana Fish, Wildlife and Parks in Kalispell, who spent an afternoon introducing me to grizzly bear management, including a culvert demonstration. Thank you also to John Waller, carnivore ecologist at Glacier National Park. The information you provided was invaluable, as was the time I spent in the park. (And I will never forget the difference in size between the black bear skull you showed me and the skull of the grizzly!) Thank you, Kat Sarensen, U.S. Fish and

Wildlife biologist in Spokane, Washington; Franklin Pemberton, Colville National Forest public affairs officer; Roby Bowe, sheriff of Lincoln County, Montana; and Jim Hagler, assistant service manager at Ed Reilly Subaru in Concord, New Hampshire. Particularly memorable is my interview with Dana Base, Washington Department of Fish and Wildlife biologist based in Colville, and our conversation about the woodland caribou. The image of the *gray ghost* has stayed with me. Many thanks to all of our wildlife biologists for the work they do.

Important publications that inspired my research for this novel include: *The Psychopathic Mind: Origins, Dynamics, and Treatment* (Meloy, 1998); "Grizzly Bear Connectivity Mapping in the Canada–United States Trans-Border Region" (Proctor et al, 2015); "Scat detection dogs in wildlife research and management: application to grizzly and black bears in the Yellowhead Ecosystem, Alberta, Canada" (Wasser et al, 2004); "Board of Review Report: Fatality of Mr. John L. Wallace from a bear attack on the Mary Mountain Trail in Yellowstone National Park on August 25, 2011" (Frey et al, 2012); *Stalemate: A Shocking True Story of Child Abduction and Murder* (Philpin, 1997); "America's Gray Ghosts: The Disappearing Caribou" (Robins, 2016); "Periodic Status Review for the Woodland Caribou" (Washington Department of Fish and Wildlife, Wiles, 2016); and *The Shadow of Death* (Ginsburg, 1993).

Epigraphs for a novel can provide both inspiration and direction. In addition to the novel's opening epigraph from Carolyn Forché's poem "The Garden Shukkei-en," Part One's epigraph, attributed to The Baroness De Staël-Holstein (Ann-Louise-Germaine Necker), is from *Germany* (De Staël-Holstein, 1813); Part Two's epigraph, attributed to Sam Berkowitz, is from *Confessions of Son of Sam* (Abrahamsen, 1985); and Part Three's epigraph, attributed to John Philpin, was written to me in an email.

A writer's world can be a lonely place without the solidarity of others. Thank you to my readers and to the bookstores that have supported my work and invited me to be their guest; it's been delightful connecting with you. I am also grateful for my neighbor and friend, Cate Regan, a retired psychiatric nurse practitioner. Thank you for the lively, sometimes hilarious conversation, and for sharing your and Jim's screened-in porch. Thank you, Michael Herrmann, owner of Gibson's Bookstore in Concord, New Hampshire, for early feedback on the novel, and to my mom for reading multiple drafts and brainstorming with me on titles.

And yet these pages would not be a book without my agent and my publishing home, Berkley. Thank you, Michelle Brower, my agent, fierce ally and advocate. I'm unbelievably fortunate to have landed on this path with you. Thank you, Danielle Perez, both teacher and editor. Your deft skill and guidance have opened up worlds to me. This book is ours. Heather Connor, you are a dream! Could there be a better publicist? I think not! I am grateful to Amy Schneider for her excellent copyediting skills, and to Vikki Chu for the beautiful original cover design. And loads of gratitude to the rest of my Berkley team: Jeanne-Marie Hudson, Claire Zion, Craig Burke, Fareeda Bullert, Jenn Snyder, Diana Franco, Christine Ball, and Ivan Held. And thank you to Penguin Random House's incredible sales and distribution team.

Thank you to my writing compatriots: Bob Begiebing, Richard Adams Carey, Alison Taylor-Brown, Katie Towler, John Searles, Wiley Cash, Mitch Wieland, Craig Childs, and my former student and newly published author Marjorie Herrera Lewis. There are others, of course: Karen and

Martha, who find me when I've disappeared too long; Glade and Susan, who have no problem with me pitching a tent in their backyard; and my late husband, Shaun, who first sparked the idea for this novel. Thank you to my sons — Nate, Seth, and Jake — and thank you to all my family and friends for their emotional support and understanding, especially my husband and best friend, Gregg Mazzola, who accompanied me on the Utah leg of my research, backpacking with me into the Nokai Dome wilderness unit. I love you all.

ABOUT THE AUTHOR

Diane Les Becquets is the former director of the MFA Program at Southern New Hampshire University and an avid outdoorswoman. A native of Nashville, she spent almost fourteen years living in a small Colorado ranching town before moving to New Hampshire.

The employees of Thorndike Press hope you have enjoyed this Large Print book. All our Thorndike, Wheeler, and Kennebec Large Print titles are designed for easy reading, and all our books are made to last. Other Thorndike Press Large Print books are available at your library, through selected bookstores, or directly from us.

For information about titles, please call:
(800) 223-1244

or visit our website at:
gale.com/thorndike

To share your comments, please write:

Publisher
Thorndike Press
10 Water St., Suite 310
Waterville, ME 04901